Paul Fleming

GASSELLO

Cover: Roman cavalry helmet found, Cumbria, 2010

Cast of Main Characters

Romans:

Domitian	The emperor. Mad, bad and dangerous to know.
Salustius Lucullus	The governor of Britannia
Decimus Tammo Vitalis	The legate of the Second Augustan Legion (first in command of the legion)
Titus Livius Colusanas	The senior (broad-stripe) tribune (second in command of the legion)
Ulpius Senicianus	The legion's camp prefect (third in command of the legion)
Quintus Robigalius	Commander of the Fifth cohort
Plancius Vallaunius Rufus	Commander of the Eighth cohort
Tadius Naratius	Commander of the Tenth cohort
Cressido Saenus	Decurion of the Eighth cohort cavalry
Luti Bassus	Decurion of the Tenth cohort cavalry

Non-Citizens:

Raselg	Household slave of Rufus, a Briton
Cybele	A Druid
Dendus	Household slave of Rufus, a Lusitanian
Mus	An auxiliary recruit, northern Briton
Tuathal	An auxiliary recruit, southern Briton

Places Referred to in the Text

Brigantia	Northern England
Carvetia	Cumbria, Lake District
Calleva Atrebatum	Silchester
Clausentum	Bitterne, Southampton
Clavinium	Radipole, Weymouth
Corinium	Cirencester
Dumnonia	Devon & Cornwall
Duronovaria	Dorchester
Gesoriacum	Boulogne
Glevum	Gloucester
Isca Augusta	Caerleon, South Wales
Isca Dumnoniorum	Exeter
Klocha Fhasach	Dartmoor
Lindinis	Ilchester
Londinium	London
Mai Din	Maiden Castle, Dorset
Nemetostatio	North Taunton, Devon
Noviomagus	Chichester
Ordovicia	North Wales
Siluria	South Wales
Sorviodunum	Old Sarum, Salisbury
Venta Belgarum	Winchester
Vindocladia	Badbury

FOREWORD

I did not want this story accessible only to afficionados of ancient Roman life and Roman military systems but to be enjoyed by a more general readership of thriller-lovers not wanting to be baffled by quaint technical jargon and Latin words. Some similar-sounding words are in any case misleading. For instance, at the time this story takes place, a 'century' of Roman soldiers could have been anything between seventy-eight to eighty-six men, never one hundred men. Because the word *century* is so embedded in our minds as meaning one hundred of something, I decided to use the word *company* instead.

It might help to think of a *legion* as a regiment, a *cohort* as a battalion, a *legate* as a many-starred general, a *centurion* as a captain of a company, an *optio* as a sergeant-major (not an officer). The six *tribunes* and the camp prefect would be like staff officers or adjutants. A *vexillation* means a detachment or 'wing' of a regiment.

There were so many tribes and subtribes in Britain at the time, that I apologise for the necessary diversity of tribal names and adjectives. Similarly, there were so many different gods worshipped by Britons, Roman legionaries and auxiliary soldiers from all parts of the empire, and so much confusing overlap between them, that I consciously made the decision to play down the role of religious worship in order not to bog-down and confuse the text with hundreds of deific names and an overabundance of blasphemies. In reality, the religious aspect of everyday life would have been so much more prominent than I suggest, and far more vocalised.

Bear in mind that a week could mean eight days, that the hours of the day lengthened or shortened depending on the time of the year as daylight was always divided into twelve equal hours, and night-time always divided into twelve equal hours. A Roman mile was a little shorter than what we would now call a mile.

Dates were measured with reference to the upcoming Kalends (beginning) of a month, or the Nones (nine days before mid-month) or the Ides (13th day if the month was short and 15th day if the month was long). The twelve months of the year were the same as we have now, the year starting at the beginning of January (but fixed to a particular moon phase).

Roman society was class-ridden but sometimes flexible. The elite and aristocratic men (previously the sole property owners of Rome) were the patrician class, also called senators. The rest were plebeians (commoners) but some of these were rich and owned property, such as the *equites* or equestrian class (knights). The emperor himself was from a plebeian family, which might explain his disrespect and paranoia towards the class of senators.

PART I

"In an island of the Ocean stands a sacred grove, and in the grove a consecrated cart, draped with a cloth, which none but the priest may touch".

Tacitus: Germania and Agricola, Ch.40

Part of Southwest Britannia showing main roads, towns and forts

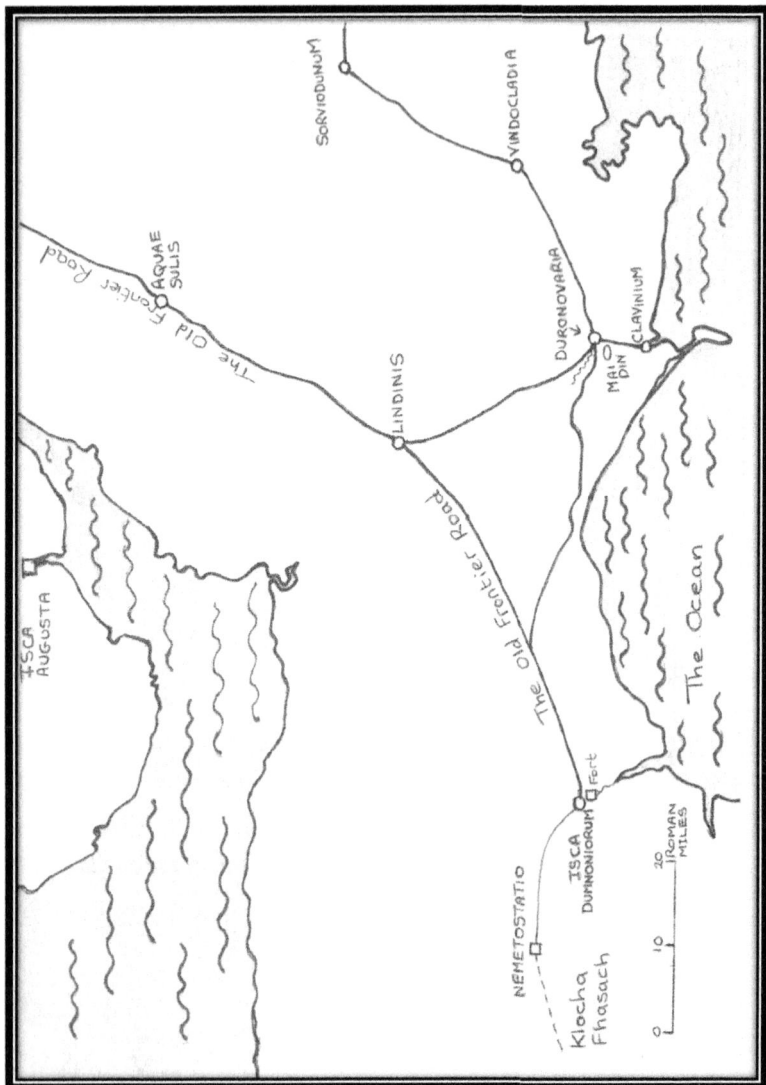

CHAPTER ONE

THE eyes could gather light better than those of any creature, and certainly better than those of a hideous Ankow. The extra reflective membrane in the natural design was key. They hunted at night, and because they could see things their prey could not, they were already ahead of the game before they started the final approach. Their long slender legs and soft, padded paws were adept at the silent stride. And the final insult: *they cooperated.* They knew the position of each other, of every other member of their hunting group, and they killed in concert. It was more like a choreographed dance than an attack, at least when it started. Graceful, beautiful and altogether deadly.

Their noses too, many times more sensitive than a man's, could detect, if the breeze floated the scent, the smallest rodent or a spray of *cuckoo-pint* berries or *ragwort* half a mile away, and a man's or a horse's sweat from even further. Here, as they approached the huge, square ugly Men's Earthwork, the dark walls and the fringe of wood planks silhouetted against the purple sky, they detected the sharp stink of burnt Men-Dens, from a fire that had consumed the structures a vague time earlier. And there was also iron and oxidated rust, and decomposed pigs.

More discomforting but just tolerable at this level, was the background scent of *Wolf's-bane*. It came up from the ground where they trod, and it emanated from the turf walls of the ugly earthwork. It was an offence in the damp air. This was not a place to stay too long. They should finish the hunt and retreat to the wholesome atmosphere of the heath as soon as possible but it was necessary to put up with the nausea in the meantime. There were Ankows inside the earthwork, so it was worth the risk.

Fortune does not always favour the brave. A half-moon shone in the sky, and it would have been better without it tonight. The advantage they would have enjoyed was compromised. They might be seen. There were at least two Ankows in the place, so it was worth the risk.

An approach from the side which was away from the Men's Track was better. Darker, more shrub, the rise of the moor behind them helping obscure their shapes.

The four hunters crept forward, a few hundred paces separating them, the alpha female slightly ahead.

Now the ditch impeded them. They sniffed at it, and it was dry but deep. On a good day with a slope helping to propel them, they could have jumped the ditch but the ground beyond it, pinched between the base of the wall and the edge of the ditch seemed too narrow to serve as a landing, and instinct told them that they might, and probably would, fall back into the ditch if they tried to jump. The alpha female constrained herself from whining or growling in frustration. Silence was everything. They would have to find a route over the ditch, somehow. This was not going to be as easy as they hoped.

Two of the beasts turned towards the eastern corner, the other two like a mirror image, turning the opposite way. The large south gate of the men's place smelt of brushed wood, lamp oil and grease. But no Ankows. The hideous Ankows had not touched this gate yet. This did not stop the alpha female baring her teeth at it, for this was where men came in and out normally. She sniffed at it again. No one had used this gate for a long time. The grease on the pivots smelt rancid but no men's hands had touched the securing bars or the wood for a while. In fact, she could not smell men on this side of the place at all. No men, and no Ankows nearby.

She was processing this information when she heard a very loud thud, followed almost immediately by another similar sound. Two of her hunting group – the two that had crept away from her towards the other corner of the earthwork - snapped into different shapes, no longer on their feet but heaped instead in a grotesque sprawl. They emitted a frightening yelp as they morphed. Then they lay still. Even from this distance she could see something like a stick protruding from the necks of her prostrate comrades.

And she knew they were dead and rotting quickly. The bite of *Wolf's-bane* and silver was dissolving them.

Up on the palisade, half-hiding behind the two large ballistae, Guilio and Cassian let out a noisy burst of triumphant whoops and laughter. They shook each other's arms in mutual congratulation and did a little improvised jig. Then, hastily, they began to reload the machines carefully with two more customised bolts.

The alpha female and her hunting group had not smelt the two Ankows above them on the parapet. The air must be moving in a different direction at that height, and they were not to know this. It does not always work out right.

She turned and barked at her remaining comrade and, even as the two *she-wolves* retreated quickly from the dark place, retching at the reek of their dead relatives and the shock of it, the ballistae were turning towards them already, and their ropes were being wound taut by the ratchet handles. An ordinary man could not crank a ballista bolt-firing contraption with the speed and strength that an Ankow such as Guilio and Cassian could muster.

They fired again and struck one She-wolf in the flank as it ran away, the flank of the Alpha-female, herself. She fell immediately while the other ran off into the night.

Guilio and Cassian were delighted. They had seen off the wolves. The improvised bolts they had found near the ballistae devices, which smelt of silver-metal and Wolf's-bane and which made them sick to handle, had worked well. They danced again and span each around in a tight circle, and nearly fell off the parapet, even though it was wider at this point. They ended up on their backs, shrieking with joy and hilarity. They had not felt this good for a while. It would have been a perfect moment if it were not for the terribly hunger. The urge to guzzle blood was always with them in the background.

"Come on, Guilio, let's celebrate with a feast!"

"Yes, killing wolves gives me such an appetite, my friend!"

They climbed down off the wall and headed to the *via praetoria* and then along it past the commandant's house, where they normally slept in the daytime, and past the cohort headquarters, and beyond these buildings towards the tall north gate, where the guardhouse held the last of the people.

There were only four of them left in the little lock-up now. Three emaciated and weakened men and one almost skeletal shrieking woman. These should last them for a couple of weeks and take them past the next full moon. Then they would not be alone in the fort any longer. There would be enough of them to venture outside the fort and look for fresh food. And of course to fight more wolves if need be.

CHAPTER TWO

DUMNONIAN people were known for two characteristics more than any other. They proudly believed a good proportion of them were born with a gift for seeing into the future. Secondly, they spurned the use of money whenever they could. Between themselves, the Dumnonii exchanged goods and services for other goods and services, seldom using money in the transactions. Those living in the civil town of Caer Uisc, as the locals preferred to call Isca Dumnoniorum, and in the hovels around the army forts and other towns in their kingdom, had grown accustomed to accepting coinage from the soldiers and their retainers because soldiers seldom had anything else to exchange. So, coins were now circulating freely amongst the natives. But, whereas the unsophisticated Durotriges and the arrogant, Roman-loving Atrebates and Regni loved money, the Dumnonii only suffered it as a necessary expedience. Such an indirect gain, they bemoaned when they handled the small, round, fiddly metal tokens. You could not season or spice your food with coins, and they did not lay eggs for you. They gave you no immediate use or gratification. You always had to buy *something else* with them further down the line. The Romans thought they were so sophisticated, but they often made life a whole lot fussier and more complicated than it need be. It was as if they wanted to make the world impractical and *artificial* on purpose, just because they could.

Raselg had associated with Romans for only a few months by now, but she was already a convert. She was a slave and so, when dealing with other Dumnonii, she was forced to use coinage because, like the soldiers, she owned nothing else to exchange. She possessed no assets at all, well nearly none. This sometimes led to awkward situations.

Take the soothsayer she encountered this morning, for instance. It was the Feast of Diana, and slaves were traditionally given a day off work. They were free to roam. Raselg had taken the opportunity to seek out the soothsayer while her master, Plancius Vallaunius Rufus, was attending the Funerary Eulogies of his friend and predecessor, the late Bruccius Natalinus. She had slipped out of the commandant's house in the auxiliary fort, joyous with the sense of freedom, bypassed the civil town where the eulogies were taking place in the forum, and steered herself towards the seedy quarter of the shantytown next to it. Here the majority of Britons resided and some of the poorest hovels were situated. The best soothsayer would be found here. The civil council had banned him from the main town itself. The two sons of the old king, who were now persuasive members of the town council, had never forgiven him for accurately predicting the early demise of their father, but more particularly because he failed to warn them that the temper of the king's second wife, their stepmother, would send him to such an early grave.

After asking directions, Raselg arrived before an especially run-down hovel. A sign outside the little house was scratched with a crude drawing of an eye and an entreaty to enter to anyone who wished to learn their fate or that of somebody else. She went inside.

She was surprised to find herself not in a house but immediately into a little courtyard. The house front was a mere sham for there was no interior, as such. Instead, she was inside a circular enclosure, ringed by a high fence that bent inwards. A tree grew in the middle and, at the base of the tree stood a bed and a little table and, on the bed, lay a little old man. He sat up when he saw her, and he stared wide-eyed.

Raselg was beautiful, and men usually reacted in this way when first encountering her. Noting her Roman clothes, the old man spoke to her in Latin but she replied in good Dumnonian dialect. He asked why she was not at home on the Feast of Diana, washing her hair as a votive offering to the Huntress, and she responded by telling him that this was because she was not a Roman woman, and did not care for such silly traditions. This had the effect of producing a massive smile on his face. He looked a little more excited.

Raselg showed him the little bundle in her bag. It was one of her master's loin clothes, which she had smuggled out of the house. "Will you tell me this man's future?" she asked. "How much to do so?"

The old man looked her up and down. "No money," he said curtly. "You are of the Dumnonii and we do not trade with coins, as you know." He almost spat the words out. "We have to maintain some standards, do we not? No, a service for a service, as it should be." As he said this, he nodded towards her ample chest as casual as he could. The inference was obvious.

"Money. How much?" she persisted.

"No money. A *service*. Or find yourself another soothsayer!"

"Then, I will." And she turned to leave.

He watched her try to find the handle of the door she had just come through. It was hidden underneath drapes of unwashed greasy cloth and required some searching. "Fine, so be it," he shouted testily. "I will take your master's lousy coinage. Give me the cloth!" He had already surmised from her lack of jewellery and the thin slave collar that she was not a freedwoman, and that any money she carried was hardly likely to be hers.

"How much?" she asked without turning.

"As much as you think it is worth," he answered. This was a shrewd tactic because slaves and servant women liked to show off their master's wealth with tokens of generosity and he could bank on it. She would probably feel compelled to give him more than the going rate.

Raselg turned and handed him the loin cloth, and he beckoned her to sit herself on the ground, upon a little square of woven goats-wool.

The man unfolded the cloth and lay it over the little table. He produced a small pouch from his tunic and opened it carefully, pouring the contents into his right palm. It was a small collection of polished bones, probably from human hands or human feet. Pressing the bones to his eyes and then shaking them in his clenched fist, he dropped them on to the loin cloth.

Both Raselg and the soothsayer stared at the result. After a few seconds, the man nudged a couple of the bones into a slightly different pattern. He then purported to look concerned. "That same pattern appears in the sky," he muttered.

"A group of stars? What do you see?" Raselg asked.

"It doesn't work like that – you have to ask me questions?" replied the man. "Have you not been to a soothsayer before, my dear?"

"Surely, you would know the answer to that already?" she responded sarcastically.

"A figure of speech. Don't get uppity. I know you have been to one soothsayer before me, around a year ago. He was travelling through Dumnonia and he stopped at your village. No, hold on, not so much a village as a *vicus*. Let me see – it was – in the Nemeton valley, at the soldiers' fort they call Nemetostatio."

"Yes," responded Raselg breathlessly. She was impressed.

"You lived with your mother and father at the time. No, hold on, your mother's spirit only. She had passed by then. A little sibling perhaps. I cannot tell whether it was a brother or sister. This sibling has since passed too." He was watching her as he spoke. He might have been adjusting his words after noting each of her reactions.

She gasped. He looked up at her. His eyes roved from her chest to her bare lower legs and then finished on the bulge in her dress where she kept the little purse of money.

"About this man," she began, pointing at the loin cloth and the pattern of bones laying upon it. "Will he be favoured in his career? Will he retire healthy and live a good life? Do you see him with a wife and children in the future?"

"He is a good man. A soldier. An important man. A very brave man." The soothsayer stopped himself, suddenly. He looked up at Raselg's face, and it was his turn to appear surprised. "He has fought *Blood Ankows*! And lived! By all that is blessed, you do indeed have a very brave master! And he fought the fiends *here*, at Caer Uisc! He was one of the soldiers to survive that great battle!"

Raselg nodded in admission. Yes, he was one of the soldiers, one of the few left standing: just her master, and his handsome decurion, and the fat curator and the standard bearer who flirted with her and taught her how to shave men, and around ten of the best and luckiest foot soldiers; that was all that was left from her master's beloved Tenth cohort of five hundred fighters. And not a single man from the similarly populated Eighth cohort had survived that night of dread and gore. One thousand and ten soldiers were said to have perished in that battle and in the bitter struggles of the previous month.

She asked: "One more question: will I always be a slave? Do you see me as this man's wife?"

"That is two questions. No, I am sorry to say it, but I do not see you as his wife. I see somebody else. And…"

The man seemed intrigued by something. He tilted his head as if to view the bones from a different angle. "I see no retirement either. His life as a soldier will end very soon. No riches, no glory, and certainly no wife."

"But you said you saw somebody else in his future – I don't understand!"

"Neither do I."

"But that is what I'm paying you for! You haven't told me anything, old man! Are you a fake?"

The soothsayer saw his pieces of silver at risk and hastened to make amends. "Look, I cannot tell you what I do not see. I have told you a good deal already, but not how you might want to hear it! I tell you, this man's life as a soldier will end soon, in a violent way. He will not grow old. And you will not grow old with him, nor bear his children."

Raselg stood up. Fumbling in her purse, and in some distress, she threw down a clutch of coins, several denarii, perhaps too many. Judging by the soothsayer's face and his craving gesture, she had been too generous.

She took one more look at the bones and loin cloth, as if memorising the pattern, and then, unceremoniously, she snatched up the underclothing and shoved it back into her bag, scattering the little bones as she did so. She knew that Dendus would notice if one single item of their master's wardrobe was unaccounted for.

She found the handle of the door eventually and left the old man in his little courtyard, finding and collecting the little bones from the ground, and placing them back in his pocket. He put the heavy silver coins in his special hiding place. He was entirely engaged in his own thoughts and hardly noticed Raselg's departure. He continued to look perturbed long after she had gone. He muttered to himself and stood up and looked around his little yard. Then he sighed, resignedly. It was a pity but if the beautiful woman's master, who he had correctly guessed was the commandant of the auxiliary fort, were to stay in Caer Uisc, then he may have to leave this town. The commandant's future was bound up and blighted by the Ankows, and, wherever he went, the blood-sucking devils would be there too, causing devastation.

The soothsayer had seen it in the bones. They showed constant war, with a great deal of killing and sorrows still to come; and innocent civilians like himself caught up in it and sacrificed in the turmoil. Nowhere would be safe wherever the man known as Rufus took himself.

CHAPTER THREE

THE camp prefect, Ulpius Senicianus, paused in the delivery of the first eulogy, and blinked his moist and sore eyes at the audience assembled in the forum before him. The senior ranks were in the first row, just the other side of the funerary urn containing the ashes of Bruccius Natalinus. The deceased's centurial helmet with its arc of red horsehair had been carefully placed on top of the urn. The most senior tribune of the legion stood in the middle of the first row, and, on either side of him, the commanders of the Eighth and Tenth cohorts. Next to them stood their seconds-in-command, the two cavalry decurions. Outermost in the front row, holding up the tall staffs upon which the crests and emblems of the Eighth cohort were mounted, stood the new standard bearers who the prefect did not yet recognise. The second row was taken up with the deceased's two male servants, some of the aristocrats and other dignitaries of the town council, and a couple of rich merchants who had benefitted from the deceased's protection and his occasional averted eyes. Further back stood the common soldiers and a collection of town-dwellers, come for the spectacle. A woman at the rear of the crowd was crying in a demonstrative way, pulling at her clothes as if to tear them apart but never quite causing any great violence to them.

"And in the discharge of his many duties," the prefect continued in a solemn tone, "he discharged them with a calmness and an efficiency that were an example to the best of us!"

"*Calmness*?" muttered Tadius Naratius, the commander of the Tenth cohort. His wry comment was overheard and taken up by others standing around him, and converted into barely restrained mirth.

Senicianus was on to it immediately, and he departed from his script. "When I say calmness, I do not necessarily mean *quietness*!"

It was fine to laugh loudly now, as the prefect had made a joke of it and legitimised the absurdity. It was funny because everybody knew that Bruccius Natalinus had been irrepressible, ebullient, excitable and very, very noisy. 'Calmness' was a word that the old prefect must have left in accidentally from a previous eulogy.

Senicianus was viewing his notes as if to check for anything else that might be challenged. During this second pause, the woman at the rear of the crowd emitted a loud wail and pretended to fall over – nearly - because of faintness in her head.

"Who is that woman?" asked the senior tribune, Livius Colusanas, sharply.

"Bruccius Natalinus's so-called grieving mistress," answered Rufus next to him. "I will get rid of her."

"No, leave her be," snapped the tribune. "Perhaps the embarrassment she is causing will hurry up the proceedings. And why isn't she with the rest of the household? Why is she back there?"

"I had to dismiss her from the household," explained Rufus. "She was acting like that all the time, and she was disturbing the hearth as well as the other servants. She was disturbing *me*. I know for sure that Natalinus had misgivings about her and was about to dismiss her, himself. He was going to replace her with a younger woman. He told me so himself."

"Well, you would know all about that," Colusanas responded pointedly. "Not a slave, presumably."

"A whore from one of the brothels, I believe."

Colusanas glanced at her again and then turned back to the prefect, who had found his place in the notes once more.

"Our dear friend, Bruccius Natalinus, was the bravest of the brave! He died as he would hope to die: his sword in his hand, charging at the enemy! Only a cowardly crossbow bolt could pierce that lion's heart, pierce that *not-so-quiet* heart, a heart that had stirred us to win a hundred battles! And no-one will ever say that Bruccius Natalinus lost a hand-to-hand fight in his life! For he never did! No, he never did! Remember that when you think of his sweet face. A crossbow bolt…" Senicianus shook his head to denote the sheer nonsense and unfairness of it.

Rufus looked aside to his decurion, Cressido Saenus, who had been the first on the scene and found the body of Natalinus, moments after he had been killed. Saenus was nodding, a tear blossoming in the corner of his eye.

"Bruccius Natalinus joined the Roman Army at the age of seventeen," continued the prefect. He had reached the part of the eulogy that summarised the deceased's achievements. The audience shifted contentedly, knowing this was the final stage of the first speech. "He enjoyed a glorious campaign as part of a vexillation of the Second Augustan Legion in Germania, where he distinguished himself right from the outset. Natalinus became a standard bearer within a year, and then attained the rank of junior centurion shortly after that; most probably because his commander had noticed our dear friend's mellifluous voice and gentle nature (more salutary laughter from the crowd at this obviously deliberate irony). *Britannia* then beckoned! No – I get ahead of myself – it's the eyes! Natalinius then, er, moved with the vexillation to Gaul; spent a year there and was quickly promoted to chief centurion. I believe Plancius Vallaunius, here, campaigned alongside him in Gaul and acted as his standard bearer. Is that right?"

"No, I was never his standard bearer," corrected Rufus. "I was a junior centurion at that time. But in the same cohort."

Colusanas, the broad-stripe tribune, tutted and swore under his breath, next to Rufus. Rufus was sure he heard the tribune mutter to himself: "*The old fool*!"

"Britannia then beckoned! He came over in the Year of the Consulship of Novius and Commodus, eight hundred and thirty-one, *ab urbe condita*, and joined the main part of the legion. I think you came over at the same time, did you not Plancius Vallaunius? Did I get that bit right, at least?"

"Yes, you did, prefect! On the very same ship!"

"Bruccius Natalinus's most notable achievements were still ahead of him. Oh, what exploits they were: Caledonia! Brigantia! Ordovicia! Particularly Ordovicia, where he gained the nickname *Ajax* because of his extraordinary vigour in the midst of battle…"

Rufus could not help casting a side glance towards Tadius Naratius, standing on the other side of the tribune when he heard this. Tadius too looked puzzled and shook his head slightly. Neither of them had heard of this nickname for Natalinus before now, and Tadius would have known *all* his distant cousin's nicknames. It was known in the legion that they were related, and therefore comrades loved to talk about the colourful chief centurion of the Eighth cohort to him and regale him with comical anecdotes. The prefect must have been given incorrect information or else was mixing up two different deceased commanders. Tadius choked back an urge to laugh.

"Twelve glorious years of service in Britannia. A hero to his men. A friend to all his men. They loved him! The walls of Isca Dumnoniorum rang with his booming laughter! Those walls are dreadfully quiet now…!"

"Well done! Well done!" shouted Colusanas quickly. "I believe that Tadius Naratius also has a eulogy to give!" The tribune was beckoning Tadius to ascend the stage and give his speech before the old prefect might think of continuing with his. Senicianus had not quite got to the end of his notes but saw that the momentum had been taken away from him by the broad-stripe tribune's intervention. He admitted defeat to himself and snatched the writing boards off the lectern. He stepped aside to give way to Tadius, still managing a gracious smile.

Tadius placed his notes on the lectern but did not look at them. He addressed the audience. "Bruccius Natalinus was my dear cousin!" he began. "And when we played as children, in the woods of Camerinum: climbing trees, damming streams, raiding birds' nests, stealing figs, building dens and trapping rats, there was no finer play fellow than Bruccius! When later, we stood as soldiers, facing the onslaught and murderous frenzy of the Ordovices, or the dashing chariots of the Brigantes, there was no finer comrade to stand next to than my dear Bruccius! When we bathed and partied in Glevum or Isca Augusta, or we rode our horses across the hills of Carvetia, there was no better companion than Bruccius. I will miss him. The family will miss him. The men of the Second Augustan Legion will miss him! Yes, it will be a dreadfully quiet province now! Bruccius Natalinus longed to see the hills and woodlands of Italia again, and he will never do so, but we know that he will look over to us with contentment but with no envy from the Elysian Fields. We in turn will one day carry him gloriously in our memories back to his beloved homeland!" After a moment's reflection, and barely supressing a smile, Tadius added: "So, farewell, our *Ajax*!" He took up his unread wax tablets and stepped down from the stage to grateful cheers from the crowd.

Rufus congratulated him and whispered: "Not a single mention of the *Ankows*, from anyone! Do you note how we all seek to push the fiends from our minds as if they are too diabolic to be real, or to have had any sway on recent events?"

"A deliberate omission, Rufus. I will not sully my cousin's memory in the minds of those listening, even with the word. To do so, would give the monsters a kind of victory -"

"I will miss him more than anyone!" wailed the woman from the back of the crowd suddenly, and she pretended to swoon and to need holding up by kindly strangers nearby. Colusanas ordered two legionaries to accompany her out of the forum.

Tadius, at a nod from Rufus who was officially the master of the ceremonies, lifted the urn containing Natalinus's ashes ever so cautiously, keeping the crested helmet balanced on its lid, and slowly marched it across the square towards the camp prefect's house. Here in the civil town of Isca, there was no longer any army headquarters or a commandant's home to carry it into: those had been transplanted to the auxiliary fort, half a mile downstream of the river. As Tadius marched solemnly, the male members of the devotional crowd, and the soldiers accompanying the urn, began a low, ululating bout of concerted groaning in conventional respect. The miserable sound only stopped when the urn had been carried through the front door of the house by Tadius.

The camp prefect, whose house it was for the time being, stepped down from the platform and came to Rufus and the tribune. "That went well, I think," he said. "I will see to the urn being buried alongside the road to Lindinis, and of course the erection of the tombstone. You can get on with the preparations for the Festival of Jupiter and Domitian, commander."

"You are so kind," replied Rufus, ambivalently. "Will we have the pleasure of your company at the festival?"

"No, I will depart for Isca Augusta next week and accompany Tadius Naratius as far as Lindinis."

"Has the wording for the memorial stone been decided upon?" Colusanas asked.

"I am working on that, but would welcome your suggestions, of course."

"Perhaps we will leave off the reference to Ajax," offered Rufus. "I confess, I was not aware of that nickname for Natalinus, and I thought I knew him well enough."

Senicianus looked surprised, then suddenly sheepish. "Damn it! That was Germanicus, wasn't it?"

Colusanas nodded and said wearily, "Yes, it was Marcus Germanicus."

"Never mind. I don't think anybody really noticed, and the appellation suits your predecessor just as well."

"It does, prefect," concurred Rufus politely.

The crowd was dispersing. The old prefect watched them go for a few seconds, nodding first to the two sons of the Dumnonian king who still occupied the bulk of the palace adjoining the prefect's house, and then to the other members of the town council. "How are the new recruits, Vallaunius? Are they shaping up?" he asked when the dignitaries were far enough away.

"They marched in, day before yesterday," he replied. "Quite a challenge. Eighty Coritani, eighty Catuvellauni, eighty Cantii, eighty Dobunni, eighty Cornovi, eighty Corieltauvi, and yet another blasted tribe that I never even heard of! All swearing and spitting at each other, and being pathetically *tribal* when we're not watching them and hitting them with our vine staffs. We will mould them into the semblance of Roman soldiery – eventually, I dare say."

"Hence the new cohort will be called the *Eighth cohort of Brittones*. But it's nothing you haven't encountered before," pointed out Senicianus.

"On the contrary, it's very different this time," countered Rufus. "Before now, we always had a backbone of legionaries to act as role models and to give it proper structure. The legionaries in an auxiliary cohort are like the wooden framework we put in place in turf walls before we fill the spaces with clods of earth to form stout walls for our forts. It steadies the heap and stops it shifting out of shape and lowering and becoming squat and lumpen. And in the past, I have trained nearly a whole cohort of Tungustrians, and at another time a mix of Lusitanians and Batavians. They managed from the outset to act as one cohesive, like-minded group of kindred spirits, keen to be Romans and proper soldiers. These new recruits you have given me are like a microcosm of everything that is wrong about Britannia – divisive, grudge-bearing factions that cannot put their differences aside, even when circumstances strongly suggest they do so. Do you imagine we Romans could have conquered these populous lands if the Britons had ever stood up against us together? No."

"These Britons will be like-minded and cohesive because they know what they are up against. They know better than anybody about Blood Ankows," contended Colusanas. "When you drum it into them that they are to form a specialist and esteemed unit of

Ankow-fighters, they will surely put their differences aside and listen up. Their lives and their pride will depend upon it."

"Don't count on it," replied Rufus. "They live and breathe to squabble with other tribes, and in any event, the Britons relied upon *Druids* to fight Blood Ankows."

"But that was because they never had the right weapon. Our men know they have the Druids' special lance now! The *Lucullan*, in their hands, will make all the difference, and they will know it. Britons are fighting-men by nature, and they will feel stronger than the Druids ever were. Discipline and camaraderie make the Roman army the best in the world," said the tribune.

"Let us hope so."

"And archers too," offered the prefect. "I hear that the Cornovian archers will make as fine a set of sagittarians as we know of in any army."

"Yes, archers too, thankfully. And I never thought I would ever say that!"

The prefect laughed. "Yes, yours was the last cohort to turn your back on archers," said the prefect.

"Oh, I never turn my back on archers!" replied Rufus, wryly. "Yes, until now it is true. Both the Tenth *and* the Eighth cohorts have avoided having them. In any case, in the twelve years I have spent in Britannia, I never came across many Britons using bows and arrows against us. Natalinus couldn't see the point of introducing archers into his battalion, bless his soul. Nor did the legate for that matter. Tammo Vitalis only eventually introduced them to the Second Augustan Legion because he felt under pressure from the governor, who expects us to adapt and use the specialities of native recruits. Things have changed now. I cannot see any real solution to those damned crossbows than to have sagittarians keep them at bay from a distance. We move with the times, as we're never sick of hearing from our superiors."

"The governor would be pleased to hear you now. Already, Lucullus boasts to everyone but the emperor about his new, special forces - the *Ankow-Killers*, as your two cohorts are nicknamed!" The prefect looked around for Tadius, the new commander of the Tenth, forgetting that he had gone into his house. "So, a new lance – the *Lucullan* - and new archers! For once, the misty province of Britannia might be regarded as the cutting-edge of the empire! Our noble army is not doing particularly well anywhere else, if truth be known."

"Our governor is afraid to boast of ankow-killers to the emperor?" questioned Rufus, surprised.

The camp prefect waved the query away, irritably. The senior tribune too looked uncomfortable about the careless admission. After a few moments, Rufus did not press the point and said instead: "I fear that Tadius Naratius and Luti Bassus are going to find themselves with a similar ragtag of discordant recruits, when they go to fetch them from Lindinis next week." He lowered his voice so that his decurion could not hear him. "And Tadius won't have the benefit of Cressido Saenus beside him – he'll have Luti Bassus, for all that is sacred; a legionary who cares more for horses and herbs than he does for men, well, most men!"

Rufus noted how the aged prefect and the senior tribune glanced at each other when he uttered these last words. He had long suspected that Luti spied on behalf of the camp prefect and the tribunes. It was a common device. The legion was spread around in various parts of Siluria and Dumnonia, and only the First and Sixth cohorts were actually based at their main headquarters in Isca Augusta these days. So, having spies in place to report back to headquarters from the remote vexillations and outposts was often the only way of finding out what was really happening. All the senior centurions' regular written reports were collected at the headquarters and then sent on to Rome to be read by the Senate, so these reports were usually written with that in mind; adapted to make things sound better and more proper than perhaps they were.

The reflex glance at each other when Rufus mentioned Luti, reinforced his suspicion. He wondered what Luti got back in return, as Luti did not really care for money, prestige or promotion.

"Two things make an auxiliary join the imperial Roman army," ventured the senior tribune, redirecting the conversation. "The wages and the promise of becoming a Roman citizen after they have served their years. Use these as your tools for moulding them, Vallaunius, and to curb their tribal natures."

"I have already thought of that. Our illustrious emperor wants our auxiliaries to enjoy three-quarters of the wages of a real legionary, whereas before now they always managed on a *third* of the wage. The rise in wages is ill-thought through as it applies equally to the rawest recruit as it does to the seasoned auxiliary. It is inherently wasteful and profoundly unfair. So, until I see these new recruits acting in the image of real Roman auxiliaries and not as hooligans, they will receive but a third of a legionaries' wage, as in the old times. If I see so much as one Coritani spit at a Cantiaci, they will *all* continue to have their wages cut! They must know that they stand or fall as one mass, together. Secondly, I have informed them that I do not yet regard them as Roman auxiliaries yet but, instead, no more than *prospective* auxiliaries – one step removed from the real thing. And so their measure of twenty-five years' service to the imperial army, before they achieve entitlement to become citizens of Rome will not even begin until I say it does!"

"By the gods, Vallaunius, did they believe that when you told them?" asked the prefect. "You don't actually have the authority to determine that."

"They don't know that, unless Luti Bassus disabuses them of the notion. Anyway, whether they believe it or not, a lot of them won't want to take the chance of testing it out."

"Well, good luck to you," said Colusanas. "I'm sure you will manage it, one way or the other."

The old prefect nodded in agreement. He shivered in the cold even though he was wearing almost all his full uniform, including wool tunic, leather jerkin, long cloak and chainmail jacket. He would have done better to have kept on his helmet which was lined with warm, wool-padded leather, and he regretted deciding to go bare-headed for the eulogies. It felt like the late summer was turning uncharacteristically damp and cool as if the Kalends of September were already upon him, not eighteen days away still, and every one of Senicianus' bones of fifty-six years was feeling the change. "Let us go in and rest, before we come out to attend the splendid feast that I've arranged for later in the basilica - with the help of the town council. My man, Axum, has found wine that invigorates a fellow, rather than lulls him, and we have a long day ahead of us still. Come, let is enjoy some good wine before we must politely suffer the swill the town council will serve."

Rufus ordered his second-in-command, Saenus, to dismiss the other legionaries of the Eighth and to march them back to the nearby fort. Colusanas did the same in Tadius' stead for the Tenth cohort's assembled subalterns and soldiers. Rufus and the tribune followed the old man into his house, making sure to take off their crested helmets as they navigated the door.

CHAPTER FOUR

WHEN the long, narrow road between Lindinis and Lindum was still the frontier road of the province, it was extended south-west to Isca Dumnoniorum to incorporate a chunk of rich, arable land into the realm. It later fell out of use largely when most of the Roman soldiers in the province went northward or westward to conquer new vast tracts of the island. They were gone for years, and the land to the south and east of the frontier road resorted mainly to the tamer tribes again, though now these lands would be governed, if that was really the correct word for it, by Brittonic kings who had sworn allegiance to Rome; client kings who had adopted its clothes and culture and gratefully received its money. The towns were governed notionally too by the officious councils of similarly converted native men; men who also liked to wear togas and take regular baths and who had adopted the habit of reclining on couches when they ate. With the soldiers pushing the frontier ever northwards, the old road grew less and less relevant. Some people even forgot that it had once been the official frontier road, but not Nepos Censorius. With uncanny instinct, he forewent the comfortable villa in Glevum that was earmarked for him at a cheap rent when he retired from serving as a soldier in the Second Augustan Legion, and instead he sank his money and his cash from his war booty into a new venture. He built a modest-sized inn, a *mansio*, a third of the way along the stretch of the old frontier road between Lindinis and Isca; a stopping place for travellers, complete with stables, baths and a well-equipped games room. People thought he was crazy to do this but he proved them all wrong in the end. The soldiers did come back in their thousands and, with them, their retainers and, wherever there were cohorts and detachments of soldiers, so too there would be merchants and traders and senior ranks and adjutants of the army, travelling backwards and forwards, and needing a good road and a comfortable inn along the way.

After ten lean years of making do and relying solely on the traffic to and from the lead mines of Durotrigia, Nepos's inn became a prosperous venture just as he had predicted. He congratulated himself on his foresight, although in truth it was nothing more than logic and pragmatism. If he had learnt anything else in his twenty-five years of army life, other than fighting and how to build houses and stack walls and lay down underfloor heating systems, it was this: that an army always needs twice as much in the way of supplies, and much lengthier and expansive supply lines than the average commander ever predicts in a campaign. So, no army could sustain itself and stretch so far outwards for more than a few years. Eventually, as it did in Germania and as it had done in Gaul and countless other places, the Roman province retracted again. Indeed, the whole empire ebbed and flowed in this way over time, like a giant breathing animal, and, when it ebbed, it tended to resort to its earlier dimensions. He had seen what it was like in the north and in the west, and it was obviously untenable to stay out there for too long. Many of the people out there could not be bribed with Roman money or Roman prestige, they were just too self-sufficient and too uncouth. Why should the new governor and new emperor take the risks and make all the extra efforts with an expensive army, when there was excellent land and a milder, more congenial climate back south, populated by peoples who appreciated Romans mostly and knew a good thing when they saw it. Yes, the people paid taxes – heavy taxes – but they got a lot back in return, such as peace and protections and laws. And, in any case, why would an emperor, who owned the province personally, want to see it become ragged and worn out along its edges, torn at and frayed by vulgar people who failed to see the indubitable worth of being civilised? In any event, the tin, gold, silver, iron and lead, and the best pastoral farmland were mostly in the south and Siluria. The southern mines, excavated expertly by the Britons, could be managed, supervised, taxed and pilfered easily from the retrenched position behind the old frontier road. The main trading ports of Isca Dumnoniorum, Din Albion, Clavinium, Clausentum and Londinium were all nearer to the Old World, providing the shortest and least risky passages by sea, and they were all the right side of the old frontier road. As Nepos predicted, the traffic came back in abundance. He just bided his time and waited for the inevitable to happen.

Nepos had a young wife, and three healthy children, two boys, and a girl. One of the boys would take over the running of the inn when Nepos himself was too feeble to do so, and Nepos would have enough money put aside by then to give it to the two sons so they could build a second inn further along the road and expand the family business. Nepos had it all planned out, even a strategy to compete with others who might try to build inns of their own in competition.

After years of waiting, the family fortunes were looking up. Hardly a day went by without at least one or two customers calling at the inn, needing lodging, food, a warm bath and stables for their horses. They came at all times of the day or night. A loud knock on the front door, even after darkness had fallen was now a common thing. As on this night.

Nepos answered the knock, opening the door to find himself facing sixteen soldiers, resplendent in the uniforms of his old regiment, the Second Augustan Legion. The large, wide-chested soldier nearest the door was wearing the red arch-crested helmet of a senior centurion. His breast was full of badges and torcs, the awards for bravery. Nepos found himself straightening his back and correcting his posture automatically. He bristled with pride to see his old regiment's colours again here displayed on his very own doorstep, and a senior centurion, no less, standing there. Judging by the chest full of badges, the officer must be one of the most esteemed soldiers in the whole legion.

"I am Mavritius Varro, chief centurion of the Fifth Cohort, Second Augustan Legion, and I require your hospitality for my men for one night," stated this man. "And do not fear, we intend to pay." Nepos saw that the centurion's left eye was red and watering, and looked sore.

"It will be my pleasure and my honour," stammered Nepos, very perplexed all of a sudden, as he had noticed something else and was trying his best to hide it. Nepos looked out on to the road, beyond the men. "Where are your horses?" he asked.

"No horses," answered the chief centurion curtly. "Just men."

"Of the Fifth cohort, you say?" asked Nepos, standing aside to let the first of them into the house.

No one answered him, which in itself was not unusual. Soldiers could be very gruff, verging on ill-mannered, especially when they were tired. And if they had marched all this way on foot, they would surely be very tired. The soldiers moved past Nepos into the house without another word. Their footsteps were heavy, the studded sandals tapping noisily on the tiled floor. The armour clanked and creaked, sixteen-fold, and they were accompanied by a waft of cold, damp air and the odd smell of wet leaves and something pungent, like mould.

It took him several minutes to show them their lodgings, the room where they could recline and be fed, and the baths. "I will fire up the hypocaust at once," promised Nepos. "And I expect you will be in sore need of good food and plenty of wine! Make yourselves at home and I will send my servants in to you very soon."

Varro nodded morosely, despite Nepos's attempt to sound like the merriest host possible. The soldiers waited for him to depart the room.

He was relieved to do so, and went straight to see his wife, who was lighting lamps in the atrium, where they retired to every evening. The room had comfortable seats and couches arranged around its edges, facing a large and colourful rectangle of fabric stretched on the floor at the centre. On this was displayed a painting of a hunting scene in the Etruscan style, the exact same picture that would eventually become the tracing for a fine mosaic in its place. Nepos was saving up the money to get this done.

"How many are they?" asked his wife, evidently pleased by the arrival of the new customers. "There sounded like a lot of them. I will summon the servants and get them firing up the heating and fetching foods from the larder."

"A centurion and most of two platoons from the Second Augustan. Sixteen in total," Nepos answered in a distracted manner.

"Wonderful. Common soldiers staying overnight in a travellers' inn?" she laughed. "Whatever next? Not like in your day, husband!"

"No, and not like these days either."

"Did you tell the centurion that you are a veteran of the very same legion?"

"No."

"Why ever not?"

"Because to do so might get us killed," he whispered.

His wife looked shocked. Nepos was careful to close the door tightly behind him. "Something isn't right about it, Perennia, and I fear these men are not what they say they are."

Her hand came up to her mouth as if to stifle a cry while she waited for her husband to explain.

"He calls himself Chief Centurion Mavritius Varro of the Fifth cohort of the Second Augustan but I think he is an impostor. Such a high-ranking officer would not be travelling the road at night in the company of only two platoons, and with no cavalry with him. And travelling this long road on foot in so few a number! It doesn't make sense. It cries against everything I know about the army. Plus, if they were soldiers of the Fifth cohort, why is their centurion wearing the badge of the *Eighth* cohort?"

"We must get the children away from here to safety! Are they brigands, pretending to be soldiers?"

"I don't know but for sure we must get the children to somewhere safe. But we must not make it look like we suspect these men to be impostors!"

"Are you certain about this, Nepos?"

"Very certain. He looks grand and authoritative enough, and he wears the badges and regalia of a centurion, but he has his sword on the wrong side! He wears it on his *right* hip like a common legionary or an officer of the cavalry, not like a centurion!"

"Perhaps it is his personal preference?"

"There is no room for such personal preference in these matters, Perennia! He might, in his own time and at his leisure, prefer fish to pork, or Gaulish wine to Rhenish wine, or olives to capers, but when it comes to his uniform and his rank, he has no choice whatsoever! And he especially doesn't have any choice when he is held up to be the very model of the best of soldiers – the commander of a cohort!"

"Are we in so much danger, you think?"

"I fear so, but they appear to have come here for our hospitality, and I think that if they mean to rob us of our food, and rape you and our daughter, they would not have acted so prettily and politely on the doorstep. I'd be dead already! My hope, but it is a nebulous one, is that they are on some secret business of the legate or governor or procurator and therefore acting in an unusual way, travelling in a very small group and not making marching camps. But it still doesn't explain the sword!"

Perennia was reeling with fright. "Neposius and Censo must shackle the horse to the cart right away, and then they must take themselves and Censoria northwards to the soldiers at Lindinis. Are there still soldiers at Lindinis?"

"I think so," replied Nepos. "A large batch of new recruits have come down from Isca Augusta from what I gathered from the wayfarers this week. There will be legionaries with them, and probably a tribune or even the camp prefect. Proper legionaries! Neposius and Censo must ride there as fast as they can. Tell them to pass a message to whoever is in charge of the soldiers, that Mavritius Varro has been here at our inn, and likely to be an impostor. They can explain that their father is a retired veteran of the legion and can tell the difference. The tribune will know the whereabouts of the real chief centurions of the various cohorts. Meanwhile, get the servants to look upon our guests before they suspect anything is amiss. And for all our sakes, they must not let it be known that I was a legionary!"

His wife was shaking her head, evidently struggling to accept the truth and gravity of the situation. "You are so very certain about this, Nepos?"

"I am."

He opened the heavy wooden door to let his wife out of the room so that she could go to instruct the servants immediately.

The large and menacing figure of the chief centurion was standing just the other side of the door, his large bulk filling the whole frame of it, with his wide chest, armoured shoulders and large exuberant plumed helmet. Varro's face was cold, stern and deathlike. He had probably been listening to the conversation between Nepos and his wife.

"Chief Centurion Mav..." began Nepos, but the vicelike hands were already around his neck before he could go any further, and were stifling the life out of him. Moments later, Nepos fell to the floor like a ragdoll, and Perennia finally let out the scream she had been holding in for the last couple of minutes. Varro stepped over the body of her husband and advanced upon her.

CHAPTER FIVE

TWO days later, another chief centurion rode past Nepos's inn: Tadius Naratius of the Tenth cohort, accompanied by his second-in-command, Luti Bassus, plus the aged camp prefect, Ulpius Senicianus, and ten riders made up of a mixture of light infantrymen who could barely ride a horse and a handful of real cavalry men from the Tenth's horse squadron. Apart from the prefect, the other twelve men comprised all that remained of the former Tenth cohort. The cohort was now five hundred men short of its proper complement. It had never been so depleted.

Luti was also diminished, having lost around half his former weight since he was impaled by a Roman sword. His recovery had been difficult and slow, and even now he was prone to wince when his horse stepped forward too vigorously or stumbled slightly, though he was a very accomplished rider. The old frontier road was in need of resurfacing but at least they had an excuse to ride at barely more than walking pace today: the two-horse carriage in which the prefect sat or possibly slept could only trundle along at a slow speed, and it was piloted by the prefect's laconic black slave, Axum, who could never be hurried, it seemed. And nor did the prefect want to be hurried. Despite his discomfort, Luti was as happy as he ever got. He was counting the days until he got back to his herb gardens in Nemetostatio, and the chance to ride out on to the moor again on his favourite horse and with his favourite horseman. The new greaves of a senior commander shone brightly on his shins, mirroring the untypical smile on his face. If truth be known, he was simply glad to be alive; something he had not counted upon when he looked down that terrible night a few weeks ago and found the legionary's sword getting intimate with his innards.

They hardly gave Nepos's inn a second glance as they passed it, although it looked strangely quiet, and the flowers in the window boxes were evidently neglected. Senicianus looked out the porthole of his carriage and wondered why his favourite inn along this road was closed at this time of the season. He even said to Axum, although not aware of the irony in his words: "Nepos and his family must have gone away. I do hope they have not met with some misfortune, Axum."

"Must have," came the answer from the driving seat, which was a long sentence for Axum.

A few miles up the road they stopped and built a small marching camp for the night, and Axum pitched a tent for his master while the men dug and raised a wall. The height of it was barely up to their knees and could not have stopped a hedgehog, but that was not the point.

In the morning, they set off again after flattening out the salutary wall and scattering earth on the campfire. They only had a few more hours of riding to reach Lindinis, even at their laboured speed, and they expected to be there by mid-afternoon.

About three miles short of the town, Tadius spotted several men digging what appeared to be a trench in a field a hundred paces off the road. There were eight of them in the trench, stripped to their linen tunics, busy with spades. Discarded on the ground to one side of the labouring men was a bright oblong of red material. It looked like a soldier's cloak, the colour of the Second Augustan Legion. A seated man, perched on a little stool at the other end of the excavation, was holding a long thin pole vertically, the height of a man, with a spherical knob of iron at the top end – an optio's vine staff. Tadius guessed that he was seeing a punishment detail, a platoon of auxiliaries sent out the town in order to accomplish some arduous and wholly unnecessary job in their own time, making a hole in the ground that they would inevitably be ordered to fill in once they had dug it deep enough, or the optio had grown tired of it. Tadius rode over to speak to the men. Luti ordered the others to stop and then they followed Tadius into the field.

The optio stood up from his stool and saluted when he saw that a centurion was approaching. More out of form than need, Tadius asked him who he was and why the men were there.

"Titus Marcello, chief optio of the Sixth cohort, Second Augustan," he began. "These men are being punished for insubordination and causing an affray."

Tadius nodded and introduced himself, adding: "So these wretches are part of my new recruits, may the gods help us!"

"I'm sorry to say they are," answered Marcello.

One of the men, his lower half hidden in the deep ditch, was staring at Tadius in an impudent way. His face, besmirched with soil, seemed to be weighing up the centurion in front of him, as if he were thinking to himself what nature of new commander was about to be foisted upon him. He spoke up: "We were attacked by Brigantian shits, so we defended ourselves." He then added out of decorum, "Commander Naratius."

"Did I say you could speak?" shouted Marcello. "And you forgot to mention to the chief centurion that you lot *are* of the tribe of Brigantes, yourselves!"

"What is your name?" asked Tadius.

"Mus."

"Mus? Is that it?"

"Yes, sir. That is all my parents gave me. And to put the legionary right – sir -, we are *not* of the Brigantes, we are *Carvetii*. They lump us together with the Brigantes, thinking we are all the same tribe, but we most certainly are *not*. We are meant to rub along nicely with them, but what should we do, do you suppose, when we are assaulted by the Brigantian shits as soon as the legionaries turn their backs on us?"

"These Brigantian shits, as you call them," replied Tadius, "are your brother-soldiers now! You are not Carvetii, they are not Brigantian, you have signed up as Roman soldiers and, by the gods, that is what we will make of you!"

"Try telling that to the Brigantian shits."

"Shut up!" shouted the optio and he shook his vine staff threateningly, looking up at Tadius for the permission to swing it at the impudent recruit.

Instead, Tadius turned to Luti. "Decurion, take a note of all these men's names. Mus, here, has assigned them their new duties when we get to Nemetostatio. The latrines will no doubt be in need of a good scraping and clean out when we arrive. And we have found our new latrine detail."

Luti daintily climbed off his horse and unbuckled a pannier bag to fetch out a writing board and stylus. The eight Carvetii men looked at him with distaste.

There was a sudden noise behind them on the road. They turned to see the horses at the front of the prefect's carriage rearing up and kicking in the air. They had been panicked by something. The horses bolted forward and turned themselves and the carriage off the road and into the stubble and rough ground of the field. They were heading with the carriage obliquely in the direction of the men in and around the trench, and towards where

Tadius sat on his horse. The wheels of the carriage bounced off a rock and the black slave sitting on the driving board at its front was thrown violently into the air. He landed heavily on the ground, while the carriage, almost tipping on its side but righting itself with a crash, altered direction and headed deeper into the field away from them. The startled head of the camp prefect within it, poked out of one of the ports momentarily and shouted for help.

There was a movement next to Tadius, and he turned to see the recruit called Mus leap out of the trench and, in a split second it seemed, jump on to the saddle of Luti's horse. He kicked the horse robustly on its flanks with his heels and galloped off to intercept the pilotless carriage. Tadius kicked his own horse into action and joined the pursuit.

Mus, with uncanny skill and control, had managed to reach the carriage and pull alongside the spooked horses. He jumped off Luti's saddle and directly onto the back of one of the panicked horses. He slid off it almost immediately but managed to keep on his feet, running abreast of it, his arms hugging the horse's neck. Within moments, the horse relented and slowed down, the other horse following suit.

Tadius caught up and could hear Mus soothing the animals with words he did not understand. The carriage came to a halt. The head of Senicianus popped out the portal and swore loudly.

He seemed to think that his slave, Axum, was still sitting on the driving board out front.

"Axum was thrown off," explained Tadius. "But I think he is unhurt."

The prefect had wrenched the door of the carriage open, and he climbed out of the vehicle. "What happened?"

"Most likely, the horses were spooked by an adder," replied Mus. "There are plenty of them 'round here for some reason. The fields are riddled with them."

"Who is this man?" demanded the prefect.

"He calls himself, Mus. Just Mus. He is one of my new recruits. And I think you possibly owe your salvation to him," answered Tadius.

The black slave now ran up to them, his tunic smeared with dirt, sticks and shrivelled leaves. "Are you alright, sir?" he asked of his master.

"Yes, in one piece, Axum. How about yourself?"

"A bit sore and shaken."

"What made the horses act like that?"

Axum shrugged.

Senicianus looked from his slave towards the distant town, longingly. "Do you know, I think we will walk the rest of the way," he muttered.

Axum nevertheless took the reins out of Mus's hands and attempted to get the horses to turn and drag the carriage back towards the road. Mus helped him. After some coaxing, the horses were persuaded to cooperate.

When the carriage had moved away, Tadius turned to the prefect once more. "Are you definitely unhurt, prefect?"

"Yes, I think so."

Tadius got down from his horse. "I will walk with you."

Mus had started to return towards the trench and his colleagues. When he was out of earshot, Tadius said, "That man acted in an extraordinary way, prefect. Bellerophon could not have done it better! He leapt on Luti's horse without a moment's thought and was able to reach your carriage and bring its horses under control before anything worse could happen! Your carriage was bound to turn over, eventually, the gods forbid! I think a commendation is due."

Senicianus thought about this. "He is barely an auxiliary yet, but I will make a note of it."

Tadius was deep in thought. "You know, prefect, better still. I am in need of an optio, am I not? And I think I have found just the man."

CHAPTER SIX

CRESSIDO Saenus was in love but he could not tell anybody about it, because the target of his ardour was the household slave of his immediate commander, Plancius Vallaunius Rufus, and he knew that Raselg's domestic duties were not confined to cooking, cleaning and fetching errands, but stretched to more intimate services, not surprisingly. She was Rufus's servant and she was his lover. For with her hair the colour of jet, her complexion as smooth and unblemished as ripe olives, her body young and lithe and her beautiful face habitually cheerful with a twinkle in her eyes of mischief and challenge, who but the lamest master would not want such intimacy? What warm-blooded man would not want to raise and extend his expectations of such a woman and widen her curricula?

For several delicious days during the Kalends of the month of Julius, Raselg had stayed in his quarters, looking after Tadius and him, and notionally Luti too, and Saenus had taught her how to shave them each morning. He remembered with fondness the touch of her fingers on his cheeks and throat and the urges this stirred in him. Sometimes their eyes would meet when she tended to him, and he detected an intrigued and slightly confused expression on her face. She was aware of the attention men gave to her but it seemed that she did not know at times what to do with it, whether to welcome it, spurn it, encourage it. That was the sense he got from her puzzled face when their eyes locked. But just when he began to think she was attracted to him, he noted with a covetous envy that she was just as warm and open to Tadius Naratius. He did not know what to make of it, and he saw with deep regret that Raselg was edging her bedroll nearer to Tadius' bedroll by inches each day, and, by doing so, further and further away from his. Thankfully, when the jealousy was getting too much, Rufus took her away and replaced her with his Iberian male slave, Dendus. The intrigue, the temptation and the frustration were temporarily relieved, and soon there were more pressing matters to fill his hours.

After the great battle on the wharfs here at Isca Dumnoniorum, when all but a handful of their cohort was destroyed by the Blood Ankows, and all their sister-cohort, the Eighth, was obliterated, Rufus had made him his second-in-command. Saenus had distinguished himself on the battlegrounds that month and been mentioned in despatches to the legate and emperor. He had been promoted to decurion, a senior commander of the Eighth cohort, the captain of the horse squadron; just as soon, that was, as a new batch of four hundred and eighty new infantrymen and twenty-nine new cavalrymen had been sent down from Isca Augusta to be reformed into the cohort. Now that they had arrived, and what a discordant, chaotic hoard of young men they were, Saenus was busier than ever, trying to knock them into a fighting unit, curbing their instincts to fight each other and to fight the enemies of Rome instead. Each day was a round of shouting, knocking heads, repeating the same mantras, punishing offenders, teaching them to speak in better Latin or at least to understand the most basic orders in Latin. His feelings for Raselg, were pushed aside out of necessity and there were whole chunks of the day when she did not enter his thoughts, only to find in his precious hours of leisure and sleep that her beautiful face returned once more with a vengeance, like an indomitable foe that had merely gone to hide somewhere and now regrouped and emerged to assail him in greater force.

And being Rufus' right-hand man, there were many occasions when he found himself summonsed to Rufus' quarters to share a meal and talk tactics and review the progress of training, and decide what was to be done with particularly troublesome factions amongst the recruits. On those occasions, Raselg would come to the courtyard where Rufus and he reclined on couches, and serve them with wine and dainties, and stir up all the difficult but frankly welcome feelings in him. Raselg, aware no doubt of the effect she had on him, would flirt with her eyes, or was he just imagining it? Her leg would touch his when she bent to pour wine into his beaker but was that just innocent coincidence? She smiled at him with slightly parted lips, or was that just the way she smiled at all the guests? Did she remember those lovely days when she cared for his household and shaved him in the morning, and he treated her with more respect than either Tadius and Luti did? Was theirs a special friendship now, a bond between them that only obedience to her master kept the right side of proprietary?

Raselg, of course, knew exactly what she was doing, and what feelings she had engendered in Saenus, and since she had visited the fortune-teller, it seemed sensible to keep her options open, not burn her bridges. The young decurion was handsome and quickly gaining a reputation in the legion for bravery. The men would look up to him; he pleased his seniors. He was bound to advance in the ranks. Already, at the age of twenty-two, he was higher than a centurion: he was a deputy commander with greaves on his legs and a flourish of stiffened horsehair over his helmet. And hopefully he would not die soon, contrary to what the soothsayer predicted was Rufus's fate. On the other hand, Saenus was barely halfway through his term of service to the army. His opportunity for retirement or to take a wife was so far distant in the future that it was barely imaginable. Centurions and commanders could not take a wife until their service to the army was completed. It was strictly forbidden. The prospects with this new decurion, Cressido Saenus, were very much a long-term investment and Raselg knew herself well enough to doubt she had the staying power. It would take many years of slaving and biding her time, while other opportunities went by, or Saenus got himself killed in the meantime! She could not see the worth in merely being the mistress of an ambitious and progressive young man for such a length of time. On reflection, therefore, Saenus was wholly unsuitable for her requirements. She would still bat her eyelids and smile at him and brush his leg with hers, if only because it was fun and empowered her, and kept her options open. But if Tadius Naratius were to come within her sphere again, that would be entirely another thing, she would employ even more subtle tactics. Tadius was only six years from retirement, and he was a chief centurion, and better still, she suspected that Rufus would bequeath her to Tadius in his will, should he die before his own retirement from the army. Her predecessor, the slave Silpunia, had informed her confidentially that this was her own destiny at the time. Rufus had no family or anyone closer to him than his old friend Tadius Naratius, and it seemed likely that Rufus' will had been altered, or it would be altered in time, to substitute Raselg for Silpunia. Either she would be set free by manumission or, more likely as she was a woman, passed to Tadius by testamentary mandate. Practically speaking, there were little or no prospects with Cressido Saenus in comparison to Tadius: she was bonded to Rufus, and she could become no man's mistress or concubine until she was free or else transferred to a new master upon his death.

These last few days, she would steal glances at Rufus and sigh. By no means an ill-looking man or a bad man, undoubtedly a very attractive man in all respects but that damned soothsayer had seemingly placed a noose around his neck, a shroud about his shoulders, a sword of Damocles above his head. If only Rufus would stay alive and reach the end of his service, and take her and Dendus to his retirement villa in the hills of Italia, and make her his wife, and lead her assuredly into many comfortable years of fine sheets, splendid mosaics, good food, polite society, warmth and security, a free woman of Rome, a thousand miles and worlds apart from the hovel of her father, who went short on food, himself, in order to keep her and her young brother healthy when they were growing up in squalor. That damned soothsayer had spoilt it all, put doubt in her mind, upset her neat plans, made her restless once more, and casting around for alternatives.

One day when she and Dendus were fetching wood to the hypocaust bunker and stacking it tidily to the side of the little room, she asked, "Dendus, what is to become of us if Rufus is killed in battle, as he nearly was last month when the Ankow set upon us, or he falls ill of some plague and perishes? Where will we go then? Who will be our new master, or will we be set free?"

Dendus looked uncomfortable and finally answered: "Our fate is provided for in our master's will and letter of wishes."

"Do you know what provisions they are?"

"I do, but it is not for me to say."

Raselg flinched with exasperation. "Silpunia told me what was to happen with her, so you must have told Silpunia!"

"Or our master told her, himself. Perhaps she asked him."

In time, Raselg found an opportunity to broach the subject with Rufus. It was when he was at his most malleable, after a session of lovemaking. She leant over him, her long hair brushing his sweating face. "Don't ever die." She uttered breathlessly.

"I'll try not to."

"You say that, but you're a soldier. There's a fine chance you will! You nearly did two months ago! In that scenario what is to happen to me?"

"You'll be provided for."

"Will you set me free? Or will you gift me to another man, to slave under him every day of my life – and night?"

He pushed her off him but not angrily. "Look, I don't intend to die, let's leave it at that."

"But you have made a will – why make a will unless there is a chance you might get killed? You know there is a good possibility."

"I wouldn't call it *good*."

"You know what I mean. Shall I tell you something? I don't want to make you angry but can I tell you something?"

"Go on," said Rufus.

"Sometimes when you make love to me, and sometimes in your half-sleep, when you turn over to me, you call me Silpunia."

Rufus's face flashed with pain momentarily. "Do I?"

"What provision did you make for her in your will? Do I not please you as much? Were you going to set her free?"

"It was a different situation. And Silpunia had been a slave all her life. You, on the other hand, have only been a slave for, what, six months?"

"Yes, and before that, I was free! I knew what freedom was! Which hand, anyway? This one?"

She placed his left hand on her breast.

"Raselg, I'll tell you something," he replied. "A centurion cannot take a wife, it is forbidden. So what does a centurion do? He takes a slave instead because that is not forbidden. It's a neat way around the prohibition."

"But a wife has status, she has possessions and money! She goes to dinner with her lady friends and chooses the frescoes in the house and what foods will be eaten. I am nothing like a wife and never will be. I am a chattel!"

"As chattels go, one of the more beautiful types."

She ripped his hand away from her breast and lay on her back away from him, seemingly furious. "And worse, still, you never tell me anything! I don't know *anything* about my future: where I will be, who I will be with -"

"You will be with me. Well, yes, you do not have all the perks of a wife but, in most things, there is little difference between a servant and a wife. Both are bound for life to a man. Both are servants in a way."

"That is ridiculous! A wife has her own slaves to boss around, and to pamper her. She runs the house when her husband is away."

"If our household were bigger, you could have slaves to lord over. Although I am the commandant, my household must be pared down to the minimum, normally only two or three servants. Here, we have three servants because I have retained one of the freedmen of Natalinus as well but, naturally you are the lowest placed of them." After a moment's reflection, he added: "Perhaps later, when I am the *governor*, we can have some junior slaves too, to be bossed around by you."

"Now you treat me like a stupid girl! I know something of your Roman class system. You are of the equestrian class and legates and governors are always of the senatorial class."

"And the emperor, Domitian, is of a *plebeian* family. The Flavians were never senators. They came from a lower class in society."

"Is that true?"

"Yes, strange as it seems." He turned and leant over Raselg, although she tried to ignore him. "And Domitian hates senators! But he likes equestrians! He favours equestrians and, if it were up to him, he would fill the Senate with them and make one the governor and one the procurator of this province!"

"So, you will be an important man one day. Or a dead one!" she concluded peevishly.

Rufus laughed. "In some ways you are just like Silpunia. She wanted to know as well."

"And did you tell her?"

He dropped back on the sheets again and looked up at the ceiling. "Yes, after many years of her asking me. After she had asked me a hundred times."

"So I will ask you a hundred times, starting from now. What is to happen to me? What is to happen to me? What is to happen to me? What is to happen to me? What is -"

"Cressido Saenus."

She stopped her chant and could not speak for a few seconds. "Cressido Saenus, not Tadius Naratius?"

"No, I have changed my will. It will be Saenus, my second-in-command. If I were to die and he survived me, the likelihood is that he would become the new commandant of the fort and the senior centurion of the Eighth. And he will then have the right to live here in the praetorium, and he will need a household and at least two or three servants to run it. So, I have provided for you to go to my second-in-command. It used to be Tadius but now it is Saenus, as it should be. Are you content now? Shall we sleep?"

After a few seconds, she muttered to herself, "Saenus?"

CHAPTER SEVEN

"I don't want to be a stinking optio!" shouted Mus with conviction.

He and Tadius were sitting on the wooden boards of the open-air latrines, a few holes apart at the time. It was not the most fragrant of places in the section of the town set aside for the soldiers, so Mus's words carried a certain irony.

"Well, that's your misfortune," countered Tadius. "Do you really think you have any choice in the matter, Mus?" In truth, Tadius was not sure whether Mus had any choice in the matter, as it was unheard of for a soldier to turn down such an opportunity. There was no precedent for it in his experience.

"But the men will hate me!"

"It'll mean an increase in wages to one-and-a-half that of an ordinary legionary," reasoned Tadius. "That's more than *twice* what you can get as an auxiliary. Do you really want to reject that sort of pay rise?"

Mus thought about it. "So what? More money but I won't have anything to spend it on, except perhaps drowning my sorrows in a victualler's or a brothel in my spare time because I've got no friends and all the men hate me!"

"Not all the men will hate you. The centurions and standard bearers and the tesserarii and the cavalry decurion won't hate you. Well, perhaps the decurion will, because he hates *everybody* unless they're his special friend. It'll mean I can put your Carvetii brethren in the first company with me, and you'll be able to look after them better. *They'll* be happy with your promotion, surely?"

Mus was impressed with this notion. "Will I be able to clobber Brigantians with the big, iron-weighted vine staff if they step out of line?"

"Well, we'll put the Brigantians in another company away from you but, yes, you'll be the *senior* optio of the cohort, with a good degree of authority over the whole cohort, except the centurions and men of the horse squadron. It won't all be honey and sweetness, though: You'll have to be up with the second watch of the night, to relieve the tesserarius and the men of the first watch. That's how we've always done it in the Tenth cohort, and I don't intend to change that.

"I can't read Latin," Mus pointed out, as if Tadius might hitherto have missed some fatal aspect of the idea.

"That's unfortunate but we don't need you to do so, to start with. You can attend lessons and learn how to write reports. All in good time. The priorities will be to get the new recruits looking like soldiers and march them to the Nemetostatio outpost as soon as possible. Do you think you can assist me in that? I've put in a commendation for you, because of what you did to save the camp prefect and his carriage."

"I know you have. And because of that, the decurion has asked me whether I want to join his horse squadron. To be honest, I might prefer that. I've always been good with horses, you see. I love horses. It makes better sense to put me on a mount and have me help run the stables."

"Luti Bassus has spoken to you about this?"

Mus nodded and wondered why a smile was playing at the corners of the senior centurion's mouth.

"If Luti Bassus gives a man attention, there is usually only one reason for that," Tadius added. "And it won't just be your horsemanship."

"Oh, I see."

"Think about it. It's your choice. You're right, it does make sense to use your talents in the horse squadron. I was the decurion before Luti Bassus, so I can see it from his angle as well. But I must warn you: I do think you'll have your work cut out, stopping him from trying to saddle you too. And you might not be able to go to the latrines as safely as you can now."

"I'll think about it," said Mus but now he looked less certain of himself. "Thank you for the offer."

Mus grabbed a sponge-stick and used it on his backside efficiently. Returning the stick so that it stood in the water channel, he rebound his loincloth and adjusted his tunic and leather jerkin. He began to walk away, back to the barracks. Finally, he turned to Tadius.

"One-and-a-half a legionary's wages, you say?"

"More than twice what you would get as an auxiliary horseman."

"The decurion suggested I might be his optio, actually."

Tadius laughed. "Did he? His *chosen man*? Makes sense, knowing Luti. I think he's fallen in love with you. I was wondering why his face was so moonstruck after you accomplished your heroic rescue of the camp prefect. Go and be the decurion's chosen man, then. I suppose your Carvetii friends will understand your particular choice. A bit of pederasty might be worth it if you can be near the horses."

Mus kicked the dirt of the ground in frustration. "Why does this always happen to me?" he rued.

Tadius pretended to be too busy with the sponge to respond to the lamentation. He was tidying up his cloths and replacing his leather belt when he noticed Mus returning.

"Can I have some days to think about it?"

"No. We must be ready to start for Nemetostatio the day after tomorrow."

"Why the hurry?"

Tadius was taken aback momentarily by the young auxiliary's audacious question. "That is not for you to query," he said. "That is not even for me to query. It is up to the tribunes and the prefect. I'll let it go this time, you cheeky bastard! Look, I need your decision tonight, otherwise I will find myself another senior optio."

Mus turned again and, this time, he did not stop walking away.

Tadius watched him for the moment. He could have explained to Mus the reason why the new cohort needed to get to Nemetostatio as quickly as possible: how it was against army sensibilities to have an auxiliary fort which was meant to be an outpost, monitoring the west road into Dumnonia Inferior, unmanned for so long; how it was against fiscal policy to miss the opportunities to check goods coming and going along the road and to collect tolls and to tax the tin shipments from the mines, but he was not going to share strategic legionary business with an ordinary soldier, let alone an auxiliary recruited from a native tribe.

ONE week later the reconstituted Tenth cohort of Brigantians, as they were now called, reached their garrison headquarters at Nemetostatio, and Tadius's optio was not Mus but instead a legionary he had known for a long time: Lugnensus Parius, a half-

Gaul, a child of a Roman soldier and native mother, who had been in the army since he was sixteen. Parius was a hybrid, reared from the start to become a soldier as soon as he reached recruitment age. He had known no other life than the army: first sixteen years of developing and preparing for it, and then ten hard years of the real thing. And none of it had been harder than the last two months: fighting fiends and seeing all his comrades die, one by one. Some said that Parius was changed because of it, was shaken to the core, but Parius was not the only one who woke up with nightmares, to find the rest of his platoon staring at him, blurry eyed in the middle of the night, concern or irritation in their countenances. Tadius was not sure whether Parius would make a good optio, whether the men would respect him or be frightened of him sufficiently but, to be frank, he did not have a lot of options. Eleven legionaries only had survived the battle on the wharfs at Isca on the twelfth day before the Kalends of Augustus. One survivor had since gone insane and the others were spread amongst the six new companies as junior centurions, optiones and standard bearers. The most literate of them was appointed as the cohort's *tesserarius*, to set the watches and the daily passwords and generally act as the commandant's clerk. Luti and Tadius had scratched their heads wondering how to fill the other traditional roles. They had no trumpeters, unless the standard-bearers doubled-up; they had no one to teach Latin to the new recruits. Worse still, they had no medics. If they were lucky, the camp prefect would send them a new medic, but this could take weeks or months. So, when they rolled up in front of the north gate of Nemetostatio, many logistical problems relating to the reformation of the cohort had yet to be resolved. Luti was refusing to assign anyone to the rank of cavalry optio until Mus said no, definitively. Despite Luti's legal brain and natural tendency towards vindictiveness, he could not decide whether Mus should be sanctioned for prevaricating.

The fort gates were locked and no one stood sentry on the large gatehouse. Tadius had one of the standard bearers-cum-trumpeters blow a signal to announce that they were all collected outside the north gate. It was just after midday, and it seemed inconceivable that their arrival had failed to create some excitement inside the fort. They must have been visible for miles, advancing along the long road from the east, a force of over five hundred men, thirty-eight horses and four carts. But the fort was just how the scouts had reported it: quiet and seemingly empty, apart from the ravens and jackdaws perched on the palisade fences and the tiled roofs of the gatehouse, with more of the creatures cawing bad-temperedly within the four turf walls. There were many more birds than Tadius remembered.

Eventually, there was a grating sound behind the double gates, and one of them swung open slowly. Tadius and some of the junior centurions pushed through the gap and went inside quickly, their short *Lucullan* lances poised in readiness. They were met by several civilians, who at least seemed gladdened at the sight of soldiers, more so when they recognised Tadius and other familiar legionaries. Weapons were lowered and a great deal of arm clasps and hugs followed. The centurions pushed the gates fully open, and most of the cohort came in, marching in rough approximations to the lines of four expected of them, and accompanied by much cheering from the civilians.

Tadius looked around. He knew nearly all the bakers, cooks, stonemasons, tile and brick fabricators, metalsmiths and woodworkers gathered around, and he counted forty-six of them. He was glad that they had stayed and been content to wait for the soldiers to return to the fort eventually. "It's good to see so many of you safe, if not a little thinner and paler," he said. "It's unfortunate that you have had to let the fields of wheat and barley go to rack and ruin this season. Did you not think of getting the harvest in? I assume the estate slaves ran away when there were no longer any soldiers to keep an eye on them."

The senior tilemaker nodded and confirmed: "We did what Caratius Lunaris told us to do. We kept inside the fort as much as we could, locking the gates at all times, and only venturing out to buy food from passing traders or to collect water from the river every few days. Some of the estate slaves remained, and we have put them to other uses." The tile maker seemed puzzled when he scoured the faces of the auxiliaries who had come through the gate. He turned back to Tadius and asked, "Where are the Tenth cohort, decurion – who are these soldiers?"

"These men *are* the Tenth cohort, now, or *Tenth cohort of Brigantians* as we are now called, and I am no longer the decurion. Luti Bassus has that privileged position. Do you not recognise the uniform and crests of a senior centurion?"

The tilemaker studied Tadius' helmet and chest and asked, "And Plancius Vallaunius? Is he well?"

"Well enough. He commands the Eighth cohort now. The Eighth cohort of Brittones, as they are now named. It's a long story, one you will hear about before long." As he said this, Tadius at last spotted in the distance some of the figures of the eighty auxiliaries and legionaries who were scrambling on to the top of the parapet over on the south side of the fort. He had sent them to scale the south wall by stealth and to enter the fort on that side, as a precaution. These men stayed on the south parapet, awaiting further orders. "Any visits from Blood Ankows," asked Tadius.

There was a general shaking of heads and mumbling. One of the civilians answered: "Some of the people who had been in the vicus, and some who were in the hospital, have lived in here with us as well, and others came from farms when they judged it safer to be here."

Tadius looked around but he could not spot the people referred to. He thought no more of it and gestured to Luti to direct his men and horses to the horse squadron's stables. He ordered Parius, similarly, to lead the infantry auxiliaries and the men standing on the south parapet across to the barracks, keeping three of the foot soldiers with himself to act as his escort and to accompany him along the street. When the soldiers and civilians were dispersing, Tadius and his escort walked to the praetorium, the commandant's house, which would be his own lodgings from now on. Some of the civilians tagged along with them. It now occurred to Tadius for the first time, that he had no domestic servants to assist him in running his new home. This was something he could sort out later, and, in the meantime, he would eat with the men in the barracks, which would be his preference, anyway. He was not used to living away from the soldiers and horsemen.

Seeing the familiar doors of the commandant's house, opposite the cohort's headquarters and the secured storeroom where the insignia standards and money chests were usually kept, Tadius could not help himself from thinking of it as the house of Rufus. He had been through the praetorium door on countless occasions but always as a visitor, as the second-in-command and the captain of the horse squadron. There was so much new he would have to get used to now. Tadius found himself encountering an emotion he had never experienced before, a sudden pang of loneliness.

This momentary sensation was arrested by a further discovery. The doors of the commandant's house were not locked. The chain and padlock that should have sealed it were missing. The doors opened inwards without resistance, so neither had they been bolted from the inside. Withdrawing his short lance from the improvised loop of leather on his belt, he pushed one of the doors open with his foot. An odd smell came from within, not the fragrance of lamp oil, food and perfume that he had known in Rufus's house before this date, but the odour of dried blood and mould. He was not unduly worried about this. The house had been unoccupied for nearly three months, and the smell of blood could still be from when the fort was the scene of the massacre of a third of the cohort. Tadius remembered the doors of the praetorium splattered with gore, and how Raselg was given the unenviable task of scrubbing it clean.

He knew the interior of the house well, had been in every room and even contributed to building it last wintertime. With his escort close behind him, he checked every part of it. The doors to several rooms were accessed directly from the inner courtyard, the most pleasant part of the house. The pond in the centre of the yard was green and stagnant, the fountains muted. Large cobwebs were interlacing the branches of a vine which grew from a pot, the size of a bathtub. He noticed that the two reclining couches were moved into a different position, as was the dining table. They were not where Rufus liked to have them.

He concluded that somebody had been using this house while Rufus and the soldiers were away. To find more evidence for this, Tadius directed himself to the back of the kitchen, and to the larder rooms. As he opened the first larder door, an intense smell of rotten meat and fungus assailed his nose. Mould fur was growing on barely recognisable shapes upon the shelves. Two rats were scampering backwards and forwards, shocked by the intrusion and trying to find a bolt hole. Tadius slammed the door shut to cut off the smell and stop the rats escaping.

Some of it did not make sense. If civilians had broken into the commandant's house, why had they not stolen the food in the larders, possibly the best cuts of meat and the finest cheeses in the whole fort? Or had they only broken in long after the food had already gone off? He moved to the wine cellar and checked that. To his amazement, the wine amphorae looked untouched, all of them covered with a reassuring layer of dust. This was perhaps the biggest surprise of them all.

They inspected all the remaining rooms and found them empty. The beds in two of the master rooms were stripped of their linen and blankets but two greasy cushions appeared to have been recently used as pillows. The main bedrooms reeked of wet leaves and mildewed leather. His escort soldiers were looking at Tadius for orders, now that the house had been fully searched. He ordered them to go to the barracks.

He went back to the servants' wing and into Dendus's room. Something had caught his eye when he had been in there. Yes, the hook was released on the window, as he had half-noticed, and the dust on the inner window ledge had been scuffed clean very recently. It seemed that somebody had used this window to come into the house or else to leave it. Judging by the absence of any new dust, this could only have occurred within a few hours, some time that day; perhaps when the cohort was spotted approaching along the road. It seemed that one or several of the civilians were not as innocent and respectful as they pretended, or else that the actual culprits were hiding.

Feeling the pang of loneliness again, mixed with some hunger, Tadius went to find company and food at the barracks. He would not use Rufus's house, as he still referred to it in his mind, or feel that it was truly his, until it had been cleaned from top to bottom, rid of vermin, and until he had commissioned a couple of household servants from amongst the civilian retainers or the remaining estate slaves.

Afterwards, Tadius was to chastise himself harshly for missing the clues and not seeing the obvious when it was staring him in the face. He could only imagine that he had been too tired that day, too daunted by the novelty of finding himself the new commander of the military base, or he had been too eager to cling to familiar things and the anticipation of routine and normality.

CHAPTER EIGHT

MUS and the platoon of Carvetii had been placed in the first company despite Mus's rejection of Tadius' offer, and this was fortunate for them and carried an element of privilege. They were separated from the Brigantes, an improvement in their fortunes by itself. They also had Tadius as their immediate centurion, for he doubled up in this role as well as being the overarching commander of the cohort. And they had Parius the Gaul as their optio, a man who was not at all frightening as a disciplinarian, and if anything seemed hesitant and timorous. A legionary named Diodorus had been appointed as standard bearer. A Lusitanian named Asempero held a position unique to the first company, which seemed to carry with it several different functions, including arranging the watches, writing reports and settling upon the daily passwords. He seemed to do everything administrative apart from deal with the cohort's accounts, a job which fell to the standard bearer by convention.

Mus's company occupied the long barracks building nearest to the centre of the fort, the building partitioned into ten interior spaces with a platoon of eight men sharing each, and each with its own door leading outside. Every room was furnished with eight wooden beds and a central table. Hooks across three of the walls carried pots and pans, ladles and various types of knives, skewers and small tridents for grilling. The platoon rooms were intended to emulate field tents and encourage the men to be a self-sufficient unit, akin to a household. The precious goatskin platoon tent itself was neatly bundled up in a corner of each room, placed alongside the stack of wooden struts that made up the tent-frame, and a large bag full of one hundred carved wooden pegs. Outside each door in the barracks block stood a little stone fireplace, upon which the 'household' cooked food in the evenings and kept themselves warm when off duty. If the Brigantes had occupied the same building, no doubt they would be urinating in the fireplace of Mus's platoon as often as they could, and Mus's platoon would of course be reciprocating. Tadius and Parius had done well to put the several platoons of Brigantians in the fourth barracks building, far enough away to avoid the worst of the tribal friction.

Asempero set the shifts of sentry duty this first night in the fort and, having been a legionary in the Second Augustan for sixteen years by this point, he needed no training in the quirks and logistics of arranging four equal watches per day. He knew that the six hours' period this created notionally would almost always bear no parity with the official hours and minutes of the day, for hours stretched and shrank in the Roman calendar depending on the season. Between dusk and dawn, or dawn and dusk, there could only ever be twelve hours, whether they be stretched long or crammed short. The length of an hour of night-time was only equal to the length of an hour of daytime on the day of the equinox of September and the day of the equinox of Martius. In order to ensure that watch-duties remained the same length throughout the year, and that everybody concerned did a fair and equal stint, Asempero and every other *tesserarius* in the army would need to burn a watch-candle, lighting a new one as soon as the last spluttered out. The trickiest part of a *tesserarius's* role was then to ensure that, when they slept, they woke in time to light the next candle. He had to have at least one good friend or be able to delegate to the senior optio when there was a chance he might oversleep. The *tesserarius* was undoubtedly the busiest subaltern in the cohort for, when he was not writing reports and despatches, and taking care of the watch-candles, he was having to rouse the next men of the watch and impart the newest password to them.

The first night spent by the cohort in Nemetostatio, saw Mus and the rest of the first company taking the second watch, during the darkest hours. Tadius posted himself on the north gatehouse, the one nearest the road. It was not beyond the Britons to try to sneak past the fort in the dead of night, the wheels of their carts greased and silent, in order to avoid being stopped and their cargo checked. If they could not pay the road toll or cargo tax in coins, part of their cargo would be officiously confiscated. The heaviest taxes were imposed on the carts carrying newly mined tin from the mines to the west and, consequently, these carts were the most likely to travel along the road past the fort in the most surreptitious manner, and seemingly always at night. Fortunately for the transporters these last three months, it had been possible to get past the fort without being hailed and inspected, the inquisitive soldiers all being away. Tonight, it would be different, and Tadius and the second watch encountered many frustrated transporters who had assumed that those good days would be continuing. They were suitably shocked when the unexpected shout came from the gatehouse. Some did not have the means to pay. A great many rough ingots of tin were wrenched from the bewildered cart drivers and overseers and taken into the fort. The second watch kept themselves busy, and it was not the six hours of deadly boredom the new soldiers had been expecting. If anything, it was fun.

When the first dawn light was tickling the eastern horizon, and it was nearly time to end their watch, Tadius and Parius were surprised to find that one of their number had vanished. As the soldiers had been coming and going between the gatehouses and some were out on the road, confronting cart drivers, while others were busy carrying heavy baskets of ingots, lead pigs and sometimes iron to the secure shed annexing the headquarters building, a head count had not been possible for a while. It now transpired, as the third watch came to relieve them, that a

Dobunnian recruit was nowhere to be found. His colleagues in his platoon were puzzled but it became apparent that this recruit had not been entirely content with his new life as a Roman soldier. The conclusion arrived at, which was not unheard of, especially during the first few months of an auxiliary's induction and training period, was that the recruit in question had deserted. The north gate had been open for lengthy periods during the night and the man could easily have sneaked away through that outlet. The seven remaining men in the deserter's platoon were immediately put on punishment detail. They were meant to look out for each other.

Tadius took the loss hard. He could not help comparing himself to Rufus, who had been the commandant of the fort during the first six months of its existence, and, during that period, they had not lost a single man to desertion. Although the missing man's dissatisfaction with his lot was not something Tadius could have prevented, the incident troubled him. It seemed that the gods did not favour his enterprise as well as they had for Rufus. Tadius went to the little shrine of Silvanus and made a dutiful offering. As was his habit, he slipped a silver denarius into the crack at the base of the altar, and he vowed to be a better devotee in return for some upturn in fortune. This god had been good to Tadius before now, indeed could be credited with saving his life as well as that of Rufus. Tadius went off to the barracks to share breakfast with his soldiers, hoping he had mitigated his fortunes with his votive offering.

It was not to be. The next night and during the second watch period, another soldier absconded during the watch. Tadius returned to the Silvanus shrine in the morning and prayed again and left a second coin stuck inside the altar's base.

On the third night, Mus and his platoon were part of the second watch again, only this night the guards had been instructed differently. The sentries on the walls were to stay where they were throughout the six hours and not get involved in the business of extracting tolls and inspecting carts that came by along the road. Only ten soldiers were engaged in that, and two of them were tasked with the job of watching the north gate constantly. The hope was that nobody would find the opportunity to vanish into the night, if they were minded to do so.

Mus and his comrades were posted on the south-western corner of the fort, the part of the walls situated by the utilitarian part of the base, where the granary, bakery, workshops and storehouses were situated, and where most of the fort's retainers slept. It was the quietest part of the fort at night. Although the fort was relatively small, this corner of it felt remote, being away from the bustle and chatter of the barracks and horse squadron's stables, and not near the secure storeroom where goods were being dumped and locked away throughout the night, the heavy iron-girded door and padlock clanging and clanking frequently.

It was a surprise therefore when Mus, standing above on the wall, spotted two figures tiptoeing between the storehouses below. He could easily have missed them in the dark but as his eyes were accustomed to total darkness, there being little moonlight or other source of light in these early hours of the morning, he picked up the moving shadows in the corner of his eye when he happened to turn in that direction by chance. He was sure that he had seen two men move down there.

He beckoned his comrades silently, pointing down towards the building where the movement had been observed. Mus and his platoon mates quietly descended the steps from the wall and spread out to encircle the area in question as best they could, given there were only eight of them.

Two soldiers were soon found with their backs up against the wall of a workshop, hiding. Mus and his friends pulled them out from their hidey-holes and surrounded them. They appeared to be two horse-soldiers, judging by their chainmail shirts and leather leggings.

"Present yourself to the watch!" ordered Mus in both Latin and Brittonic. "No horseman should be out and about this time of the day! What scurrilous activity are you up to?"

The two horsemen stayed silent for a several seconds. It was difficult to judge the expressions on their faces in the darkness: whether their countenances were frightened or brazen, embarrassed or carefree. The quietness and posture they maintained seemed to indicate a challenging demeanour. They did not appear to be cowered by the situation, nor the eight soldiers of the guard surrounding them. Mus sensed anger and malice but did not know how and why he felt this.

Eventually one of the men spoke up. His accent seemed to be that of a Durotrigan. "I'm Callio of the horse squadron, and this is my friend Guissian. We have some business to attend to, if you don't mind."

The other man, referred to as Guissian, stifled a laugh.

"And what business is that at this hour of the night?" asked Mus, harshly.

One of the horsemen whistled and, a moment later, the door of the workshop near them squeaked open. Out from it came a young woman, wearing only loin and breast cloths.

"*This* business," said the man who called himself Callio. "To comfort a soldier in exchange for two denarii. She is a lovely young companion for an hour or two. Tell you what, let this go and she is yours for free, my friend. I'm sure she can cater for a whole platoon. I've seen her in action. It probably won't be her first time. What do you say?"

Mus replied in the native language. "You have been in this base for no more than three nights and, already, you have arranged this shady type of commerce? That is very enterprising of you, for sure, and I don't doubt that this woman should be very engaging for lonely soldiers at night. But I am afraid that I must put you on report and leave you to be dealt with by the decurion, and the gods help you, as the decurion won't see the worth of your enterprise." Mus laughed. "Not with a woman, anyway."

"You won't do that to us, surely?" asked the man called Guission. He nodded at the woman, and she unbound her upper cloth and exposed her breasts. The men trying to observe this rued the fact that there was not more moonlight. Mus sensed the frisson of excitement around him.

One of Mus's comrades said, "Let it go, Mus. What harm is it doing?"

Mus was going to relent but a loud voice behind him suddenly shouted: "What's going on here?"

It was Tadius Naratius and, alongside him, several more soldiers.

Mus answered: "We have come across these horse soldiers, commander, engaging in, well, you can see for yourself…"

The two apprehended horsemen said nothing. The young woman did not bother to cover herself up. If anything, the three criminals seemed unperturbed.

"You know what the sanction for this is, soldier!" said Tadius. He had already ordered a man to fetch a torch from the south gatehouse. The man and the lighted torch now came back. Tadius took the torch and lit up the offenders' faces. Then he stepped back quickly. "Cassian and Guilio!"

"Yes, decurion," said both of them, standing to attention.

"Not decurion now!" replied Tadius. "Luti Bassus is decurion now. I am the senior centurion and commandant, and where the fuck have you two been all this time?"

"Here, commander," answered Guilio. "We got lost and came back to find the fort deserted. We've been making do and looking after the place since then."

"Lost? Lost for so long that Caratius Lunaris and the remainder of the cohort had left for Isca? That doesn't make sense! You must have been lost for *weeks*." Tadius paused. "*Deserted*, more like!"

"No, not deserted!" replied Cassian, indignantly. "Never deserted! We – we even kept the wolves at bay!"

"Wolves?" uttered Mus.

"Shut up!" ordered Tadius.

"There are wolves on Klocha Fhasach," declared Guilio, pointing vaguely southward. "When the fort was deserted, they tried to get in. We stopped them."

The Carvetii recruits began muttering between themselves.

"I said be quiet!" shouted Tadius.

The woman bound forward, took hold of the head of one of the soldiers who had escorted Tadius and twisted it violently until there was a sharp crack. The soldier dropped to the floor and the woman shrieked with delight. She had pounced on the next soldier before anyone had reacted. At the same time, Guilio and Cassian leapt into action, attacking Tadius and the men near him.

Tadius felt strong hands begin to throttle him, and his vision exploded immediately into a parade of lights, and his ears sang with a crescendo of noise. All the soldiers were unprepared for the sudden attack, and none had their weapons drawn, but there were twelve of them and only three Ankows. Several arms came to Tadius's rescue and managed to wrench Cassian away from his neck. Mus drew his *Lucullan* lance and thrust it into the back of Guilio, who folded immediately but was not dead, as the spearhead had missed his heart.

Once free of Cassian's stranglehold, Tadius fetched out his short lance and prodded it into Cassian quickly and clumsily, and very angrily. Cassian too dropped to his knees, his face showing the surprise and sudden nausea caused by the wound. The woman had turned to try to run away once she realised that the soldiers possessed poisoned lances, but she only got one pace before a soldier pushed his lance forcibly into her back with all his strength, its tip piercing her heart. With a moan of anguish, she collapsed and died, and immediately began to decompose, the air in her lungs squeaking out through the ruptures in them; a sickening sound like that of a trod-upon bladder.

Tadius croaked an order for Cassian and Guilio to be tied up and taken to the guardhouse. "Prick them with the lance if they struggle at all. It will sicken them for a minute or so!" he counselled while trying to catch his breath. "And kill them if they look like they might escape!"

The air was filled with the reek of rotting flesh. The soldiers gagged and were keen to move far enough away from the heap and smell of the shrivelling corpse. They picked up the dead soldier whose neck had been broken by the woman and carried the body solemnly towards the hospital building in the northeast quadrant. The rest of them, including Mus and his platoon, helped bind the two Ankows and drag them towards the north gate where the lockup was situated.

Mus turned to Tadius after a little while. "Are you all right now?" he asked. "They are amazingly strong, and, by the sacred gods, extremely fast! I thought you were about to get your neck snapped."

"It's not the first time an Ankow has tried to strangle the life out of me," answered Tadius.

"Really?" Mus was impressed.

"Over there, by the Silvanus shrine. The night I killed my first Ankow." There was no triumph in his voice, only sadness and regret.

Mus looked in that direction. He whistled with appreciation and awe. "It's true then?"

"What's true?"

"We're Ankow-fighters!"

CHAPTER NINE

THE children loved it. The ordinary soldiers hated it. You drew a square on the road with a lump of chalk, three-feet by three-feet in size, then two squares beyond it and nearly touching. Then you drew a single square again beyond that, then two beyond that, and so on. When you had enough squares drawn symmetrically in one long line, single squares alternating with double squares, you numbered them **I** to **C**. You could make it longer if you wished. Rufus had known such courses to be numbered up to **CC**. The Roman soldiers called it *Gassello*, and they hated it beyond words.

Girls and boys tested themselves on the course when the soldiers had stopped training on it and gone back into the fort, staggering with twisted ankles or carried in by comrades. The girls and boys wore light linen tunics and enjoyed the challenge of trying to complete the course, giggling joyfully and sometimes falling over; careful always to try to avoid the splashes of vomit on the squares towards the end of the line. In contrast, the soldiers were required to attempt the course in full armour, carrying swords, spears and shields and heavy backpacks. Most of them got half-way to two-thirds of the way along the line, and then in the advanced stages of fatigue, heartbeats drumming in their ears, their bodies as heavy as lead pigs, and their legs no longer obeying them, they would usually throw up their breakfast: hence the pools and splashes towards the end of the course. The soldiers hated it. It was intended to improve their fitness, strength, agility and foot-placement, all skills essential in the heat of battle, but it turned most of them into blubbering, nauseated lumps of exhausted flesh. It was so despised that it was often used as a punishment. An optio would shout: "Right, you lazy, good-for-nothing wretch – get out there on the Gassello squares! And you won't be coming back here until I've seen you complete it without putting one foot wrong, no matter how many times you fall over or puke your guts out!" The foot-placement skill came from the rule that only one boot could be placed in each square when a soldier ran along it. This meant he had to hop on one leg then land on two feet and then hop on one leg, continuously *ad nauseum*, literally. If he went too slowly, the iron knob of an optio's staff would hit him in a crucial or painful place, like the back of his knees or top of his helmet, leading to an inevitable collapse or a constellation of stars in his vision, which in turn would cause him to miss his foot placements. Either way, he would have to start again from the beginning. Optiones used the course to hone their skills at landing the knob of a long vine staff accurately on a certain part of a soldier's body. It was good training, all round.

The soldiers could not understand how the children could do it voluntarily, let alone make a game out of it. The key of course was doing it without leather jerkin, chainmail or other body armour, helmet, shield, spear and a pack that was, in itself, half your body weight. Or by using only part of the course and then challenging yourself to pick up a feather or hen's egg placed partway along the course, without standing on it or squashing it in your hands. The children loved it. If you said: "How about some Gassello?" to a child, his or her face would light up in delight. Say the same to a soldier, particularly a recruit who was on the wrong side of the fitness spectrum, and his face would be transfixed in an expression of foreboding, if not terror. It was more accurate to say that children *and optiones* really loved it.

The recruits who had come down from Isca Augusta were unfit, clumsy in their heavy uniforms and armour, and consequently fodder for the Gassello squares. This was the same version of the course etched on the road next to the civitas of Isca Dumnoniorum that Rufus had seen scratched there ten years earlier, before they all went north to Deceanglia and Ordovicia. More recently, Bruccius Natalinus had used it to terrorize his troops.

The tribune, Exuperatus Helius, had arrived in Isca, replacing Livius Colusanas who had gone to Duronovaria on some undisclosed business. Helius was young and new to the legion, and altogether more pleasant and much less pompous than the senior tribune. Rufus had met him for the first time in the summer, at the palatial residence of the governor, near to Noviomagus. Tribunes used their time in the army as a steppingstone to some, more important position. A young, ambitious man with talent, and of an equestrian family, was expected to go into the army at some early stage in his life, and many chose to be a narrow-stripe tribune rather than bind themselves to twelve years of tedious and risky service as a real legionary. It also kept a man's options open because, if they found that the army life was in fact to their liking, it was an easy jump from being a tribune with five years' military experience to being the rank of decurion or senior commander. He might even achieve the post of senior tribune, effectively the second-in-command of the legion. A tribune's responsibilities were for the welfare and discipline of the soldiers and ensuring the smooth running and efficacy of a legion placed far from Rome but, more often than not, it just meant a great deal of travelling between military bases or carrying reports to the governor of a province, and the chance to be bombastic to all he met along the way. Helius was not in that mould, thankfully, and Rufus found he liked the young man. This junior tribune would, for instance, acknowledge when he was ignorant of some aspect of the army.

"It occurred to me," Rufus began to explain to him, while they watched the spectacle of a third of the cohort attempting the

Gassello squares one morning, "that this particular ordeal might serve two purposes. First, it might improve their physical prowess, which is generally pathetic, and, secondly, it might knock some of the divisive, tribal instincts out of them."

"How so?" asked Helius, evidently entertained by the spectacle. One recruit had collapsed on the road, amid the squares, and was being carried back to the beginning of the course by two other men. He seemed unconscious. They were carrying his shield and spear for him.

"It won't be over for *any* of them until everyone has completed the course without putting a foot wrong. They might be there until after sunset, if they have to be. No food, no rest, just water. So, we mix them up: a platoon of Belgae with a platoon of Cantii, a platoon of Dumnonii with one of Atrebates, and so forth. We team them up so they are forced to cooperate with each other or face eternity on the Gassello squares! They learn that they are all the same, they puke up or black out in just the same way, and they learn to need each other, and to help each other, even a man from another tribe. Allegiances are formed, even friendships."

Helius shook his head in wonder. He was watching a man further up the course, doubled-up and vomiting. "We Romans have come up with some awful things, don't you think? There is no limit to our diabolical imaginations, it seems. Crucifixion is a good example and now this, what do you call it - Gassello?"

"They say that the emperor Vespasian invented it, when he was a young man and the legate of our legion here in Britannia. I don't know whether that is true, but his son will be proud of the legend, nevertheless."

Helius laughed. "Oh yes, it will appeal to our glorious emperor Domitian's finest instincts!"

"Come on, let us not ruin our appetites anymore."

Helius understood the suggestion. It was midmorning and a couple of hours since their light breakfast in Rufus's house. They climbed onto their horses waiting nearby and rode to the auxiliary fort. They were let through the east gate without needing to shout the daily password, for the guards on duty saw the helmets and crests of a tribune and a senior centurion approaching.

At the praetorium, Dendus took their guest's helmet and cloak and placed it in the bedroom reserved for him.

"Where is Raselg?" asked Rufus.

"I sent her out to buy beans and pork fat," replied Dendus.

Rufus nodded and directed Helius to one of the couches in the atrium. Rufus's other servant, Luperus, a slave who had been freed under his old master's will and was now retained in the household, offered Helius a plate of pastries and fruit. Helius took a pastry and waved the man away. Luperus was back a few seconds later with a goblet of wine for the guest.

"Vallaunius, now that we have an opportunity to talk, man to man and discreetly, as it were," began Helius when he was ready.

"I thought I ought to tell you that your fortunes are very much on the rise these days, and you are back in favour. There was a time, I don't mind telling you, when you were quite out of favour, particularly after that incident with Silius the Younger, and when your slaves ran amok and killed no less than a senator -"

Rufus bristled to hear this description of events. He was tired of correcting the wrong versions of it but, on this occasion, he could not be bothered to do so. The young tribune saw the pained look on Rufus's face and said: "Well, that was how the governor and tribunes saw it at the time, whatever really happened. Anyway, I meant to say that I think you are quite forgiven on account of your exploits and heroism in the battle of the Julian Ides, here at Isca Dumnoniorum."

"Thank you for informing me, Exuperatus Helius. It seems that one must get oneself slaughtered, maimed or cut to ribbons to enjoy an upturn of fortune and favour in this army – if one doesn't have the right connections, that is."

"I think that is true," said Helius. "In your case, and I know this from the briefings I received from the legate and broad-stripe when I enlisted as a tribune, your reputation did not help you. You were seen as a captain who was irreligious, insubordinate, arrogant and who gambled too much. But who was always a bloody good soldier."

"I have tempered my nature these days," replied Rufus in defence.

"I hope not!" said Helius brightly. "As I was quite looking forward to meeting you!"

"I also pray to my god, Silvanus, regularly", added Rufus. "I choose my religion carefully. I can't abide all these other selfish deities, most of whom I'd like to punch on the nose if I bumped into them."

"You and many others!"

"I can't help thinking this is leading up to something," said Rufus.

"Well, yes, it is. Now that you are the hero of the hour and mentioned in despatches to the emperor, Lucullus is considering sending you to Rome with the new lance, to show it off to the emperor."

Rufus thought about this. "Then I would rather we renamed it the *Domitian*."

"Why so?"

"The emperor will be furious! He is the son of the famous and distinguished general of the Second Augustan Legion, Vespasian, but when the very same legion invents a new lance – a weapon that will be the salvation of men and revolutionise the army - we call it the *Lucullan*, not the *Vespasian* or the *Domitian*!"

"Then, why did you call it that?"

"I didn't. It was my decurion, as he is now."

Helius searched his memory. "Luti Bassus?"

"Yes."

"Then it is for Lucullus to rename it."

"He won't, he's too proud and egoistic. He has embraced the name."

"This does put another slant on it," pondered Helius. "Perhaps the legate wishes to send you to Rome to test out how the new weapon will be received; whether the messenger might be blamed for the bad news. Perhaps Lucullus thinks it might come better from you, an equestrian: knowing that the emperor thinks more highly of equestrians than senators."

"Do they not know about it, yet?"

Helius shrugged. "Word might have got back about some new lance but perhaps not its name."

Rufus was surprised. "And the Blood Ankows – do they know about them?"

"They will know something but not all the details. That is why Lucullus is thinking of sending you to Rome to make a full report. You are the best man for it, when you come to think of it."

"I am not sure about that. Why not Colusanas?"

"Because Livius Colusanas has not fought them at first hand! He has not even seen one of the devils. In fact, none of us have!"

"I will go if they wish to send me. But I would rather report it to the Senate, not the emperor. They at least have some brains between them."

"They also have Silius the Elder! And, in any case, Britannia has little to do with the Senate. It is part of Domitian's personal estate, not a territory of the people of Rome."

"What happened about Domitian's planned visit here?" Rufus asked upon reflection.

"He keeps putting it off. He's too distracted by what is going on in Dacia, and with the new palaces and public buildings he is constructing everywhere."

"How advanced is this plan to send me to Rome?"

"A suggestion, an option, no more. Think no more of it for the time being. I haven't been sent here with the purpose of telling you about it, I merely mention it in passing as it concerns you. I have been sent to oversee the reformation of the two cohorts, the Eighth and the Tenth, as you might have guessed."

"And what is your assessment so far?"

Helius pulled a wry face. "You have your work cut out, that's for sure, but I don't suppose there is a better man for the job. You have a great reputation for soldiering, and the men look up to you. You are also, dare I say it, known for being ruthless and as cold as iron when you need to be. The fear that such a reputation causes in recruits is no bad thing in the circumstances."

"An example being?"

"Letting a whole village of Britons be slaughtered under your very nose because you decided that no Roman assets or lives were at stake at the time. And having done this, not just the once - but twice!"

"I don't feel happy or proud about that. But let us flip it the other way: Had I sent in my infantry on those occasions, and it turned out that some of them got killed, I would have been reprimanded for risking good Roman lives without a just cause. So, it was neither ruthlessness nor cold-heartedness, it was nothing more than simply obeying standing-orders and being in fear of sanction."

The servant returned to check on the men in the atrium, his jug of wine ready to administer. Both Helius and Rufus waved him away again. When Luperus had departed once more, Rufus said: "I seem to have more servants these days than I need. I inherited three from Natalinus. I sent one back to the brothel she came from, the others became freedmen, including Luperus who you have just seen. The other servant preferred to return to his folks in Venta, and mercifully so for my part, because I would not have known what to do with him. I already had two slaves before I inherited Natalinus's post and his house as well."

"One from Lusitania, who you've had for years, if I recall," said Helius. "We met him in the porch, and a rather beautiful young Dumnonian. The prefect and broad-stripe are quite irritated by your reputation and good fortune in that regard, but I do not see anything wrong with it. Would they rather you dallied with another man's wife or caught the clap from constant use of the brothels?"

"As many have! No, it's a neat way around the prohibition against marriage."

"And far cheaper than a wife!"

THE slave in question, Raselg, was at that moment visiting the cavalry buildings in the north-east quadrant of the fort. She had purchased the beans and pork fat from a shop nearby and taken a circulatory route back towards the praetorium that conveniently passed the stables on her way. Yesterday it had been mutton and barley but the decurion had been absent. Today, on a second attempt, her luck had improved, and the captain of the horse squadron was standing just within one of the stable rooms, brushing down his horse.

She started to sing as she passed the spot, to draw attention to herself. And, as expected, he hailed her.

Purporting to be surprised at finding herself outside the stables, as if her daydreaming had led her astray, Raselg returned the greeting. Saenus had stopped brushing his horse and come to the stable door to enquire what she was doing. She showed him the pack of food items in her basket. She feigned shyness and went to continue on her way, then, changing her mind supposedly, said: "I hear you are a brave man, Cressido Saenus, and distinguished yourself here at Isca, and that we slaves and servants all owe our lives to you. Is that true?"

"Some say so, but I did no more than your own master at the battle of the Julian Ides, probably less," he replied.

"Yes, he is undoubtedly brave too, but…"

"What is it, Raselg?" he asked when she did not continue with the thought.

"I was going to say that he may be as brave as you but he is not such a good teacher. Far from it."

"What would you have him teach you? Your Latin is surprisingly good, and I am sure you are adept at everything else required of you."

She returned his ironic look in equal measure and walked through the stable's door, passing him nonchalantly, and went to pat the horse on its large, chestnut rump. "About horses, decurion. I would like to learn how to ride one."

"And what good will that do a domestic slave? Do you mean to fetch the groceries, wash pans or to peg up washing from a horse's back?"

She laughed heartedly. "Those would be fine tricks but not any that Dendus would approve of, let alone Plancius Vallaunius! No, I mean to know how to ride a horse properly. The first time I was astride a horse was when we travelled together to

Noviomagus, and you will recall what great efforts and difficulties I created for everyone, clinging on to the back of whatever poor soul I was shackled to. Slowing the cavalcade down each day."

"You caused me no such difficulties, if I recall. Far from it. It was a pleasure, not a burden."

"Oh, Cressido Saenus, you are too polite!"

He began to blush. "Raselg, I would like to teach you how to ride, teach you everything about horses, but a decurion's free time is very limited. Presently, I am having to teach more than twenty recruits how to ride properly, in the Roman-cavalry way. And when I am not doing that, or tending to my own horses, I am asleep in a stupor of exhaustion. The new recruits are proving very problematic, it is worse than breaking in horses. And I don't imagine you have much free time, either!"

"I know. I don't. I'm only able to sneak here today because I pretended that we needed something to buy for the larders. And I can only do that because the commander is also so busy, and he doesn't bide where half his household is. He is with the recruits from dawn to dusk, every day."

Saenus was surprised and evidently excited. "You sneaked here?"

She nodded and looked around as if to emphasise that this admission should not have been overheard. She was pleased to see that they were alone in this part of the building.

"You see, these are not the days for trifles and selfish pastimes," he said after a moment. "Not yet. Neither of us have the leisure or the opportunity. Let us place the idea to one side then, Raselg. I promise, if somebody else has not done so already by then, I will teach you how to ride a horse. Like I taught you how to shave a man. Do you remember?"

"I remember it well, and I have put it to good use. You are improving me, stage by stage, Cressido Saenus, because no one else has the patience or the kindness to teach me things. I will always be grateful." Her smile was lingering, distracting, provocative, as it was intended to be. He smiled back at her in earnest, like a pack animal mimicking a contagious yawn, making the emotional connection. There was an awkward, unseen lump of something hanging in the air between them for a moment. She barged straight through it and kissed him warmly on the lips. It was quick and she stepped back the moment she had done it.

Once he had regained his composure, he said quietly, "I am patient and kind to you because, frankly, I have grown to love you."

For days afterwards, he was unsure how to decipher the expression on her face: whether she reacted to this sudden declaration in a good or a bad way, to admonish him or encourage him. The ambivalence was of course designed to baffle him, manipulate and hook him. She looked down at the floor and stepped outside the stables, but she turned to look at him eventually and say in a business-like tone, "Let us place the idea to one side, then, Cressido Saenus."

CHAPTER TEN

THE great moor of Klocha Fhasach was at this time of the year as dull, dark-green and spongy as the moss that grew on the sides of old canals. Its vast landscape seemed to swallow up what little colour remained in the year. Dark bruised hills and sodden hollows appeared to spurn the rain that fell relentlessly upon them, pushing the wetness away in scornful rivulets that ran ever downwards. Even the wildflowers that grew there were of a kind that shrugged and elbowed enquiring life away: spiky thistles and prickly wild rose; stinging nettles and skin-tearing brambles. It was September and the cursed and indignant land was in an even fouler mood. It had turned its back on joy and dragged a cloak of dank mist sulkily over itself.

The soldiers viewed the moor with various opinions but with a common denominator of loathing. Most of them held the blighted land in deep suspicion, believing it to be the abode of evil spirits. A place not meant to be visited. Others were not in such awe of it but hated it anyway because it was the venue for twenty-mile forced marches and because the ground was very wet underfoot, which meant hours of trying to dry leather sandals near a brazier, afterwards, and then more time rubbing copious amounts of fat into them to make the leather supple and wearable again.

Some of the soldiers were even more reluctant to go to the moor today because they knew they had grim, judicial killing to do there, and were dismayed by the prospect. Most of the men avoided investing such scruples or compassion, willingly disengaging feelings and prepared instead to mindlessly follow the orders of the commander and decurion. After all, that was what was expected of them. Some felt angry and vengeful because they had received deep claw marks on their faces or necks in the fight that had just occurred in the fort, or else they reproached the Ankows for a childhood full of fears and nightmares. A minority relished the thought of the slaughter this damp morning.

The Ankows had numbered forty-eight when they had surrounded them at dawn and proceeded to capture them. The fiends fought back ferociously: spitting and cursing and clawing at the soldiers, trying to strangle them. Only the poison lance kept them at bay. Five Ankows died in the melée. Two soldiers who were throttled within an inch of their lives were only saved by the quick action of their comrades, and quick thrusts of the new weapon. But it did not end there. Forty-three Ankows were eventually led out of the fort and towards the rise of the great moor to the south but, knowing that they were being marched effectively to their oblivion, the captives refused to go quietly. It was a slow and arduous ordeal. Each few paces, one or other of them, or a group in concert would turn and hurl themselves at the soldiers, as quick as an African cheetah and as strong as a lion. An auxiliary infantryman died in the skirmishes during this fatal march. The soldiers were highly jittery and began to take on the look of devils themselves, bug-eyed with tension, their faces rigid and glistening with sweat. Rain fell continuously, seeming to grow worse the nearer they got to the moor.

Tadius had ordered that they march their captives one mile only and then set to executing them, but that relatively short distance turned into an eternity and began to feel unachievable. By the time they reached what Tadius judged to be an early and auspicious place to do the killing, yet only half a mile beyond the fort, thirty-two of the fiends were still left walking. The others lay in suppurating heaps of bone and dissolving flesh in the wake of the grim procession. And on the heath, one dead soldier who had not changed but looked asleep would have to be fetched and carried to the hospital furnace when the soldiers came back this way.

Tadius and Luti who had known seventeen and twenty-four years of soldiering respectively, could not remember anything quite so desperate and unsavoury as this morning's task. They had watched prisoners being executed in groups before, particularly under Agricola's stern governance, but this was worse. All but two of the prisoners were civilians and people they had known for years. They looked the same and spoke the same as they did before, even if they did not act the same, and it felt very wrong, instinctively, to march them out into open country and officiously slaughter them. Similarly, it appalled them to think of killing two of the horsemen so familiar to Tadius and Luti; men they had billeted with during the last ten winters. It was an obscene day.

There was a hushed silence when Tadius gave the order to stop. A stand-off developed immediately. The air between the raised points of the soldiers' special lances and the chests of the shaking, spitting and cursing prisoners was so turgid as to be capable of slicing up like a pig's liver.

Cassian shouted in plaintive tones, "Decurion, tell me you are not going to do this to your old comrades! We served with you in Ordovicia and Deceanglia! We shared our bread and drank and whored together in Isca Silurum! For the gods' sake, have pity!"

"You have no gods now!" answered Tadius. "Or none that I recognise. In truth I do not hold you in any blame, Cassian. It could be me standing there. I know that very well. But you have seen what you've done to all these people, made them as wretched as you, and it must stop."

In a less friendly voice, Cassian replied, "It was *you* who led us to this! You ordered us to go find the Eighth cohort, which placed us in jeopardy of being attacked alongside them, and, if it were not for that, Guilio and I would be standing where you are now, on the other side of your precious lance!"

The rain was cascading off Tadius' helmet steadily now. Through the veil of water, and after a pause, Tadius turned to his optio, Parius and said with a heavy heart: "Get on with it."

The remaining Ankows attacked all at once. A final desperate campaign to preserve what was left of their lives. Although the soldiers were already highly alert to the danger, they were taken by surprise by the suddenness and speed of it. Many had carelessly lowered their spears during the exchange of words between Cassian and the commander, and they could not raise the points quickly enough to arrest the charge. Several soldiers went down with a savage opponent upon them, and a terrifying snarl filling their ears. Only the cheek guards of their helmets prevented the monsters' teeth biting off a chunk of face or an ear. There were many more soldiers than fiends as, otherwise, the odds would have been clearly with the Ankows. They were at least twice as strong as any man and twice as fast.

Above the crescendo of snarls, screams and shouts, another sound now erupted: a wild chorus of excitable howls and barks. Dark beasts had appeared out of nowhere, from every direction off the heath, and they began attacking the Ankows immediately. Flashes of fangs and wild glittering eyes and a maelstrom of claws and dark fur everywhere. It seemed at first that the Furies themselves had descended upon them, but the soldiers could see within moments that it was a pack of large wolves or, more bizarrely, a clan of hyenas. It was difficult to discern which in the chaos and vortex of movement, and the beasts appeared to own features of both predatory species. They were targeting the Ankows and not the men, and the soldiers scrambled away as soon as they could and watched the spectacle unfold - the massacre for that was what it was. It lasted less than a minute, at the end of which, the torn bodies of thirty Ankows lay upon the rye grass in various grotesque shapes, mottled and streaked with bright red blood.

One wolf-hyena seemed to be the alpha. She barked a command and the frenzy stopped at once. Then the beasts turned their frightening heads to look at the soldiers, a mix of bright gore and saliva dripping gloopily from their bared teeth. The animals did not appear satisfied with the killing so far.

Tadius had pulled Guilio and Cassian away from the killing spree and placed them behind himself as if to hide them. He was not sure why he had done this. It was perhaps an automatic reaction, when he saw men wearing the remnants of the uniform of Tenth cohort horse-soldiers being attacked before him, and his mindless instinct to rescue them had kicked in. In the heat of battle, another part of his brain tended to take over, it had given him the knack to survive the closest, most chaotic and violent confrontations so far. His actions in those moments became the product of repetitive training, animal instinct and an urge for self-preservation. Reason was suspended.

Tadius saw that the beasts were aware that two more Ankows were hidden amongst the one hundred and twenty-three soldiers standing and shaking before them. The large animals sniffed the air and the heckles rose on their broad muscular shoulders. They began to hiss like cats and stare-out the faces of the men. Guided by smell more than any other sense, the beasts could not distinguish Cassian and Giulio amongst all the taut, bulging-eyed faces paraded before them, not able to pinpoint the hateful smell amongst the crowd. Now that they were still, the creatures could be seen better. The men were still unsure what they were witnessing: whether wolf or hyena, or a sinister mixture of both. They were as ugly as hyenas, that was for sure.

The large alpha amongst the creatures bent her neck and sniffed at a *Lucullan* lance that lay broken on the ground near her. She shook her head violently and whined in frustration and indignation. She barked something at her comrades and they, too, began to whine and howl. If anything, they looked even angrier.

Luti spoke up, his voice high-pitched and tremulous but the words confident and verging on arrogant. "They sense we are armed with poison lances, men! These lances will work just as effectively against wolves as they do against Ankows! Remember, they contain the dreaded *Wolfs-bane*, after all!"

As soon as he said this, a hundred or so soldiers pushed their lances forward in the air, threatening the beasts. Several could not help themselves shouting "*Wolfs-bane*!" like a taunt.

"If they *are* wolves, that is!" shouted a soldier. It was Mus. "They don't look like any wolves I have ever seen!"

Several men turned to him in surprise, wondering where he had encountered wolves in his life.

"Hold your mouth, soldier!" shouted Tadius. "Keep tight order, and don't turn your faces or your weapons away from the beasts for one moment. And we will slowly retreat in the direction of the fort. Tight order, do you hear! Every one of our lives depends upon it!"

And so began a macabre dance of men and she-wolves. The men walked backwards, and the animals advanced proportionally to preserve exactly the same distance. After this had gone on for a minute or so, the wolves fanned out and encircled the men on all sides. They hoped to stop the men's progress by doing this, but Tadius quickly issued orders and turned the men into a tight, compact disc, every soldier facing outwards towards the ring of drooling animals, lances bristling outwards. They continued to walk ever so slowly in this awkward configuration, the two Ankows hidden amongst them.

Minutes passed. Men stumbled occasionally, sometimes when their feet stepped in or became snarled in the bones of the decomposed bodies of Ankows, heaped on the ground every few hundred paces. These men were pulled up on to their feet again by others, quickly. It was agony and took every ounce of their concentration, but it seemed to be working. Only, the fort seemed hardly to grow any nearer for all their efforts and the time that passed.

When they had covered around half the distance back to the fort in this ungainly and precarious fashion, a cornet blast blew from the south gate of the fort, and Tadius saw to his immense relief that the gates had been flung open and men were streaming out of the fort in rows of eight, together with twenty-odd cavalrymen on their horses, who were already galloping towards them. The horsemen had their long cavalry lances poised horizontally in front of them. It was a sight designed to chill the hardiest soul but it brought nothing but joy to the soldiers alongside Tadius. There were cheers and noisy cries of gratitude to the gods.

The she-wolves, seeing the sudden change in their situation, appeared to decide it would be less risky to run off southwards towards the rise of the great moor. But after covering a couple of hundred yards or so, the beasts stopped abruptly and together all in one instant, presumably at a command from their leader, and stood still to stare back at the men.

Tadius had the good sense to find Guilio and Cassian, who were still cowering amongst the crowded soldiers, and he placed them back under arrest. "Skewer them like pigs if they try anything!" he shouted sternly. For some reason, perhaps because the soldiers were ecstatic with joy and a feeling of life-affirming triumph, and they would find anything and everything worth cheering about, they whooped with delight at hearing their commander's words.

Luti's second-in-command arrived with the other members of the squadron, and pulled up his horse. He greeted Tadius first, as proprietary demanded, and then his captain, Luti, with a concerned but happy smile. Everybody knew where Viterius's affections and preferences really lay.

"One of us dead, lying out there some three hundred or so paces," said Tadius, regretfully. "Can you get the poor soul back into the fort and cremated?"

Viterius nodded. His head was turning backwards and forwards, from his cherished captain to the pack of animals still standing and observing them from a distance. "Wolves?" he asked, incredulously.

Tadius laughed, not that it was funny in any way, but the absurdity seemed to call for it, as well as the welcome release of tension. "Yes, wolves."

CHAPTER ELEVEN

HELIUS was departing. Not to Nemetostatio, as per his earlier orders, but back to Duronovaria, the capital town of the Durotriges region. Messengers had arrived carrying new orders for him, and hence a change of itinerary. He was circumspect about the reason for the change of plan, mainly because the order had been vague itself. It said only that he must meet with the Fifth cohort and the broad-stripe tribune urgently, as trouble was brewing amongst the Durotriges: a possible but petty rebellion, led by the remnants of the subjugated Celtic aristocracy. There had long been tension between the ethnic people and the Romans in that area, the bloodshed at the great fortress of Mai Din, not yet forgotten or forgiven.

Rufus checked the orders himself, in case they had missed the part of it that mandated the Eighth cohort to go as well.

"Your cohort is not deemed ready for action yet, and, in any case, it has a special function now, as you know," suggested Helius.

Rufus sighed. "But the Fifth cohort vexillation don't have the numbers to contain any uprising," he pointed out.

"Not yet. I suspect that we will be reinforced before long."

Rufus handed back the letter. "I know Duronovaria very well. This order is ill thought through."

Helius responded with a wry shrug, as if to say: *our elders know better*. "I will be leaving this afternoon. I am sorry that I will not be able to observe your fine efforts any longer or go to see how Tadius Naratius is faring with his at Nemetostatio. I am convinced, nonetheless, that the new cohorts are in good hands, especially if Naratius is as fine a commander as you say he is."

"Both he and Luti Bassus are the best," said Rufus.

"Well, then. I must get my bodyguards ready for the journey. And we will meet again soon, I do not doubt."

They shook arms like old friends rather than saluted.

"One last thing before I go," said Helius, on reflection. "I was hoping not to have to bring this up so early, until I was sure about it…"

Rufus waited for him to go on.

"You know I have my scouts, looking around and keeping a close watch on things. You might call them *spies* -".

"All tribunes have them, if they are any good at their job," pointed out Rufus

"Well, yes, that is true." Helius clearly looked uncomfortable. He paused before going on. "Your decurion, Cressido Saenus, has been getting intimate with your domestic slave. She has been visiting the stables, disguised as a boy."

Rufus's face flushed pink with anger. "How long has this been going on?" he asked.

"A week or so, that's all. There is even a possibility they have met out in the countryside. Saenus has been known to ride out on his own recently, with spurious explanations. I suspect he has been encountering her there."

"Encountering? Are you sure he has not just been teaching her to ride? She has asked me to teach her about horses so many times, recently. It has been quite an irritation. I don't know why she thinks she needs to learn, although possibly it is in the hope of being less of a nuisance when she travels with me…"

"Well, let us hope so. It was a little more than that in the stables, however. Unless he has a strange way of teaching a woman how a beast should be ridden!"

"They have been seen in conjunction?" stammered Rufus.

"I am afraid it is the case. More than once. My, er, scouts are certain about it."

"She is a Dumnonian," mumbled Rufus, confused. "They believe they must provide a service in return for another service. It is their nature."

"That might excuse *her* diversion but, not perhaps your decurion's breach of subordination."

These last words appeared to make Rufus even redder. He could hardly speak. Helius took the opportunity to pat him on the shoulder and say in a final tone, "I'm sorry."

He left Rufus on his own.

THAT same afternoon, when Helius was putting the final touches to his packing in the room laid aside for him, Rufus appeared again. He seemed hardly any calmer than before.

"She is with your escort, placed on a horse and ready to go with you! One of my ironic touches," announced Rufus.

"I don't understand..." said Helius.

"You need a servant. She is yours now. Take her as a gift from me. I have too many servants. I will get my subaltern to send on the written confirmation in due course."

"You are giving Raselg to me?"

"Yes. I will deal with my decurion, separately!"

"But, Rufus, I cannot just turn up at Duronovaria with a slave in tow! What will Colusanas say? You need to think this though."

"Colusanas cannot very well criticise you. Most tribunes have at least one slave back at their headquarters. Yours will simply be on her way to Isca Augusta and accompanying you in the meantime. And Colusanas took Natalinus's mistress with him when he departed from here some weeks ago! You will *both* have a new servant in tow."

"Rufus, are you sure about this?"

"Take her, get her out of my sight! It won't be the first time I have given my servant girl to a tribune!"

Helius laughed. "But look how that one turned out!"

The two men stared at each other. "My mind is made up," said Rufus with finality.

Somehow, word got back to Saenus as to what was afoot. He came to the praetorium and craved a meeting with Rufus. Rufus told Dendus to send him away. When the male servant had turned the flummoxed decurion back to the stables eventually, he came to ask Rufus what was happening.

"But what has she done to bring this about?" he asked his master.

Rufus was pacing about the little courtyard within the house. He stopped and answered, "This is precisely why we do not have wives, Dendus, when we are supposed to be devoting all our time and energies to governing soldiers and maximising their chances of survival and success! When they are not being needy, wives would be distracting us with this kind of conduct!"

Dendus appeared confused. "She has been going missing of late, popping out to buy food and to do errands when the same did not seem necessary, I have noticed that. I have suspected something was going on, sir. I would have informed you but you have been so busy, yourself, and…" His voice trailed off.

"I am reformed, Dendus. No more distractions! I have a reputation, you know? Always a beautiful slave near me, they all

121

say. Lucky Vallaunius, how does he always manage it? Did you know I have a reputation? The tribunes and prefect have told me I do."

"No, I did not know, sir."

"We have enough servants now. You and Luperus. I do not need Raselg." He could barely utter the last word. "It was bad enough with Silpunia! They bring me nothing but woe!"

"But, Rasclg, sir? Are you sure about this? I must confess, I have rather got to like her now. She seems very talented."

"Yes, and I am helping her with her ambitions! She won't stop here! It won't stop with my decurion. She is, well, devious!"

"That much is true. She had me quite fooled for a time into thinking she could not speak a word of Latin."

"She has had us all fooled. And she will make bigger fools of us, yet!"

Dendus nodded.

"Get her away from here, Dendus. I am not going to see off the tribune. You do it for me. And keep that damned decurion away from her, if you can."

"I will try my best."

"And Dendus…"

"Yes, sir?"

"It's about time I made you a freedman! I will see to it as soon as I can. I don't want Luperus thinking he has airs and graces above you. He shouldn't."

A tear formed in Dendus's eye. He struggled for words.

"Well, go on, then!"

The male servant bowed and left the courtyard.

CHAPTER TWELVE

"YOU seem to know a lot about wolves, tell me what you know," said Tadius Naratius. They were standing in the dank courtyard of the cohort headquarters, the principia, Luti Bassus and Asempero too. And Mus, who had been summoned on Luti's suggestion and just been asked this question.

"We have them still up in the mountains in Carvetia. Not many now, but enough to keep the legends and fears alive. And we have serpents in the great lakes and wild cats as well. Wonderous and mysterious things!" Mus appeared very proud of it.

"I am not surprised to hear that," replied Tadius. "I have been to your country, and it is indeed an enchanting, if not a foreboding land."

"Foreboding, sir? Far from it. They are the most amenable and beautiful lands in the world!"

"And what lands have you actually seen?" asked Luti, pointedly. "Have you seen Italia, Germania, Gaul, Iberia,

Lusitania, Mavritania – like some of the people assembled here in this courtyard? No."

"I have not," said Mus, abashed.

"You said that these wolves we have just engaged with on the moor here, are not like any wolves you have seen," continued Tadius. "I must confess that I have never been face to face with a wolf at such close quarters. What do you make of them?"

"They are wolf*ish*," Mus tried to explain. "But bigger and stockier and these creatures seem to be feline too, as if they are half-cat and half-wolf."

"Like a hyena," ventured Asempero. "I have indeed been in Mavritania, myself, and seen those animals. I would say that the beasts here are *more* hyena than wolf."

"I have seen hyenas in captivity in Massilia and the arenas in Rome," said Tadius, and I agree with you. Is it possible that there are hyenas living out in the wild hills of Klocha Fhasach?"

"They could be living all over Dumnonia Inferior, for all we know," proffered Luti Bassus. "We hardly know anything about those remote lands. I have heard that there is another great moor further along the peninsula, even more mysterious. Divorigenin used to talk of it."

Tadius's head turned to look at Luti, enigmatically. "The Celtic horse dealer, the gods preserve his soul."

"Yes, a man of useful knowledge at all times," replied Luti, regretfully.

"Could this Divorigenin be found and questioned about the creatures," asked Asempero.

"Hardly," answered Tadius. "On account of Plancius Vallaunius killing him!"

The tesserarius's mouth clamped shut.

"He became an Ankow," explained Tadius, and then turning to Mus, "he was the very same Ankow who tried to throttle the life out of me, that I told you about. Vallaunius saved my life."

"We could send a delegation out to speak to the High King," suggested Luti. "His court will know as much about the creatures as anyone."

"And how do you suppose we do that without putting our lives in danger?" countered Tadius. "The High King, as far as we know, is not inclined towards us Romans, and we would be five hundred against thousands!"

"There is no evidence that the High King is so ill-disposed towards us," replied Luti.

"There is no evidence, either way! We simply don't know how we might be received. That is why we have left him and his people alone for the most part. I suspect that our advance into his country might be seen as an incursion, if not an invasion. We would need a whole legion to venture that far without risk, and even then…"

"We could send a friendly invitation to parley," suggested Luti. "Enquire of any traders who pass this way, and see if they would carry a message to the High King's court."

"And hope it does not get garbled along the way," said Tadius in irritation. "If they had a damned written language, we could at least put it in writing, and make it flowery with diplomacy."

After half a minute of further contemplation, Tadius said: "There is another possibility. Luti, remember that weird Druid we met up on the moor this summer?"

Luti nodded. "It's worth a try. If we can find him again."

"I suspect he will find *us*."

After a pause, Tadius added: "Good, let's do it as soon as we can."

That seemed to end this part of the discussion. Luti then spoke up: "Commander, there is another reason why I wanted Mus to be at this meeting. I want him to be my standard bearer."

"Standard bearer? Is that suitable?" queried Tadius, surprised.

"Eminently so. He does not need to deal with finances, nor even write Latin in the horse squadron. And you have seen what he can do with a horse."

"Indeed I have. But, Mus, what do you say about this? I thought you wanted to be with your Carvetii compatriots?"

"Well, that's just it, commander," continued Luti, interrupting before Mus could say anything. "It just happens that I have eight trainee-cavalrymen who, let's face it, are never going to be much good for my purposes. I was going to talk to you about it, anyway. Then we have Mus and his Carvetii brothers, who are keen horsemen, all of them, and I suspect very qualified for my purposes, but who have landed in the infantry by accident! They love horses in Carvetia, horses and deer. They're known as the *Deer People*, by the way. With your consent, commander, I would like to have the platoon transferred to my squadron by exchange. You know from your own time as decurion that it makes sense."

"I'm willing to give it a go," said Mus, finally having the opportunity to speak.

Tadius could not find an argument against the idea. "Very well, make it so."

He dismissed the meeting. "One last thing, Mus, before you go."

"What is it, commander?"

"Enjoy the riding, try not to get too saddle sore, and mind how you go, that's all."

Mus looked bemused. "I will, sir, don't you worry."

"TO Plancius Vallaunius Rufus, Senior Centurion and Commander of the Eight cohort of Brittones, from Tadius Naratius, Senior Centurion and Commander of the Tenth cohort of Brigantians, on the eighteenth day before the Kalends of October, Greetings and may Jupiter and our Master and God, Domitian, find favour with you on this their joint Festival of Ascendancy.

Our news in summary: The new Tenth are shaping up. We have some very fine horsemen in the Carvetii and some fine infantrymen in the Parisii. I reserve my judgment on the Brigantes as, although they form a large part of our cohort, and we are indeed named for them, they are a troublesome and divisive lot. If I could get them to fight Ankows like they love to fight other tribes, I will have succeeded in something! Parius is my optio now, Asempero my tesserarius, Diodorus my standard bearer. We have no discrete signallers or medics. Luti is proving a useful decurion and has Viterius as his optio and a young Carvetian, called Mus, as his standard bearer. Mus is the man who saved the life of the camp prefect with some astounding horsemanship when the prefect's carriage went feral outside Lindinis. You have probably heard of this incident already.

We have killed some Ankows and have two in captivity, being my previous legionaries, Guilio and Cassian, who perished, as it were, alongside Natalinus's two maniples of the Eighth. Not all Ankows went to Isca and attacked us on the Ides of Julius it seems.

Now for our strangest news: We have discovered new creatures living on Klocha Fhasach – a cross seemingly between a wolf and a hyena. We call it a Wolfena *for want of a better name. They attacked our captive Ankows and killed them all except Cassian and Guilio who I managed to save, although I will probably regret it. Yes, it is true, I rescued two Ankows!*

Luti and I intend to find the Druid on the moor and seek his knowledge of the Wolfena for we need to know how to contend with them, or else Klocha Fhasach may become too dangerous for us. C and G say that the Wolfena have attacked the station already, but they fought them off with ballistae. The Lucullan works just as well with Wolfena.

I challenge you to have more exciting news than this, friend, and of course I pray that you take care to keep yourself well."

Asempero looked up from his paper. "Any more?"

"No, that should do. Get it delivered."

"Good," replied the tesserarius, shaking his weary hand.

It took five hours by horse to travel between Nemetostatio and Isca Dumnoniorum, and, surprisingly, Rufus's reply was already back with Tadius the following morning. It did not have all the flowery introduction and flourishes that Tadius's letter had, that was not Rufus's style. It simply said, in Dendus's recognisable handwriting:

"Do not go to find the Druid until I am with you. I leave for N tomorrow. Yes I have news but nothing happy or exciting. S A V, a.d.XVIII Kal.Oct."

Asempero, who had brought in the daily password and night report to Tadius with the letter, said ruefully: "Clearly, Vallaunius's scribe will not have such a tired hand as mine!"

Tadius laughed. "That is typical of my friend the commander of the Eighth cohort for you. Morose and curt!"

He called for the two auxiliaries who were acting as his temporary household staff, to prepare a room for the arrival of the commander of the Eighth cohort of Brittones, and to be ready to accommodate Dendus and Raselg, as he assumed. There was already room enough in the stables for Rufus's expected escort of cavalry.

But when Rufus appeared the next day, he was without his servants and accompanied by just half the horse squadron. Tadius was not altogether surprised. He knew Dendus hated travelling and he assumed that Raselg could still not ride a horse. The slaves would have been a drag on the journey. It was only when Rufus cleaned himself up and reappeared to join Tadius for a meal in his atrium, warmed by the underfloor heating, and he had drunk a few beakers of wine, and rather too quickly at that, Tadius noticed, that Rufus began to explain what had happened.

Tadius heard him out. Finally, he said: "You gave Raselg to the tribune, Helius?" He appeared piqued. "You know I would have gladly taken her off your hands, Rufus. She was fond of me, I think, and in all honesty, I harboured certain feelings for her too, admittedly of the carnal sort."

"I may have acted rashly," replied Rufus. "Not in passing her on to somebody else, that was the right thing to do, but in passing her to Exuperatus Helius and not you. But, then again, I would not have been doing you any great favours. She is devious and ambitious. She will prefer to be with a tribune now. That is for sure. If I had passed her to you, she would have been on the lookout for the next tribune who passed through."

"Did she show any interest in Helius, then?"

Rufus looked perturbed. "No, in truth she did not."

"Are you sure the blame does not lie then with Cressido Saenus rather than Raselg?"

"I am not sure of anything!"

"Take another drink, my friend." He poured Rufus another beaker full. "You know, at this rate you will have every tribune in the legion calling by so that you can give them each a beautiful slave girl! First it was Silius, then Helius. Next it will be Tammonius, Valerius, Vitinus, Silvanus – even Colusanas!"

"Not Colusanas, he already has his hands full. He took Natalinus's old mistress off with him!"

Tadius guffawed and nearly spat his wine across the room. He choked a little on it and had to right himself. When he had stopped laughing, he said in a strangled voice, "I do not know the woman, is she so old?"

"No, not really, perhaps thirty years. Younger than us."

"I never knew the wooden, sour-faced broad-stripe had any blood in him! Not enough to erect his manhood sufficiently, anyway!"

"The point is, Tadius, I am done with it. My reputation now post-cedes me! Before long, people will think of me as a eunuch, dedicated to soldiering only. In fact, knowing my weakness for a pretty woman, it would be better if I make myself a eunuch properly. Do you think it will hurt so much?"

"I should think so! And if I were to discover that you were a eunuch suddenly, I would have a *Lucullan* lance put straight through your heart immediately, just in case you were an Ankow!"

"I had not thought of that! I had better stay intact then, and hope I can maintain abstinence through ethics and self-discipline!"

"You know, there are always brothels. I would have thought there are some of those still in Isca. Maybe the same whores we visited will still be there for you!"

"I hope not. That was ten years ago, Tadius!"

"Rotten with disease by now, then."

Rufus raised his wine. "Here's to *new* whores!"

They clanked beakers.

"In six more summers you will have licence to marry, Rufus, and will have more time and energy to put up with the mischief of a wife. And children, little *Rufi* running around, like a bunch of radishes."

"There is little chance of surviving till then. This is my life now, Tadius, as it is and always will be."

"Perhaps, but console yourself with the thought of how much you love the army!"

"I do love it, Tadius, though it may appear at times that I hate it. It is everything to me."

"You know, it is more like old times now. Like when we first soldiered in Germania. We do not have a single civilian or retainer in the fort now. We bake our own bread, shoe our horses ourselves, make our own weapons, build fences and repair roofs. We plant crops and tend the fields so something might grow, with the will of Ceres and Flora, next spring. My household servants are two auxiliaries from the Dobunni. In a way, I like it like this. It is more - what is it?"

"Pure?"

"Yes, less complicated."

"Talking of less complicated, let us hope we find that mad Druid quickly enough."

Tadius was staring into his wine. After a few moments, he said: "That night – the Battle of the Ides of Julius as they call it…"

"It was actually the fourteenth day before the Kalends of Augustus, if you remember, but that doesn't fit so readily on the tongue. Yes, go on."

"Well, I have dreams about it now. I see visions of it. I remember Druids being there now."

"Me too. I know there were Druids there, for the one from the moor told me so. I have disturbing memories too. They are happening more and more now, and I don't always understand them, because there are other, frightening aspects of it that I cannot see clearly. There were other elements, as if the Furies were present too."

"I am glad I am not the only one. I have imagined gods were there, fighting for us: Silvanus and Mars, and the heroes from old. But then I realise I am not seeing forces in the image of *men* at all, but something less tangible – the embodiment of anger in some other form! I have tried to push it all from my mind, and the visions trouble me little during daylight, but then…"

Rufus waited.

"The creatures we encountered on the heathland this week…what we have rudely called Wolfena – I think, Rufus, they were there too on that night! I recognised them, although at the time, I did not realise this!"

Rufus closed his eyes and tried to arrest a vision that his memory might have preserved from a recent dream of it. Had he seen animals too? He shook his head because it was all too dim and black now, beyond reach.

"Perhaps when you see them yourself, you might recall them," suggested Tadius.

"We have so many questions for this damned Druid, when we next meet him."

They drank to that.

CHAPTER THIRTEEN

IT was not the first time that the horsemen of the Eighth cohort of Brittones had felt pride and rivalry. After all, they were of the tribe of Catuvellauni, whose High King had once ruled all these lands, at least on its surface, and who had gone further than anyone else to try to unite the peoples against the Romans, and to nearly send them back from where they came. They felt pride, and aggressive rivalry with the horsemen of the Tenth cohort of Brigantes, not because they were Roman cavalry in a competing cohort, notionally, but because of a natural enmity that ran deeper and longer into the past. The treacherous Brigantes had sold their heroes into Roman slavery, their bitch of a queen had sided with the enemy and filled her coffers with Roman gold and silver. When they had been forced to billet with the horsemen of the Cohort of Brigantes, yesterday evening and night, they were ready to tell the bastards what they thought of them, straight to their primitive, northern faces. They had not been prepared to find, however, that the horsemen of the Tenth were just as contemptuous of the mainstream Brigantes as they were, and just as scathing about the sordid history of Cartimandua and the

Romans. "We are not of them!" they persisted. It turned out that they were instead of the Lopocares, Gabrantovices, Tectoverdi, Setantii and Carvetii tribes, names that the southerners had never encountered. The Romans in their ignorance had lumped them all together and called them Brigantes. It was like calling a fish a frog and then hoping that it would croak and jump from rock to rock. Their optio, himself a Carvetian from the watery mountains on the fringes of the Brigantian kingdom, had brokered a pact, if not a truce, with his counterpart in the Eighth squadron. It was meant to hold until the men went back to Isca, and to be enforced viciously. The two optiones were adamant about that, though neither of them was Roman. It helped to be on twice the wages of an ordinary auxiliary and have a big stick, and to be keen to keep these privileges.

Today, when they headed off for the great moor, following the meandering river along the flatlands that led to it, the rival horsemen of the two cohorts had been able to keep themselves apart. Only half the squadron had come with Rufus from Isca, and now an equal number from the squadron of Nemetostatio set out with them, mirroring them at first; the Catuvellauni riding along to the east of the river with the two senior centurions and the chubby decurion beside them, while the optio with fourteen of the Setantii and Gabrantovices rode abreast of them to the west of it. Later, as they reached the edges of the rising heathland, the separate wings of riders fanned out to scout the rough land and mostly lost sight of each other.

The rain was holding off for a change but clouds of various hues of grey swirled in the sky above them, and a breeze was growing stiffer as they gradually ascended. The horses were unhappy, their feet struggling with the soft and uneven ground, and their nostrils flaring at scents they picked up in the dynamic air.

It was first time that the horsemen of the Eighth cohort had seen the notorious heights of Klocha Fhasach. It was known as the Cursed Land to the Catuvellauni, and its notoriety had become merged with the general area known as the Land of Giants or as the Land of Holes. The people from these parts were themselves referred to as the People of the Holes. Legend had it that, when the Romans came in great numbers, the natives had burrowed under the Cursed Land, and there they still resided for safety, emerging only to dance around stone circles and to sell tin-laden rocks and jewellery to passers-by. And over the years, the people had shrunk in stature and were now more akin to moles, and nearly as blind. They were known to eat worms, disguise themselves as bundles of rags and to snort like little piglets in order to entice inquisitive children and steal them away to their underground grottoes.

No little people to be seen today, when the soldiers on their horses reached the first sweep of the great moor, no dancing around the occasional stone circles or standing stones of great provenance dotted about the landscape; only the bleak sway of the land and the large birds wheeling silently around the ash-coloured sky. Gusts of rain now blighted their travelling, like cold gravel thrown in their faces suddenly. They wrapped their cloaks about themselves and tilted their helmets into the wind. The commanders and subalterns had been wise enough to leave their plumed headgear back in the fort and adopt the plain but more practical helmets of the cavalry. Thankfully, the weather was not settled into any one mood.

Mid-afternoon, when the rain abated and the sun even appeared for the best part of an hour from behind the ragged clouds, the centurions called a halt to the riding and the men sat about, eating, resting the horses and trying to dry their cloaks by spreading them on the smooth rocks of an outcrop. The ground below them, away from the escarpment, was marked with the unmistakable rectangular outline of an old marching camp. Rufus told the assembled horsemen, those that were not away scouting the land still, that here was the very spot where they had met with a Druid, and it was this very same Druid who they hoped to find again. The decurion added that it was here too, more importantly, that the secret of the poison lance had been imparted to the Roman Empire. "Wisdom changed hands, from one culture to another, in this very same spot!" The decurion seemed almost overcome with the significance of this. He held his own lance aloft and stared wistfully at the iron point of it, punctured with its rows of tiny holes.

Rufus and Tadius thanked the decurion for reminding everybody of this auspicious event, and, not forgetting that they, as commandants of the forts, were masters of religious ceremony, then ordered the men to stand and raise their *Lucullans* in the air and give thanks to Mars for the special gift of the new weapon. After that, they hailed Vulcan and Silvanus and invited the auxiliaries to add their own connotations. Without hesitation, the Britons all raised their lances and praised their god, Lugh, and the goddess, Morrighan, shouting their names at the top of their voices. Rufus and Tadius joined in enthusiastically.

When they were all sitting again, the assembled soldiers felt invigorated and happier with their lot. It was as if they had found some common thread to weave them together: the northerners and the southerners, and those from Germania and Italia. Rufus got up and went to the pannier of his horse, and drew from it the small wooden plaque of Pegasus which they had dismantled off the cohort standard. He held it aloft and asked the men what they thought the winged horse was called. Some dutifully, replied "Pegasus".

Rufus nodded and asked them what this magical horse was also called. The men looked confused, so Rufus prompted them by adding: "Perhaps it is *Enbarr*. Or perhaps *Morvarc'h*?"

The auxiliaries looked astounded. He had also managed to pronounce the names in a decent enough accent.

"Do not the horses called Enbarr and Morvarc'h fly in the air, over sea and land, too? Who is to say, therefore, that this is not a picture of one of those, and not Pegasus?" he contended.

"What you are saying, commander," interrupted Luti's optio, Mus, "is that your magical horses are our magical horses too, just with different names?"

Rufus turned to the young optio. "Yes! And Lugh is also Mars, and Morrighan is no other than Pallas Athena, herself! Or, if you find that too difficult to believe or accept, they are sufficient equivalents for our purpose."

There were grumblings and all shades of agreement or contradiction.

"Sufficient equivalents?" queried one man aloud.

Rufus held the plaque high in the air. "When you are marching into battle under the glorious standard of the Second Augustan Legion, and you look up and see this icon, think to yourself that you are seeing Enbarr or Morvarch'h! Your gods go into battle with you, not just the spirit of Domitian and the gods of the empire."

Rufus saw that he had taken the discourse as far as he should and went back to his panniers to put away the plaque. The seated soldiers continued their muttering. It was not clear whether Rufus's spontaneous sermon had made any converts or just created bafflement. Even Tadius looked in two minds. Luti was still staring at his lance and rubbing his stomach. Unbeknown to anyone but himself, he was reflecting on the benign favour his own god had bestowed upon him, when, as the Ankow's short sword had entered his midriff that dreadful night, a spontaneous entreaty to Nerthus had erupted from his lips. He was not one for praying, or could be described as religious, but the prayer had come out: "Oh, Nerthus please preserve me, and I will forever be your servant!"

And he had lived. The medic was surprised. The men laughed afterwards and said it was all his fat, and the modern infantry sword, the *gladius*, was simply not designed to go through so many folds of it before entering a vital organ, but Luti knew better. The mother goddess had preserved him.

They continued on their journey, heading further into the uplands. The rest of the day passed without event and the sun soon began to brush the western ridge of hills. They halted again and set about building a camp for the night. A rock-crowned edifice stood out majestically against the dusk sky to the west. The river, which they were still following, had petered out to a narrow stream by now. The scouts came back to report that they had found the source of the Nemet river but nothing else of note.

Roman soldiers in an overnight marching camp do not make any noise when they are preparing themselves for the stay, save for the inadvertent fart, or clank of a pot or an iron utensil. There is little conversation and no singing. Their ears must stay alert for other sounds. The campfires must be minimal, lest they ruin the vision of the men on the watch. Once you have eaten the evening meal, and if you are not called to be on watch, there is nothing else to do, or indeed want to do more than climb into your bedroll and sleep, especially when you have been travelling all day and have just helped build as quickly as possible a long thigh-high wall on four sides, and have dug a perimeter trench.

Sleep was fitful for some: Tadius and others who were unsettled by the prospect, and indeed anticipation, of hearing wolves on the moor and being ready for the shock of it when it inevitably occurred. They woke occasionally, wondering why no howls had yet pierced the night, why such a normal level of relative quietness prevailed. It was like stumbling upon a familiar comrade, finding him as still as death but seeing no murder weapon or sign of wound: reassuring but at the same time raising the question, why and how such stillness could exist against all expectation. Or it was like looking over a friend's shoulder to see what they were reading, expecting to see words but seeing a blank board where there should be writing.

It was not total quietness. The wind, battering against a nearby lofty configuration of rounded, layered rocks, caused a fluting note that rose and fell. The eerie call of a goatsucker bird could be heard in the far distance, occasionally the strangulated, coughing bark of foxes, and always the low, night-time familiar background of men snoring. The hours of night were equal to those of the day at this time of the year, and they passed slowly for some people.

Rufus was always a bad sleeper. He often rose and went for a walk at night, a habit which at least ensured that he could go back to bed and sleep another shift. He decided to emerge from his tent and join the men of the second watch when they were stirring themselves for the six hours of duty. He first paced alongside the salutary wall on all its four sides, which seemed to take a minute, then set off into the moor alone on foot. The soldiers on guard assumed he was going off to relieve himself.

He headed for the river, which was narrow now and had cut a trench in the acidic turf nearby, and was flowing faster because of the gradient. The sound of the water whispering along its deep channel grew louder as he approached. There was a second purpose to his outing: he hoped that it would provide an opportunity for the Druid to appear. Whether it was the case or not, Rufus expected that the man would try to convene a lonely meeting with him first, as he had done on the ramparts of the fort at Isca. They had a special relationship, the Druid and he, or so Rufus assumed. They liaised because of a common interest. The Druid could in all reality be just about anywhere in the country at this point, so Rufus was aware that his assumption might, on the one hand, be a stretch. But a calming faith, verging on a religious one, impelled him to believe it.

When Rufus at last spotted a white figure, standing in the river trench some two hundred paces downstream from him, he breathed a sigh of happiness and congratulated himself, and quickened his pace.

To his astonishment, however, on drawing nearer to the spectral shape of the person, he saw that it was a woman, and she appeared white because the diffused moonlight through the thin clouds was reflecting off her skin from head to legs, and she was completely nude. She looked for all the world like an alabaster statue of Venus. He approached no further and watched. She was wading very slowly along the river away from him.

After a minute so, he decided to follow her. His superstitious mind warned him that this could be nothing but a supernatural entity, perhaps even an Ankow, for a natural, mortal woman does not wade along a river in the dead of night, in the middle of a wild, cold moor, naked as a new-born baby. The apparition was far more likely to be ghost, a siren, a nymph, an Ankow, a decoy. A trap. He opened his cloak and unfastened the *Lucullan* lance and placed it ready in his right hand. He was till walking nearer to her, but she had stopped wading. He was perhaps only a hundred paces from her now.

She turned and looked at him. She began to watch him walk nearer with an inquisitive and not unduly concerned countenance. This, in itself, was uncanny, wholly the wrong reaction in the circumstances. She should have been shocked to the core to see a man approaching her suddenly from out of the darkness.

His soldiery instincts froze him but heightened his senses. He was sure, more than ever, that it was a trap, and he had fallen into it. He waited for it to spring, knowing it would.

She smiled warmly and dropped her arms to her sides, and waited for him to come nearer.

He calculated that he was far beyond a point where he could turn and run back to the fort, if this was indeed an ambush, and he would do better to brazen it out, defy the situation, stand or die without flinching. Part of him, despite the surprise for feeling it, did not really care.

They were near enough to talk now. He could see her clearly and form some idea of her age and possibly her ethnicity. Her skin was very pale, which was normal for the people of these parts, her hair very long and of a fair colour. Her proportions were pleasing, and suggestive of an athletic strength, her face less attractive, perhaps plain in comparison. Rufus judged her age to be around thirty.

"Don't be afraid," he said, which was a ridiculous thing to utter, as she appeared less fearful in the circumstances than he felt.

She said something in reply but it was meaningless to him, spoken in a thick Dumnonian accent in the local language, and he recognised the voice, just a notch higher than a familiar one.

If the trap were to spring, it would have done so by now, and Rufus realised with a feeling of relief that the woman was a Druid. She could of course still be an Ankow. He approached her further, so close that she could bend and sniff the perforated tip of his lance. She looked up in surprise, significantly the first actual surprise she had shown. He did not understand the word she said then.

She turned and began wading back upstream. He followed her. At a point roughly where he had first spotted her, she stooped and picked up a heavy robe or cloak from the bank. Rather than put this garment on, she spread it out on the spongy turf and climbed out of the stream to lay herself down upon it. She opened her legs and placed her arms flat on the ground beside herself, and stared up at him, waiting. She was offering herself to him.

Rufus stared in wonder for a moment, then his soldier's instincts caused him to whirl his head around to check that he was not about to be jumped. But there was nobody else there, and nowhere for anyone to hide. They were alone. The seconds passed while she lay still, never once taking her eyes off him. He put the point of the lance to her chest, directly over her heart, if only to see how she reacted to this. He would expect an Ankow to show fear, perhaps even swipe the lance away. Her expression showed agitation, but it was not fear, more like anger, or hurt, perhaps arousal. Her breathing had quickened, her chest rising and falling rhythmically. He pushed the point of the lance into her skin, feeling the resistance of the breastbone. She cried in pain but still did not move. He withdrew the lance. A spot of blood bubbled up from her skin and a thin line of it ran down between her breasts and on to her abdomen.

At least two minutes had gone by since he approached her. It was unlikely to be an ambush, and he felt reassured that the woman was not a fiend, or fey, but an ordinary woman of flesh. A Druid. He bent and scooped the edges of the heavy robe and overlapped them over her body to cover her. He knew some words of the local language, so he said enquiringly, "Father?" because he did not know how else to describe the Druid he was looking for.

She responded to the familiar word, her eyes widening. She began to get up from the ground, putting on the robe and then pointing to a dark rock some hundred or so yards away. She took hold of his hand and pulled him into the watercourse. He was right, she was strong. He felt the cold water immediately around his feet and ankles. She pulled him further, up on to the opposite bank and led him towards the dark rock. He freed his hand and stopped. She grabbed it again, immediately and smiled as if to reassure him that it was safe and not a trap. He relented and let her lead him.

Although he half-expected somebody to appear from behind the rock when he drew near to it, the rock itself suddenly moved and stood on its feet. The large hood went back, and Rufus saw at once that it was his friend, the Druid. They shook arms, and the Druid said: "Daughter, this is the man the Romans call Plancius Vallaunius, or Rufus, who I told you about."

Noticeably, she appeared to understand the Latin.

"You are her *father*!" stammered Rufus.

"So I am told," the Druid replied with a wry smile. "I had only enjoyed fourteen summers of youth when I found myself so blessed. I still don't know how it happened. Her mother was a very beguiling woman, that's for sure. A lot older than me. Believe it or not, man-they-call-Rufus, I was a handsome fellow when I was a lad. Turned a few lasses' heads in those days."

"What is her name?" asked Rufus without thinking.

"You know better than to ask me that," he replied.

Rufus acknowledged his mistake with a nod of his head. "She offered herself to me. And you were watching us all the time, weren't you? Was I being tested?"

"Tested?" laughed the Druid. "No, she's probably just feeling a bit randy tonight! She doesn't get much opportunity, living up here!"

"I can imagine that."

"I often accompany her to the river at this time. She likes to bathe herself in the water of the sacred groves and convene with God."

"Who is her god?" asked Rufus.

"*Your* god too. I believe you might call her Cybele or Magna Mater."

Rufus turned to look at the woman, recalling her naked form. "Cybele? The name suits her."

"If you say so."

"Are you not frightened of the wolves, Druid?"

"Wolves? Are there any in these parts?"

"Yes. You know there are! You once told me that Ankows are not scared of you Druids but scared of something else. Were you referring to wolves?"

"Not wolves as such, *she-wolves*."

"I don't know the difference. Will you tell us about them? What we need to know? It will help us. The creatures have already attacked our soldiers and killed a great many Ankows who we were holding. It's all new to us. Your knowledge will be invaluable."

"Yes, by all means." The Druid pointed to the large stack of rocks on the nearby hill, silhouetted against the grey-purple sky to the west. "Meet me up there after dawn, today. Bring your friend, the one you fought alongside on the night we had to rescue you. And the German one who grows herbs."

"Luti?"

The Druid smiled like a parent patiently suffering the nonsense of a child. "If you say so."

CHAPTER FOURTEEN

PUTTING it in context, although the change had been sudden, extreme and daunting, Raselg could at least announce to the spirit of her father, as she rode her horse alongside her new master, that all had now transpired as he hoped. He had wanted nothing better than that she become the wife or consort of a rich and important Roman. He would be dancing with joy to think of her in the household of a tribune.

Exuperatus Helius seemed a good man. She had met him back in the summer at the palace of Noviomagus, one of the six tribunes there for a war counsel with the legate and the governor of the province. He had acted kindly towards her then, better than he was doing now in fact. He was young and good-looking, and, as a narrow stripe tribune of the Second Augustan Legion, he should be financially secure and well-favoured for promotion or for an eminent post-army life of luxury. He was also not in any particular danger of being killed while serving his empire. Junior tribunes were destined after retirement from the army for an important civilian post. Not politics, as that was reserved to the patrician classes, but an esteemed functionary of some kind, such as a tax collector, an aedile, a banker or lawyer. He would live in a villa, and he would be respected, feared, left alone. All Raselg had to do was please him, stick with him and be there when he turned his back on the army and left this island of occupation, this stepping-stone. She sighed with pleasure when she imagined glorious Roman towns beyond the Ocean, even the great city itself. Would the palaces be even grander than the one she had stayed at in Noviomagus? That had been a real taster of the magnificence she could expect in the real Rome.

Helius did not seem to know what to do with his new slave. It was as if he had never had a servant before, but that could not be true. He largely ignored her for the first part of the journey from Isca Dumnoniorum to Lindinis. He glanced at her sometimes but, when he did, he looked confused and even bashful. He spoke to her sternly but this seemed a pretence. Oddly, he appeared embarrassed to have her there. He sent her back to the rear of his escort for the second half of that day's travelling.

At Lindinis, she was placed in a tent that was not too near to his. On her own, and unsafe. They were outside the town walls in a temporary and deserted military camp adjoined to it. Here, a cohort of new recruits, destined for the Nemetostatio outpost in Dumnonia, the very one she had grown up near and later lived next to, had been housed for a week. They were gone now, but the walls and trench the new recruits had built on three sides of a rectangle, were still there, enclosing a large, mainly empty field.

Nearly seventy tents had been pitched in rows but now there were only a handful: Helius's tent, the tents of his bodyguard, and hers on the outside. They shared the field with a herd of pigs, thankfully fenced off to one corner. Their horses were in another corner.

Helius did not need her to wait on him in the evening He ate with the men. Her food was brought to her tent. She sat in there, listening to the noisy and sometimes ribald conversation of the soldiers. Occasionally, when the voices became hushed, she suspected that the men were talking about her. Why else would a group of soldiers need to whisper?

The next morning, they continued the journey towards Duronovaria. It was a road she had travelled along previously, ironically in similar circumstances, with a new master who went out of his way to be indifferent towards her. Once again she would have to be patient.

She had plenty of time to think, to reflect and plan. Riding was far more comfortable now. She could sit on a mount by herself since Saenus taught her how to do it. How not to be such a burden on the road.

She persuaded herself that she was content, although truly she was missing the people she had grown fond of: Rufus, Dendus and Saenus in particular. She could not think of Rufus without drawing breath quickly. She had been able to take his company, even his affection, for granted, when she knew he would always be there. Now that he had cast her off permanently, the wrench to her innards felt like nothing short of trauma; like she had felt when she was dragged away from her father and little brother and turned into a slave. She found herself weeping, for all her losses and, most surprisingly, for being separated from Rufus more than anything. This made her miss a beat in her breathing. It was shocking.

They reached the town of Duronovaria by evening, again familiar. The approach road had crossed the long, unfinished, meandering aqueduct at several points. This prospective water course was said to be twelve miles long, she remembered Dendus fondly telling her, as it followed the contours of the land and slithered snake-like towards the town, eventually to service its public fountains and baths. The imposing profile of the old Durotrigan citadel, Mai Din, craned to peer at them bombastically from one of the two nearby hills, four miles to the south-west.

She remembered there being a tension in the town when last she was there, a stand-off between the civilian town council and the Romans. The Durotriges loathed every Roman. The natives spat on the ground when soldiers walked past them, afterwards pretending it was innocent and coincidental. They spilled stinking animal guts in the road when they saw a detachment of soldiers coming along it. They shouted abuse before disappearing down a side street. The children mocked the marching men, trailing behind them, making rude gestures in their wake. The more the

Durotriges learnt how to write Latin, the more common became the offensive graffiti in the town. The civilian council cared little to put a stop to it, even secretly encouraged it. Memories were long, grudges were deep. There was not a native in the town or in the fields around it who did not have a recent ancestor who was a victim of the massacre up on Mai Din. In retrospect and in the official record, the Romans called it a glorious battle, even pretended there had been great bravery and honour on both sides, but the locals knew this was putting a gloss on it. Mai Din had not been the impressive Brittonic fortress the Romans later claimed they had stormed so brilliantly, it had been a relatively peaceful and thriving village which just happened to nestle within the imposing ramparts and ditches left over from much earlier times, when the Durotriges feared the nasty slingshots of the invading Veneti.

The vexillation of the Fifth cohort who manned the town had one of the more unenviable posts in the province. They would have to be stationed in Ordovicia or Siluria, or perhaps some parts of Brigantia these days, to receive a similar level of loathing. They were a nominal force, a token of Roman superiority, whose limited numbers would be snuffed out in an instant if the natives turned upon them. Outnumbered one hundred to one, each of them, they might be forgiven for feeling they were living on borrowed time. Only the expectation of draconian reprisals preserved them from day to day.

When Raselg entered the town this evening, the tense atmosphere was still there. She could see it in the predatory eyes of the town dwellers, as they studied the arriving soldiers, and in the weary eyes of the garrison. As a slave of a Roman, and a Dumnonian one at that, she could not expect to receive any less animosity from them.

For safety, they were billeted amongst the Fifth cohort's barracks, even the tribune himself. Solid walls and roof, and a room shared with her new master. Helius was absent from the room until the middle of the night, then returned, staggering and reeking of wine and dropped straight into bed. He might even have forgotten she was there too. She slept on a mat of straw in the corner. He snored loudly all night.

In the morning, she emptied his piss-pot while he still slept. She brushed down his leather jerkin, wiped the ornate breastplate of his armour and polished his decorative helmet. When he woke, groggy and bleary-eyed, he did not seem to notice her efforts, less appreciate them. He went off for breakfast with the men without saying a word to her.

She began to wonder whether he liked women at all. Did he prefer men or boys? She would look out for signs of this from now on. This would be a major setback and she would need to find a way round it, become the best servant ever; hopefully become indispensable to him for other reasons. Perhaps she could find boys for him. She had heard that many pederastic men used their female staff for that purpose, sending them out to befriend and round up a pretty boy.

Duronovaria was a ghastly place to stay but they would have to do so for several more nights while they waited for the arrival of the camp prefect, Ulpius Senicianus, and the broad-stripe tribune, Livius Colusanas. On one of the rare occasions that she saw Helius, she asked him how long they were planning to be in this miserable town. He answered her brusquely: "Until I know what is happening."

The prefect and senior tribune finally arrived. Raselg was not asked to attend on them when they met with Helius in the public baths. They had their own servants. Once again, she was left to bide her time back in the barracks. She could not even venture out into the town as it was unsafe. She would be easy pickings for a disconsolate Durotrigan wishing to get one over on a Roman tribune by despoiling or destroying one of his assets by way of a bit of rape or murder.

They were possibly the most tedious days of her life so far. She dared not even talk to the soldiers in the barracks. The trouble with young men was that they saw any attention from a young woman as an invitation to flirt, or they might even interpret it as subtle flirting on her part. And an indignant man, who saw his assumptions and advances duly rejected, would twist the situation round and seek to blame her. After what had happened with Cressido Saenus, she was not going to risk it. Only women, very old men and homosexuals could be her friends now it seemed, without them seeing it as an opportunity for carnal commerce.

In the long hours at her disposal, she practised writing Latin, using some books she found amongst her master's bags. She scratched the letters out repetitively on a wax tablet until she became quick and adept. She began to try to associate the groups of scratchings with words she only knew phonetically. But without a teacher, it was largely guesswork. Although she could be quite sure that two of the words handwritten consistently on to the front of all his books was his name, *Exuperatus Helius*, she could not be sure of the words that preceded them. At least she could now write his name with confidence.

On the third day after the arrival of the prefect and senior tribune, when Helius came back to sleep and was not too drunk this time, she resorted to the ploy of feminine weeping. This would either send a man into a fury or reveal his soft side. She sat in the corner, her face in her hands, and waited. Secretly she felt a surge of triumph when his large hands peeled hers from her face and he tilted her chin up. "What the hell is wrong?" he asked.

"I have nothing to do," she replied. "I am of no use to you, and I want to be!"

"Oh yes, of course," he said in a distracted way. "Look, polish these or soften them with fats," he added, handing her a pair of stout, studded army sandals.

She took hold of them, and, turned one over so that its sole faced her. She picked up a nearby stylus, one that she had been using earlier that day, and scratched the words 'Exuperatus Helius' on to the sole quickly.

He looked at her handiwork. "What use is that?" he asked. "The hard ground will rub it off before long!"

She dropped the sandal into her lap in exasperation. "Send me back, then!" she retorted.

"No, I will not!"

She burst out crying again.

"Oh for fuck's sake!" he exclaimed. "Perhaps you *are* of no use to me!"

He went over to the other side of the room and began to take off his toga, keeping his back to her.

"Exuperatus Helius, do you by any chance, prefer boys? If so, I don't mind. It's not a reason to ignore me. I can be a very good house servant. Even Dendus used to say so."

"Who?"

"Dendus, the slave of Plancius Vallaunius."

"Oh, him, the one from Lusitania."

"Yes, and you could have someone teach me how to write and then I could be your secretary. I am very good at learning. I can assure you I will be very good."

"We'll see," he grunted. "Look, I haven't had a servant for a few months, that's all. I am not ignoring you. We have our orders now from the prefect and broad-stripe tribune, so I will probably be in better humour. Like you, I do not like to hang around, wondering what is happening."

"Are we leaving this god-forsaken place?"

"Yes, we are waiting for a vexillation of the Fourteenth Legion to arrive from Gaul, and then we head north with them, quickly."

"North?"

"Yes, to reinforce the Ninth Legion at Eboracum. There is trouble up there. The main part of the Second Augustan Legion is heading up that way with the reinforcements from Gaul, to be ready to put down a rising."

Raselg thought about this. "*All* of the Second Legion?"

"No, the Eighth and Tenth cohorts stay where they are for the time being. Look, I have told you too much already. I am only doing so to try to stop your pitiful weeping."

"Thank you – sir."

"And I don't prefer boys."

"I didn't really think you did."

He climbed into bed and ordered her to fetch him a jug of water and then to put out the lamp.

CHAPTER FIFTEEN

THE senior centurion of the Fifth cohort and Helius hosted the prefect and senior tribune the following day at the barracks. Raselg now found herself called to duty, one of four servants on hand. Her arrival in the small atrium of the centurion's quarters, caused a stir. Senicianus exclaimed, "By the gods, is this not the slave of Plancius Vallaunius?" He turned to Helius for help. "I hope there is a good reason for this!"

"On this occasion, a better reason," replied Helius with an awkward smile. "Vallaunius thought he had too many servants, and she, being the most junior that he had, he kindly off-loaded her onto me."

"Are we talking about the same Vallaunius?" asked Colusanas, pointedly. "That must have left him with one aged Iberian and two male freedmen, courtesy of his predecessor. So, yes, I can see he would have too many. But to send away his most *becoming* domestic, is not like him."

"The very same man, 'though mellowed. More conscientious these days," ventured Helius. "Intent on wiping out the Ankows without distractions."

"A female slave like that can be far too distracting, that's for sure," agreed Senicianus. "But now that we've admired the state of your new household, Helius, to the matter in hand..."

Colusanas cleared his throat as if he were about to deliver a speech. The Fifth cohort's commander, Robigalius, scratched his breeches and leant forward on the couch in readiness. One could tell from his manner that the next bit directly concerned himself and he was looking forward to hearing it.

"We lost another infantryman of the Fifth cohort to desertion last night," began the senior tribune. "At his rate, the Fifth are losing a man every other day. Robigalius would agree with us when we say that the morale of the Fifth cohort is irrevocably shredded. It's a symptom, no doubt, of being posted here for so long. So, the camp prefect and I have decided we would like to move Vallaunius and the Eighth cohort here to Duronovaria, and swap them with the Fifth, so as to give the latter some respite and hopefully stop the rot." He turned to Helius. "This does not affect your orders one jot. You're still going north."

Helius studied his hands for a few seconds, stewarding his thoughts. "The Eighth cohort of Brittones are a specialist unit. They are nick-named the *Ankow Killers*. They are trained in unorthodox tactics. They are, as far as I can see, not comparable to an orthodox unit like the Fifth cohort, not naturally exchangeable."

"What difference does that make?" interrupted Senicianus. "And, in any case, we have had no problems whatsoever from the so-called Ankows since the month of Julius. Two and a half months ago. It's not exactly active warfare."

"They may be amassing their forces as we speak, waiting to strike in force. Having one of our specialist units in transit from one base to another at the time that happens is not ideal."

Robigalius spoke up. "With respect, tribune, the army moves all the time! That's what it does! When trouble appears, the army travels to meet it. It's designed to be in transit from one place to another, not meant to stay in any particular garrison all the time, waiting for trouble to come to it. That's why we have tents and platoons of tent-buddies, and spend so much time learning how to build marching camps. We are supposed to be moving units!"

"He's right. Your argument is misconceived," said Colusanas.

"So be it," conceded Helius. "I suppose it won't harm us to have a commander of Vallaunius's reputation stationed here, and twice the number of soldiers as well. It'll shake up the sour-faced council, who think they've got the moral and de facto upper hand."

"That's decided then. The barracks here will need to be expanded to house four hundred and eighty men, and extra stables will have to be built at the same time," said Senicianus. "Robigalius, before you lot leave here, can you organise suitable builders to do that? You know the civilians better – who to trust amongst them. Make sure it's done properly. Only when the new accommodation is ready, can you leave."

"I don't trust *any* of them, but I will do my best."

With one eye on Raselg, who was standing in the corner, Helius said: "So, Rufus is coming here. Do we have any idea when the reinforcements from the Fourteenth Gemini will arrive, prefect?"

"Could be days, could be weeks. Depends upon the weather and the tides. Can't wait to go north, I take it?"

"Never been north in this island. Should be interesting," he bluffed.

"Perhaps some real fighting," Colusanas added.

Helius had to stop himself from commenting.

The old prefect snapped his fingers and Axum came over to help him on to his feet. The meeting was over.

"Stay for some food, prefect. We have an excellent pork stew in the pot," offered Robigalius. "Soldier's fare but you will find it excellent."

"I would but, talking about being in transit, if I don't keep this body moving, it will seize up with arthritis. I need to get on to Isca Dumnoniorum and inform Vallaunius of the decision. I'm not sure what he'll make of it."

The camp prefect was on his feet and heading for the door.

"Me too, will you excuse my not taking up your kind offer?" said the broad-stripe tribune. He was much younger, thin and

165

angular and energetic. He gave the impression of hawk, perhaps even a vulture. They made a contrast, he and the amiable third-in-command of the legion.

"Isca too?" asked Helius, conversationally.

"Londinium," Colusanas answered. "The governor is back there for the winter, and I must check in with him and return part of his bodyguard." He clapped his hands, and a woman came forward to collect his empty beaker from him and set it down on the side table.

"Can I ask, before you go," started Helius. "The new lance. I understood that somebody is due to go to Rome to present it to the emperor. Has it been decided who is going?"

Colusanas and Senicianus, both by the door, exchanged glances. "It has not been decided yet. I intend to speak to Lucullus again about it when I am in Londinium," said the tribune.

Helius nodded and pretended he was satisfied with the answer, but he was fairly certain they were being circumspect and that it *had* been decided. The second-in-command of the legion was going to see the governor, the third in command was going to see Rufus. It seemed likely that they would be sending Rufus, himself, back to Rome to present the new lance to Domitian.

When the senior commanders had gone, Robigalius turned to Helius. "What was that about?"

Helius pondered whether he should answer. "They are caught in the horns of a dilemma, Robigalius. Somebody must go to

Rome to do it but they are fearful of the reception there. They expect that Domitian will be furious, possibly murderous, when he finds out that the new lance has not been named after him or after his father, Vespasian. Lucullus won't go for that reason, the legate is obviously reluctant too. They are both senators, of course. Some other mug needs to do it, someone not of the patrician class. So, Vallaunius fits the bill. Only, it could be the last we ever see of Vallaunius!"

The senior centurion of the Fifth cohort was a simple soul. "Just rename the lance, then."

"One would think that was the easy solution, wouldn't they? But Lucullus likes it named after him. He is a vain man."

"You care for Vallaunius?"

"I do. He is my friend." He looked around at Raselg. "I care for his welfare, and he is the best soldier the legion has."

Raselg returned a thin smile.

BUILDING work on the barracks began that day. The soldiers could have accomplished it themselves; they were skilled, amongst other things, in joinery and tiling but it would take too long. Robigalius was keen to shorten the time before their overdue departure. They drafted in civilians from the town to help: carpenters and masons and fit men who could haul and manhandle heavy beams of wood and dressed stone into place.

Raselg sat in the doorway of Helius's quarters and watched the work beginning. Helius, himself, was amongst the throng of activity, helping supervise the planning of it. She watched him with a curious expression. Was he her future now? How easy would it be? How far would this man go in the realm? Had she fallen on her feet with him? Was this destiny playing out? She could not keep the face of her father out of her thoughts. He seemed ever present, watching her, nodding approval from the spiritual plane where he now dwelt. She felt his benign approbation. With a shock, she saw that one of the men, now helping the soldiers with the building work, looked like her father. She took this as a sign that Fate was really behind the recent events. If Fate could do such a thing, send her a sign, then surely this was it.

Helius looked over to her. She smiled back. It was a sunny day, even warm for this time of the year and the men looked happy and purposeful as they set about the task of building new stables, especially the men of the Fifth cohort.

Some of the civilians working with them were talking together. The man who looked like her father was trying to communicate with them, using hand gestures. He evidently could not speak. An awkward feeling descended upon Raselg. This was too much of a coincidence for comfort. Her father too could not speak, after Rufus ordered that his tongue be cut out in punishment. She stood up, hesitantly.

Her urge was to walk over and take a closer look, if only to satisfy herself that she was imagining things. By standing up, her movement caught the attention of some of the men. They turned and looked at her. They looked her up and down and smiled lecherously. Only the man who looked like her father did not. His face registered shock. His hand came up to his face. He stared at her, even craned his neck forward.

Raselg could not resist the urge any longer. Helius would reprimand her but she did not care. She ran over to the men, just as the man himself, stepped forward towards her. They were both transfixed. When they were barely ten paces apart, Raselg screamed. The man put his hand up as if to counsel her to be quiet. The others had stopped what they were doing and were gawking at the spectacle.

"How can this be!" shrieked Raselg.

"What?" shouted Helius.

She pointed at the man. "My father but he is dead – he should be dead!"

Helius's head span round to look at the man. He was still standing there, his arm up to stop Raselg coming close. Anguish covering his face.

Raselg was backing off. Nobody seemed sure what to make of it, no one but Raselg. Her reaction, to back away from the very man she said was her father, finally informed Helius what she meant. "*Ankows!*" he shouted. It was the last word he uttered.

The civilians attacked the soldiers. The soldiers fought back with saws and chisels and hammers, anything to hand, but they were no match. They died one by one, although there were more of them and they were trained fighters.

Raselg had run back to the barracks but there was nowhere for her to hide effectively. She ducked into Helius's room and slammed the door closed and hooked on the restraining bar to lock it. She could hear footsteps approaching. She turned around, searching for a weapon. Helius's sword was on the desk. He did not possess a poison lance, unfortunately. The sword would have to do. She snatched it up and headed for the window. It was barred by wooden mullions. She pushed them loose, savagely, and cleared a hole just big enough for her to climb through. If she did so, she would be hidden between two rows of buildings, out of sight of the civilians. It was her only chance.

She clambered through the gap between the broken mullions and stood for a moment on the ground. She was just considering which way to run, when a man appeared around the corner of the building. A large man, with grim intent showing on his face. She was going to scream but she saw that it was her father. She was about to be killed by her own father. She stabbed the sword at him but he grabbed it and whisked it out of her hand. Suddenly she was off her feet, being carried. Her father was carrying her, and he was doing so with a strength she had not experienced since she was a toddling infant. She began to blubber, her face wet with snot and tears.

He carried her briskly away from the barracks, away from the chaos that was happening there, the killing that had started there and would now be spreading to the town.

A cart was standing ahead of them. The horse had been untethered from it, and the cart was tilted towards the floor. Her father threw her into the back of it and covered her quickly with a large sheet of fabric. He piled things over her. She could feel the weight increasing upon her body. Bricks and tiles and tools. She lay still and wept as silently as she could. She felt the cart right itself horizontally and begin to move. Her father was wheeling her, was rescuing her. Perhaps he was not an Ankow, after all.

Minutes seemed to pass, as she continued to feel the motion. There were shouts coming from various parts of the town. She could hardly bear the weight pressed down on her, it was squeezing the breath out of her, and the pain was increasing but she dared not move. She was a dutiful daughter again, doing her father's bidding even though she did not understand it and it was against her immediate inclinations. She wanted, with every painful inch of her being, to shout out to him. To call him father. To show that she loved him.

The cart stopped. The weights began to lessen. The cover was ripped away from her. She gasped at last and threw her arms up to hug him. He let her do so, lifting her lightly out of the cart at the same moment. He placed her down on her feet and pushed her away. She turned to look where she was. They were outside the town, hidden from the walls and the south gate by a clump of trees.

He pointed somewhere. She turned to look where he was gesturing. To the citadel on the hill to the south. Mai Din. He wanted her to run there, to be safe.

She tried to run back into his arms but he pushed her away, roughly. Desperately, he pointed again to where he wanted her to go. He pleaded with her with frantic grunts. He was weeping too.

Reluctantly, she obeyed.

PART II

CHAPTER SIXTEEN

"WHEN the world was young and even our distant ancestors were yet to be born, behold a different order. The Cave-hyena ruled the earthly plane and the Great Goddess smiled down from above."

"Does she at least have a name?" asked Rufus. He shifted his legs as he was sitting awkwardly on a rock that slanted backwards, and for the first time in his life, he felt an ache in his spine. It accompanied the more familiar throbbing sensation in his legs that sent a shooting pain up to his left buttock. He winced.

"Great Goddess," answered the Druid. "Britons, but not Druids, call her *Danu*. Romans might call her *Magna Mater*. Not a useless label for a change."

"What's this about names?" asked Tadius, impatiently. "When I asked a simple question, this morning, like what's the daughter of the Druid called, my comrade here, Plancius Vallaunius, gives me a reproachful look as if I am wrong to ask it? What's that about?"

"The Druid thinks names are very silly," explained Rufus.

The Druid pointed to Rufus. "Man. Soldier. Centurion." Then pointing to Luti, "Man. Soldier. Horse-rider. Decurion." Then to Tadius himself. "Man. Soldier. Centurion."

Tadius looked scornful, a little triumphant. "Yes, precisely. You pointed to him and said exactly the same things as you did when you pointed to me. How are we meant to distinguish one person from another? It's ridiculous. How can I say to somebody, for example: 'It's Vallaunius's birthday today', or 'Make sure you give this thing to Vallaunius and not to Luti Bassus? Am I supposed to say: 'It's the soldier's birthday today? Which soldier would I mean, when I said that? Or am I supposed to say, 'Make sure you give this thing to the soldier not the soldier'?"

Rufus laughed. "He's got a point."

The Druid sighed. "Why do you need to distinguish yourselves in the first place? You are presenting a position that is halfway along the reasoning, and which misses the starting premise of the reasoning."

"I'm doing what?"

Rufus tried to make it easier. "I believe he is saying that we can still refer to ourselves as what we are and what we do, not by some extra label that some third person, like our parent, gave us when we were born, which might not even be appropriate for what we do. I could still therefore issue an order like: 'Send the Eighth cohort there, keep the Tenth cohort here. Inform the commander and decurion of the plan', et cetera. Do you see?"

"I do but I don't know who is being very silly, here. I suspect it is him, not us."

"You are learning," said the Druid, good-humouredly. "You say *him* and *us* and it is quite sufficient for us to understand you!"

Tadius seemed unimpressed. He got up from his improvised seat and moved to a gap in the tall rocks, where he could look down on the marching camp scratched into the earth in the distance, where miniscule men were busy making breakfast and brushing horses. From this stack of rocks, piled one on top of each other like massive loaves of grey bread, he could see a great expanse of the moor in all directions. It was beautiful in the morning light but a place of daunting mystery. A land beyond the civilising empire, beyond the surveyors and road builders where nature governed itself. He heard Rufus behind him, take up the thread of the enquiry once more. "Where does this fit in with the she-wolves, anyway?"

"Well, the cave-hyenas were all dead, long before even we Druids arrived in these lands. They lived and they all died in the times before that, when the great stone circles were made, and the standing stones were put in our landscape."

"Who do you say put the stone circles there?" asked Luti Bassus.

"Those people are gone too."

"We Romans say that the Druids made the stone circles," explained Luti.

"The Romans are wrong about that! There is no one alive now who is related to the race that put the stones there. It wasn't even a proper island when some of the oldest sanctuaries were built, it was that long ago. It was a different world. A different shape. You could walk from here to the lands you now call Gaul and Belgia, and the water would only come up to your hips at the highest point! The earth was white with permanent snow, and giant hairy elephants roamed about. Men hid from the hyenas, and women carried their little ones permanently on their backs to avoid them being scooped up by savage teeth. Have you thought why babies are soothed by a rocking motion? It is because it reassures them that they are being carried by an adult, and thereby kept away from the jaws of a pouncing hyena. It all goes back to those distant times, long, long before any Druids, Dumnonii, or whatever tribe you wish to call it, populated these lands. So, you Romans need not keep pulling the stone circles down and dismantling them in the hope it will bother us and compromise our power, as if it were like knocking the nose or the phallus off a holy statue. They have nothing to do with us. It doesn't make us angry or weaker, it just makes us believe, even more than we did before, that you are just a load of ignorant, superstitious foreigners."

Tadius returned to the group. They were huddled in a natural gap between two parallel stacks of rock, three times the height of a man. Luti was nodding, looked uncommonly benign as he sat there on a smooth stone, away from the wind, listening to the Druid, and even though some of what the Druid was saying was frankly insulting. "Does this history accord with your sense of things, Luti?" he asked, surprised to see his decurion so amiable about it all.

"It does. I think the Druid is right. In Germania, we have a name for the Great Goddess. We call her *Nerthus*. She protects me. She preserved me for some great purpose. It started with the lance." He patted his leather jerkin, just over the scar on his midriff.

"Then we were acting as Her agents when we took you from the battlefield and carried you to the Roman's healing place," said the Druid.

"Thank you," mumbled Luti.

The Druid's daughter now joined them. She had been standing behind the stones nearby and listening. She sat down, cross-legged on the ground near her father. She spoke some words to him in a language that even Luti could not understand. He was mouthing the strange words to himself, as if he were memorising them for later.

"My daughter thinks I should hurry up and get to the point, as she does not think you have the patience or the intelligence to hear a lot of old history from me."

"She is correct, at least about the lack of patience. We are indeed still waiting to hear about the she-wolves," said Tadius. He sat down again in the space reserved for him.

"Then stop interrupting me." The Druid patted his daughter on the head, affectionately.

Rufus was appraising her, seeing her for the first time in daylight. Her hair was the colour of sand, her face as pale as it had seemed the night before, but her eyes were astonishingly green now in the daylight. She wore a large robe of the same colour, to enhance them by reflection, possibly. Her face had appeared plain and ordinary last night, when darkness shrouded her eyes. Today, she was arrestingly attractive, if only for those eyes. But for those she might still be called ordinary.

"Cybele," he muttered. "In some parts of the world, they carry a white marble statue of her from the temple down to the river at night, so that the goddess can bathe."

The daughter turned and looked at him, the emerald eyes startling him even more. "And there she was found," she whispered in precise Latin to him.

"In Germania, people believe she resides in a sacred cart. *Nerthus*, the Bringer of Peace," continued Luti. "The sacred cart lies on a holy island, covered in a cloth, somewhere in the Ocean."

The Druid nodded at Luti. "I have also heard Her referred to as *The Bearing*, for she gave birth to everything. In the old language, *Dheghom*."

"That sounds like a name to me," said Tadius, tetchily.

"It is a description," countered the Druid. "And Vallaunius here, has fallen under the spell of my daughter, it seems."

Rufus blushed in embarrassment when the others turned towards him.

"See Druid, it is you who are wrong, not us! You call him 'Vallaunius' but we call him *Rufus*, the red one! It is a description!"

The Druid slapped his knees in delight. "You have me there, centurion!"

The daughter now spoke. "I think my father tiptoes around the subject because he is embarrassed about the she-wolves, aren't you, Father?"

"Perhaps," he admitted. "Why don't you tell them, my dear?"

Her emerald eyes scanned the waiting faces. She shifted position, to kneel rather than sit, and placed her hands on her knees. When she was comfortable again, she began to explain. "Some of the Druids have tried to bring the cave-hyenas back. A faction of them believe the Goddess wants them to, and that they must do so in order to help fight the Ankows. They believe that the cave-hyena is an earthly embodiment of Her and that they exist to do her bidding. They are misguided of course. No one can bring the creature back. It is difficult to get a grey wolf to mate with a spotted hyena, very difficult, but it can be done if the beasts are drugged and helped along with chants and coaxing. It is a special skill that some of the Druids attempt from time to time. The result is a creature that is very similar to a cave-hyena, so similar in fact, that the misguided souls think they have actually succeeded in the endeavour."

"How do they know, how do *you* know, that the offspring is so similar?" asked Tadius, not unreasonably.

"Paintings of them in hidden caves, and a modicum of self-delusion on their part," she answered, equably. "But the product of the mating is always female and always barren. They cannot reproduce. They live for around twelve to fifteen years and then they die."

"It is a ghastly creature," the Druid interjected.

"I know, I have been close to them!" replied Tadius.

"And the Ankows fear these creatures more than anything? Do they think they are real cave-hyenas?" asked Rufus.

"They do or they don't, what does it matter? The grey wolf hates Ankows, anyway, and will go out of its way to kill them. Always has, always will. It is exactly the same with the spotted hyena. Natural enemies. So naturally the she-wolf, being the product of both parents, inherits the same hatred for them."

Luti spoke. "The drugs that they use to bring about the mating, are they made from plants grown around here, in the Scared Groves for which the Nemet valley is named? Is that why the she-wolves are here, on Klocha Fhasach?"

"Now, that would be telling, wouldn't it?" chuckled the Druid. "It is archaic and esoteric magic, jealously guarded by the Druids. Not even written down anywhere. As my daughter says, this is a phenomenon created by a certain faction of Druids. I am not one of them. But I will tell you this much, decurion: No, the drug is not made from plants grown in the valley down there."

"Then it seems to be a limited problem," Tadius pointed out. "We are not going to be overwhelmed by these creatures, however ghastly they are."

"No, and they can actually be helpful in some respects. They work with us Druids, as we have a common enemy. We know how to call them when we need them. They go into battle with us to fight Ankows, and during that time, there is a truce between us and them."

"The night of the battle on the wharfs at Isca – they were there as well, weren't they?" asked Tadius in a tense whisper.

"I knew you might remember, eventually," replied the Druid.

"I didn't until I saw the creatures again!"

"How many are there?" asked Rufus.

"One hundred or so – here. I cannot say for other parts. You won't find them, certainly not during the daytime."

"We don't want to find them," said Rufus. He stood up with a wince of pain. "I'm glad they help kill the Ankows. Is there a way that we can call them to help us, if need be?"

The Druid shrugged his shoulders. "I doubt it."

"Come on. I think we know what we need to know now." Rufus was bringing the meeting to an end. The others got to their feet, except for the woman. They shook arms and thanked the Druid. Nodded to the woman.

When Tadius and Luti had started the long descent from the pinnacle, the Druid stopped Rufus with a pull on his shoulder.

"In Dumnonia, they say 'a service for a service'. I need one from you, he-who-they-call-the-red-one. A big one."

"You are not strictly a Dumnonian, Druid."

"They also say, 'When in Rome, do what the Romans do'. Is that not right?"

"What is the service you ask of me? I owe you my life, of course."

"You do, which is why it is a big one." The Druid gestured back to his daughter, who still sat within the rocks on her own. "She is getting on, some thirty years old by my reckoning. I've lost count. I don't want her to become a hag. I have kept hold of her long enough, and it is not like the old times, when there were many of us and we could pass freely in and out of society and sustain ourselves. I want you to take her with you, protect her. She will be of value to you, a sort of guide. You need it."

Rufus was surprised. He was going to object, find excuses, politely refuse, but when he perceived the Druid's earnest expression and realised the context of it, knowing how much he owed this man, how much they all did, he stopped himself. "If that is what you want."

And this was why the others were astonished to see Rufus descending the hill behind them, with the woman close behind him. They stopped and waited for them to catch up. Tadius glanced at Luti, expecting to find a scowl on his face, but the decurion looked merely curious. These were strange times.

CHAPTER SEVENTEEN

THE town behind her had grown quiet again. Who knew what dreadful things had unfolded there this morning? She stood and looked through the gaps in the trees towards the gatehouse and low walls, watching the cart recede and disappear through the gates. Her father was oddly vigorous and purposeful. The town walls were neglected and minimal, hardly defensive walls at all, but they were tall enough to hide what she wanted to see. The fate of the people within it. Her face, besmeared with tears and mucus, her gown torn where she had clambered through the broken segments of the window, her mind a frenzy of thoughts, she finally turned and began to walk towards the distant hill. Today, she seemed to have regained her father, in some form, but lost her new master. Her past had returned to some degree, but her future was up ended. She could not believe that Helius had survived that mayhem. He must be dead. Then again, she had been entirely sure her father was gone for good but somehow that assumption no longer held. She had to remind herself that he had not actually returned to her, not in any way that she could fit into a normal structure of things. Some of him was there, no doubt: his body and appearance, his love for her. He had saved her. He could not be completely gone if he could still do that. He was still a father of sorts.

Joy seemed to be the wrong emotion, it was swamped by an awful feeling of bewilderment and terror. She wrapped her arms around herself to feel rooted and earthed and present-bound. While she still had herself, she had enough for now, she told herself. This was where it must start again. She was the spring, emerging from the barren ground, and all her future would now trickle from her and find its way where it could.

The ramparts of Mai Din were black against the pale blue sky, the tops of the tallest roundhouses upset the otherwise smooth profile on its west side. Every step she took towards it felt like a step in the wrong direction, she – a Dumnonian – edging towards the egocentric and patriotic symbol of all that was Durotrigan. If anybody was living in the old castle now, the chances were that they would be averse to anything Roman and anything not belonging to Durotrigia. Raselg – a household slave of a tribune - was sufficiently Romanised now to be loathed, she was also of the wrong tribe, of the tribe that failed to come to their ancestors' support when the Romans came and slaughtered them. She ignored her intuition and her fear only because she was obeying her father again. While she did that, she still felt like his daughter. It made her feel oddly satisfied, a rock to cling to. She was not even averse to dying while carrying out his final stricture.

A hundred paces and no more from the first deep ditch of the earthwork, a large white stone pinged off the chalky turf near her feet. It kicked up a small swirl of white dust. She stopped walking and stood still. A second stone hit the ground a step away, bouncing and glancing off her right calf. She felt a sting of pain and a cold, wet slice of nausea. Shock.

She was being sling-stoned from the nearest rampart. They were not aiming to kill her or blind her; her head would have been the target for that: they were aiming to wound her, to maim her, to stop her coming. In loud Celtic, she shouted that she had escaped from the Romans and needed sanctuary.

The response was a stone into her leg, shattering her kneecap. She fell to the floor, screaming.

She lay there for some minutes, panting and grimacing with pain. Eventually, six men came and stood over her. One prodded her with a stick, sharpened at the end, like a stick people used to herd pigs. She swore at the man with the stick. She might as well have her say before she died too.

The largest man of the group, a black-haired brute with a face that was three-quarters coarse hair and one quarter bellicose red, began to laugh when he studied her more closely. "A fucking woman!" he hollered. "And a fucking pretty one at that!"

They lifted her up and carried her up to the ramparts. She felt herself being carried in one direction and then shortly in the opposite direction, along an intricate and complex path through the concentric walls of earth and deep trenches.

The men dumped her on the ground finally. She put her hand on the pulp of her knee and cupped it in a futile gesture of protection. She had never felt a pain like it.

For some reason, they thought she needed wine. It was brought over and poured down her throat, almost drowning her. Her spluttering brought on a round of great mirth.

"What is she?" asked one man.

The large brute said: "Bolgoi - Regini – something foreign."

"A slave," she wheezed. "Dumnonii."

"A whore. A Roman whore. Look at her clothes. She even smells Roman," averred one man.

"I am not a whore!" shouted Raselg. "I am a Roman general's slave. A slave in the household of an important man! I can be ransomed! I'm valuable!"

This haughty declaration was challenged and laughed at, but the large brute did not join in. His head was tilted to one side while he studied her. "I never heard of a slave being ransomed. She must be very special." His tone denoted that he did not believe her for one moment. "Let's ransom her, like she says. Eventually."

He began to drag her by one of her feet along the ground, over to a roundhouse nearby. She was pushed through a rush door, inside the house. She found herself next to a tiled hearth, stinking of damp ash and old fat. Her hand instinctively went out to grab an iron poker lying next to it, but she quickly withdrew her arm, thinking twice about encouraging more violence. She sat up and looked around. Two women and a child were gawping at her from the edge of the hut. The brutish man jammed a rough, earthen vessel of some kind into her mouth, and she tasted more wine. It was all over her face and running down her neck into her dress. The women were asking who she was. She was going to answer them, herself, but the man slapped her across the face to shut her up. Her lower lip was pulp now as well, and a tooth, or part of a tooth had come out and was rattling in her mouth. When she recovered from the initial shock of the blow, she looked up and saw him loosening his woollen trousers. And she knew what was going to happen next.

THE brute's name was Tasuatas, and he was the High King of the Durotrigans, or so he said. Any tribal leader who refused to succumb to Roman authority might call himself a *High King*. That was the easy part.

His kingly palace was a round hut, admittedly one of the biggest ones. He had a harem of three wives now, Raselg having just been added. Only one heir, the boy who kept staring at her and who watched his father while he raped her. There were no internal walls in this hut, not like the stone houses the Dumnonians built. Everything was watched. Look, this is how you do it, my son. Watch and learn. One day you will be a great king too.

The other two 'wives' tried to mend Raselg's knee. She was not sure why they did this, as they were not friendly towards her. They did not care for her. She could only imagine that they were told to do it, under some threat of sanction. They also kept her intoxicated, forcing wine upon her every few minutes. The interior of the roundhouse was a blurry place, full of harsh words and sexual violence. The man kept appearing at various times of the day and coming to her, never to the other two women. At least not that first week. She tried to speak to him but he would not listen.

At the start of the second week, when Tasuatas was away, Raselg said to the women: "The king is a fool. I keep trying to tell him something important but he won't hear me out. Time is running out and we will, you will *all* lose out because of it."

The women did not take the bait, just told her to keep her mouth shut if she knew what was best for her.

But a couple of days later, one of the women who called herself Belena asked, "What is this important thing you think the king should hear? Let me judge if it is important."

Raselg was ready. "I came to Mai Din to tell the High King that the Romans have a great hoard of gold and silver coins hidden in the town. It is due to be shipped north with the soldiers, when the soldiers all go north for a new war, but at the moment the treasure is there for the taking, and there are very few soldiers! The coins are wages for the soldiers – enough coins to last a whole year! I came here to tell the High King this because I hate the Romans and I want their gold and silver to be stolen from them. The bastards! But instead of listening to me, the king hits me and refuses to hear me. The shame is that he would be an even greater king than he is now if he were very rich too. And we would have fine clothes and live in a fine palace, not a roundhouse in an obsolete castle." And then, breathlessly, Raselg added. "I have seen the hoard of gold and silver coins myself! You would not believe it! The boxes, full to their brims, are stacked as high as the ceiling in a large room, which has a very high ceiling, I might add. In the middle of the town. In the Basilica!"

The two women looked at each other. "We will tell him, ourselves."

The following day, Tasuatas asked Raselg to tell him more about the Roman hoard of coins. She explained it all again, adding this time that more soldiers were about to arrive from Caer Uisc from the west, and another thousand soldiers, from another legion, fresh from Gaul by ships. Then there would be too many soldiers in the town for them to fight. For the moment, however, there were barely two hundred of them. The Romans had kept the bank of coins very secret, and thought they were safe from attack, but she had learned of it from her master who was a Roman tribune.

The king asked her, "When is the latest we can act?"

She thought about this. "You must attack the town no later than a week after the next full moon. All the reinforcements are due to arrive after that. Best to do it one or two days after the moon is at its fullest."

Tasuatas counted his fingers. "That is within two weeks!"

She nodded.

There were around three hundred men living with the king in Mai Din, about half that number of women, and about half that number again of children. The community did not strike Raselg as being especially warlike. Yes, the men carried weapons and practised with them but the village amongst the ramparts looked more like a farming community. They kept pigs and cows and grew vegetables. They sent goods to market in the harbour at Clavinium. Perhaps this is why Tasuatas was not rushing to do what she suggested, to attack the town to steal the gold and silver. There seemed no evidence that they were preparing for it. They looked very poor. The women and children were very thin but, notwithstanding, the men were not preparing to steal the money and make themselves rich. They were not warriors, just proud. Dogs that barked a lot but did not bite.

Yet the king kept asking her questions about it, which kept her hopes alive. Where was the hoard of coins actually kept? How many soldiers guarded it? What in her opinion was the time of the day when the soldiers were least ready to defend themselves? She honed all her answers to suggest that she had inside knowledge, better than most because of her position, and that she had a motive based on vengeance. She made up stories of how her master had treated her so badly, and how cruelly the soldiers treated the civilians.

The full moon arrived. She estimated that it was three days before the Ides of October in the Roman calendar. Surely more soldiers must come to Duronovaria soon. Even if all the Romans had been wiped out by the Ankows, including the camp prefect and the senior tribune, and even if there had not been an opportunity to send messengers out to tell of the massacre, surely the traders who came and went in their ships in the nearby busy port would quickly find that something was wrong, and go to alert the Roman authorities?

Her dread was that a merchant, trader or travelling Durotrigan would stop at Mai Din and tell the king of the massacre of the Romans in the town and spoil her plot. None came. Perhaps they never got out of the town alive. Whatever the case, the longer Tasuatus hesitated and did nothing, the more likely Raselg's lie would be uncovered.

She thought she was rumbled one day, when merchants came to see the king. She sat in the corner of his house and listened to what they said. They had come to pay their respects and had arrived directly from visiting the Roman town. She braced herself. This must be it. But, no, they just expressed surprise that there were no soldiers evident in the town today. The Romans had gone away. They also had other news. There was a storm raging in the Ocean and the ships could not leave the harbour and neither could any ships arrive. They had heard of ships full of Roman soldiers, waiting in the port over in Gaul, destined for *Prydein*, as they and many Britons called this island. The storm might still last for some days yet by all accounts. Tasuatas scratched at his beard and sometimes cast glances at Raselg.

When the merchants had left, he was angry with her. She had told him that they had until a week after the full moon to attack the town and steal the coinage, but it appeared that the Romans had already gone north, no doubt with the money.

That cannot be, she reasoned. They would not go north until the soldiers arrived from Gaul and those soldiers were still stuck in the port in Gaul, waiting for the storm to subside. The Romans were probably away on training manoeuvres. There would still be some of them guarding the money inside the Basilica, and the merchants had not seen these.

Tasuatas looked less than convinced.

"What are you waiting for?" she risked asking.

That slap opened the cut on her lip again.

CHAPTER EIGHTEEN

WHEN the praetorium, the commander's house in the military base at Nemetostatio, was Rufus's principal accommodation, which in context was less than six months ago, he applied a strict rule never to allow a Briton inside it, nor in the headquarters building next to it. Tadius remembered it well. His friend was very different then. Even though the same house belonged to Tadius now, and Tadius set new rules, it amused him to see how compromising and accepting his friend was of the new order. Rufus was content to have not only a Briton living there, but a Druid! In fact, he had requested it. She was to be a special guest of them both.

Rufus called her *Cybele*, and the name caught on. She eventually went along with people calling her that. Tadius was entertained by the novel arrangement. Who would have thought a year ago that they would be so willing to have a Druid staying with them in Roman property, sharing meals with them in the atrium and inner courtyard; making conversation with her and trying to make her comfortable.

She proved useful at times. When the full moon arrived, three days before the day of the Ides, she-wolves began to bay all through the night just outside the fort. There had been no evidence of the beasts while they had stayed out on the great moor, but here they were now, just outside the walls of the road station, a large group of them, perhaps sixty to seventy. Cybele called them a clan. She was puzzled at first why the beasts were there in such numbers, so excitable and persistent, until a possible explanation occurred to her. She went to Rufus's door and knocked on it in an agitated fashion, waking him up in the dead of night.

"Do you have Ankows in the fort?" she asked, when he opened the door.

Tadius had woken too because of the knock. He came into the corridor, enquiring why the woman was standing there in the middle of the night, banging on doors.

"Centurion, do you have Ankows in the fort?" she asked again. "If you are going to tell me that you haven't, I must recommend you search again! The baying of the she-wolves suggests they have picked up the scent of Ankows here! There cannot be any other reason! I am afraid that the blood-sucking fiends are in our midst, here in the fort!"

"I know there are," replied Tadius equably. "We have two of them locked up in the guardhouse, or what's left of them. They were our soldiers, Cassian and Guilio. Now they are our prisoners."

Cybele looked surprised. "Are you mad?"

"They are pitiful wretches now. They didn't eat for a long time, rejected everything we gave them until we finally thought to bring them raw meat. They grabbed at that. They will eat that, and it gives them some nourishment, but they tend to vomit it out eventually. We now give them animal blood too. They get by with it. They are very weak and in no state to cause us any trouble. It seems, we have found a third way to kill Ankows. By slow starvation."

"A *fourth* way," she corrected. "You are forgetting that beasts such as grey wolves, hyenas and she-wolves can also annihilate them. Such animals like nothing better than to rip an Ankow apart. That is why the she-wolves will not go away until you get rid of the, er, prisoners."

"I see," muttered Tadius.

She turned and went back to her room.

Rufus said: "In truth, there is no good reason to keep them alive, or undead, or whatever state we care to call it, Tadius. It is probably cruel as well and serves no purpose. We don't want those creatures wailing outside our walls every night from now on. Let's decide what to do about Cassian and Guilio in the morning."

Tadius did not reply.

When Rufus broached the subject in the morning, Tadius cut him short by announcing: "I am keeping them prisoner, Rufus, because I am ordered to do so."

"By whom?"

"By the governor himself."

"And how does he know that you are keeping two Ankows in captivity?"

"Because I told him. If I hadn't, Luti would have informed the prefect or senior tribune anyway."

"But why imprison them in the first place rather than dispose of them?"

"I think it was the realisation that I might have found myself with the only two specimens of them in captivity in the whole empire. I wanted to seek the prefect's opinion about what I should do with them."

"And Senicianus told you to preserve them?"

"Look, Rufus, I am sworn to secrecy but, as it possibly involves you directly, and I know I can count on your discretion, I will tell you. Here..."

Tadius went and fetched something from his room. It was a letter. He handed it to Rufus. After he had read the contents, Rufus said in an accusatory tone: "They want them taken to Rome to exhibit to the emperor?"

"The thing is, Rufus, I don't think Domitian or anyone in Rome actually knows about Ankows yet."

Rufus was flummoxed. "But after the so-called Battle of the Ides of Julius, we were both mentioned in despatches to the emperor for our bravery!"

"Yes, we were, but according to Luti, all that is known is that we battled against a new adversary, a blood-thirsty cult of Britons, never encountered before, who had been hiding out in the moors in Dumnonia and came to attack us. A host of cannibalistic savages, who worshipped devils was how it was described. And we stood up to them and put them down. It was *our* glory. Not even any mention of Druids!"

"Why the secrecy? The emperor needs to know! These are his lands. This is more than just a new adversary! Rome must be prepared!"

"Lucullus thinks, Domitian being as he is, that he will react in a very strange way. Overreact. The emperor is deluded and paranoid. As you know, he insists on being addressed as *Master and God* by everyone now. He also believes that all senators are out to get him. He might – and I can quite believe it myself – issue some impossible orders that will mean we find ourselves, all of us, subject to the punishment of decimation at best, or executed on mass for treason, at worst."

"What type of impossible orders?"

"Orders directly from the emperor to us commanders in control of cohorts of soldiers and cavalry. From an emperor who fears schemes and tricks on the part of the senatorial class. It won't take much for him to jump to the misguided conclusion that the governor, the procurator, the legates and the broad-stripe tribunes – all the high-ranking senators he believes have it in for him and his Flavian family - are planning to build an army and overthrow him. If one of them should come to him now with news of a terrible army of fiends amassing in Britannia, there is a good chance Domitian will regard it as nothing other than a subtle threat. That is the way his mind works now, his tortured, nervous mind. Imagine how he might react when a powerful senator such as Lucullus comes to him to inform him that he is aiming to control an army of blood-sucking devils with his new weapon, a lance called after himself! Domitian will perceive it as a declaration that an army of ungodly monsters will one day be unleashed against him! How else would it unfold, if trickster senators are in control of them! The subject is therefore very delicate, Rufus, and needs to be addressed in a sophisticated way."

"I still don't understand. What *impossible* orders?"

"For all us plebeians to stop the generals! To get rid of the patrician class. To kill all of them! Apparently, it has something to do with a dream or a prophecy. Domitian believes there is a plan to raise a great army of monsters and devils, led by senators, somewhere on the fringes of the empire!"

Rufus put his head in his hands. "And so his madness extends even this far!" He looked up again. "What has this to do with me?"

"You are likely to get the delicate mission. To go to Rome with samples of the new lance and two miserable specimens of the fiends, and explain the whole thing to Domitian. It is hoped that, hearing it from you, an equestrian, and seeing how weak the wretches really are, his burning paranoia will not be fanned. That, apparently, is the plan. Until then, everything is being kept under wraps."

"And you got all this from who – Luti?"

Tadius nodded. "Luti Bassus has always been their spy and their instrument."

"Utter madness," exclaimed Rufus. "And what are they going to do with Cassian and Guilio once they have been *presented* to the emperor? Am I to demonstrate the new lance upon them: summarily execute them in front of Domitian, for his entertainment? Or will they be put in the gladiatorial arena, or used perhaps for spectacular slaughtering of Jews and heretics?"

"Who knows? Anyway, that is why they are my prisoner, Rufus. I am under orders to preserve them for the time being."

Rufus turned and walked out of the room without a further word. His cheeks and back of his neck had grown very red.

Inevitably, he was pressed on the subject of the prisoners by his new guest. She intercepted him when he was on his way out to see to the arrangements for returning to Isca Dumnoniorum the following day. He told her that the decision was to keep the two Ankows imprisoned, and alive.

She was astute enough to guess the reason, or near enough. "You cannot put them into a zoological garden like a lion or an elephant! They are far more dangerous! I know what you Romans like to do: collect and keep novelty creatures for entertainment or watch them die in crowded arenas. You are famous for it. Do you not appreciate the extreme risks you are taking?"

"It is not my decision."

After reflecting some more, she said: "Do not tell me they are being transported somewhere! Where? Rome?"

Rufus's expression gave her the answer.

She appeared to make a decision, her face serious, worryingly so. She said slowly and deliberately: "If that is going to happen, they won't get very far. I must warn you. They will be stopped and destroyed, and people will probably die. Your friends and comrades may die. *You* may die. My people will not let those fiends leave the country, whatever it takes!"

The import of this was not lost on Rufus. "I believe you," he muttered. "But the soldiers are not frightened of Druids, far from it."

"Then let them be frightened of a confederation of my people *and* the she-wolves! You have no idea what forces will be brought to bear!"

CHAPTER NINETEEN

IT could not have been a better disaster if she had managed it all herself. In all aspects of it, it was doomed from conception. The time they chose to launch the attack, for instance: an hour before dawn, when they assumed the soldiers on the watch would be at their most careless, tired and bored and thinking about their breakfast and warm beds; the soldiers who were to replace them on the next watch, still deeply asleep. The tactic might have borne some fruit, with normal soldiers, but Ankows hunted at night and preferred the dark, and their eyes were sharp enough to be able to watch the marauders with amusement and delight from the moment they left the safety of the hillfort and descended the hill to cross the flatland towards the town.

The walls of the town were easy to assail, the peripheral ditch long neglected, and Tasuatas and his army chose the northern part on the assumption that this would be the least expected place for an incursion. They kept together in a tight group, nearly three hundred of them, and silently negotiated the Roman ditch and ramparts. They lowered themselves to the ground with impressive stealth, noting the absence of guards. It was a short distance from there to the basilica where the chests of coins were purportedly kept. They expected some resistance at the basilica, the security there proportionate to the value of what was locked away. They never got that far. More than six hundred Ankows emerged from the shadows of the buildings and cut them down with swords, javelins, lances, hammers and axes, and with strong pincer-like hands. It was short work.

Raselg and the women could hear the battle unfold from where they waited. To all of them except Raselg, the sounds were those they expected: Their men were wiping out the small Roman guard. Raselg took the opportunity, when the women were concentrating on the noises, to slip away. She could not run, because her leg was badly injured, but she could hide. She found a hollow and burrowed down under the damp infill of leaves, old nutshells and twigs.

She waited there until she heard, ten minutes or so later, the first consternation in the voices of the women. They were not concerned that Raselg had slipped away but bothered by the sounds of triumph coming from the town. The exclamations and cheering did not sound like their men, there was something foreign, sinister and unnerving in those sounds. The Durotrigans should be singing their familiar song of victory by now while they rounded up the civilians and corralled them away from the basilica, so that the plundering could begin. Some of their men should have appeared on the parapet of the southern wall, waving their arms to affirm the victory to the waiting womenfolk. Instead, there were no visual signs of life and only unfamiliar noises.

Within a few more minutes, the women had dispersed. Raselg assumed they had decided to go back to Mai Din, back to their children and to consult with the old men there who had been too infirm to fight.

Raselg was under no illusions. It would quickly be concluded by the surviving community, that the king and his son, and the other men had been led into a trap – by that Dumnonian woman the king took in. She would be stoned or ripped to pieces on sight by a baying mob. They would be setting out to look for her within minutes. She had to move.

The problem was that her leg was stiff and painful, and she was in poor health. Her diet over the last few days had consisted mainly of sour wine and dry bread, some lightly boiled pulses but hardly a mouthful of meat most meals. Like with the mules, they had kept her subdued, low-spirited and malleable by withholding energetic nutrition.

She reckoned it was under sixty Roman miles to Caer Uisc, or Isca Dumnoniorum as the Roman's called it, by the most direct road, and that would theoretically take her three days if she hobbled steadily and she barely slept. But she was without food to sustain herself, and would inevitably grow weaker over time, and her leg might seize up completely before too long. Her pursuers would also expect her to take the direct road towards Dumnonia, back to her own people.

Raselg decided to act contrary to expectations and take the road north-westward to Lindinis instead. This was a more circuitous route to Caer Uisc, perhaps more like seventy to eighty miles, and it would mean staying in the area of the Durotriges for longer, but she could disguise her accent if need be. Her clothing was Roman and would not give her away. She quickly formed a plan to make for Lindinis, present herself to the town council there, or hopefully a centurion or other senior rank of the army there might be, and declare herself the slave of Plancius Vallaunius Rufus, commandant of the Eighth cohort at Isca Dumnoniorum. As far as she was aware, from what Helius had told her, the legal document transferring the possession of her to Helius had never arrived. Perhaps it had never been signed.

She climbed out of her hidey-hole and keeping as low and crouched over as her bad leg would allow, she headed in the direction of the town, planning to skirt its walls on the east side, the more illogical side, and pick up the road to Lindinis eventually which headed off near to the west gate of the town. The old road to Caer Uisc and the road to Lindinis unfortunately started off near to each other on the west side of the town so she would need to take this tortuous route in order to keep well away from the search area.

The town was quiet now. She hoped Tasuatas had suffered a horrible slow death in there. It pleased her to imagine his lifeless, ragdoll body now being abused by Ankows. She wondered what her father was doing at the moment, whether by providence or fate, he had had some part in the murder of the brute, Tasuatas, who had tormented her during the last few days. Then, when her imagination conjured up the horrible image of her beloved father gorging on the dead bodies, his face painted in bright red blood, she forced herself to shove the unwelcome thoughts away.

It took her most of the morning to walk slowly around the east side of the town and to negotiate the flat wetlands on its north-eastern side. Here the way was far more difficult than she had expected, leading her to wade through boggy marshes and to cross several water channels. She had to swim along the river at one point. By the time she spotted the Roman road heading off towards Lindinis from the west side of the town, she was already exhausted, soaked through and shivering with cold. But she dared not rest. She headed in a tangential direction, across fields of neglected farming strips to meet the road eventually some three of four miles from the town. Placing her feet finally on the welcome, hard paving of the road, she collapsed and lay still for an hour, panting, in pain and drifting in and out of sleep.

When she felt stronger again, she looked on the road surface near her left hand, where she had dropped the handful of orange mushrooms foraged during her journey that morning. She ate them greedily and lay a little longer, staring up at the grey sky. Eventually, she was able to get up and consider walking again. The road stretched out to the horizon in front of her, empty of traffic and seemingly endless, but pointing to salvation. For a moment, she could not move her legs, a sense of hopelessness and self-pity engulfed her. She did not believe she could do it: limp thirty or so miles to Lindinis. All that way. She was weeping again, like she did when her father picked her up and carried her out of the town.

She bit into her torn lip, admonishing herself mercilessly for being so weak. She must start to walk, as painful, tiring and hopeless as it seemed. She would do it for him because he had always planned her future and he had returned to rescue her and had put her back on the path to it.

CHAPTER TWENTY

THERE were several days in the life of Plancius Vallaunius Rufus which were defining turning points in it, and none more so than the day of the Ides of October in the Year of the Consulship of Domitian and Nerva. The day his friendship with Tadius Naratius ended.

As usual with Rufus, the turning point involved a woman; this time one he hardly knew at all, had known only one week; eight days of transition which defined him irreparably as someone else. People were later to opine that she had placed an enchantment on him, after all she was a Druid. He should have known better. Rufus to his dying day would argue the opposite. There was nothing fey, there was just reason. Reason when folly and many deaths were possibly the alternative, and none but he and Cybele saw it and cared for the obvious risks.

Perhaps it would have been better if the soldiers that Tadius put on the guardhouse had stood up to Rufus when he threatened them. One of them would survive the day, and certainly regret his actions afterwards.

"Let us in to see the prisoners," Rufus demanded.

When they hesitated, Rufus strapped on his senior centurion's helmet and said through gritted teeth: "I will tell you again. And, if you defy me, the tribunes will want to know why you disobeyed the order of Plancius Vallaunius, Commander of the Eighth cohort of Brittones! And why you preferred to be whipped and thrown out of the army in disgrace!"

"We do not mean to defy you, commander," one of them uttered in a timorous voice. "We request that you wait here until we check with Tadius Naratius or the decurion. You see, we are under strict orders not to allow *anyone* in to see the prisoners." They looked from Rufus to the woman standing beside him.

"And when did you get those orders?" Rufus demanded.

"Those are standing orders to all the men who take a stint guarding this place, commander."

Rufus's face reddened some more. "*When* were those orders made?"

The two men looked at each other. One shrugged, the other said: "The day we brought them in here, after the attack by the wolves."

"I see," said Rufus, conclusively. "Then those orders were issued before I arrived. *Before* a more senior commander than Tadius Naratius was in the fort. Well, so be it. Let us call for Tadius Naratius and we will have him confirm to your stupid faces that you are to be whipped and thrown out the fort and out the army for gross insubordination. And without any backpay, I will add. Go and get him!" Rufus stood aside.

But the men did not move at first, until slowly they turned, reluctantly lifted the heavy restraining bar on the guardhouse door and opened it. The door creaked on its iron pivots, top and bottom. Rufus, ensuring he kept the scowl on his face, pushed them aside and went in.

Cassian and Guilio were indeed in a pitiful state. They lay in their own filth in the corner of the lockup, each shackled by an ankle chain to a thick iron ring cemented into the wall. It had not occurred to Rufus before now that Ankows must still defecate and urinate. They evidently did, and what was excreted was foul and liquid, like diarrhoea. Rufus and Cybele gagged when the smell hit them.

The prisoners did not recognise their former commander. They stared with blank, angular and toothy faces at the visitors, not even registering surprise or interest. Their heads were hardly more than skulls, covered with brittle skin. Their hair had fallen out. Lips had shrunk, causing a permanent snarl, eyes had sunken, like they were backing up out of the light and away from human society. When Rufus saw them, any semblance of doubt he still had immediately evaporated.

He was about to issue the cue to Cybele next to him, but she was already moving across the room towards the wretches. As she did so, she withdrew the *Lucullan* from out of her robe. When she reached Cassian, seemingly within a second, she sank the head of the lance through his chest into his heart. She twisted the lance quickly to snap off its head and leave it in Cassian's chest. It was a strike requiring both strength and precision. Cassian, with almost a fleeting expression of relief on his face, before the pain engulfed him, collapsed back onto the earthen floor.

Rufus had no time to marvel at the Druid's efficiency as he followed suit and plunged his lance into Guilio's chest. The wretch made no effort to avoid the anticipated strike. Rufus dropped the headless shaft of the lance on the floor.

The flesh was already beginning to curl, shrivel and turn dark, as the Ankows' bodies quickly decomposed. Rufus and the Druid backed away, pinching their noses and turning for the door.

The two guards were standing in the frame of the door, and one of them, for some mad reason, thought it necessary to rush at Cybele with his lance. Rufus, in an instant, barged him aside and grabbed at the lance. The two men lost balance and sprawled on the floor.

The other guard turned and fled, just as a loud crack heralded the end of his comrade's life. Rufus had snapped the other guard's neck.

They left the guardhouse and made their way back towards the commandant's house. Tadius and the praetorium guards were already heading over to where the killing had taken place.

"It's true then?" he said curtly to Rufus as they passed.

"Yes."

Rufus and Cybele continued to the house without saying a word. Her face was pale and her lips trembling. He went to his room, she to hers.

Some minutes later, Tadius returned and came to Rufus's room.

"You know very well that I was under orders from the camp prefect to preserve those prisoners!" he pointed out.

"And I was under orders from the governor to kill Ankows!" retorted Rufus.

"Did you have to kill one of our men?"

"That I regret but he attacked Cybele, and I promised her father to protect her."

Tadius thought about this. "Rufus, if I had told you one year ago that you would kill a Roman soldier because of a promise you made to a Druid, what would you have said?"

"I would not have believed you, and I would have said you were crazy! But things have changed, Tadius, and I warned you that you were about to commit a grave mistake. One soldier died today. Many more may have died if we had tried to get those fiends on a ship over to Gaul and then attempted to transport them all the way to Rome. A very long journey with possibilities and opportunity for one or other of the Ankows to escape. You know how cunning they are. It was a risk I was not prepared to take. If one of them had got loose, they could have caused a scourge on the lands we love! The idea was absolute folly!"

"Since when did we put our personal opinions before our strict orders, Rufus?"

"Many times, if memory serves me right."

But Tadius was not placated. He shook his head, resignedly. "What has happened to you?"

He turned and walked down the corridor to his room.

CHAPTER TWENTY-ONE

IT was slick and in marked contrast to the naïve and feeble campaign of Tasuatas and his men at Duronovaria two days earlier, and the auxiliaries of the Belgae tribe timed it well. Cressido Saenus was in the Basilica in the civil town of Isca Dumnoniorum, meeting with the council. His optio and standard bearer, at leisure in the stables of the auxiliary fort half a mile away, were quickly overcome by forty of the Belgae of the third company. All the remaining horses were stolen. Two of the Belgae donned the uniforms of the optio and standard bearer, and, resplendent in the feathered helmets, coolly led the mutineers out of the fort and turned left to head in the direction of the nearby town. Twenty-four of the mutineers peeled off quickly on foot and made for the wharfs. At the town's east gate, the remaining forty Belgae auxiliaries were undergoing the torment of the Gassello course on the road near the gate, wearing their armour and carrying their weapons and full packs. They had been waiting to spy the horses coming across from the auxiliary fort. And when they spotted them approaching, it was an easy thing to overcome the centurion and optio of the third company. They carried ropes in their packs to tie up the officers. Nobody was killed, for they wished to avoid the repercussions of doing so in case their mutiny and desertion were unsuccessful. By the time that Saenus learnt what had happened, the culprits were riding two per horse and had long gone up the east road towards Lindinis, or apparently so. There were no horses left in the fort to give chase.

The mutineers added a sophisticated touch to the enterprise by delivering a letter to the commandant's house and handing it to the servants. In it, the Belgae explained to the acting commander why they had vacated the army and stolen the twenty-eight horses. They cited the withholding of a third of their promised pay as the main reason, the harshness of the relentless Gassello training, their second. The third reason was profit: They intended to take the horses north and sell them to the Brigantes tribe who were rumoured to be arming themselves.

This latter part of the letter was clever. It gave the impression that the deserters would head north directly by road along the frontier road towards Ratae and Lindum, whereas in fact their real intention was to double back through the cover of the wooded countryside and make for the wharfs on the Isca river. Eighty armed men would easily take a ship from the port, and a large vessel had already been earmarked for the plan.

As Saenus and the officers of the Eight cohort were to concede later, the Belgae's operation that day was executed remarkably well, and nobody was hurt. Unfortunately, however, they had lost probably the best contingent of native soldiers from the Eighth cohort and dented their own careers at the same time. They were not looking forward to informing Plancius Vallaunius when he returned from the west, let alone the camp prefect and tribunes of the legion.

A sombre and edgy mood descended upon the camp at Isca. Everybody knew they were in trouble. Despite their being no indications, whatsoever, of what the Belgic auxiliaries had been plotting, the army's way was to visit sanctions on the innocent. The officers and the remaining auxiliaries would take the blame for letting it happen. Somebody would have to pay. Rumours of punishment in store for them ranged from stoppage of wages, through to mass floggings and even the dreaded and ultimate penalty of *decimation*: the execution of every tenth soldier at random. It was no wonder that the atmosphere was sombre and edgy. Indeed, the chance of further mutiny and desertion became extremely high.

Saenus could not believe what was happening. His commanding officer was away for only a couple of weeks, and he found himself presiding over the unravelling of the cohort. It was now minus a sixth of its soldiers and all its horses save for those currently with Rufus in the west, and it was manifesting a worrisome mood of malcontent and insubordination. The centurions and subalterns reported to him over the next couple of days, that the men obeyed instructions and orders hesitantly and begrudgingly, with scornful expressions on their faces, as if to say, 'Well I'll do it for you on *this* occasion but don't push your luck'.

Saenus took the executive decision to reinstate the auxiliaries' wages in full. They would now be receiving three-quarters of a legionary's standard wage, just as the emperor had decreed it should be for all his provinces. He also excused the men from Gassello training for the time being. The mood immediately and noticeably improved.

These remained troubling times for the acting commander, however. He was unenthusiastic about Rufus's return due to the coldness that already existed between them. Rufus was contemptuous of Saenus because he perceived him to have seduced his slave, an offence perceived to be even worse than borrowing a beloved horse without consent. Saenus was contemptuous of Rufus for sending Raselg away when he could have discussed the matter and come to some gentlemanly accommodation, and because he felt he deserved more respect than Rufus showed him. Under the cloud that Saenus presently found himself in terms of his immediate commander, he had no doubt that the mutiny and desertion of a sixth of the infantry would be presented by Rufus to the tribunes as entirely due to the acting commander's woeful negligence. Saenus had been in Rufus's shadow for so long, that it was almost as if he was following in his footsteps as well, making the same mistakes as his mentor: setting back his reputation and otherwise promising career by compromising himself over a low-based woman, and giving his immediate superiors the excuse to be upset with him, and to be critical of unrelated things.

When it transpired that the ship had been commandeered by the Belgic mutineers, and had sailed off eastward along the coast, its captain presented a formal complaint and a request for compensation to the auxiliary fort commander. He was incensed that their soldiers had been allowed to steal his boat which was laden with goods ready to be taken to Gaul once the storms died down. The Law expected atonement to be made, and the captain and shipowner would have it. Saenus took delivery of the formal written complaint with dignified calmness, then kicked the captain out. He shredded the papyrus letter immediately the man was gone.

The stables were absurdly quiet and roomy. A good many of the expensive saddles and bridles had been stolen. It was sad to see all the unworn wood and canvas hoof-protectors laid up on the shelves neatly. The men looked forlorn without their cherished horses, and most of the daily tasks they were used to doing, such as brushing and wiping down the animals, trimming manes and nostril hair, and scraping out and sanding the floors were unnecessary and missed too.

One whole barrack building was empty in the infantry section of the fort and, whether the Belgae contingent had been particularly noisy and bellicose, or it was just the serious and subdued aftermath of such a shocking rebellion, this quarter of the military base was also noticeably quiet too.

It was Saenus's duty to report the incident to the tribunes and requisition replacements from the recruit pool to make up the missing complement, but he was without the usual mounted messengers for this purpose. He was forced to hire horses from the civil town in order to send two men the long distance to Isca Augusta. He could just imagine how his shameful report and request would be received there.

The hired horses were checked over carefully and appeared healthy and robust enough to make the long journey to the legion's headquarters in Siluria but it was not possible to know anything about their character, whether they might have a tendency for obstinacy, which was a common trait of the little horses bred in the south of the province. The two messengers, who were of the Dobunni tribe and therefore from the very region they would be passing through near Glevum, were acquainted with the nature of this local breed. They found to their cost but not their surprise that the horses in question were strong-willed and typical sticklers for routine and warm hay. When they tried to ride past the inn on the road to Lindinis that first afternoon of the trip, both horses protested with a whinny and stopped. Even when they were beaten on the flanks sharply, they walked no more than a few begrudging steps and halted again. They even tried to shake off their riders. Evidently, they were disinclined to pass up the chance of a habitual overnight stay in one of their favourite stables.

The messengers decided they would need to alter their plans slightly. They might initially have hoped to reach Lindinis before stopping that day but, on reflection, it would not lengthen the overall time of the journey if they went along with the horses' preference and made up for it with a longer ride the next day. They could still reach the familiar town of Glevum for the second night.

They turned towards the inn and made their presence known to the innkeeper by knocking briskly on the front door. The door was opened by a tall pale man, who smiled broadly at the sight of the horses and stepped outside immediately to take hold of their reins. He said cheerily, as he led the horses around to the stables at the rear of the building, with the messengers following on foot, "I see a lot of horses, and a great many of them time and time again. I don't claim to recognise them all, but I know most of them, and they always know me!"

There were two stables' buildings, one was shut up and probably only used at the busiest times, the other was open and occupied already by some fine-looking horses. The men waited while the innkeeper undid and removed the saddles and bridles of their mounts and hung them up on large hooks protruding from the roof beams. The unburdened horses then walked over to the corner manger and began nuzzling contentedly at the hay, obviously at home in a familiar place.

Inside the inn, after they were shown their rooms, the innkeeper asked them conversationally, "Where are you heading, then?"

The messengers replied that they were carrying letters to the camp at Isca Augusta.

"Ah, Isca Silurum," the innkeeper replied, using its older and more established Roman name. "I know it very well. I am a retired veteran of the Second Augustan Legion. I see you belong to a horse squadron. Let me guess, the Eighth cohort, am I right? Auxiliary recruits, judging by your Dobunnian accents."

"Yes, Eighth cohort of Brittones, stationed at Isca Dumnoniorum. What's your name? We'll mention you when we get to headquarters. Perhaps they'll still remember you."

"Nepos Censorius is my name. I know your camp prefect very well. Ulpius Senicianus. He often spends the night here. Very amiable man. If you see him, tell him you stayed the night at old Nepos's inn. He would always recommend a stay here. Never misses a chance himself to sample my wife's pork stew."

"We'll do that."

"I am a Durotrigan by birth," continued the innkeeper, "but I did my twenty-five years in the army, mostly serving up north. I was with Agricola. I'm surprised that I managed to survive so long!"

"I'm surprised too, from what I heard! You must have been one hell of a good fighter," one of them answered.

"Practice and discipline, practice and discipline. It's the difference between life and death, boys. Remember that when you're cursing the monotony and repetition of the training."

"We will."

"Sorry, I forgot my manners. Let me take those lances off you."

Nepos gently took the lances from the messengers and stood them carefully against the wall. The horse squadron's *Lucullans* were longer than the ones carried by the infantry.

After he had taken off his heavy chainmail shirt, one of the messengers asked where the shitter was, using the army vernacular for the benefit of the veteran. He was shown to the little window in the room and directed towards an outhouse outside. It was still light enough for the messenger to see a plank laid over a deep hole in there. The messenger went outside to visit the facility immediately. After he had removed his cavalry leggings and loin cloth, and had crouched over the hole, he was surprised to see the innkeeper still watching him through the window from inside the bedroom. He closed the door of the outhouse for privacy.

Nepos waited until he had done so and then turned to his other guest. He smiled like a good host and then strangled the man quickly and efficiently. By the time the other came back from the outhouse, Nepos was ready to kill him too.

Afterwards, he dragged the two dead men around to what appeared to be an unused stables building. He unlocked its door and hung the men on the large hooks protruding from the roof beams inside. Next to the other guests.

CHAPTER TWENTY-TWO

THE glummest of salutes at the north gate of the fort informed Rufus that something was amiss. He turned to Cybele, who was riding on the back of the horse with him and said as much. Her green eyes were turned upwards, viewing the guards on top of the gate with interest. When Rufus began to explain the layout of the fort she should expect inside, telling her that it was much the same as the one called Nemetostatio, but here the commandant's house – the building they called the *praetorium* – was his own official residence and it was where she would be his guest, she looked down and smiled at him and surprised him by whispering: "I have been here before, centurion."

He was going to ask her when, but realised he knew the answer. The night of the battle they called *The Battle of the Ides of Julius*. So, it was not just her father and other male druids, and she-wolves.

"Did you fight?" he asked her. It would not be the first time he knew of a Celtic woman involving herself in warfare but he felt a pang of awe, nevertheless, as he looked at her blithe, innocent face.

"Of course."

They rode through the gate, now it had been opened to them, and trotted along the road to his house, followed by the fifteen men of the horse squadron. Dendus and Luperus both appeared at the door of the house with notable expressions of relief. Luperus took the horse and headed for the cavalry stables, following the other horsemen who were ahead of him along the road, and in for a shock when they got there.

Dendus appeared to have aged, or else Rufus had not noticed before how the years were placing lines and gauntness on his old servant's features. Likewise, Dendus was appraising his master with extra interest. He had not even looked at the strange woman beside him.

"What is wrong?" asked Rufus.

Dendus took this to be a question about why he was studying Rufus's face so keenly, and answered: "Only that you look altered, sir."

"It has been two weeks only, you old fool. No, I meant to ask why the troops act so, well, tensely."

Dendus shrugged and turned to Cybele at last.

"This is the Druid's daughter. We call her Cybele," explained Rufus. "She is to be our guest from now on. Officially, should anyone ask, she is our interpreter and adviser. That is what you will tell Luperus."

The servant nodded and let them pass through the door. He fussed over them, nervously, apologising for the house feeling so cold. He and Luperus had felt reluctant to waste wood on heating the rooms when it was occupied only by the two servants. They had not known when Rufus would eventually return. Dendus would get the hypocaust working immediately, and then fetch wine and food to the atrium for when they had both changed. Did the woman – Cybele – have a change of clothes? Did she want to borrow some of Silpunia's gowns, which were still boxed up somewhere?

"Yes, back at Nemetostatio," pointed out Rufus. "Not here at the fort of Isca Dumnoniorum, surely."

Dendus apologised for the mistake, what was he thinking, it was age? He was delirious with happiness that Rufus had come back, fit and well. All of a muddle in his head, he explained.

"That's quite alright, Dendus. I'm sure you will find a change of clothes for Cybele, or Luperus will do so. Perhaps a warm bath for Cybele?"

"Don't trouble yourself. I will use the river tonight," she said.

"The river?" queried Dendus.

Rufus reminded his servant that the woman was a Druid, as though this fact might excuse all manner of eccentric behaviours. "We'll make our way to the atrium in due course. I won't need any help changing."

One hour later, almost to the minute, Cressido Saenus arrived to make his report. He was shown into the atrium. Cybele had not yet appeared, so Rufus was alone. Whereas, before Rufus's departure, Saenus had been perfunctory, verging on haughty, when he addressed his commander, today he showed more deference. Time had taken the edge off his anger and recent events meant that Saenus needed Rufus's understanding, not that he expected it. He gave his account of the mutiny and disappearance of the auxiliaries from the Belgae tribe awkwardly, tactfully avoiding the obvious defences on his part: ignorance about the well-kept plot, and the surprising and admirable speed and efficiency in which it had been undertaken. Those were elements that the senior officer would need to consider and fill-in objectively himself in the circumstances. In any case, a report from one officer was never enough to get the true picture. Saenus ended by confirming that he had sent two messengers on hired horses to Isca Augusta to inform the legate, Tammo Vitalis.

Rufus listened silently. When the decurion had finished, he amiably offered him a couch and some wine. Saenus took them gratefully. When he sat on the edge of the seat, tears appeared in his eyes. "May I ask, commander, why you are taking such a grim report so calmly?"

Rufus thought about the answer, himself. Part of it was knowing that none of it was anything that Rufus could not have let happen himself. The gods themselves knew how many times he had been blamed for circumstances beyond his actual ken and control, like this. Part of it was also from a sense that these incidents and setbacks were not worth worrying about any longer, in the grander scheme of things. The largest part of it, however, came from the knowledge of what he had done in Nemetostatio, the day before. In comparison to that, nothing Saenus told him could be so grim.

"Any news as to where the camp prefect or broad-stripe might be these days?" Rufus asked, without answering the question.

Saenus shook his head, negatively. He sipped at his wine, appreciatively.

"I may be going to Rome, Saenus. Some ill-born notion about me presenting a report to the emperor about the menace of the Ankows, and about the new lance. I was apparently to drag a couple of the actual fiends there with me. Cassian and Guilio."

Saenus's eyes widened immediately. "They were not here at Isca, at the battle?"

"No, they went back to Nemetostatio, and there they were still there when Tadius Naratius and Luti Bassus returned with the new Tenth cohort. Cassian and Guilio had slaughtered all the civilian retainers in the fort and turned them into Ankows. Luckily there were only about fifty of them and Tadius and Luti were able to contain them. But that's only half of it, Saenus. Creatures, not yet encountered, called *she-wolves* – massive beasts that make grey wolves look like kid-goats – came off the great moor and killed the Ankows. Every one of them except Cassian and Guilio. Our former horsemen were then clapped in irons and held in the guardhouse in a wretched state. If they were not Ankows by then, I would call it cruel. The plan was, apparently, for me to take these two Ankows in a ship from either the port at Isca Dumnoniorum or Clavinium through Gaul, all the way to Rome, and there present them with the lance to Domitian, himself! What do you think of that?"

"I would call that utter madness," confirmed Saenus. "What if they had escaped?"

Rufus nodded. "Such madness as to call for drastic intervention, don't you think? You have not met her yet, but I have a Druid woman under my protection. She is here now. By the gods, Saenus, she is an enigma! She persuaded me, not that I needed much of it, to help her kill Cassian and Guilio! We sneaked *Lucullans* into the guardhouse with us and did it. Tadius Naratius will not forgive me for it. We are no longer friends. And you ask me why it is that I take your relatively anaemic report about a mutiny and the loss of a ship so calmly?"

"And it could have been worse. At least we got the horses back when they were abandoned at the wharf. Tell me more about these *she-wolves*."

"They are the spawn of hyenas and wolves, bred by a faction of Druids who think they are doing their god's bidding. The creatures hunt Ankows with a vengeance. Indeed, they surrounded the fort for several nights while we had Cassian and Guilio incarcerated within it."

Just when Saenus thought he could not be surprised any more, Rufus added: "And Saenus, believe me, the *she-wolves* were here, at Isca on the night of the *Battle of the Ides of Julius*! They fought alongside the Druids!"

Saenus placed his empty wine beaker carefully on a table. "I don't remember anything of that night, well not much, Rufus. The medic says I must have been stabbed by a *Lucullan*, or some other poison that sent me off into delirium. I remember the start of the battle, and I just about remember there being but a few of us left standing at the end. After that, it all seems black."

"No dreams?"

"None."

Rufus got up and filled the other man's beaker with more wine. "Eat with us tonight, Saenus."

"With pleasure, commander."

They shook hands.

THE ship was called the *Egeria*, one of the finest vessels to ply the trade route between Gaul and Britannia, and the leader of the Belgic mutineers, Tuathal, knew the ship well. Its normal port of call was the harbour the Romans called Clausentum, where he had once lived, and he had helped load and unload it as a jobbing worker before he joined up as a Roman army recruit. He had even been aboard it on occasions. When he learnt that the same ship had blown off course in the storms and was taking shelter in the estuary at Isca Dumnoniorum, it was as if the gods were talking to him. Providence had given him the opportunity to alter his fortunes, correct his mistakes. All he needed to do was talk the others into coming with him. He promised them riches, better than it seemed they would ever achieve in the Roman army now. They had all signed up as recruits on the promise of three-quarters of a legionary's wage and the chance of war booty. What they had got instead was reduced pay, harsh discipline and cruel bullying from officers. And once they found themselves assigned to a specialist unit, trained to fight the fiends called Ankows, of all things, they knew they were facing a precarious and ghastly future with little or no chance of any profitable looting. Suddenly, twenty-five years of service to the army was something that could and should be avoided at all costs, whether by death, maiming or, preferably, by effective desertion. It had not been difficult for Tuathal to convince the others to come with him. He lied a little and told them he had crewed on the ship called *Egeria* and knew how to sail it. If they had any doubts about what they were doing, these were dispelled by the brilliant way the mutiny was plotted and implemented by Tuathal.

There was not a man among the Belgae contingent who had actually been on a ship out at sea. A storm on the ocean was therefore an abstract and alien idea to them, the nearest notion of what it meant being high winds encountered inland, causing trees to lean over or, at worst, roofs being blown off roundhouses or tiles coming loose from some of the buildings the Romans or the Atrebates had raised. The notion of a ship being bounced around mercilessly by a sea, fatally engulfed by a deluge of water or split apart on rocks was not something within their imagination. And Tuathal told them that he could sail the ship. It did not occur to them that the same ship was laid up in the safe haven of the Uisc river for a very good reason.

Their plan was simple from this point: sail the ship along the coast eastwards until they found themselves between the coast and the large island called Vectis, and then turn into the wide estuary of the river that led up to the port of Clausentum. There they would spin some story about how they had been blown of course, trying to make an ill-advised crossing to Gaul with their cargo; how the over-ambitious captain and most of the officers had been lost at sea, unfortunately, how Fate had looked kindly upon the rest of them and allowed their salvation. Tuathal would pretend to be the last surviving representative of the shipowners. He had watched and seen how they talked and acted when he was a stevedore at the port. In the unlikely event that they did not manage to sell the ship and its cargo at the port on the black market, they could still vacate the vessel under cover of darkness and make their way directly north towards Venta. Venta *Belgarum*. Their home. If they got that far, their Roman uniforms and weapons would be left far behind, in the sea, never to be found. At best they would all receive a lucrative share of the sale of the ship and cargo, and, at worst, they would be back home with their people, with a chance to start again and, in some cases, reunite with sweethearts they had left behind a year ago.

But when the ship edged out of the river mouth of the Uisc, they were not prepared for the sheer violence of the sea. They turned eastward and hugged the coast, with half a sail unfurled, most of the men intending to take turns down in the galley on the long oars. Tuathal and two others stayed up on deck to wrestle with the rudder-oar and stop the boat crashing onto the shore. The deck began to pitch terrifyingly towards the foaming water on its left side, while huge waves thumped the exposed flanks of the vessel. The oars were useless and were abandoned. No one dared climb up the diagonal mast to decrease the surface of the drenched sail, although Tuathal screamed for volunteers to come up on to the deck and do it. Probably his anguished shouts were ripped away by the wind and nobody heard him.

The large and sweeping bay kept them from the worst of the tempest at first but as they ploughed further eastward, the wind and the fury of the ocean seemed to increase. Most of the men came up on deck. Some were cajoled into attempting the ascent of the mast but hung helplessly from the horizontal spar, their unskilled hands unable to pull up and furl the sail. They climbed down the ratlines again to the deck and hung on to any handhold they could find, occasionally casting pleading and bewildered looks towards their new captain, the one person who claimed to know anything about ships.

They spied what appeared to be a small island through the grey murk ahead, and Tuathal naively imagined he could steer the ship between it and the shoreline. But as he grew nearer to it, he realised it was merely more of the land tricking him, possibly a peninsula joined by a long stretch of low, gravelled beach. The wind was trying to hurl the ship against this beach with increased vengeance, and the three men on the rudder, pushed it desperately to one side as far as it would go, trying against all the odds to bring the nose of the vessel out towards the sea again. It was hopeless, and with a low rumbling scrape beneath them, the *Egeria* came up on to the gravel and stopped. It lurched over even further so that its mast was skimming the surface of the white, brothy waves as they tormented the beach.

Tuathal untied the rope around his waist quickly and shouted to everyone to abandon the ship. His might have been heard but it was no matter, everyone had come to the same decision already. Eighty men in chaotic fashion, plunged into the water on the leeward side. Most merely needed to slide off the rail of the ship into the frothing water lapping the boat's side. The men swarmed on to the beach and were just clear of its mast and rigging, when the ship lifted suddenly into the air and crashed down onto the sweep of pebbles. The mast and spar groaned and snapped, and the sail dragged its ropes and netting further up the beach as the wind filled it and gave it one last push.

Not bothering to watch the spectacle any longer, the men clambered over the bank of the spit and into the leeward shelter of the beach on its other side. Here the wind was a fraction of its former force. The bay to the east was relatively calm. There were ships and boats in the entrance of an inlet, one to two miles away, their masts swaying in the gusts but comparatively safe. Tuathal rounded up the men. They seemed all to have survived. He urged them to sink to their knees and pray to the goddess Cliodna for their deliverance. After this quick benediction some enquired where they were. No one was sure.

"I never came this way," bluffed Tuathal, "but judging by the distance we travelled, I would guess we are still on the coastland of the Durotriges somewhere."

"There seems to be an entrance to a harbour over there," pointed out one man.

Another was looking back where they had trudged from and said in a regretful voice, "We left our fortunes on the beach back there. That cargo is very valuable."

"There's nothing we can do about it right now. Likely the Durotrigan bastards will come and try to rob it all as soon as the wind drops, and they'll put up a fight if we try to stop them!" reasoned Tuathal.

Nobody disagreed. They had lost their armour and weapons, and had nothing to fight with at the moment except bare hands and pebbles. At least they had their lives still, and freedom. For now.

"We must get out of this shit weather," said Tuathal. "Let's find a farmhouse and make ourselves at home for the night. We'll come back tomorrow morning with tools and try to get the cargo out the wreck. We must hide it. Some of it, at least. There's tin, iron, lead and coal in there, and it's not going anywhere till somebody shifts it."

"I'm hungry!" one man complained.

"I'm wet for some reason!" answered another, causing a round of laughter.

CHAPTER TWENTY-THREE

IT was three months to the day since the auspicious but misnamed Battle of the Ides of Julius, a battle that had happened four days afterwards. The titular date had fixed in the minds of people as it coincided with the time of the full moon that month: the night that the bulk of the erstwhile Eighth cohort had risen from the dead, joined forces with other ghastly vexillations of evil, and started on their march towards Isca Dumnoniorum. To Rufus and the senior ranks of the legion who were in the know, this was the date they had stopped looking for the bodies of the dead cohort and had braced themselves instead for war.

The auxiliary fort of Isca, visibly the same three months later, was in all other respects markedly different. Gone was the booming voice of Bruccius Natalinus, gone were the legionaries of Italia, Lusitania, Germania and Gaul. All dead. In their stead, four hundred unfamiliar faces, a hubbub of Celtic dialects and a brooding air of tense resignation. Now that the commandant was back, the atmosphere had quietened. Whether or not he deserved such a reputation, Plancius Vallaunius Rufus was feared for his harshness. Rufus himself had fostered it when it suited him. On the morning after he had returned to the fort from his trip to the west, he did not hesitate to punish the soldiers who had been on the watch on the north wall of the fort on the day of the mutiny, for failing to raise the alarm when a large group of Belgic auxiliaries ran to the wharfs in plain view of them. His heart was not in it, but he had to stop the rot growing. He needed them to know that even though his acting commander had been generous and raised their wages and excused them from the Gassello course, he himself was cut from a different tree. Rufus employed the old general's approach to training new recruits: scare them to death in the first six months, then after they were as malleable as soft clay, work to get them to love you in the fullness of time.

This ploy was predicated on having sufficient time, however, and events now appeared to work against Rufus. The day after he had returned to Isca, a Dumnonian merchant, fresh from the town of Lindinis troubled the guards on the door of the commandant's house, requesting he be allowed to pass a message to the commandant, one of utmost importance. It had to be delivered personally.

Rufus ordered the guards to leave the man in the road. He might be housing a Druid but he still wanted to maintain his policy of keeping anyone who was not Roman or an auxiliary outside of his house or the army headquarters nearby. Leaving a sufficient interval of time to demonstrate that he was not falling over himself to entertain the entreaties of passing merchants,

Rufus finally came out of the front door to meet the man in the street. Dendus went with him to act as witness.

The merchant was a proud man. His clothes were fine but not showy; travelling clothes good enough to wear on a long journey but not too sumptuous as to invite robbery. He wore a beard, trimmed in the Arabic style but when he spoke, he was obviously a native of these parts. He looked a little put out at having been left waiting so long in the street, and by not being welcomed into at least the vestibule of the building now. When he realised that he was expected to deliver his message there and then, with no hospitality in the offing, he eventually spoke to Rufus.

"Commander, I have just come from Lindinis. The town councillors there, knowing that I was travelling the road to Isca, asked me to bring a woman with me. She had been found lying outside the home of a senior town official, more dead than alive. They assumed she was just a beggar, and were going to let her perish, until she told them that she was the household slave of Plancius Vallaunius, the commandant of the cohort at Isca Dumnoniorum. Hearing this, they decided to care for her, and, the following day, they fetched me in order to bid me to take her with me. But, seeing what wretched state she was in, and suspecting at once that she was likely to die before I ever got her here, I refused the councillors' request. I promised instead to bring you this report. Do with it what you want."

Rufus demanded sternly: "You are misinformed. I do not have a female slave any longer. However, tell me exactly about her appearance. Was there any indication where she had come from?"

The merchant bristled at the cold way his well-meaning report had been received. "Sir, no one knows where she had come from. She was alone and could hardly speak. She was wearing a Roman dress, torn to shreds and muddy. Her bare feet were blistered and bleeding from walking. She looked to me like she had not eaten for days. One of her knees was very swollen and bore the signs of a wounding. Her lips were cut. Her hair was, or should have been, the colour of beechmast. I heard only one sentence or two from her, and she sounded like a child of Dumnonia. I felt sorry for her but could not, in all conscience be complicit in killing her. She was in my opinion not up to travelling in my cart to Isca, nor up to living a few hours longer as it was."

"What did she say to you?"

"When she heard me promise to bring a message to you, she grabbed my arm weakly and spoke to me. They might be the last words she ever spoke, as far as I know. I remember them well because I was repeating them during the journey here. She said: 'Sir, my name is Raselg. I am the slave of Plancius Vallaunius at Caer Uisc. Tell him, Helius is dead but my father is not.'"

Rufus, reeling from confusion asked the merchant to repeat the words. After that he asked, "Did she say anything else before that? Did she indicate where she had walked from?"

The merchant shook his head, noting the anxious expression on Rufus's face. "Believe me, commander. I could not have brought her here safely. A corpse, yes, but not a slave."

"She is not actually my slave, as I told you already. She was confused. If the tribune, Exuperatus Helius is dead, then she will pass to a new master by action of his written will, and I very much doubt it will be back to me. She is no longer under my governance or responsibility."

At this point, Dendus, who had been standing listening to the side, said, "Sir, we did not complete the transfer papers. So, if the tribune is dead, she will have reverted to you."

"So be it," muttered Rufus, icily. "Dendus, pay this man for his troubles. I will send someone to examine her at Lindinis. If she is still alive by then, I will have her brought here. If not alive, well, we will have to find another way of getting to the bottom of this puzzle."

He nodded to the merchant and went through the door, back inside. The meeting was over.

Later, after Dendus had given the merchant some money, he went to find Rufus in the house, knowing that he would be in some agitation about the news. He found him pacing about the inner courtyard. There was no roof to the yard and it was open to the elements, and seldom used this time of the year except to snatch some fresh air after using the latrine or to walk off a sudden onset of indigestion. The couches and tables had been moved to the outer edges of the yard, partly under the eaves and out of the worst of the rain which seemed to fall regularly but perhaps not so frequently as it did at Nemetostatio. When Rufus spotted Dendus, he said, "Why is Helius dead?"

Dendus knew a rhetoric question when he heard it. He shrugged. "Sir, let me go to see Raselg. 'Though I am not quick on a horse, I could reach Lindinis in a day, at a push."

"Yes, Dendus, I have been thinking that could be the best action. If she is still alive, find out from her what has happened. Why is she not with her new master, or with the army for that matter."

"*If* she is still alive, sir. I did not like the sound of it. He said, 'more dead than alive'. He even said that she might have spoken her last mortal words to him."

"*More dead than alive?*" came a voice from the side of the courtyard. It was Cybele, who had come out of her room immediately adjoining it. "Centurion, let me go with Dendus. I should be able to tell whether she is now an Ankow. If she is not, I have healing knowledge. I can try to get her better."

Rufus had stopped pacing. "Have you been listening, Cybele?"

"You have been going backwards and forwards across this courtyard, saying the same words over and over again out loud: *My name is Raselg. I am the slave of Plancius Vallaunius at Caer Uisc. Tell him, Helius is dead but my father is not.*"

"An Ankow?" exclaimed Rufus. "That had not occurred to me. You are right, of course."

"It must occur to you, centurion! It must *always* occur to you!"

She walked into the centre of the courtyard and tried to put a hand on Rufus's arm. Dendus noted that he flinched slightly.

"I cannot let you go, Cybele. I promised your father that I would protect you. To keep you with me."

For a moment, an expression came to her face that reminded Rufus very much of her father: a bemused, slightly mocking look.

Dendus interrupted, saying, "I will go alone, sir. I don't mind. I will willingly do that for Raselg. Tell me how I can ascertain whether she is one of the fiends, and I will try to get to the truth."

"It is too dangerous," said Cybele. "If the people at Lindinis are not aware of it, they will not be taking any precautions."

"She's right, Dendus. It could be dangerous. I need to send some horsemen there to warn them as soon as possible. They need to keep a strict guard on her, till you arrive. Dendus, tell the quartermaster to give you the fastest cart he has. Set out within the next hour. Our horsemen will have got there well before you and seen to it that she is placed in the strongest chains – if she is still of this world. If she is dead, then you will have to make sure that her body is treated so that she cannot rise again. When is the next full moon?"

"Not for many days," answered the Druid. "We are only six days beyond the last one. Centurion, I want to go with him. One of the reasons my father wanted me to accompany you, was to keep an eye on you foolish Romans. I know for sure he would want me to go in this situation."

"I am not so sure of that."

She laughed. "I know him better. He likes you, centurion. He says you are a good man. But, with him, the fight against the scourge of the Ankows will always come first."

Rufus was unconvinced. "Dendus, go to the quartermaster and get things ready to leave for Lindinis right way, while I think about this. And ask one of the guards to fetch the decurion urgently, while you're at it."

When the servant had gone way, Rufus would have resumed his pacing but for Cybele standing there, expectantly. He invited her to sit down on one of the couches to the side, albeit that they were cold and damp and it was not surprising that she declined. He offered her a wooden bowl of apples instead. She took one and said, "You are very agitated. I am sorry to see it. This woman – Raselg as you call her – she has brought you pain."

"Some", he answered, not wanting to elaborate.

"I can be ready in a few minutes. I wish you would reconsider."

"Cybele, you say that, with your father, the fight against the scourge of Ankows will always come first, but I don't think that is true. If he had a choice between your welfare and killing Ankows, what would he choose?"

He was surprised that she needed to think about this question for so long. With relief on his part, she replied eventually. "He would choose my welfare, but it is more nuanced than that. In some circumstances, for instance, if the choice was between avoiding a hundred innocent deaths and my welfare, then he might choose differently."

"You Druids are well known for your liking of human sacrifice! It has been your downfall as far as the empire is concerned. It was one of the main reasons the governor decided to cull Druids and destroy their culture and religion, rather than apply the normal Roman diplomacy of tolerance and absorption."

A cold expression transformed her face, hints of anger and resentment he had not seen before. Even the green eyes seemed to turn to flint. "Human sacrifice is necessary when it is for the good of all, for the good of the lands. You killed a soldier without hesitation in the prison in Nemetostatio. What was that if it was not human sacrifice? What was your motive for doing that, do you think?"

He did not want to be reminded of that incident. Its repercussions were manifold and yet to play out, and it hung over him every breathing moment. The worst of it was not knowing the form the inevitable sanctions would take. The legate, Vitalis, would rein back on the punishment but the governor might not.

Rufus had defied the orders of the emperor's delegates, although the emperor himself would not yet know about it. The penalties could range from demotion to death. He might be ordered to fall on his sword. Suddenly, despite himself, he felt a surge of anger and bitterness towards Cybele and her damned father, for bringing him to this point, possibly ruining everything. He might owe his life to her father but what kind of life would that be now?

"Go with Dendus, then!" he snapped.

He left the inner courtyard and found Dendus packing a bag in his room. "Why have you not yet gone to see the quartermaster about a cart?" he hollered. "And while you're at it, explain to me, Dendus, why you had not prepared the document transferring Raselg to the tribune, Exuperatus Helius!"

Dendus looked abashed. "I'm sorry, sir. Selfishly, I spent my time preparing my manumission document and a change to your will instead. And you were away at Nemetostatio, so I thought the other documents could wait. You weren't here to sign anything. And, as for the cart, I was about to go there, now."

"Why is Cressido Saenus not here? Did you at least send for him?"

"I did, sir. Told the guard to tell him it was urgent."

"Good. The Druid woman will be going with you to Lindinis."

He was out of the room again before Dendus could answer.

CHAPTER TWENTY-FOUR

"BUT Luti, we already have two shrines in what is a relatively small fort. And we've only been able to fit those shrines in because we stopped using the west and east gates and the Via Principia street, here."

The rain was falling lighter now, and Tadius and Luti, wearing their helmets and wrapped in their water-proof cloaks hardly noticed it. Normally, Tadius would undertake his daily tour and inspection of the fort with his optio, Parius, and his standard-bearer, Asempero, but, today, Luti Bassus had requested he accompany him. It was obvious that the decurion had something he wished to bring to the commander's attention.

They started the tour at the door of the headquarters' building in the centre of the fort, walking from there to the south gatehouse along the street, and then turning left to approach the six parallel barracks blocks. Tadius liked to stop and check that the ballistae were in good order in the south-east corner of the fort, with a neat stack of large, heavy iron-tipped bolts in readiness. When they had inspected these machines together and walked past the barracks, where auxiliaries were busy cooking their breakfasts on rows of small firepits, Luti had halted their progress at the round Mithras shrine to make his request.

"We can place it where the Mithras shrine currently is, commander. No one worships here at the Mithras shrine any longer. These new recruits have never even heard of that god. And I know you don't make any vows here. You've always done your devotions to Silvanus on the other side of the fort."

"Yes, it's true but, you know what a deity is like when he or she thinks they are not being worshipped enough, or they perceive themselves to be offended. Are you prepared to take that risk? I am not sure it is a good thing to dismantle a shrine without some compensating act to appease the god. Things are tricky enough without having a vengeful Mithras to contend with!"

"Who is this Mithras, anyway?" responded Luti, sneeringly. "What power has he got in these parts? I never understood the soldiers' obsession with him. He's a Persian deity, as I understand it, and it's a long way from Persia to here! I'm prepared to take the risk. I think we're safe in the depths of Dumnonia from a god who resides in the far east of the world. In any event, it's Nerthus who rules here, and She will protect us."

Tadius waited for the next part. It was becoming all too inevitable and a little tedious by now.

"Look, commander," continued the decurion. "She preserved me when I was skewered by that sword. I looked down and saw it impaling me and, 'though I'd never prayed to Nerthus before in my life, it came into my head all of a sudden! She would be my protector, but She would require something back from me in return! I called out to Her and I promised that if She saved my life, let me live, preserved me, I would be her servant for evermore! And She did! She saved me for some great purpose, that is obvious, commander, and I am beginning to understand what it is!"

It seemed that, every time that Tadius heard this story, it had become enhanced and embellished. In the latest version, it had Luti making a pact directly with the goddess, there and then as the sword pierced him, whereas on previous tellings, he had just shouted out her name spontaneously, if not accidentally in his morbid fear of death, and probably because he was German and it was the first native goddess that popped into his head. In the earlier versions, the realisation that he had been preserved for some great purpose had only come days later, while Luti was recuperating in the hospital.

"Hold on, decurion. Nerthus is a German god, isn't she? Why do you think she rules around here? And won't you be on your own, worshipping her at your shrine, with a bunch of Britons looking on, bemused?"

"Nerthus, Isis, Terra Mater, Cybele – it's all the same god! She is one of the pantheon of recognised deities worshipped by Romans, and we ought to be encouraging our recruits to worship a good Roman god rather than their multitude of unauthorised ones!"

"Cybele?" muttered Tadius.

Luti's eyes began to sparkle with zeal. "I asked Her to give me signs. Tell me what she wanted me to do. And she did send me signs! The lance, the she-wolves, the Druid and the woman called Cybele. Even Mus saving the camp prefect. It's all pointing to my mission. I am fated to help rid the lands of Ankows! In these times, when the God is due to intervene, there are no coincidences!"

"But it was Vallaunius who named her that, because he found her bathing naked in the river alone, and it amused him to call her Cybele."

"He was guided unknowingly. We are all agents of Her. These things come to pass for a reason. She is unfolding her plan. Look, it makes sense. The natural order of our existence is that we live, we die and then we corrupt into compost. Our bodies feed and enrich the land while our spirits are released to journey on. But the Ankows stop this natural cycle. They prevent us dying and providing our dutiful boon to the earth. They are the opponents of nature in its purest form. And their numbers are growing like a cancer. The earth is a citadel that lies besieged. It is no wonder that Nerthus is planning her intervention, and will come amongst us again; to rally Her troops to fight back! And we will finally win against mankind's greatest foe once we have Her leading us."

"Hold on, you think the Druid's daughter is a manifestation of the god?"

"I think it is more than a possibility. Do you not feel it? Have you not felt that a new season is upon us?"

"Oh, Luti, I cannot hold with such an interpretation. Next you will be telling me that you are appointed as her high priest."

Luti's facial expression moved from ambivalent to scornful within a couple of seconds. "I am her soldier, *you* are the nearest we have to a priest in this place. The Master of Religious Ceremonies. That is why I am requesting permission from you to build a shrine to *Nerthus-Cybele*. It is a reasonable request in the circumstances. The adherents of Mithras have gone. That god's shrine is already neglected. Look at it. The offence has already been committed. Our duty – your duty in particular – is to guide and nurture the recruits in ways of religion as well as martialism. Do not forget that this is one of your main duties as commandant here. Let me build the shrine, commander. There is really no argument, legally, regulatory or ethically that you can use to deny me this!"

It was typical of Luti, when trying to get his own way, to begin with soft honeyed words, but, once he encountered resistance, resort to a more legalistic and threatening tone. It was a tone that carried a thinly disguised warning about the consequences. The legate may get to hear of your dereliction of duty, it implied.

"Very well, decurion. Build the shrine."

Luti smiled and nodded. Back was the obsequious inferior officer. They continued their tour of the fort, walking past the hospital towards the north wall. After a few moments, Tadius asked, "What has this got to do with Mus?"

The decurion seemed unwilling to answer. Eventually, he said in a measured, deliberate voice, much like he was delivering a homily: "The Goddess dwells in a sacred chariot, in a temple next to a secluded lake. Many have wondered where that place is. All that is known is that the temple lies on an island in the Ocean. The location must be remote enough to be hidden from common folk and it must lie next to a lake that is barely ever visited."

"You think it is on *this* island?"

"I know it is!"

Tadius could not help himself turn and look towards the distant hills of the great moor and the mysterious lands of tunnels and giants beyond it. Vales and grottoes that no civilised person had yet visited.

"No not there," interrupted Luti. "At first I thought it was there. Until Mus appeared with his Carvetii comrades. Then I remembered a land we went to years ago. You will remember it too. A land of mountains and wondrous lakes, remote and shrouded in mists! In just such a place, a great mother goddess would dwell! It is the perfect place for Her sacred temple to lie, until the day the priest can find Her again! When I remembered our being there in Carvetia, Tadius Naratius, I felt a strange tingling vibration grip my body and such overwhelming happiness consume my being! It was as if I had known it all along!"

Tadius felt slightly perturbed, if not mildly disgusted at the fervour of this revelation. He had spent years alongside a pragmatic, unemotionally legalistic man called Luti Bassus, and now he was presented with a maniacal, orgiastic religious fanatic in his stead. Everyone knew the decurion had altered since that day he received the sword thrust, and the Druids had carried his limp body to safety and succour, but this was far too extreme for comfort. This was worse than the change that Lugnensus Parius had undergone since that same day; the hesitant, gloomy and nervous man where once there had been a brave, cheeful and assertive soldier. Tadius would not have believed he would ever think it, but he found himself actually *missing* the old, vicious, irreligious version of Luti.

"I have spoken to Mus about it," continued Luti. "And he believes he knows the exact place in Carvetia! I hope to go there together with him when this present stage of the battle is completed."

"I would have thought you would need to go where the army sends you, decurion," retorted Tadius, impatiently. "And Mus is signed up for twenty-five years yet."

"Then I will go alone, guided by his description of the place. I have less than one more year of service left, not even one year."

"So you have. Perhaps we will not have completed our present inspection before you retire? Shall we continue this tour of the fort, or do you wish to delay us more?"

Thankfully, Luti was finished on the subject for the time being.

CHAPTER TWENTY-FIVE

THE Druid's daughter had been to many parts of Dumnonia. She knew its moors and valleys, its hills, estuaries and craggy, dynamic coasts. She had walked across to the magical island, only accessible on foot at low tide, and she had gone as far afield as Caer Uisc on the country's easternmost fringe. For a middle-aged Druid, she was comparatively well-travelled. She still felt a thrill, however, contemplating the sheer magnitude and audaciousness of long straight Roman Roads like this one that stretched as far as the eye could see to the horizon ahead. Dendus reckoned this ancient Road, one of the earliest built by Roman hands, was so long as to divide effectively the whole giant island of Albion diagonally into two; with a tamed, civilised and strictly governed part to the south, and a troublesome, wild part to the north. Her country lay mostly on the untamed side.

Dendus chattered contently and sometimes whistled a happy tune as they rode along. He informed her that it was a melody from his homeland of Lusitania, which he was surprised today that he still remembered. Cybele did not understand half the things he said to her, with his thick foreign accent swilling about and knocking over the already difficult Latin words. She nodded when she thought it appropriate to do so but said very little in return.

He liked to flavour his everyday mundane existence with reflective peppercorns of personal significance; contextual notes and milestones along the way. Today, he was pretty sure that this ride to Lindinis on a cart was personally significant to him for being the last time he made this well-worn and familiar journey as a bonded slave, and he was not wrong in that. The future looked exciting. Although he was certain, the gods permitting, that he would want to continue working for Rufus as a freedman, he could take a wife and receive a wage for his labours once he was no longer in bonded servitude. The latter seemed easy, the former more difficult to contemplate in his particular circumstances. Ironically, today, while processing these cheerful thoughts for the first time in his life, he happened to find himself in the highly unusual position of sharing a long ride next to a single and, as far as he knew, unmarried woman. He judged her age to be around thirty years, which made her around twenty years his junior. She was not a great beauty but she was pleasant enough to look at, and he grew excited by the intriguing image of what it would be like to roll around naked with her, trying to make children. She would have several more years left to bear them and, perhaps at her advanced age, she would not be quite so fussy about her suitor.

He had never been brave enough to flirt with a woman, and it did not come naturally to him now, but he had to start somewhere. Rufus would sign his manumission papers in the next week or so, and Dendus would be released like a hawk to glide away on the rising breezes and find a mate. He settled his beady eyes on the woman sitting on the driving board of the cart alongside him.

But whenever he said anything to her, she just grunted and nodded and looked slightly uncomfortable. She was pretending not to understand half of what he said. On reflection, it was probably impossible to take a Druid woman as a wife. They kept to their own, and their own mysterious society. He was a fool to even think that she would be available for betrothal. They had strict rules about that, to be sure. He gave up on the idea after about an hour of fruitless chatter, and fell silent instead, staring ahead up the road where he noticed that they were now approaching the one and only travellers' inn on this stretch of the ancient highway.

As they were passing the set of buildings, a woman ran out from one of them and into the road to urge them to stop the cart. She wore Roman clothes and no slave collar, and she seemed respectable enough. Probably not a whore on this occasion, therefore, even though they were passing an inn and it was not unusual for prostitutes to wander out, looking for commerce from passing traffic. The woman was in a heightened state of distress, unlikely as well to be the deliberate tone set by a whore touting for trade. Dendus brought the horse to a halt and waited to hear what she wanted.

"I am Perennia, wife of Nepos Censorius the innkeeper," she began, on the verge of panic. "Please take my daughter, Censoria to the medics in Lindinis! She is very ill with the falling sickness and we fear she will die! I will pay you for your troubles!"

"Why can't Nepos the innkeeper take her?" asked Dendus.

"He is away at present, in Lindinis already on business, and I only have my two young boys to help me run the inn. I cannot go to Lindinis with Censoria myself, and I therefore implore you to help us! Please sir, I will carry her into your cart and all you need do is take her to the medics in the town. It will not be out of your way. They know her already, as our inn is very well known in these parts, and she has been inflicted with the same illness before. She only survived on the last occasion because my husband was able to go to Lindinis with her, and the medics could help her just in time. Please sir, she may die if she is not taken to them again, straight away! I have no one else to help us in this situation! Travellers with carts are infrequent on this road at this time of day! Please, I beseech you!"

Dendus turned to Cybele to see what she thought about the request. Cybele's expression was ambivalent but she asked, "Where is your daughter? Show her to us."

"Yes, off course. Please follow me and I will take you to her."

"No, bring her here," countered Cybele.

The woman looked puzzled suddenly. "Are you a Druid?" she asked. If Cybele was not mistaken, the woman appeared slightly frightened by this notion, but this was not unusual in her experience. Her people were more feared and tolerated than loved.

"Yes, I am a Druid. Bring your daughter here so we can see her."

Perennia eventually obeyed and ran quickly back to the inn. After a couple of minutes, she reappeared, wheeling a small two-wheeled handcart, on which lay the prostrate form of another woman, this one around fourteen or fifteen years of age. She was unconscious, her face covered in a film of sweat. Her mother had nevertheless wrapped her in a blanket.

"Have you given her anything?" asked Cybele. "It looks like a sweating sickness or fever of some kind, not the falling sickness."

"That is normal. She complains of being terribly cold immediately after a fit. Her body becomes icy and she begins to turn blue and shiver violently if we do not try to keep her warm. Have you a salve or some magic that can help her, Druid?"

"No I have not. Put her in the cart. We will take her to Lindinis. Be quick about it."

Dendus spoke up. "We will take her to the medics, that is all. After that, we are not responsible for her. We will ask the medics to arrange to fetch Nepos the innkeeper."

"Thank you, sir. My husband will pay you for your troubles."

"No need for that," said Cybele. "Put her in the cart now. We must be on our way. There are only three more hours of daylight."

The young woman was placed in the back of the cart. Her mother whispered some comforting words to her and Dendus flicked the reins to start the horse. They left the older woman standing in the road behind them, weeping and staring at them, her hand to her mouth in apparent wretchedness.

They had not gone more than a hundred yards when Dendus tried to engage Cybele in conversation again. "It was very kind of you not to ask for money," he said.

"What would I need with money?"

Dendus laughed and flicked the reins again to quicken the pace of the horse.

After a moment, his eyes on the road, Dendus said, "I can't help thinking about how strange this is: the merchant, telling us that he could not carry Raselg to us in Isca because she was too ill to travel and might die on him. And what are we doing now? Carrying another young woman in the opposite direction, who might die on us just as easily! If we're unlucky, we might deliver one corpse to Lindinis and find another one waiting for us to collect."

"Hopefully, this one will be strong enough."

Cybele began to turn to check on the passenger in the back of the cart. As she did so, she caught sight of a quick movement, the shifting of the thick blanket, a flash of metal, and then saw the pointed end of a dagger emerge from the front of Dendus's throat. His eyes widened and he uttered a weird gurgling sound before his head slumped forward. The cart did not alter speed even though its driver had let go of the reins. There was a scream of triumph from the young woman behind them. She was kneeling and viciously shaking Dendus's head. Cybele saw the point of the dagger blade withdraw back into Dendus's throat and realised that the young woman was extracting it quickly from the neck of the first victim in order to plunge it into her second victim. Herself. In that same instant, Cybele leapt sideways off the cart.

She hit the ground with a violent crash that knocked the wind out of her and sent flashes of light dancing before her eyes. She could still discern the cart riding on without her along the road, the innkeeper's daughter now clambering into the front of it to occupy the space Cybele had just vacated, probably in an effort to grab at the reins. Cybele knew she had but moments to get up and run, and to try to hide.

But when she moved, a sharp tearing pain erupted in her side. She had fallen on to the short lance that she had concealed in her robes, and the point of it had gone into her flesh deeply. How badly she did not know but, it was not just the wound and the hole in her torso that she pictured, and which shocked her, it was the knowledge that she had impaled herself on a spear that contained poison. *Wolf's-bane*. Any moment now, the toxins in the spearhead would hit her blood stream and start to pump around her body, sending her into spasms of nausea, cramps and delirium.

She felt for the shaft of the lance under the folds of her clothes and yanked the point out of her side. She could not help herself scream at the pain this caused. Her vision began to dissemble and float about, her head going light. Then the sickness hit her with a wave, and she vomited bile which was bitter and burnt her throat and tongue.

The cart had stopped up ahead and was beginning to turn around. The innkeeper's daughter was coming back for her.

Cybele tried to get up but her body would not obey her now. She flopped down on the paving stones of the road as the symptoms of the poison gripped her like a vice. She could only stare helplessly up at the undulating clouds above her, and wait for the inevitable.

CHAPTER TWENTY-SIX

THE iron of the narrow slave collar around Dendus's neck had worn so thin over the years that it was in danger of snapping of its own accord as it was. Censoria's dagger had split the band in two, and the violent shaking of his head and gleeful mock-strangling of the dying servant's neck had caused the broken band to drop off and fall to the road. It may have lain unnoticed or been kicked eventually over to the verge had it not fallen within a quarter of a mile of Nepos's inn.

On the second day after Dendus's and Cybele's departure, the two horsemen Rufus had sent to Lindinis set off to return to the fort at Isca. They had seen Raselg and she was still alive, possibly in a better condition than they had expected. They told the town council to hold her in heavy irons and await the arrival of the delegation of their commander. When Dendus failed to appear in the cart that evening and the following day, the horsemen assumed there had been a change of plan or else some misfortune had befallen him. They returned along the road, half-expecting to find the servant's cart laid up beside the road somewhere with a broken wheel. There was no sign of it.

They stopped at the inn along the way to enquire whether the slave and his companion might be staying there. The innkeeper's wife, Perennia, confirmed they had put the slave and his companion up for the night and that the two guests were currently in the stables to the rear of the inn, shackling the horse to the cart in readiness to leave.

The two horsemen went with the innkeeper's wife to the stables. When they were shown into one of the stables blocks, they found a couple of carts in there and a row of dead guests hanging from hooks from the rafters. The sight was so appalling that they were momentarily inattentive to the danger they were in, and were quickly overcome by Nepos who was waiting in there to ambush them. The soldiers fought back but could not use their lances in time, clasped as they were to their thick leather belts. The outcome was two more bodies hanging from the rafters.

Three days after the day that the horsemen, Dendus and Cybele had all left to go to Lindinis, it was apparent to Rufus and Saenus that something had gone wrong. The horsemen themselves were under strict orders to return to Isca once Dendus had arrived and taken control of the situation concerning Raselg. Consequently, they should have been back the day before, at the latest.

If it had been a year earlier, the commanders would have suspected foul play at the hands of brigands or some hothead Britons who wanted to stir up trouble. Now they were forced to contemplate by default, and by the report the merchant had given about Raselg, the probability that *Ankows* were involved somehow. There were no soldiers stationed at Lindinis these days, the vexillation of the Sixth cohort having returned to Isca Augusta a month earlier, so the peaceful civil town would be easy prey to a hoard of the fiends.

It was decided that Rufus would take half the cohort, comprising two hundred and forty of the light auxiliary infantrymen and fifteen men of the cavalry squadron, north to Lindinis. At top marching speed, it would be possible to reach Lindinis on foot in one day, as soldiers could cover forty miles along a good road. Whether they would be fit to fight when they got there was another thing. Rufus doubted it. These auxiliaries were not hardened soldiers. He had watched them with dismay flopping about with exhaustion and lack of fortitude on the Gassello course. He would therefore dig in for one night in a temporary marching camp alongside the road, perhaps two-thirds of the way.

Saenus remained at Isca to command the auxiliary fort and guard the civil town. He was disappointed to have to stay behind, especially after being told that his beloved Raselg was but a day away and suffering in very bad health, if she was alive at all.

The scouts Rufus sent ahead to Lindinis during the march there, came back in the early afternoon to report that the town seemed peaceful and in good order, which was a surprise to some extent. The scouts had found no sign of their comrades or Rufus's slave and the Druid's daughter. Their comrades had last been seen heading off along the road back to Isca on their horses.

Approximately two-thirds of the distance along the road was also where Nepos's inn was situated. Since Lindinis was reported to be peaceful and under no threat, Rufus was by then scouring the fields with his eyes just beyond the inn buildings as he marched at the front of the infantry column, looking for a suitable place to stop and build a camp for the night. It was then that he spotted the broken slave collar lying on the road. He picked it up and recognised it to be Dendus's collar at once. The wording engraved on the collar had long since been worn away but there was no mistaking the object's provenance.

Rufus ordered the auxiliaries to step off the road and search the verges on either side for signs of a cart or anything else unusual. When the road was empty and he had retraced his steps a few hundred yards, Rufus found three patches of dried blood staining the road slabs. He felt the stains with his fingers and ascertained by the iron taste on his tongue that it was blood.

He stood and looked around, the adrenaline ramping up his heartrate. There were woods on one side of the road, thick enough for people or fiends with ill intent to hide in. Dendus and Cybele could have been ambushed by attackers emerging suddenly from these trees, but this seemed unlikely in the situation. Dendus should have had time to put the carthorse into a face pace, if not a gallop, and to race out of harm's way. The attackers would have had to be waiting on the road itself and, in some way or another, have taken Dendus and Cybele by surprise. Or be on horses. But Rufus had never seen an Ankow ride a horse for some unknown reason.

His eyes returned to the huddle of buildings in the distance. Was it just a coincidence that the inn lay only a quarter of a mile away? Rufus stared at it with growing suspicion.

His new optio was a likeable, conscientious recruit of the tribe of Parisii, from the windy eastern coast of the province, who had adopted the Roman name of Tullius. Rufus called him over and shared his suspicion. The two men looked at the buildings in the distance for a couple more minutes, while Rufus laid out his plan.

The two hundred and fifty-seven men easily surrounded the inn buildings and drew in on them like a tightening iron band. The men at the rear of the assault broke into the stables buildings and there found the grim larder of hanging guests, as if meat slabs hanging upon hooks. They recognised four of their comrades from the horse squadron. There were also several horses in the stables next door still alive, and the carcasses of others. The soldiers could barely keep themselves from becoming frantic and vociferous because of the horrors. The optiones' long vine-staffs were employed vigorously to remind them that they were meant to be competent and disciplined soldiers, even in a crisis like this.

Rufus searched the faces of the corpses and was reassured to find that none of them was Dendus or Cybele. All the dead were men.

Next, they turned their intentions to the main inn building itself. Every door and window had been tightly shuttered. Rufus ordered the soldiers to smash through the portals. He was reluctant to set fire to the place in case Dendus and Cybele were still alive inside.

He and Tullius went through the front door and helped search the interior. No one was inside. The soldiers ripped the flooring up and checked the roof spaces to ensure that nobody was hiding. When they were sure that the building was empty, Rufus considered billeting the soldiers there for the evening and night. On reflection and because of the mood of the men, he ordered it set ablaze instead. Consequently, it became the crematorium for the poor souls hanging in the stables, twenty-three of them in total. Rufus was not acquainted with Nepos and his family and could not be sure whether the innkeeper himself was amongst them. If he was, the innkeeper must have become a widower prior to this massacre as there was no sign of a wife.

Once the buildings were fully alight, the soldiers set about building their camp nearby, an activity that would keep them occupied for the best part of two hours and hopefully steady their nerves. They chattered constantly, while working, in a range of Brythonic dialects, which irritated the three centurions and their subalterns no end but could not be curbed easily. The early evening air was tainted with the smell of burning wood and flesh from the inferno they had created.

Rufus paced the outer dimensions of the temporary camp, over and over again, seemingly etching it out on the ground with his hobnailed sandals like an aedile or surveyor. He was still carrying Dendus's broken collar in his hand. He appeared very angry. The only time the men ceased their inane chatter was when he happened to approach on one of his rounds. Consequently, the noise in the camp rose and fell depending upon where the commander strode.

CHAPTER TWENTY-SEVEN

THE horses struggled with the sticky bank of the river on its eastern side, and, at one point, a horseman had slid down into the water, causing the horse to panic and protest indignantly and the rest of the patrol to laugh uproariously. Viterius, in command of the scouting group and the only one not to find the accident humorous, relented and pulled the patrol further away from the river and they headed in a north-easterly direction across more benign countryside, scattered with small native farmhouses and the occasional little village of roundhouses.

Mus and all his compatriots from the mountainous lands of Carvetia where on this patrol. It was customary practice to take half the squadron, fifteen men, out on such expeditions daily; the others staying back in the fort to rest the horses and to dry and repair tackle. Viterius, much like his direct commander, Luti, favoured taking the Carvetii out on patrols, as they were competent riders, less complaining by nature, and worked together well with manifest camaraderie, pleasant to witness when you were not the actual butt of their jokes.

It rained every day this time of the year, and horses' shoes could become mired in mud and act like anchors, bringing the horse to an abrupt stop and risking a snapped leg. The horse would have to be slaughtered on the spot if a leg broke, and they could not afford to lose another one that way. Consequently, they walked the beasts slowly across the fields, using any native trackways they could find and which went in roughly the right direction. Spotting a village in the distance was always a welcome sight as it meant a good chance of a well-trod track somewhere nearby.

It was mid-morning when the patrol spotted smoke a few miles ahead of them, a substantial amount of it that suggested roundhouses or a farmhouse on fire. They went to investigate and, much as they expected, found the smouldering remnants of a village that had once comprised eight or nine homes, fences and sties and a storehouse. All were destroyed by fire and twenty or so dead bodies lay strewn amongst the miserable wrecks.

Viterius and the standard bearer, Mus, got off their horses and checked the corpses. They had been stabbed through with swords, mostly through their necks. They looked like the victims of a group of brigands, scouring the land and laying waste to tribal communities they hated. In these parts, such brigands might be from the Dobunni tribe to the north or the Durotriges to the east, or possibly Belgae. They would rob, rape and slaughter without scruples, much as their fathers, grandfathers and earlier ancestors had done. There was only so much the *Pax Romana* and occupation of the country could do to stifle the inbuilt and ingrained cultural instincts of the natives.

Mus was just getting back onto his horse when he spotted something in the corner of his eye. He reckoned it had been a head bobbing out from behind a distant tree and then retracting itself in the same instant. He said, "Come" to Viterius next to him and headed towards the tree before the optio could even respond.

It was obvious that Mus was leading the soldiers to the tree where somebody was spying upon them, and the culprit now decided to climb the tree to a height where he assumed he might be safer, a forlorn hope if he was at all aware of the long lances Roman cavalry men carried with them, and their throwing accuracy that came from hours of daily practice with the weapons. But climb he did.

Mus saw that it was a lad of around thirteen years of age. Mus stopped under the tree and ordered the boy down, or else be killed on the spot. After some reflection, the youth slid down to a lower branch as a kind of compromise. He was extremely frightened, his face a mess of tears and snot.

Viterius, who had caught up, asked Mus to proceed with an interrogation, as he was not a proficient speaker in Brythonic himself. Mus therefore asked the lad to explain what had happened to the village.

The answer came back, between gulps and hiccups, that Roman soldiers had attacked the village and killed everybody, and then set the village alight. The lad had been searching for an errant pig some distance from the village when it started, and he was forced to watch the ransack and murder from a safe hiding place. He had been waiting until he judged it safe to come out of hiding again, when he then spotted the horse squadron from Nemetostatio approaching from the south.

"So it has only just happened?" asked Mus, incredulously.

The lad nodded. "This morning." A glob of snot or mucous fell from his face and narrowly missed Mus' horse.

Mus turned to Viterius and translated.

"Ask him what direction the soldiers went," suggested Viterius.

Mus did so and the lad pointed northward. As if by intention, the exact direction he indicated coincided with a new plume of smoke which had sprung up, perhaps four or five miles way. The lad saw it at the same time and let out a cry of surprise.

Viterius muttered the word, "Deserters".

"From where?" asked Mus. "The only soldiers in these lands are at Nemetostatio or Caer Uisc. And there are certainly no deserters from our fort."

"It's called Isca Dumnoniorum," corrected Viterius irritably. "Then they must have deserted from Isca, from the Eighth cohort."

Mus was not convinced. "Why head to these parts?"

Viterius shrugged. "How many soldiers did he see?"

Mus translated the lad's reply. "Between fifteen and twenty, he says. All on foot."

"On *foot*?"

Mus was looking puzzled, if not incredulous suddenly. "Including a centurion."

"A *centurion*?"

The lad was indicating the arched crest of the man's helmet with his hands.

"Not like our helmets, he says, but curved like this. But *red* horsehair instead of white."

Comically, Viterius repeated Mus's words once again. "*Red* horsehair?"

"That's what he says. An important centurion, with large badges on his chest, and very strong looking."

They stared towards the new plume of smoke in the far distance, which had increased in volume in the last few seconds.

"We must give chase," urged Mus. "There are fifteen of us but we have the advantage of horses."

A flash of fear and uncertainty crossed Viterius's face. Eventually he nodded.

"What do we do with the boy?" asked Mus.

"Leave him."

Mus asked the lad whether he had family somewhere near, some place safe to go. The lad shook his head miserably.

"Then stay here," ordered Mus. "In this tree, until we return, do you understand? We will take you back to our fort where you will be safe, and can find work there, and food."

It was evident that the boy sorely wanted to believe this but could not be sure. He nodded his head tentatively.

Viterius rounded the men and then, finding a fortuitous native trackway approximately in the right direction, they cantered the horses towards the source of the distant smoke.

When they were underway, Viterius shouted to Mus, "I don't understand," and then, as if to answer the very question occupying his thoughts, he added, "But it makes sense in a way. If deserters were to find themselves in a territory strictly governed by a civil authority or military base, they would quickly come unstuck, be rounded up and executed. Every town council in the southern part of this province is beholden to the governor and procurator and they would have no hesitation in reporting the deserters to the Roman authorities. So, they must head for a remote, ungoverned part of the province instead, like the great moors of Dumnonia, where they can hide and eke out a relatively risk-free existence, living off the thin benefits of the land. Raiding villages, stealing food and having fun with the women."

Mus looked sternly ahead. "We Carvetii would head for our homelands, where we could go back to our sweethearts and families, who would protect us and help us to pretend we never went near a Roman recruitment centre."

"Yes, but the Durotriges, the Cantii, Regni, Belgae, Atrebates and so forth – the peoples of the south – would not have that luxury. They would have to live at home in the strictly governed zone where they would forever run the risk of discovery."

Mus nodded and could not help looking at his right arm, where the army had tattooed him on his skin in a specific place with the bold letters *SPQR* when he had agreed to twenty-five years' loyal service as an auxiliary soldier and in order to receive his first wage. Deserters might pretend to be somebody else but they would always risk some inquisitive official demanding to see their right arm. And a convenient scar in the exact place reserved for the tell-tale tattoo would be seen for what it was.

"Have you ever heard of a centurion deserting the army?" Mus asked after a further minute or so had passed.

"No, and it's highly unlikely to happen, signifer. A particular place in Hades is reserved for such a man, and the gods help his carcass if he was caught by the army! In any case, men who become centurions are of a certain breed. Such men do not shirk their duties and obligations, and do not dishonour themselves."

"That's what I thought."

"More likely, a centurion has been murdered and his uniform and crests stolen."

Mus was going to openly muse about why such a man would dye the horsehairs on his centurial helmet the colour red to pretend to be a commander, but noises ahead of him arrested his attention. The wind was carrying from the north, and they could hear the shrieks and screams of what sounded like murders and destruction unfolding a mile or so in front of them.

The trackway seemed to run between the previously ransacked village and the one presently being assailed, so the horsemen could risk kicking their mounts into a conservative gallop. It took all Viterius's efforts to keep up with the adept horsemen of the Carvetii at such speed.

As they closed in on the imperilled village, the grim sounds grew louder and they could now see the red and brown uniforms of infantrymen moving around the hellfire, searching roundhouses, bent on slaughter. Mus let out a sudden terrifying shriek, immediately echoed by his compatriots. Viterius had never heard anything like it before, and it terrorised him too. The noise carried to the attackers in the village ahead and they stopped what they were doing and peered up the track towards the men of the Tenth cohort. Viterius and Mus counted sixteen of them. A large, impressive soldier came to stand at the front of the group of marauders. Broad-chested and resplendent in a centurion's helmet, with an arch of stiff crimson horsehair mounted atop. Like the others, he took hold of one of the long javelins which were produced by someone in their group and being passed out quickly. The large centurion raised his, ready to hurl it. If these were Roman soldiers, deserters or otherwise, they would be very adept with such weapons. The horsemen of the Tenth almost slowed their horses when they saw what they were heading towards. Some gulped and some winced with dreadful anticipation.

A Roman javelin had a long thin iron shank and a small, pyramidal spearhead, designed to go straight through most shields and to pierce the man behind it. It's first third would pass through the wood and leather of a common shield and stop only when the thicker, wooden shaft that comprised the rest of its length had struck the shield. Although those of the Eighth and Tenth cohorts had been reinforced with a thin layer of beaten iron to withstand crossbow bolts, the adapted shields were wholly untested in battle. Viterius and the other horsemen could not help but feel that something extremely nasty was about to happen to them, fatal at worst and injurious at best, when the weapons were unleashed in their direction. Sixteen of the things whistling towards them and their fifteen unprotected horses. The speed of the horsemen's approach, which had picked up significantly by this point, would also add to the velocity of the projectiles hitting them. They might be able to protect themselves with their large reinforced shields but not their poor horses.

"Shields!" shouted Viterius at that moment and the men raised their oval protections.

When they were within eighty yards of the centurion and his comrades, the javelins suddenly flew towards them with astonishing speed. The horsemen who were hit on their shields were carried straight off their mounts backwards, such was the force of the impact. It was difficult to know at his instant whether the reinforced skins of the shields had successfully stopped the spears coming straight through up to the wooden haft. Most of the javelins struck the horses, rendering them dead instantly or about to die within minutes. Mus was struck off his horse and landed awkwardly on the ground, winded and helpless for several seconds. He noted that the spearhead had embedded itself near the boss on the outer skin, the tip of it showing through to the inside like a snake's tongue, the twisted projectile now latched on firmly and impossible to remove. He threw the shield aside. At the back of his mind, the surprising strength of the display of skirmishing he had just witnessed seemed to be telling him something he was yet to comprehend fully.

He turned to find Viterius and saw the optio lying on the ground nearby, obviously dead. He had fallen foul of the javelin thrown by the centurion himself. Viterius had not raised his shield to cover his face in time and consequently received the point of the iron shank right through where his nose had once been.

Mus would need to assume charge of what was left of their small squadron. He tallied it up. They were now twelve men against the sixteen deserters, and had only six horses. He was about to tell the men to get back on their mounts when instinct stopped him doing so. He knew the opponents would prioritise killing the horses, which were much bigger targets and much less protected. He had to try to keep the remaining horses alive. He shouted orders to the men to get up and attack on foot. They obeyed him and closed in accordingly. The demeanour of the enemy, particularly the big one, masquerading as a senior centurion, brought forth the delayed comprehension Mus had been struggling to grasp. The explanation for the extraordinary strength and accuracy of the throwing came to him in a rush.

"Ankows!" he shouted. "Use your lances!"

For a moment, all the Carvetii stared at Mus, as though not daring to believe him, and to check if it was some bizarre joke that he had decided to tell them to lighten the moment. It took only a second or so for each of them to realise what they had seen with their own eyes, and what they should already have known. No one except Achilles or Hercules could throw a javelin like that. But Ankows might.

"Come on. This is what we've been waiting for!" growled Mus. "We are *Men of the Deer,* and they are – what? Pathetic aberrations of Nature!"

The centurion and his ghastly comrades were charging towards the horsemen already, in order to maintain their momentum and upper hand. They came on quickly so that the first swords and lances were clashing within moments. The cutting edges of the short Roman swords wielded by the Ankows were not sharp enough to cut through the especially dense shafts of the *Lucullan* lances but they could bat the lances out of hands, and did so. Mus saw another of his comrades fall with fatal wounds. But all the others still had a lance in their hands, either the longer cavalry type or else the back-up short infantry lance kept on their belts. The horsemen had one advantage: the surprise caused by the first lances to strike home. The smell of putrefaction quickly filled the air and Mus saw that two Ankows had withered into oozing pulp.

No one was more surprised than the centurion, who stopped fighting to contemplate what had just happened. He bounded backwards to avoid the thrust of a lance at that instant.

Mus had similarly dodged the forward thrust of a sword and retaliated instantly by driving his cavalry lance up through the iron plates on his opponent's chest. He missed the heart but must have struck arterial blood with the tip of the lance, as the Ankow folded on his knees instantly and rolled on to the floor. Mus had withdrawn his lance intact in time and now drove it through the cloak deeply into the back of the fallen fiend, this time finding the heart. Consequently, a third body began to corrupt and turn into mush quickly. As it was designed to do, the perforated spearhead snapped off at its neck when it was firmly buried and twisted, and Mus threw aside the wooden shaft. He quickly unbuckled the shorter lance on his belt.

The other Ankows had grasped the situation and were suddenly less confident. Some backed off. The centurion bounded to Mus's horse and jumped on the back of it, kicking it viciously forward. He was going to try to escape.

But the horse would not have it. It whinnied and reared up on its back legs. It reeled around in a circle. It refused to cooperate with the unnatural stranger on its back. The centurion swore with frustration and jabbed the point of his sword into the horse's flank.

"Hey!" shouted Mus, leaping forward and catching up with the flailing horse and its unwanted rider. Mus could see the instant recognition in the white, panicked eyes of the horse. The beast seemed to understand the need to stop its motion and allow Mus to wield his weapon. Mus ducked the swing of the centurion's furious swipe with the sword towards his head and pushed the lancehead into the man's thigh as high as he could reach, almost near his groin. At the same moment, the horse made one further effort to unseat the heavy passenger and this time succeeded. The centurion fell heavily to the ground.

Mus ran forward to use his lance but found his legs kicked out from under him. He was up on his feet in a moment but so was the centurion. With frustration, he saw that there was pinned on the centurion's chest armour directly over his heart a large circular iron badge, a hand-width in diameter. It was not one of the decorative clasps helping attach the corners of the cloak to his shoulders but one of a pair of honorific medals attached to the chest harness. This must be, or had been, the uniform and regalia of a very senior centurion. The iron badge in question unfortunately stopped Mus delivering a killing blow from the front. The two men faced each other off, the centurion with his stabbing sword and Mus with his short infantry lance. Neither held a shield. Mus could see a flurry of violent movement to his eye side, accompanied by shouts and curses and threats, as men engaged in hand-to-hand combat in pairs. He was sure that their numbers were now equal, twelve on either side, but the tenor of the fighting had altered and segued into that part of close combat that sometimes occurred towards the end, though Mus had never experienced it himself, when combatants see no further profit in continuing, and are more concerned with extricating themselves with all their honour, limbs and lives intact. The Ankows could see that they risked oblivion from the strange poisonous lances, and they were not as aggressive in that knowledge. They were defending rather than attacking. The fiends had never wanted this fight in the first place, and fighting with men who could send them to hell and convert them into suppurating pulp was not at all the same as attacking civilians, and certainly not so much fun. Without making it too obvious, they were trying to back off.

Mus shouted, "Horses!" and everybody understood. The Deer People had remounted, two per horse, and were speeding away within seconds, and the centurion and the other Ankows effectively let them go. A couple of them hurled their daggers and struck the flanks of retreating horses but this only made the animals gallop faster away.

Mus and the other Carvetian survivors returned to where they had left the boy in the tree and ordered him down. Mus took him on to his own horse, which was the strongest and which could manage three passengers for at least a few miles. He ordered his men to shed their tools, camp building materials and rations from their panniers to lighten the loads.

Even so, it would be dark before they got back to the Nemetostatio outpost. What a report Mus would then make to Luti and Tadius. Three dead, including Luti's optio, and nine fine horses lost. And they had fought Ankows and survived the engagement even though they were outnumbered.

His comrades looked at him gratefully from time to time, smiling and trying to rally the comrades to sing a song of their homeland. But the singing never went on very long and always petered out. They were all tired and thoughtful and most just wanted to ride and get back to the warm stables.

CHAPTER TWENTY-EIGHT

MAI Din, or the great fortress as it was also known, was even more impressive than Tuathal expected. He and his seventy-nine men approached the massive hill from the south side, admiring the steepness of its outer ramparts, the depth of its trenches, the baffling maize of fence work jutting up into the sky. Most of the men kept hidden out of sight until the two scouts Tuathal had sent in advance came back to report to him excitedly that the ancient Durotrigan fort was barely occupied and was strangely bereft of adult men. There were just a hundred and fifty or so women in there, some girls, some boys no older than twelve or thirteen, and a handful of old arthritic men who were hobbling about on bad hips. There was a herd of pigs and some mules and goats but no horses. The place was up for grabs.

"Where are the men?" muttered Tuathal to himself, then added, "A hundred and fifty women would normally suggest at least that number of adult men, wouldn't it? But who cares where they are, anyway? We're here now, and they'll have a nasty surprise when they come back. We'll be in there already, ruling the roost!"

His followers agreed. They were all fighting men, although not so scary now in their borrowed clothes, and armed only with domestic knives and miscellaneous farming implements. Their army weapons had all ended up in the sea.

"Here's what we'll do. We'll invite ourselves in, nab any extra weapons to hand and put our claims on the women. They must have a forge, so we'll fire it up and make lots of slave collars and put them on the folk. They'll be our slaves now! If anybody tries to stop us, we kill them! Make an example of the first two or three! Real nasty! Chop the old men's hands off if you have to. Then, when we're established and feeling nicely at home, we'll start digging up the cargo from the ship in batches and we'll bring it all back here. It'll keep us rich in trading for months."

"I thought we were going home," pointed out one of the men.

"So we are, but what's the hurry? The longer we take, the more likely they forget what we look like. Best thing really would be to winter it out here and move east in the spring. In any case, how do you think we'll get all the cargo from the ship unless we set about it properly? There's loads of it!"

The plan had its obvious attractions, to start with, one hundred women to turn into slaves. They could live like kings. Kings of the castle.

"No time to waste then. Let's get ourselves established before the menfolk return and have other ideas on the matter," suggested another.

"Remember, real frightening now! We're terrible, we are! Don't fuck with us!"

They adopted frightening faces. Some even growled.

They skirted the southern rampart and ditches and entered the fort at its east gate. Puffing their chests out and looking haughty and not to be trifled with, they were slightly baffled by the evident lack of consternation seen amongst the women folk. Only the old men looked put out by the intrusion.

It was not long before Tuathal asked them, "Where are your men?"

The answer came back: "They went into Duronovaria to steal the treasure there, and never came back!" This spoken by one of the finer dressed women.

"And who are you?"

"Belena, the queen of these lands."

"*One* of the king's wives, or widows. Me being the other one!" shouted another woman, indignantly. This one was finely dressed too, regal in manner and wearing kohl around her eyes, possibly to distract from the wrinkles.

"The king is dead? What is his name?" asked Tuathal.

"Tuasatas."

"Well, you might have been queen or queens once, but you're slaves of the Bolgoi now!"

"That's what you think. Dead men don't have slaves!"

This was spoken by one of the old men, who had the audacity to be leaning on a stick and gulping air wheezily when he said it. The bombastic statement sat awkwardly alongside the pathetic image he presented.

"One more word from you, old man, and I'll shove that stick so far up your arse, birds'll be perching on it!"

The man spat distractedly, trying not to look hurt while the Bolgoi laughed delightedly.

"Example?" asked one of Tuathal's right hand men, stepping towards the miscreant elder.

"Let's be magnanimous!" responded Tuathal, holding him back. He turned towards Belena. She was a fine-looking woman. "Queen or slave. Your choice."

"Queen," she answered without hesitation, looking him up and down.

He smiled broadly. "I am Tuathal, and this is my fort now! And you are my subjects. What you need to know, and learn fast, is that I can be a good king and we can all live and work together to our mutual benefit. But anyone who causes me trouble will be put in a tight slave collar and chained to a post in the centre there…" He pointed to a muddy area of open ground between the roundhouses. "We'll put your eyes out and there you'll stay until the crows and rats have had their fill of you! Fair king or foul king – it's up to you! You've caught me in a good mood this morning, luckily."

"You have," added his right-hand man. "You're lucky."

"What about me?" asked the other widow with the kohl eyes.

"I'll take care of you," offered the right-hand man with a sly grin across his face.

"Right then! Take me to my hopefully rather large and luxurious house," concurred Tuathal. Turning round to address the others, he added. "Go on, get to know each other!"

Belena led him to the largest roundhouse. It was not exactly a palace but was the most prestigious residence amongst the others. It was a low standard to fulfill. Still, inside, it was comfortable enough, with a large bed and room for some goats. A hearth lay in the centre, unlit at present. Tuathal looked at it and said, "I'm hungry. Get me some cooked food."

"If that's all what you want," she responded ambivalently.

"Second thoughts, get on that bed, Queen Belena."

She hopped over to the bed, which was covered in animal furs, and started to undress. "You made the right choice," she said.

"You too."

"The other so-called wife, her with the big mouth, she gave the old king a lot of trouble."

"Well, she's someone else's problem, now. You don't sound too sorry about all of this."

She looked at him as she exposed her breasts. "He was a brute. He was only king because he was bigger and had a hairier arse."

"You don't know how hairy my arse is yet!"

She laughed. There were more clothes to remove, and she got on with it. "He wasn't real royalty like me: granddaughter of the High King. He thought that, by taking me as his queen, he would somehow qualify for the role, besides using brute force."

"And the other widow, how much royalty is she?"

"Not even a fingernail. Doesn't stop her haughty attitude, though. If you pretend to be something long enough, you'll fool somebody."

"Two wives. Must have been a brave man."

"He had three at one time, although the third one didn't last very long. She was a bitch from Dumnonia. Caught Tuasatas's eye, as she would any man's, I don't doubt. She was the one who told him about the treasure in the town, ripe for stealing. Whether it was true or not, it sent him and all our menfolk to their doom. A real vixen she was. Probably made the whole thing up. She disappeared soon enough."

She was fully naked now and Tuathal looked at her and thought to himself how the day had developed into something that was almost too good to be true.

After he had had his fill of Belena and her larder, he took himself out for a regal walk. This really was a mighty fortress, too big to defend with only eighty me; one would need a thousand at least he reckoned. There were fewer people milling about now. A couple of boys were herding goats at the west end of the plateau. They too seemed to have accepted the sudden change of regime.

None of his men were out and about. He assumed they were all getting to know their new community in various roundhouses. The wheezy old man with his stick was still pretending to be annoyed. Thirty years earlier, he would have had to fight someone like Tuathal for this very same territory, and now he had to put on a show of being just an aged version of that same fighting man. He would be harmless enough, but Tuathal would nevertheless keep an eye on him. He sensed that Belena would be the key to his ruling his new realm smoothly and safely. While she saw the personal benefits of it, she would seek to protect it. He could snore soundly without fear of a dagger plunge during his first or second sleep at nights.

He stopped to look across at the Roman town. There were soldiers down there, and that was very worrying. He wracked his brain. A vexillation from the Fifth cohort if memory served him right. If Tuathal and his men were going to stay here at Mai Din over winter, they would have to have a strategy for when Roman soldiers came calling. Eighty men of army recruitment age, with Belgic accents would be an immediate give-away, especially if it was known that exactly this number of Belgae had deserted from the camp at Isca. For now, Tuathal did not have a strategy. Perhaps, on reflection, it was not all too good to be true after all. They were less than four miles from a detachment of potentially curious soldiers, including auxiliaries who came from other British tribes and hated his type of folk, and would recognise the accent, and who had been told to look out precisely for what had now arrived up in the old Durotrigan fort. Eighty men of the loathsome Bolgoi. The soldiers would be ordering them to roll up their right sleeves, looking for the *SPQR* tattoo or the ill-advised attempt to obscure it, soon as look at them.

He looked back towards his new house. Belena was standing in the doorway, beckoning him to come back.

CHAPTER TWENTY-NINE

LINDINIS was essentially no more than a market town, but the local dignitaries had ideas above their station and treated it as if it had been granted a *civitas* charter by the governor, the right to be run by a formal town council appointed by, and acting as delegates of, the Roman governor and procurator. The dignitaries who called themselves the *decuria* and *curia* of the town council, as if acting under a charter, wanted it to be the capital of a Durotrigan sub-tribe called the Lendinienses. The locals in fact called the town *Lendiniae*. There had been a hamlet there well before the Romans came, at the spot where an ancient trackway crossed the river. That trackway was now aligned exactly with the Roman's long border road, the one that sliced the province in two. The village had prospered since the frontier road came though. A timber military post laid out thirty years earlier had been manned by soldiers on and off. The Roman camp had attracted the usual accretion of round native hovels and square Roman-style merchants' houses, all feeding off the soldiers' intermittent presence as well as their protection and the benefits of the robust bridge the newcomers built. The village had become a civil town and was now hopefully on its way to being an alternative capital. There was spare money from the manufacture of highly reputable iron, glass, ceramic and bone ware, and the aristocracy and merchants were relatively well-off and ambitious in a peaceable and civic way. They loved the Roman occupation of their lands because it avoided the bothersome risk of being ruined or killed by other tribes, and it gave them the peace and freedom to flourish. The irony was that there were many towns in the province of Britannia that had been granted civitas status which were far less deserving and far less *Romanophile* than Lindinis. Due recognition was just a question of time.

Rufus had been told that Raselg was being kept in the home of one of the *curia*. The title of the man bothered him but he went along to the house in question and was prepared, at least to start with, to show polite deference to the dignitary who, by all likelihood was a member of the local aristocracy, whatever he chose to call himself now.

Unfortunately, Rufus' irritability and intolerance, especially when he was embarrassed or feeling under stress, could often get the better of him. His bile was rising because, after knocking and identifying himself, he was told to wait outside the front door by a servant. He felt that he should have been let straight in. It did not occur to him that he had treated the merchant who called at his house in Isca in exactly the same fashion.

"Did I not just make myself clear?" he said to the servant. "I am Plancius Vallaunius, and you are keeping my slave in this house. So, why are you not taking me to her immediately?"

The servant was caught in a diplomatic dilemma. His master was a member of the curia, and a Roman officer should know that he did not have the right or jurisdiction to enter such a home unless he was formally invited. This angry-looking centurion thought he could just barge in. Letting him in without seeking his master's due consent would be tantamount to admitting, vicariously, that the army had all the authority in Lindinis, and his master - one of the two distinguished elders of the town, and *royalty* to boot - had none.

"We have kept good care of her and bound her with chains as you asked, though why we have needed so many chains I do not understand. I will pass your request on to my master."

"I hope not to have to explain about the chains," said Rufus curtly. "Yes, go and tell your master. I am running out of patience!"

"Is she prone to run away?" asked the servant, nevertheless.

"No. She is prone to other things!"

The man finally turned and walked back through the house, leaving Rufus and his bodyguard of soldiers standing peevishly outside on the street.

They were finally let in and taken to a room at the back of the house. The house owner was standing at the door of it, ready to greet his visitors, obsequiously. Rufus gritted his teeth and got through the introductions, then said in a snappish tone: "There is an inn about fifteen miles to the south of here, on the road to Isca. Are you aware of this inn?"

"Yes, of course. The inn of Nepos Censorius. It is well known."

"Did you know that it had turned into a charnel house of dead guests? We found twenty-three corpses strung up from the rafters in there, and the owners presumably gone. Did this Nepos have a wife by the way?

"Yes, and a daughter too."

"Well, they are missing. Do you know where this family is now?

"No. Nepos was here in the town only a few days ago but he is back at his inn, as far as I know. I can make enquiries."

"Well, he is not back at his inn, especially since we torched it. It is nothing but a mound of ash now. A crematorium!"

The man looked shocked. "Nepos?"

"I need to know where he is. But be careful, he is probably very dangerous."

"Surely not?"

Rufus' face caused the man to flinch. "Yes, we will take every caution," he corrected.

"My slave is missing – my other slave. A man aged around fifty from Lusitania. He has a very thick Iberian accent. His name is Dendus."

"You had *two* slaves run away? That is very unfortunate."

"No! Neither of my slaves ran away!" said Rufus, raising his voice.

The door behind the proprietor opened and Raselg was standing suddenly in the frame of it. "I recognised your voice," she said. Then she bowed and muttered, "Plancius Vallaunius. I am very happy to see you."

Rufus found himself stepping back and reaching for his sword hilt on his left hip. Then he adapted his natural instinct and found the shaft of his lance instead, ready to slip the buckle. "Why is she not in chains!" he shouted.

"We have just released her as you were coming in. You are soldiers and there are eight of you! Surely, the woman no longer needed to be chained up! Look at her. The wind could blow her over. And the window in there is securely closed and bolted!"

"Ah, but an Ankow could break through the shutters and escape, you see?" explained Raselg. Then turning to Rufus, she said, "Oh, Plancius Vallaunius, I am not an Ankow! I have *escaped* from the Ankows, and I have important news to tell you!"

"Leave me with the woman," said Rufus, addressing both his host and the soldiers behind him. He followed her into the room.

It was dark, only a weak pair of lamps illuminating the interior. The chains that had held her were still secured to the bed frame at one end. The bed was basic but comfortable. There was a chair placed near the window and a small couch in the corner for reclining, possibly eating.

Rufus closed the door behind him. He unbuckled his lance and held it lightly with one hand.

"I am speaking the truth. You don't need that," she said.

He gestured to her to sit down in the seat by the window. She swivelled the chair so that it faced away from the window and into the room.

"You are looking better than I expected," he said. "You smell better than I expected too."

She found this amusing. "They have treated me well. I was very weak and at death's door when I arrived. I walked from Mai Din with a broken knee!" She showed him the knee, lifting up her gown.

He tried not to look moved, although he had forgotten just how beautiful she was. He had been expecting a hideous semblance of Raselg, not the fair slave he had known. She was much thinner but had not changed to any great extent. He noticed that her lower lip was thicker in one place and seemed to bear the hardened skin of a scar. He was never very good at hiding his emotions and she saw the inner turmoil and stirrings of passion her presence was causing him. It made her smile and feel reassured, knowing they were still the same people and that they created the same sensations in each other. An innocent bystander would have said that Rufus was fighting the urge to run and hug her. His face was flushed and there was a hint of trembling in the line of his mouth.

"Mai Din? Duronovaria? That is quite some distance with a broken knee," he said after a while.

She nodded. "Would it be too much to ask that you hold me, Rufus?"

"I cannot."

She looked down at the floor and clutched her hands together, wringing and twisting the fingers as if wrestling with the need to hide her feelings too. "How is Dendus?"

"Dendus is missing. I think Ankows got him. He is probably dead. Well, you know, dead in the way we normally talk about it." Rufus held his hand to the broken slave collar which he had laced to his chainmail shirt beside the bravery badges.

Raselg saw where his hand had gone and recognised the broken object pinned to his chest. This brought forth her tears. After nearly a minute she muttered, almost whispered, "No, not Dendus."

"I am afraid it is the case."

She got out of the chair and attempted to close the distance between herself and Rufus. He stepped back and held up the lance to keep her at bay.

"Is that to stop an Ankow or to stop me - Raselg?"

"I don't know what you are. What you have become!"

"Oh, Rufus, I have not changed! I'm just a bit worn and roughed up by events. But I still love and respect you. I always will!"

"I'm sorry. I am past that, now!"

She sat back down in the chair, heavily. "You're right. Ankows smell of dead leaves and fungi. Of something rotten. Their breath smells of dried blood. I know because I have been *this* close to one!" She held up two of her fingers, pressed together in parallel. "My father! He carried me out of Duronovaria! He saved me!"

"That cannot be!"

"It was my father, and he was an Ankow! They are *all* Ankows in Duronovaria. The whole town!"

Rufus considered the import of this. "What happened to Exuperatus Helius?"

"Dead."

"What about the Fifth cohort: the vexillation led by Robigalius?"

"Dead! And the camp prefect and senior tribune too!"

"Senicianus?"

"Yes. I am sorry, Rufus. It was horrible. The town folk just turned on the soldiers. My father was there, and he carried me out of the town to safety."

302

"Your father died and was cremated at Nemetostatio. He cannot be an Ankow!"

"I have been thinking about that. It's all I have been thinking about while I've recuperated here. No one identified his body, and we know that the Ankows carried many of the people away. My father could have been one of them. We assumed he was in the burnt vicus, alongside my brother, but it must have been somebody else."

"We found the burnt corpse of a man and a boy where your hovel was situated."

"It wasn't my father. I tell you, he is in Duronovaria. I know my own father! I was this close to him! And why would an Ankow carry me to safety if it was not my father?"

Rufus had no answer to that.

"How many Ankows are there in Duronovaria?" he asked a few moments later.

"Three hundred, four hundred. Maybe more! And the new dead will add to their numbers after the next full moon!"

"Why did you walk here to Lindinis and not head back to Isca Dumnoniorum? It is, what, nearly sixty miles between Mai Din and Isca, directly, but it is eighty or ninety miles surely if you go via Lindinis."

"I was being hunted. I took the route that they didn't expect me to take. They would have expected me to head west, straight for Dumnonia."

"Who? The Ankows?"

"No, the community of Durotriges at Mai Din. They captured me and held me there in the great fortress. I was forced to be the king's concubine, but I got them all killed and managed to escape."

"How...what?" He was flummoxed.

"Rufus, are you going to take me from here? Take me home?"

He squirmed with confusion. "Yes, you are coming back with me. Until I find you a new position. Not Cressido Saenus. Possibly Tadius Naratius."

"I have lots more to tell. I can do so while we travel, if you would be kind enough to find a carriage for the journey to Isca."

He was taken back by her audacity, then remembered that this was how she always was. Had always been. It almost made him smile. Then he thought of Dendus and Senicianus and Helius and the smile deserted his face. "We will eat, and I will give your host some money for his troubles. My new optio, Tullius, will try to find you a carriage."

"Put that lance away. I am not Silpunia and I have not ended up like her."

He buckled the weapon to his belt again. But he waited to see whether she took the opportunity to move against him quickly. His dagger was inches from his right hand, and it was adapted too to carry *Wolf's-bane* and silver in its blade, and she would not know this.

But she did not move.

PART III

CHAPTER THIRTY

CYBELE would never forget the expression on Censoria's face at that moment. In her half-delirium it burnt into her memory like a scene from the worst nightmare.

The innkeeper's daughter had turned the cart and was trying to drive the horse back along the road to where Cybele lay; wounded by the lance in her side, and sick with the poison.

But the horse was protesting and not cooperating, and Censoria was madly whipping it with a loop of the reins. The horse had sensed the violence happening behind it, had smelt Dendus' blood and seen Cybele fling herself off the side of the driving board. It knew that something uncanny, something that smelt of rot and mould, was trying to control it with the reins. It would not accept the insult of it all.

Eventually, the Ankow gave up trying to drive the cart up to where Cybele lay, and she dropped the reins and began to climb down from the cart. Her terrifying face showed clearly her intent to get to Cybele and kill her immediately. She held the dagger in her hand already.

As she placed her first foot onto the road, something happened, and, instead of stepping down and running quickly to the Druid, Censoria collapsed in a pile to the ground. A *Lucullan* lance was sticking out of her back between the shoulder blades. Dendus was moving in the carriage seat slightly and staring down at what he had just done with the last of the strength he had summoned.

The lance could not kill the Ankow, as its tip had missed the heart, but neither could she pull it out of her back because of its position. She tried to claw at it with her hands and dropped the dagger in doing so. The poison was working its effect and Censoria vomited and shrieked. The expression on her face as she looked up at Cybele at that moment, all the hatred that Hades and its fiends might ever contain, seemingly wrapped in that one countenance, was something Cybele would never forget.

She knew that she must try to move now or be party to her own oblivion. She cried with pain as she forced her body up off the road and made her way, against all natural instincts, towards the squirming Ankow and the cart beside her. She avoided the sweeping claws of the frantic innkeeper's daughter and pulled herself up onto the driving seat of the cart, beside Dendus, who was groaning and trying to speak. Blood and lymph and mucus bubbled out of the wound in his throat.

Cybele grabbed the reins and flicked them, praying to her god, *Dheghom*, harder than she had ever prayed before, that the horse would obey her. It did. She wheeled it around to drag the cart one hundred and eighty degrees. She snapped the reins again and the cart lurched and started off in the direction of Lindinis.

Cybele turned briefly to look back at Censoria. She was still writhing on the road, trying to reach the shaft of the lance. Further away up the road, where the buildings of the inn stood, Cybele saw two figures emerge, glance up the road and then begin to run towards the frenetic form of the daughter, as parents would naturally run to a stricken child. Cybele quickened the speed of the cart for she knew how fast Ankows could run.

She carried on driving until she had put four or five miles between them and the innkeeper's family. Then, feeling safe at last, she stopped the cart and turned to try to make Dendus comfortable. She thought about trying to move him onto the flat base of the cart behind.

He was alive but dying, and he grabbed her arm when she tried to move him. It was no good. She nestled his head in her lap and stroked his face. Staring up at her briefly, with an odd and inexplicable look of what seemed to be recognition in his countenance, he breathed his last and died.

She had hardly known him, but she knew he was cherished, and she wept as if it were her own father's head that was in her lap. She wondered whether he had children somewhere, who would mourn him, or anyone else other than Rufus.

She let a couple of minutes pass and then moved his body to the side again so that she could pick up the reins and drive.

They continued on their way to the town.

When she reached it later that afternoon, the sun now low in the sky and brimming the horizon, she decided not to take the cart through the gates into the town. She turned the cart instead towards the hovels, the *canabae* as the Romans called them, at the south of the town, the poorest homes of those not worthy of being inside its walls.

There were a number of reasons for her not going directly into Lindinis. Druids were usually not welcome inside towns and, although she might claim to be the friend and ambassador of the Roman commander at Isca Dumnoniorum, it might not be seen as a good enough excuse. If the town council was beholden to the Roman governor for its authority and jurisdiction, it might well be under standing orders to capture, and even kill, any Druid that should dare to tread on its streets. Druids were still officially classed as terrorists and enemies of Rome. Thirdly, and perhaps the strongest reason, however, was that she could not be sure that she would be safe from Ankows inside the town. If the nearest inn to it was infiltrated with the fiends already, there was every chance that the town itself was infested with them, maybe even fully inhabited by them. She remembered her father's dire warning when he bemoaned, as he often did, that the Romans had inadvertently culled the very people who could stop the towns and villages of the land from slowly and inevitably filling up with the unnatural fiends. *Who is to stop it if we can no longer do so*, he was prone to say?

She pulled up the cart near to a roundhouse and stepped down from it. She stood and waited. *The wound in her side ached, but the bleeding had stopped and the nausea had long passed.*

Sure enough, people emerged from the hovels to look at her. They saw that she was a Druid by her clothes, and they stood in wonder. Most had not seen a Druid in years, and some had never done so. *seen one. They noted the patches of blood staining her robe.*

A man came over to speak to her, to ask her what she wanted.

She told him that she was a Druid but also the representative of an important Roman general, who commanded the garrison at Caer Uisc. She was careful to use the Brythonic name for it.

The man looked sceptical, as well he should in the circumstances. "A Druid – you say a *friend* of the Roman commandant at Caer Uisc?"

"Yes," she answered. "I have come to fetch his slave called Raselg. She is being kept in the town. She arrived here some days ago."

This declaration appeared to strike some resonance with a portion of her listeners. Some turned to murmur things to the person next to them.

"So why have you come to us? The gate to the town is just there." The man pointed over to it.

311

"I have a body to bury. It is here, wrapped in the back of the cart, and I would not be allowed to take it into the town, as you know. I need to bury it outside. Will you help me?"

"Are you a healer?" asked a woman. "Do you have the Druid's knowledge? I have a sick child. Can you help us?"

Cybele nodded. "I will do what I can. Show me to the child and, in the meantime, can somebody take my dead friend from this cart and carry him to where I can inter him? I will call on God to help you if you should be so kind. And She will bless your poor village."

The older members of the listeners seemed content with this deal. A youth, perhaps no older than fifteen, was less so. "The council will punish us if we help a Druid! They would lick the arse of the Roman governor if he happened by. They want to be seen to obey all the Roman laws. We will be punished if we help a Druid. I have no personal objection to you, but I know what will happen to us if the council get to hear of it!"

"Then they need not know," answered Cybele. "We will bury my friend and I will only go into the town when you are back in your homes. They will not know I have met you, or that you have helped me. They will never know I loitered here. Tell you what, I will bury the man myself. I don't need your help. I just need you to take this cart to where you think I can safely bury the corpse, without drawing any attention to it, and leave me a spade to dig with. And I will help you with salves and make your children better."

"Can you deliver a baby? My daughter is in labour and has been at it for hours. We are also exhausted with the effort, and getting very concerned. There is a problem getting the child out."

"I can do that," said Cybele quickly. It was easier to lie if she said it quickly enough.

"Yes, no one need know," said the man who had first talked to her. He turned back to Cybele. "We will want the cart as well."

Cybele sighed. "I need the cart to take the commandant's slave back to Caer Uisc."

"That's the deal," said the man, stubbornly.

After reflection, Cybele eventually agreed.

As the sun had set by now, the assembled community began to move the cart away from the town towards an area of rough grassy land a couple of hundred yards away. Cybele watched them go and then turned and followed the women towards the hovels.

Her wound ? Woundwort and Selfheal.

CHAPTER THIRTY-ONE

Before she could help the others she had to help herself. She padded and bound the wound in her side.

CYBELE remained with the villagers that night. *Then,* With a mixture of bluff and good fortune she managed to help deliver the baby in the early hours of the morning. Its shrieks filled the night. She then made up potions and helped the *other woman's* sick child and brought its fever down so that, by the time the sun came up in the morning, the child and her mother were smiling and looking gratefully at her.

Cybele learnt that the villagers called themselves *Lendinienses*, a minor tribe amalgamated with the larger tribe of Durotriges. They claimed that they had once held a special relationship with the Druids, with her people. They were very poor but they were happy to share their food with her, and the men showed her where they had buried Dendus. He was amongst a copse of trees to the west of the Roman road, not far from a loop of the river. Cybele wanted to mark the grave with something but all she had was a small bracelet of *Smooth Hawk's-beard* flowers that one of the children had woven and given to her that morning. Although she had promised the child she would wear it, she placed it gently on Dendus' grave. It was fitting because, that morning, this felt like one of her richest possessions.

Then she turned and peered at the town nearby, and reminded herself that she should not delay going into it once she was sure she would be safe. The boy's words worried her. It was a common problem amongst her people now. Druids were *non persona gratis*, officially censored and under penalty of summary death. She had felt safe with Dendus beside her, as he would have done all the talking and vouched for her, and her instincts told her that an obsequious town council, looking to curry favour with the Roman authorities, might not listen to her kindly. They might execute her first and listen second. Somehow She had to get word of her presence to the scouts from the Eighth cohort who Rufus had sent to the town in advance.

Her plan was to talk one of the villagers into finding the scouts in the town, and relay to them the message that she was waiting outside the town, and that she needed a safe escort.

She walked back towards the hovels but, as he did so, she was conscious of a cart moving slowly along the road not far from her. It too was heading towards the town. She looked over towards it casually and then yelped with surprise and fear. Censoria was sitting in the cart and staring maliciously at her. Beside her were a man and a woman, the woman being the very same who had come out of the inn to speak to Dendus and her, and implore them to take sick Censoria to the town. There were also two boys, perhaps brothers.

The cart carried on a few more yards but then stopped. The man and the two boys climbed down from the cart and began to walk from the road directly towards her.

Cybele felt for the reassuring shape of the lance hidden amongst her green robe but knew she could not feasibly fight and overcome three determined Ankows with it. She turned and began to run towards the river.

When she got to its bank, she turned to ascertain how close her pursuers were now. She was surprised to see that they had given up chasing her and returned to the cart instead. A minute or so later, the cart continued on its way into the town. It disappeared through the gate ~~inside~~ beyond the low turf walls.

Cybele was now even more reluctant to go into the town. She was not even sure she could trust the plan to send somebody in there to make enquiries about the whereabouts of the Eighth cohort scouts. A cartful of Ankows had just driven into the town without hesitation, and that increased the likelihood, in Cybele's mind, of the town being full of them.

When she judged it safe to do so, she headed for the hovels.

The villagers were readily prepared to listen to her account of the innkeeper and his family being *Blood Ankows*. After all, Druids had special authority on that subject. But they were pretty sure that the town was not full of the fiends as she feared.

"Then I must draw the innkeeper and his family out and destroy them. Will you help me? Before they start preying on you and your children."

That seemed to be taking things too far. It appeared that the special relationship between the Lendinienses and the Druids of old did not extend to helping Druids fight Ankows. It was more to do with collecting herbs and sacred plants at certain times of the year. The villagers shook their heads and enquired how they might possibly be in a position to fight, and to succeed in destroying, five dangerous fiends.

One of them asked, "Did your friend, the one we buried last night, perish at their hands?"

"Yes," answered Cybele. "But I can destroy them. I just need a plan and a little help. Give me an hour or two and I will come up with something."

One of the older villagers asked, "Do you have a Druid's lance?"

"Yes," and she pulled the lance from out of her robes.

The people cooed at the sight of it. They wanted to handle it but knew they could not, should not. She did not tell them that it was a version of the traditional lance, made by Romans not by Druids.

They asked her how it worked but, knowing that it was meant to be a long held sacred secret, she just shook her head and returned the lance to her robes. Someone asked, "Is it to do with the lines of holes in its point?"

"Something like that."

They were a little more confident now, especially when, to the question as to how many Ankows she had killed already, she answered, "Only one, but he was a big one. I walked right up to him and I stuck in my lance like that! Straight into his heart. He then rotted into stinking pieces in front of my eyes!"

"We will try to help you but we don't have such weapons," someone suggested.

"Do you have axes?" she asked.

"Gabrant has an axe," somebody else declared. "It was his grandfather's."

"Sharpen it and have it ready," Cybele counselled. "What about lamp oil or pitch?"

They shook their heads.

"Remember, not a word of this outside the village, and certainly not within the town. This must be a surprise."

Unbeknown to Cybele, while she was having this audience with the villagers, the two scouts from the Eighth cohort had given up waiting for Dendus to make an appearance in the town and had taken the decision to head back towards Isca, expecting to find Dendus and Cybele broken down in their cart somewhere along the road.

Cybele's desire to find the innkeeper's family and destroy them was only equalled by the innkeeper and his family's desire to get to her. A day unfolded when both factions waited and gathered information to aid their purpose.

Cybele sent one of the villagers into the town to find the horsemen of the Eighth cohort. It was the boy who had raised concerns about the sanctions the council might impose on them for aiding a Druid. He had come around to realising that it would be better to help the Druid in this instance as he did not like the idea of Ankows in the town, getting a foothold and becoming a scourge. He had been assured by the Druid that she was working together with a specialist unit of Roman soldiers to find and destroy the fiends. In truth, he was excited by the prospect of assisting these Ankow killers.

The boy's enquiries ascertained that the two horsemen who had arrived yesterday from Caer Uisc, had departed that morning. The horsemen had gone to the home of one of the curia and presumably this was where the Roman general's slave was being kept. When, during his enquiries, he was ever asked who wanted the information, he always gave the same answer, "A woman staying amongst the canabae outside the town, wearing green robes."

The boy went back eventually to report to Cybele. She spent part of the day sitting outside one of the roundhouses, one set aside from the others, preparing salves and medicines from plants she had been able to purloin from a nearby herbalist. Unfortunately, she had not been able to get her hands on any *Wolf's-bane*. When she was not sitting outside the little house, she walked around the village, getting to know the community better and soothing them with Druidic chants and handing out medication. A lot of a Druid's power and mystique came from playacting: seeming to be other-worldly and wise, and edifying her listeners with bombastic sayings or bewildering them with deliberately vague parables. She had learnt it from her father, who had never shed his habit of acting that way, even though he seldom had any audience out on the great moor these past years, except for her.

Gabrant's axe was found and polished and put aside in readiness.

The boy gave her the bad news that the soldiers had already departed that morning. She considered this and finally said to him in a cheerful voice, "Never mind, I must wait then. My friend will send others, or he may even come himself when he finds out that Dendus and I are missing. Yes, I think he will come himself. In a day or two. Hopefully I will have found and destroyed the fiends by then."

The boy asked Cybele if she know how much a Roman soldier was paid. She did not know the answer and said that she was the wrong person to ask. He asked her for her name. She told him that she did not know her real name, only God knew, but the Romans called her Cybele. She did not ask for his. At one point he went and picked up the axe and weighed it in his hands as if contemplating wielding it against an Ankow.

"They are too quick and too strong," she told him. "The axe is only to use when one of them has been floored by the lance but not quite destroyed. You must chop off their head before they get up."

The boy was impressed.

"There are five of them," she reminded.

"I will fight with you."

Cybele smiled. "You are a brave man. I wish the others were so brave."

He stayed with her the rest of the day. They took turns keeping a careful eye on the south gate of the town to see if the innkeeper's cart ever emerged. She wondered why the family had gone to the town. Did they have some other purpose, other than finding her? Would they dare to kill townsfolk in broad daylight? Possibly. Perhaps the innkeeper also owned a house in the town, perhaps another inn. The boy did not know the answer to that.

Eventually the sun set on the day and, as was customary for the poorest people who did not possess the means to use artificial lamp or candlelight for very long, the villagers went to bed in their little houses. They would sleep for a few hours, the first and most fatigued spell of it, and then wake and stir again around midnight.

The womenfolk would get on with some chores together for an hour or so and then go back to their beds for their second sleep.

Cybele did not get up. The boy slept outside the little house that had been vacated and lent to her during her stay. He kept the axe near him.

Nepos and his family came for her during the first part of the night, around the third hour of darkness. They knew the roundhouse where the Druid slept and made straight for it. They were quick and efficient. They broke the door in and all went inside. Censoria and her brothers, not noticing in their haste that the bed was positioned unusually in the centre of the interior, went to the bed and viciously stabbed at the blanketed form in it. But it turned out to be nothing more than bundled clothes, made to look like a sleeping person.

A noise behind them indicated that the door was being barricaded. The smell of smoke indicated that the little roundhouse had been set on fire, on various sides all at once. The flames quickly grew and turned the interior into an oven. The Ankows coughed and looked for a way to get out. But this roundhouse was made from robust material, and it was not easy, particularly as the fire was on all sides suddenly. More lighted clumps of straw and kindle wood dropped through the little hole in the roof of the house to set the bed and furniture on fire inside.

Nepos was strong and he punched a hole through the wall. He pushed one of his sons and then his daughter through it so they could escape. But Cybele and the boy, as well as a man from the village who had finally relented and agreed to help, were waiting for the Ankows to emerge from the burning house. They attempted to chop down the fiendish children when they came out and to stop anyone else emerging. The boy swung the axe into Censo, the oldest of the innkeeper's sons, hearing a shriek in return. Cybele plunged the lance into his chest at the same time but in the darkness, she could not be sure where she had struck him. There was a concerted attempt by the Druid, the boy and the adult man to decapitate Censo when he fell to the ground but the boy's swing with the axeblade went awry. The innkeeper's son rolled away on the ground, and, at that same moment, Cybele's head exploded in a shower of sparks and she fell unconscious, the lance dropping from her hands.

Censoria had managed to find a large stone and attack the Druid with it while they fought to destroy her brother. She smashed it into the Druid's head. When she saw the boy pick up the lance angrily and turn towards her, she backed off and ran. From a safe distance, Censoria turned to see the roundhouse now entirely engulfed in fire, her parents and younger brother still inside. She could hear their cries of pain and anguish. She could not tell whether Censo had escaped too.

But the oldest son had finally succumbed to the lance and the axe. The village boy still stood with the broken wooden shaft of the lance in his hands, astounded by the smell and horrible crinkling sounds he could hear from the disintegrating heap below him; the heap that had been the innkeeper's eldest son until seconds before.

The boy and the man dragged Cybele away from the heat of the burning hut and into the relative darkness, and they screamed for people to bring light so that they could see the Druid's head. But nobody had light. Some women came and felt the druid's head. It was sticky and mushy on the back of it. They suspected that her skull was broken. They carried her into one of the houses and lay her down on soft blankets. They had once urged the Druid to help nurse their ailing children and pregnant daughters but now they nursed the Druid.

The boy asked, when they were carrying his new friend into the house, "Will she live?"

"I don't know said a voice in the darkness. "Probably not."

The boy promised himself that if the Druid woman died he would sign up for the Roman army next year when he was sixteen, and spend his military career fighting Ankows.

CHAPTER THIRTY-TWO

IN the month of October, when the bitter wind blew and all seemed dank and cold in Britannia, Rufus would wear all the layers of his uniform and armour: the linen undershirt, the wool tunic, the leather doublet, the shirt of chainmail, the linen loincloth and woollen hose under his leather skirt. But he still felt chilled. Even the houses of notable town officials seemed as damp and frozen as the streets outside.

The man who had cared for Raselg, who was named Murdach, was fawning and embarrassing when he noted the two thin lines of Tyrian purple on the edges of the centurion's best tunic. It denoted a Roman citizen of a wealthy family, an Equestrian. A man with distinction and authority, someone who could perhaps put in a good word for the men of the town council.

So, even though he was anxious to get away, Rufus found himself listening to the longwinded account of Raselg's pitiful state when she was brought to the house; to the extent of the care and attention they had administered to her to bring her away from death's door and to the significantly different condition she was in now. Murdach would not have laboured so much for the slave's welfare, had spent so much money on the doctor and medication, had he not known that she was the possession of a distinguished commandant of the glorious Second Augustan Legion. Eventually the monologue came to the point: if the commander had the ear of the governor, would he in turn mention that the good men of the ordo of Lindinis craved permission to build a forum and basilica in the town? At their own expense and using their own labour of course.

If only to drive a wedge into the obsequious and extended submission, Rufus agreed that he would do so; next time he had the honour of meeting with the governor. In reality, Rufus reflected that he had, in all his long military career of nineteen years, met with the provincial governor of Britannia only once, and would possibly not do so again.

"Or the procurator," added Murdach. "For we are very efficient at collecting and paying taxes, and better than most civitates, I should think."

"I am much less likely to run into the procurator," replied Rufus flatly. "I am a career soldier. I live on a military base or in a marching camp. I meet army personnel, or I meet nobody."

Murdach glanced briefly at the Tyrian stripes and seemed less than convinced.

"We must be off," pressed Rufus. He shivered with the cold. For all the grandness of the man's large house, it obviously did not have the luxury of an underfloor heating system. Rufus was looking forward to being back on the road, feeling the warmth of a horse beneath him.

He managed to get away and step back on to the street. Raselg was already there, wrapped in a blanket and sitting pillion on the back of one of the largest horses. The horseman with her did not look displeased. Rufus nodded to her, as if to ask whether she was ready for the sway and bumps of the journey along an ancient road that had seen better days.

"I am ready," she answered.

"You will get to Isca before me. I will be with the infantry and reach Isca tomorrow. Tullius and some of the squadron will accompany you. When you get to the praetorium, you will have to inform Luperus about what has happened."

"If that is your wish," she replied. She was resigned to his coldness and perfunctory manner and knew that any plea to stay with him would not change anything.

He was about to order the horseman to proceed to the gate where the infantrymen would be lined up waiting, when he spotted a beggar boy of around fifteen or sixteen years of age approaching them along the street.

A couple of the soldiers of his bodyguard stopped the boy, and Rufus was going to ignore the intrusion, when the boy started berating him loudly and excitably.

The soldiers holding the boy turned to Rufus in mild surprise. "He says something about a Druid woman, commander. You may know her, he says. She has a head injury and is lying in one of the *canaba* outside the town."

Rufus reacted immediately. He ordered Raselg's horse to proceed to the gate and then went over to the boy. He grabbed him roughly by the arm. "Ask the rascal what happened!"

The soldiers did so. The answer came back. "They fought Ankows. Five of them but the Druid was struck by one of them, with a hard rock on the back of the head. She has not woken since. He then goes on about wanting to become a soldier so that he can fight more Ankows!"

The boy was tearful by now and evidently very angry. He was struggling to get free of the centurion's grasp. Rufus let him go. The boy stood and rubbed his arm and continued with his babbling.

"He says that the Druid turned up at the town with a dead man in a cart. They buried the man in the graveyard out front of the town. Then the Ankows came and attacked the Druid in the middle of the night. That was two nights ago. The boy and the Druid set fire to the hovel and burnt some of the fiends. Two escaped. The Druid killed one of them with the Druid's lance but the other – a woman – attacked the Druid with the rock and may have given her a killing blow."

"Take me to her!" ordered Rufus.

They caught up with the horse on which Raselg was a passenger and overtook it, half-running to the south gate and then turning left just outside to head for the collection of hovels that started a hundred yards away. The reek of burnt wood and bedding was coming from the remains of one of the hovels, set aside from the others. Rufus had noted the wreck on his way into the town but had not thought more about it.

The boy led them to another hovel. Two women were sitting outside it and appeared at first to consider objecting to the arrival of Rufus and his bodyguard of eight soldiers, when the boy admonished her for being disrespectful. This was the Roman general the Druid had spoken about. The one who would be coming, as the boy had predicted. The soldiers were not there to harm the patient.

Not waiting for permission, Rufus went into the hovel, leaving the door open to emit at least some light. It stunk inside of goats, greasy ash, unscrubbed hearth and damp blankets. He waited until his eyes grew accustomed to the darkness and then, eventually, he saw the recumbent shape of Cybele to one side, lying on what passed for a bed.

She appeared to be sleeping. The women had cleaned the blood off the side of her face and sponged it mostly from her hair, and her head appeared to be normal, her face white but reposed and animate. Rufus was too afraid to lift her head to see the extent of the damage to the back of it. Someone had come into the hovel behind him, and he turned to this person for assistance, expecting it to be one of the villagers. But it was one of his own bodyguard.

Rufus felt helpless, unsure what to do. The lack of illumination was frustrating. Eventually, he stood up and walked out of the hovel.

To one of the bodyguard, he said, "Go back to the house of the curium, to councillor Murdach, and tell him that I need the best medic here now!" Turning to Tullius who had come over to the hovels in readiness, he said, "I need a carriage – large, with clean blankets. We'll use the two horses we got from Nepos' inn. The marks on them show they are used to pulling *carrucae*. And find a lamp! I cannot see a damn thing in there!"

Tullius hurried off.

Raselg was looking over from near the gate. He beckoned her over and, when she had climbed gingerly down from the horse and walked over on unsteady legs to where he was waiting, he snapped, "You are no longer the patient, you are the *nurse*. But, on the other hand, Raselg, it looks like you might have got your carriage, after all!"

Not waiting for her to respond or bothering to explain who she should be nursing, he looked around for the boy. The youth came over promptly when he saw that the centurion wished to speak to him.

"Now, show me where the man who came with the Druid is buried," said Rufus.

It took Raselg only a few moments. "Dendus?" she asked.

"Yes. Stay here and wait for the medic!" he ordered.

ON the pitiful mound of disturbed earth, Rufus saw that somebody had placed a bracelet of wildflowers, now faded. He lifted up the dried offering and fingered it gently. Then he wept quietly.

A soldier behind him asked, "Do you want us to fetch out the remains, commander?"

"No, why? This is as good a place as any," he answered curtly.

He did not stay at the grave more than a minute. He felt another shiver go through his body, suddenly. He was falling ill it seemed. That was why he was always cold today. One side of his body felt stiff and leaden, as if the leather pieces and iron armour he was wearing on that side were twice as heavy and twice as thick as on the other. He turned and began walking back to the waiting infantry troops near the town gate, his gait a little laborious, and a buzzing noise like a mosquito growing louder in his head.

When he had covered half the distance, the medic appeared, and Murdach too. A junior centurion, marching backwards and forwards in front of the rows of troops pointed over to the *canabae*. Rufus noted the medic hesitate when he saw where the soldier was pointing. He had probably never been near such low and disreputable residences in his professional career. He looked to the councillor next to him as if to enquire whether this was the right place.

Rufus quickened his pace to intercept them. Then he seemed to become dizzy, to lose his balance and stumble. Just as a sharp headache came on as well and one of his eyes went blind. He noted the medic looking over at him, and Murdach's hand going to his mouth in surprise and concern.

CHAPTER THIRTY-THREE

"YOU managed to fill half the hospital with your cavalcade!" joked Saenus. "I have not seen so many walking-wounded since the Ides of Julius."

"In my case, without raising a hand in anger," sighed Rufus. "The Druid received her blow honourably in a skirmish. Even the slave, Raselg, can wear her scars with pride. It seems, in my case, it is just age and weariness catching up with me. Time to start thinking of my retirement."

"Nonsense. In a month from now you will be outreaching me on the Gassello course! What was it, anyway, do we know?"

"Brain fever? Apoplexy? A mild case."

"Well, you are in good company, at least."

"Julius Caesar? Yes."

"No, I was thinking Caligula, actually," said Saenus, mischievously.

"Worryingly, they say that Caligula was a fine emperor until he suffered his attack. Then afterwards, he was a madman."

"We shall have to keep an eye on you, Rufus."

"'Though, he was afflicted for three months, whereas I was gripped with it for no more than three hours."

"Well, you do appear a lot better than the day you left the hospital."

"We are well enough now," replied Rufus. He looked around at the atrium, which he still struggled to think of as being his own. It still seemed a place where his predecessor, Bruccius Natalinus, might walk into any second. "Even Cybele, but it was touch and go in her case."

"May the gods be praised."

"She is a remarkable woman."

Saenus agreed. After several seconds, he said. "I came here to give you this. It came this morning from the other Isca. From Tammo Vitalis, I think." He handed Rufus a letter.

Rufus leaned forward from the couch with a grunt and took hold of the envelope. Peering at it, he said, "You're right. From the legate. This is his secretary's handwriting."

Opening the outer covering of papyrus, he unfolded the sheets inside and began to read the letter aloud. It was almost always the case that Roman people read aloud, whether alone or not. Rufus had wondered at times whether it was the same for other cultures.

The more Rufus read the letter, the more baffled he became over its content, its assumptions and its indignant tone. It was obvious he had failed to receive some important orders from

Colusanas before the senior tribune's violent and unexpected death, but what were those orders exactly?

'We had expected to receive confirmation from you by now that you are at Duronovaria, awaiting instructions for your passage to Gesoriacum...'

Rufus looked up at Saenus. "Why are they sending me to Gaul? It doesn't make sense. I am needed here to fight the scourge of the Ankows! I am supposed to be here, training up a specialist unit!"

Saenus shook his head in wonderment. "Perhaps you are to meet and accompany a new legion back to Britannia from there. There is news of a possible uprising of the Brigantes in the north again, so it would not be surprising if a fourth legion has been sent to reinforce us."

"But why me?"

"You are one of the most senior centurions in the south of the province, an equite. Perhaps some *delicacy* concerning status must be observed and the Second Augustan Legion cannot presently spare any of the tribunes to go."

Rufus was not convinced. "I had not realised I was so far up the pecking order."

"You bely your real status. Apart from the tribunes, who else in these parts is of the knightly class? You might be posted here as a senior centurion of a cohort of lowly auxiliary foot soldiers, but you also wear thin purple stripes on your tunic or toga, and that emblem still means something to diplomats and politicians. You are, in that sense, a higher grade than even the *Primus Pilus*."

"So you think somebody who would be insulted if he were met and greeted by a poorer sort of plebeian, is going to be waiting for me at Gesoriacum? Somebody who expects to be invited to Britannia by a patrician or equestrian and nothing less?"

"Such as a sitting senator, or one of the consuls?"

"Domitian himself, incognito?"

"More likely Nerva, but we are only guessing. What else is in the letter?"

'*Is your silence connected with the same we encounter from the senior tribune, from the camp prefect and from tribune Helius?*'

"We know why they have fallen silent. They are dead," interrupted Saenus unnecessarily.

"It goes on: '*Helius was due at Corinium but he has failed to appear. There is no word from the senior tribune and prefect. The legate and tribunes therefore require your report by return.*'

Rufus asked Luperus to summon his tesserarius. The two men made small talk about Natalinus's taste in furnishings and frescos while they waited; particularly the gaudy mosaic he had laid in the centre of the room: Naked nymphs straddling rampant bulls, with the god, Bacchus, watching approvingly to one side and pouring wine into the obscenely open mouth of a prancing satyr. It was no wonder that Rufus struggled to feel that the place was his own. When the tesserarius had arrived and was sitting at the desk nearby, Rufus began to dictate a reply to the legate.

"To tribune Pilius Silvanus from Plancius Vallaunius Rufus, commander of the Eighth cohort, this eighth day before the Kalends of November, Greetings. I have received no orders from the broad stripe tribune. He and the camp prefect and the tribune Helius and the vexillation of the Fifth cohort are almost certainly dead, killed by the fiends who now occupy Duronovaria in great numbers. The Eighth cohort will go to Duronovaria within three days to confront them. Do not send messengers there until I confirm it is safe. I will report when I can. In sorrow I am at least content that the souls of our dearest dead sojourn in glory in Elysia."

Saenus admired the tone and then added, "We can be there in less than three days, I think."

"I know."

The tesserarius finished inscribing the letter and handed it to Rufus to check over. Rufus handed it back, approved.

When the tesserarius had departed with the letter, Rufus turned to Saenus and said with a heavy heart. "I said three days because I want Tadius Naratius and at least half the Tenth cohort of Brigantes to go with us as well. The last full moon was on the fourth day before the Ides of October and, despite what I said in the letter just now, we both know that the souls of our dearest comrades will not be enjoying the glories of Elysia yet. Instead, they will be waiting for us at Duronovaria, standing alongside the other Ankows. We must fight them and vanquish them and release their souls too!"

Saenus nodded. "May the gods be with us on that day. It is going to be a hellish day!"

Rufus began to look at the decurion with an earnest expression on his face. "I should hope that you would do the same for me, if it came to it."

"Of course I would."

"You know that Raselg went to see a fortune-teller, who prophesied my imminent death?"

"Yes, she told me about it," replied Saenus uncomfortably.

"I'm sure she did! It served her purpose!"

"Oh Rufus, we were led by madness! I could think of nothing but my passion for her. And when she told me that she would be mine under the terms of your will and testament, and that a soothsayer had foretold your imminent death, it was as if the gods themselves had given us licence to, well, bring about our fate and the gods' kind providence."

"She can be very persuasive."

"I hope that you can forgive me and still do my that honour. I would take very good care of her."

"You believe the fortune teller, then?"

"No, but I believe that we will only be one step from death from now on. *All* of us. The peace is over for us again. It's not the

Ordovices and *Silures* and the *Brigantes*, this time, but worse! It will be the same hideous foes we faced here at Isca on the Ides of Julius! I still don't really understand how we managed to survive that battle! They surely got the better of us. Perhaps we do not need soothsayers to tell us what *our* fate is likely to be, now?"

Saenus looked as though he felt he had said too much. He changed his tone to a lighter one. "The fortune-teller who Raselg saw was probably a charlatan, anyway. She told me he lived in a very decrepit hovel outside the town walls. If he was any good at it, he would have been inside the town and sponsored by the council."

"I heard that he had prophesied the death of the king and it had come about just as he said it would. But the king's sons, for reasons they can only explain themselves, decided that the old soothsayer was to blame to some extent for their own father's death! That it had been a self-fulfilling prophesy!"

"That is a very strange way to regard prophesies, Rufus!"

"So, they cast him out of the town and took away all his assets. But the folk here still think of him as the wisest of them all."

The two men regarded each other. What Rufus was implying was that his fate was the same as that of the old king, and that the fortune teller would be right in this instance too, that Rufus anticipated his own early death.

"You have not answered my plea," Saenus said after a minute.

"My will says that she will be passed to Tadius Naratius, so you had better help keep me alive, so I have time to change my mind again!"

"Then, go to Gaul, and we will do the Ankow-fighting ourselves! You need the rest in any case. You look worn out."

Rufus sighed and settled back on the couch. "Write to Tadius Naratius on my behalf, Saenus. Tell him that Duronovaria is occupied by hundreds of Ankows and he must join forces with us. We must set aside our differences and be prepared to march there in three days."

Saenus saw that Rufus had closed his eyes. "Be well," he said and, noting that his commander did not even respond to this customary salutation, he left the room.

CHAPTER THIRTY-FOUR

THERE was nobody more enthusiastic to answer the call of the commander of the Eighth cohort to join forces and march eastward than Luti Bassus. Even though his precious new shrine-cum-temple to *Nerthus* was half-finished, he abandoned the project with good grace and set about, with the same fervour, to organise the horse squadron for the journey and, in his view, for a potentially a long campaign.

His new optio, Mus, was impressed with his commander's proactive zeal. He had never considered the effeminate man to be a fighter but more a horse-trainer, herbalist and academic; somebody who you would expect to see in a library or stables or tending to his garden. Mus was not alone in his astonishment, everybody found themselves having to reassess the despised man. Now a man of action.

Less than a week of mourning had seen Luti get over the loss of his beloved friend, Viterius. Six days of introspection, solitude and prayers at the semi-formed shrine. In one further day, he had ensured that the cavalrymen were ready to move out: cloaks oiled, panniers crammed full of food and saddles tied with marching camp wherewithal, personal savings deposited in the bank, last minute wills scratched on scraps of papyrus, and their horses trimmed, groomed and shod with their most robust boots. The standards were fetched from the secured store and repolished. The cavalry beasts were jittery with excitement, sensing that travel was in the offing. And so were their horses.

The infantrymen faced the prospect of carrying three weeks' worth of food and equipment on their backs, as well as a long javelin and a large, curved shield made heavier than usual by the extra iron layer. They knew the toll this burden could make on them from the marching exercises undertaken every other day. Ten miles was within their comfort zone, twenty would be the limit of their abilities along a surfaced road, but thirty might be expected in a crisis.

The journey was all along a paved road so at least the troops had the luxury of seeing their sixty-one heavy goatskin tents plus wooden struts for tent box-frames and eleven hundred guy ropes and wooden tent pegs loaded into a cart.

Tadius, as commander of the Tenth cohort of Brigantes, had several roles. He was commandant of a military base, centurion of the first company and the master of religious ceremonies. He ensured that the right and proper dues were given to the favoured gods the evening before they departed: to Silvanus, Nerthus-Cybele, Mars and the abstract spirit of the reigning emperor, known as *Genius*. Secretly, the troops prayed and would go on praying to their own proper gods.

So, on the second day after Saenus's request for their assistance, the horsemen and infantry of the Tenth cohort were ready to depart; a contingent of eighty-two foot soldiers and five horsemen staying behind to guard the fort and continue the fiscal raiding of passing trade. Nemetostatio would remain open for business.

Isca Dumnoniorum was within a day's long march and Tadius decided to push all the way with only a brief stop at midday. These were not the efficient legionnaires he had soldiered alongside in previous years, and he had some catching up to do. They had taken longer than he wanted to get ready to ship out.

They arrived exhausted and footsore at the end of a long day. Many grumbles and curses rose into the grey, frosty dusk air when the men realised, or were reminded, that the auxiliary fort at Isca was very small and that there would be no space in the permanent barracks buildings for the rank and file. They had been warned about this but most seemed to have forgotten. They dragged their rolls of patchwork skins from the cart and wearily put together the box-frames and hung the tents over them, and clogged the unpaved roads with lines of brown tents. Soon the fort was thick with the stench of cooking fires.

The officers made use of the ten empty rooms in the barracks that once housed the contingent of Belgae auxiliaries. Tadius would normally have stayed in the commandant's house but on this occasion, he felt disinclined to do so, and opted to stay in the barracks with his officers.

But there was no avoiding meeting with the commander of the Eighth cohort in the evening. The men must not see that their commanders were at loggerheads. Tadius donned his plain toga and wrapped himself in his large cloak and made his way to the praetorium, not looking forward to the encounter. Luperus welcomed him at the door and showed him into the atrium, where Rufus was standing stiffly in readiness upon the gaudy mosaic. He appeared a shadow of his former self, so much so that the thought occurred momentarily and unkindly to Tadius that he ought to keep his Ankow-killing dagger close to hand. His former friend was pale and thin and somewhat aged. Rufus had always been serious-minded, if not a little grave and morose at the best of times but there seemed to be an extra dourness in his manner now. This was not surprising, once Tadius heard an account of recent events: the treachery of Raselg, the massacre at Duronovaria, the death of Dendus and the travails of Rufus's ward, who Rufus insisted on calling Cybele. The two commanders exchanged reports pertaining to army matters, not realising that their stories were linked by the same group of Ankows, led by a monster called Mavritius Varro.

When Raselg made her appearance, bringing a tray filled with wine containers, and a dish of apples and nuts, Tadius's expression lit up. If it were not for Rufus's telling of events, he would of course have expected her to be there, serving in the household as usual, but after hearing the account, and spotting the tell-tale signs of violence on her face, he felt relieved and delighted that all was relatively normal in her case, and she was as lovely as ever. They exchanged quick glances, a frisson shooting through each of them at that moment. Raselg was careful not to linger too long with her glance.

They dined on lamb meatballs smothered with fish sauce, and discussed manoeuvres and plans in a stilted tone. The wine was consumed in quantity but not in celebratory fashion, and there was no toasting. Although they had not known each other at the time, both men had grown up in Camerinum in Italia. In earlier days, when the army business had been finalised, they would love to talk about their homeland fondly, and ruminate on how the woodlands, rolling hills and green pastures must look in the milder climate at this time of year. This evening, however, the atmosphere was sombre and the talk perfunctory, for form's sake. The subject of retirement was touched upon. They were both career soldiers, bent upon service to the army for far longer than the obligatory term of years, and they knew little else, were not even sure how they might fare in civilian society when they finally returned to it. For the first time ever, Rufus was prepared to talk about life beyond the army, about the practicalities of it. His face turned sad when Tadius reflected that they must each find themselves a good wife and spawn little versions of themselves, and despite his misgivings about Rufus, Tadius kicked himself for broaching the subject, realising that Rufus still mourned the loss of Silpunia, and that it was still a raw wound.

"Come, Tadius, I want to show you something," Rufus said after half a minute's silent introspection.

Rufus was up out of his couch but not without a little grunt of pain. He seemed agitated. He went off to speak to his servant Luperus and returned, ten minutes later, wearing his large heavy cloak over his toga.

"We're going outside?" asked Tadius.

"Fetch your cloak quickly," urged Rufus.

Luperus was waiting near the front door of the house, carrying a lamp and a cloth bag filled with heavy items. They left the house and threaded themselves past the dark rows of tents filling the street that led to the north gate of the fort. The guards on the gate let them through.

Rufus was walking quickly but Tadius detected a limp. His right leg was stiff and a little cumbersome. Luperus followed them, carrying the lamp and the bag. They seemed to be heading to the east side of the civilian town.

Eventually, Rufus stopped. He instructed Luperus to open the bag and take out the items. The servant carefully removed the contents: twenty or more small ceramic lamps. They must have been nearly all the lamps in Rufus's house. Luperus spent a couple of minutes lighting each one and placing them in a long, neat line, perhaps two paces apart. Tadius saw that the weak light was revealing the left edges of the old Gassello course etched on the road.

"Is this a challenge?" asked Tadius.

"Yes, I need to prove something."

"But it's, what, ten years since I last enjoyed the pleasure of the Gassello course! This very one, in fact."

"Me too."

"There's nothing to prove, Rufus. You were always able to beat me at it. Every time."

Rufus smiled but it was too dark for Tadius to catch the wry expression. "Thankfully, we have half a moon to help us," he commented flatly.

Tadius looked up. The moon was almost exactly half its disc. The light from it hardly made any difference to them down there on the ground, and he could hardly see the lines of the squares scratched into the road. His memory and spatial judgment would have to make up for the lack of illumination.

"Can you see it?" asked Rufus, thinking along the same lines.

"My eyes grow accustomed to the dark," replied Tadius, trying to sound accommodating. "Thankfully, we are wearing light togas and cloaks, not heavy armour and backpacks."

"And no shields and javelins."

"We will dance through the whole course, no doubt," said Tadius.

"Even at our ages. A wager, perhaps?"

"Oh, Rufus, we don't need a wager. The challenge is enough."

"No, a wager," insisted Rufus. "If you win, you will have one of my precious assets. One I know you covet."

Tadius thought this through. Eventually, he whispered, "Raselg?"

"Yes."

"That is easy to promise, when you know you are the better man."

"We'll see. You go first. Luperus and I will count the squares you land on properly. Be aware that Luperus here used to officiate when Natalinus tortured his men with this course, didn't you, Luperus?"

The servant nodded in the darkness and his silence was taken as affirmation.

Tadius went to the starting end of the course. The numbers in the squares had been scuffed off by countless feet, hooves and cartwheels over the years and were now unreadable. He steadied himself for a few moments and then set off.

Without the weight of full armour and weapons and the awful burden of the full backpack, he felt as light as a feather for the first few steps. He landed on one foot and then jumped to land again on both feet, planting them neatly in the centre of the large squares. His heart began to race. The squares danced and wiggled beneath him as he advanced along the course, feeling exhilarated and fighting a surprising urge to laugh. The course had never felt so easy, and he did, indeed, feel like a gazelle.

"Suddenly, both Luperus and Rufus shouted, "Foul!"

It was true. Tadius, in his enthusiasm had planted his foot wrong in the twenty-third square.

"Twenty-two!" both judges confirmed.

Rufus now went to the starting point. After a few seconds he sprang into action. He got as far as the fifth square and fell over.

"Foul!" shouted Tadius. "Come on Rufus, that was a poor show, we will not count that attempt."

"That is very magnanimous of you," panted Rufus. "You are five years younger, and I would do the same."

"More light would help," replied Tadius, generously.

Rufus went back to the beginning and tried again. This time he reached the ninth square before stumbling and falling over. He lay on the ground and did not move. Tadius went to help him to his feet but Rufus did not cooperate and refused to get up. Tadius sat down next to him on his cloak in the dirt of the road too.

"Poor show, Rufus. But it won't stop you balling at the auxiliaries when they perform just as badly."

"No, it won't, Tadius."

"Well, it's proved one thing I feared. You're not an Ankow."

"I could be *pretending* to be pathetic."

"But you're not pretending, are you?" said Tadius quietly and seriously.

"No."

Rufus then raised his right arm to shoulder height. "See that?"

"What?"

"That is as high as I can lift it. My sword hand, Tadius. It is weak and useless. I can barely grip a sword or javelin, let alone thrust with them."

"You need rest, that's all. There have been times when I felt like that. I broke my arm and got it infected in the fight in July and it was weeks before I felt I could properly use it again. But it comes back – with time. Time and practice."

"I would like to think so. But I don't have time. We are off to Duronovaria tomorrow, to fight enemies who are quicker and stronger than us. The quickness and strength of my right arm will mean the difference between life and death. And I am going to die as soon as I find myself in the first mortal encounter."

Tadius did not reply. Finally, he cursed to himself. "It is the apoplexy, Rufus."

"I know, but what can I do? I must lead the men and not show weakness. They depend upon me!"

"They do."

"You must not remember me this way. When I am gone."

"You will be fine. You must tell your optio and standard bearer to watch out for you, to protect you, like Saenus and

Lunaris protected us over there at the wharfs this summer. You must be honest with them and tell them about the effects of the apoplexy. They will understand that you are not yet recovered."

"I know. I will."

"Is that why you made that ridiculous wager about Raselg? I won't hold you to it in the circumstances."

"The wager stands. I made it in all seriousness."

"After Duronovaria, Rufus. We will talk about it then."

Nobody spoke for a minute. The two centurions remained sitting on the dark road, deep in thought.

There was a loud, impatient sigh near to them. "Have you finished the competition? Can I collect up the lamps and put them back in the house?" asked Luperus eventually, in a long-suffering way.

CHAPTER THIRTY-FIVE

TUATHAL did not call himself king, most of the time it felt like he was nothing more than the consort of the last remaining monarch, Queen Belena, but he *did* feel the master of his new realm. Basically, this was because he had seventy-nine strong men at his command, and nobody was going to pick a fight with the edgy Bolgoi. He navigated a careful path between allowing Belena to act the part of queen to her people, whilst at the same time ensuring that everybody understood that he was the tendon that pulled the new Mai Din muscle. His men would not answer to her, and she knew it.

Life at Mai Din was shaping up very well. Each of his men had coupled up with a woman and there had been little argument or contest about the choices. Surprisingly. Time would tell perhaps, as Tuathal could already sense some resentment and envy simmering below the surface in some cases.

They forged crude iron swords and axes, ensuring they were made in the Durotrigan style, and made a brisk and lucrative trade from intercepting merchants travelling along the nearby road from the port of Clavinium to the capital town, and persuading them to buy crude ingots of tin and lead, and heaps of large quarried stones, and to release to them in return countless amphorae of wine or a premium price for the goods foisted upon them. Persuasion often took the form of outright menace. The merchants went on to the capital town, indignantly riding their heavier carts but with purses much lighter. Whether or not they intended to complain about the outrage to the town council or the Romans in Duronovaria, these merchants were never seen again.

It did not take Tuathal and Belena long to realise why the Roman soldiers in the nearby town never appeared on the roads or came to check on them. It was the same explanation for the disappearance of Tuasatas and the Durotrigan men as well as the explanation for the one-way traffic of merchants to the town. Duronovaria had been taken over by Ankows. There could be no other explanation.

For days after this dawned upon them, the Bolgoi were inclined to leave and head eastwards to their homelands. Yet they never did. They were worn out carrying boxes from the shore to the top of the massive hillfort, and by the effort of mending fences all day, and they were having such a profitable time with the passing merchants and the warm women in their midst, that they kept putting off their departure. Eventually, the plan to vacate the fortress, sooner rather than later, was forgotten. The Ankows were leaving them alone, anyway.

Still, just in case of a raid by the fiends one night, they kept on strengthening the maze of fences, and forged eighty sharp axes and robbed lamp oil in the gallons-worth from the merchants. They felt confident that they could put up a great fight if Ankows ever attacked them and, after all, they also happened to be lording it in the mightiest fortress in Britannia.

The great feast day of Samain arrived. Tuathal had put aside vast quantities of wine for all of them to consume from dawn to long past sunset this day. There would be dancing and much singing, and rough, testosterone-infused games of dare and strength-testing. A great bonfire would be lit after dusk. While the men started on the wine, and slaughtered several goats, the women baked bread and pasties to sustain them all till midnight. The weather blessed them with a bright, cloudless day, a stiff wind coming from the west. The first songs of the day came from the busy women and children, sitting round their ovens, their arms and hands, and sometimes their faces, caked in grey flour.

Belena presided over the women's tasks, and thought to herself how much it seemed just like old times, when her mother and father led the revelry at this auspicious festival, and the day gradually became uproarious, till half of them were already slumbering in alcoholic stupor by the time the great fire was lit. And the Druids thankfully kept away.

Tuathal's already hazy head partly cleared, when a voice went up from the sentry on the western gate just before midday.

He ran to that end of the plateau and peered out to where the man was pointing. Then he nearly defecated on the spot.

Marching along the road and having just cleared the furthest ridge of the hills, was a dark column of people. They filled the road from one side of it to the other, probably eight men wide, the tail end of the procession yet to arrive over the horizon. Tuathal recognised the shape and the rhythm of the walking immediately. Roman soldiers! An absolute multitude of them.

"What shall we do?" asked the sentry.

Tuathal tried to think. Finally, he said, "Nothing. We just act normally." Instinctively, he felt his face for the reassuring feel of his beard. The question really was, *is this the Eighth cohort and, if they stop here at Mai Din, will we be recognised?*

Tuathal peered at his comrade and tried to assess his appearance objectively. They had all let their head and facial hair grow and become unkempt. They were all wearing Durotrigan wool tunics and trousers. They surely bore little resemblance to the Belgic auxiliaries who mutinied and deserted Isca Dumnoniorum some weeks earlier.

"They will be expecting us to be celebrating Samain today, and I think they will go to the town, not here. Why should they come here?"

The sentry blinked and nodded.

Somebody tapped Tuathal's shoulder. It was Belena. She spotted the mass of soldiers approaching along the road and swore loudly. She said after that, in a surprisingly meek and pleading manner of voice for her, "Tuathal?"

"Wait," he replied. He was still trying to estimate the number of foot soldiers. Something was wrong. This division was more than just one cohort. His mind tried to square the length of the configuration with the number of men, if they were eight men wide. When he eventually counted the carts being pulled behind the column of men, he swore too.

"It's *two* cohorts!"

"And look at the riders!" shouted the sentry.

The horses were squirming around on either side of the procession, like flies around dung; what looked like over forty of them. Four horsemen were well ahead of the marching men, and had just left the road, and appeared to be coming towards the great hillfort.

"Scouts, heading this way!" said Tuathal. "Come on, we must act as though nothing is wrong! Then they will hopefully leave us alone."

Tuathal and Belena returned to the area of roundhouses and ovens and told everyone to shut up and listen to them. They explained the jeopardy. They must all pretend to be an innocent community of the Durotriges, enjoying the great feast day. The Bolgoi must not be exposed. Then the Romans would go to the town and, hopefully, be slaughtered or, at least, distracted sufficiently for now.

There was again some excitement at the west end of the plateau. The Roman scouts had left their horses at the foot of the trenches and ramparts and climbed up to the gate. They were trying to converse through the fences, asking to be let in.

Tuathal ran back to where the exchange was taking place. "Let them in," he shouted breathlessly when he was close enough.

The sentry obliged, and four Roman soldiers with oval shields and long cavalry lances stepped through the gate and looked around. The man at the front of them was wearing the headgear of a cavalry optio.

"Greetings!" shouted Tuathal in what he hoped passed as the correct accent.

Mus peered at him, almost contemptuously, and returned the greeting.

"Come, we are celebrating Samain," encouraged Tuathal. Have a beaker of wine with us. You look as though you have come far today."

"Not so far," responded Mus curtly. He was counting the heads of the crowd over by the roundhouses. "How many are you?" he asked.

"How many? Er, ninety or so men, the same number of women, and a few brats."

The optio looked suspiciously at Tuathal, and the latter felt his innards begin to squelch again suddenly. To cover up, he asked, "*Brigantes*, I guess from your look and accent?"

Mus shook his head. "*Carvetii.*"

Tuathal twisted his face in puzzlement but thought better to say anymore on the subject. "But now a Roman soldier, what's it like?"

Mus ignored the question. "When was the last time you went to the town?" He gestured north-eastwards.

"We seldom go there. We're not welcome," conjured Tuathal. "My wife is banished by the town council. She's on the wrong side of the old aristocracy. We of the *Durotriges* keep long grudges, I'm afraid."

"Does that count for all of you? When was the last time any of you went to town?" persisted Mus.

Tuathal puffed his cheeks and pretended to think about it. "Months ago, I suppose. Maybe a year. We keep ourselves to ourselves up here."

Then, if things were not precarious enough, Tuathal's legs nearly crumpled beneath him when the optio calmly said, "We are eight hundred foot soldiers and fifty-two cavalrymen, plus eleven centurions. We will be setting up camp here in Mai Din. And you will make us welcome, if you know what's good for you."

"Here?" squirmed Tuathal. Then, after a moment or two, "Why here? Why not in the town?"

"Don't you know?"

Tuathal's mind was racing. Should he let on that he knew? Eventually he plumped for innocence and answered, "No. What is there to know?"

An angry look appeared fleetingly on the optio's face. He turned to the three scouts with him, and said, "They would have had us go to the town and be eaten by Ankows! What do you think of that?"

"Ankows!" hollered Tuathal, innocently.

"Yes. And you would most probably have been falling prey to them these past few weeks. How many people are you losing each night?"

"Er, none. What do you mean?" Tuathal was pretending that his mind was still reeling with shock, and, to some extent, it was. "Look, if what you say is true, then the Ankows will be feeding off all the merchants that go to the town every day. Hundreds of them these past few weeks! None of them have ever come back this way, come to think of it."

"And you never questioned why that was?"

"Well, not really. There could have been any number of reasons."

The optio looked doubtful. He said to his comrades. "Let's bring this man back with us. He is lying."

"I am not lying!" attested Tuathal in panic. "Here, we will open our gates to you. All of you are welcome! We are a little the worse for drink this day, because we've started the feasting early, but we will keep out of your way and let you set up camp. The more the merrier!"

Mus repeated his order, and the four men together grabbed him roughly, and led him back through the gate, through the myriad of trenches and out to where their horses were waiting. Tuathal peered in the distance and saw that the cohorts of soldiers were now only a mile away. He was now sure that his subterfuge would be exposed, and they would all be tried and executed for mutiny and desertion. He was shackled to the saddle of one of the horses, and they began to pick their way slowly down the hill towards the road to intercept the procession. He walked with them like a man condemned, only now and then remembering to keep up some pretence at least, and to make loud protests.

CHAPTER THIRTY-SIX

AT the head of the soldiers, resplendent in their plumed helmets which arched from side to side, and sitting astride fine horses, were the senior centurions of both cohorts. Beside them, also mounted, were their senior optiones and the decurions of both squadrons, their plumes going front to back to show their subaltern ranks.

Mus behind Tuathal, said, "This man lied to us, commanders. He would have sent us on to the town to be killed in our ignorance, so I have brought him here to answer for himself and tell us the lay of the land. Since we will inevitably kill him if he lies again, we should expect him to be a little more truthful now."

Luti, a few yards away, beamed at his optio, who seemed very sure of himself and had never looked so strong and handsome. He declared, as if he were showing off his new, sparkly officer to everyone around him, "Thank you, Mus. Very well done!"

Tuathal recognised Rufus, Saenus and Tullius immediately but they did not, for the time being at least, recognise him. He kept his head bowed as if in reverence and submission. Then he realised that he was not acting like the leader of the Mai Din community, and he was showing too much humility and not enough bombastic scorn, as he might expect a free leader of the Durotriges of Mai Din to behave. It was well known all over the south, that there was no love lost between the Durotriges people descended from ancestors massacred by the Second Augustan Legion, and the present incumbents of the Second Augustan regimental colours.

"What is your name?" the chief centurion of the Eighth asked him, the man he already knew was Plancius Vallaunius Rufus. He pretended not to know him. "What is *your* name?" he blurted out. This was a knee jerk reaction to needing moments to think of a suitable risk-free answer, rather than real defiance.

The optio of the horsemen who had captured him and brought him hither, walloped him hard on his right shoulder, so heavily with the iron knob of his vine staff which Mus had armed himself with again, that Tuathal fell to his knees and cried out in pain. When the spasm of agony had passed, he growled, "Manann." It was the name of his father, a name given to his son by his seafaring grandfather when they were still back in Gaul.

"Manann, good boy," repeated Rufus as if he were congratulating a dog who had just obeyed a command to sit. "Well, Manann, I hope you are all going to make us welcome, because we are about to take over your beloved citadel. We will remain there until we have finished our business."

Rufus pointed to the town in the distance. "That town, as you already probably know, is occupied by the fiends called *Ankows*. You might be one too for all we know. So, we are going to set up camp, prepare to do war with them, and you, and your people are going to assist us. You are certainly not going to impede us. The Ankows are the common enemy now, not Romans. Do you understand?"

Mus's vine staff prodded Tuathal in the shoulder again. "Yes, I understand," he muttered.

"I didn't hear that."

"Yes, I understand!" repeated Tuathal through gritted teeth.

"Good. Who leads your people – you?"

"No, Queen Belena. It *was* her husband, Tuasatas, before that, but he and some others went to the town and never came back. Now she rules in his place."

"And you're her right-hand man, I suppose," added Mus, speaking out of turn before he could stop himself.

Rufus looked sternly at Mus.

"I'm her, er, consort as well," explained Tuathal.

Some of the men laughed. "Queen Belena is not much of a grieving widow, is she?" suggested Tadius from his nearby horse.

"No," said Tuathal, pretending to find this funny too. "But, then again, I'm such a handsome fellow. Who could resist?"

Rufus now did an odd thing. He climbed down from his horse and went over to Tuathal. It looked for one moment that he was about to kiss the man. In truth he was smelling him, especially his breath. He was about to ask the man to remove his boots but then caught the unmistakable odour of wine on the man's breath. "You've been drinking. You stink of a lot of wine, and you have spilt some of it down your front!"

"Yes, it's the feast of Samain! We always get pissed today!"

"It's barely past midday," replied Rufus. Then to the others he proclaimed, "And Ankows do not drink wine, as far as I know."

"Unless they deliberately cover the smell of decayed blood by swilling wine, to trick us," suggested Luti. "You have a strange accent, Manann. It does not sound Durotrigan to me."

"Doesn't it?" replied Tuathal, innocently.

"Bind this man," ordered Rufus. "We will release him only when we know the lay of the land. Queen Belena will lose another lover if she is not careful!"

The soldiers guffawed. If they had not been so weary from marching, the noise might have been louder.

A movement distracted Tuathal's eye. A horse was walking up the side of the column of soldiers, slowly towards him. Two women were riding on the back of it. A rather beautiful woman on the front of it, wearing a Roman tunic, wool trousers and short cloak, and an older woman sitting behind her in long, emerald-green robes with a large hood covering most of her hair. Tuathal caught sight of an iron collar around the younger woman's throat.

He was transfixed by the sight: a Roman slave riding with a Druid.

When the horse reached Rufus's side, the slave said to him, "I'm sorry, sir, the Druid insisted."

Rufus nodded. "Let her."

The Druid woman now got carefully down from the horse, the slave steadying her as she did so. She walked over to Tuathal and did exactly what the commander had done a few moments before. She sniffed at Tuathal's mouth and stared fixedly into his eyes. She checked his ears and hands with a glance. Then quickly and deftly she grabbed him by the testicles and said quietly, "Remove your boots."

"Let go of my stones, Druid, and I will," answered Tuathal.

She did so with a jerk that made him wince. He took off his boots, smiling as mischievously and confidently as he could at the Druid.

His filthy feet revealed ten grimy toes.

"He is not an Ankow," announced Cybele to the soldiers.

The soldiers were very entertained by these events and several comments and a murmur of barely suppressed giggles could be heard rippling along the road.

"Shut up!" bellowed several of the junior centurions and optiones down the line.

Tuathal was bound with leather thongs at his wrists, and a heavy chain put round his neck and fastened with bolts tightly, the two loose ends of the chain then wrapped around his arms behind his back and bolted together just under his crotch. He knew this arrangement of restraints already; it had been part of his early training up in Isca Augusta. If they needed to manhandle him, then a soldier jerking any part of the restraining chains would immediately twist and cause sharp pain to several parts of Tuathal's his body at once: his neck and throat, his shoulders and elbows, and his genitals. It was best not to give them an excuse to manhandle him.

While this was happening, the Druid woman had climbed back on to the horse, and the two women had turned and guided the horse back along the side of the standing soldiers to the rear of the column again.

Once trussed up securely, the officers ordered a cornet-wielding standard bearer, to sound his instrument. The rows of soldiers began walking again, in turns from the front. Tuathal was impressed. They had never been that good when he was with them.

Tentatively, he looked down the rows of men to the junior centurions further away. One of these would be the centurion who commanded the third company of Belgae before, that was, they had grabbed him and tied him up in order to start the mutiny. This man would surely recognise Tuathal up close. After all, Tuathal had been cocky and loud, and not exactly one of the least noticeable recruits at the time. This centurion almost certainly had

366

committed an image of Tuathal, if not all seventy-nine of his brethren from the Belgic region too, to his lasting memory. Today had quickly turned into a nightmare, when at the beginning of it, as he had climbed off Belena, his body zinging with exhilaration, it had all seemed so good.

They marched towards the gigantic hillfort. Tuathal did his best to keep in with the rhythm, to avoid the violent yanking of his chains. He wanted also to keep well up front, away from the junior centurion who would know him. During the slow ascent up the hill, he wondered about two things: how he and any of them might manage to keep away from soldiers who would recognise them and, secondly, how to stop Belena or any of his men assuming, when they saw him being marched towards them in chains, that they had been rumbled already. The reaction of the men to this might give the game away completely. He had to find a way of pre-warning them before it was too late.

Risking the torment of his captors, he shouted to the nearest officers of the Tenth cohort behind them. "You had better be careful. Every day, we expect an attack by the Ankows from the town, from Ankows who will be dressed as soldiers, just like you, and my people might suspect you of malign intent. I admit that we know the town is full of them. You should let me go ahead and speak to Belena: tell her that you are not Ankows, that you have come to defend us from the devils, and she will then welcome you with open arms."

The commander and decurion of the Tenth, were both staring at him shrewdly. The slightly fat decurion was mouthing words to himself. The two officers brought their horses closer and whispered to each other.

The commander eventually trotted his mount over to Rufus and exchanged words with him too. He came back to speak to Tuathal.

"What weapons have you got ready to fight Ankows with, Manann?" he asked.

"Axes and firebombs," answered Tuathal.

Tadius weighed this up in his mind. "Very good. Are there any Druids amongst you?"

This was a trick. Everybody knew that the Durotriges hated Druids because they had deserted them when the Roman general, Flavius Vespasian, brought the Second Augustan Legion to this very hill and slaughtered their ancestors forty-six years ago. The Druids had disappeared hours before this, when they heard of a large army approaching from the east.

"No Druids," replied Tuathal. "They are not welcome amongst us."

Tadius nodded as if he understood suddenly. "Then that soldier officer over there, the one who brought you down here, will go with you into the fort in advance. He will take eighty foot soldiers and his horse troop, and he will take you to Belena. You will then inform her of our intentions and beseech her to cooperate. If all goes well, and we set up camp and pass one night up there without incident, we will release you. You can tell her that. On the other hand, if there is any trouble, she can be assured that you will be executed on the spot. I hope for your sake that she has not grown tired of you!"

"No chance of that," said Tuathal proudly.

The orders were given, and Mus led their captive and a junior centurion of one of the infantry companies up the hill together with their troops, the horsemen dismounting when the horses met the first ramparts and trenches and could go no further.

Up in the hillfort, the Samain celebrations had by this point been put on hold and the wine hidden away. The men and women were standing around looking tense and glum when Tuathal and his escort of soldiers walked in through the gate and on to the plateau at its western end. Belena had walked halfway to meet them, and her face was a picture of anxiety when she saw how wrapped in chains he was. But it was the Bolgoi he was most worried about. Some had drawn their swords; some had even gone to fetch an axe from the large pile of them by the east gate. Before any of them could make the situation worse, he shouted out to them: "It's all good, men! They've clapped me in irons just until they're sure we will be friendly and cooperative! But I've already told them, I said to them: I – *Manann* – consort of the queen, promise you that we, *Durotrigans* will cooperate with you and not give you any trouble! And I said that it's not just me – *Manann* – saying that, we'll *all* say that, won't we?"

He looked at them to gauge their reactions. He was met with expressions that showed a mixture of confusion, perturbation, anxiety or just mindless gawping.

"So, they expect us, *Durotrigans*, to be peaceful and welcoming!", continued Tuathal to make sure the position was understood. "They're going to stay one night here and, if there is no trouble, they'll release me in the morning, and we can all get back to normal!"

Mus corrected him. "Hold on, we did not say we would be staying only one night! We said that we would be staying here in Mai Din until we had finished our business!"

"And what business is that?" shouted Belena, who was walking towards them, brazenly and haughtily. "And why have you put him – Manann – in irons? What crime has he committed?

Tuathal was relieved that she, at least, had understood the situation.

"Take those irons off him and let him go. Tell us your business!" she demanded.

Mus looked her up and down. "I assume you are the so-called Queen Belena. The so-called *widow*."

There is nothing *so-called* about it!" she countered briskly but taken slightly aback. "What were you before you sold your soul to the invaders, and enslaved yourself? Brigantes by the sound of it!"

Mus did not bother correcting the mistake this time.

The centurion with the foot soldiers now stepped forward. He shouted in a Atrebaten accent that was very much like that of the Bolgoi: "Woman, there are no kings and queens around here! You've obviously forgotten who rules these lands now!"

"Not the dumb *Atrebos*, that's for sure!" she shouted back, scornfully. "Or are you *Bolgoi* or *Regini*?" She spat on the ground for good measure as if the words were too distasteful in her mouth. "You come here from over the waters (she pointed vaguely out towards the Ocean), pretending to be Britons, and then, later, you're more than happy to pretend to be Romans! Snowflakes and leaves, blowing this way and that way in the wind with no roots or integrity. No wood, no stone, no iron! You don't really belong here and, if it wasn't for you lot, we wouldn't have these Roman bastards here in the first place! You practically *invited* them into our lands! You've ruined everything!"

The centurion went forward to teach her a lesson. Mus quickly snapped at him: "Leave her alone, centurion! She is our host! This is her fortress! You are not to touch a hair of her head until I tell you!"

The centurion turned towards the cavalry optio indignantly. He seemed at first to be bent on exercising his superior position and venting his fury on the other man. He sized Mus up. The

371

centurion was taller and wider and, in his mind, much more of a real soldier than Mus. He also had eighty men with him, and Mus had three poncy horsemen. Then it dawned on the hothead captain of infantry that this Carvetian upstart in his chainmail and primitive northern accent was not worth fighting. Although, technically he outranked him, the cavalry optio was the right-hand man of one of the senior officers in the cohort and would have the officer's ear. A wrong move against somebody with influence could ruin a career man's trajectory or, at the very least, cause his company to be placed in the worst position in the next battle. So, wisely, he said nothing and stepped back briskly.

"And, in any case," continued Mus. "She's probably right."

Belena laughed. Then she looked ahead to where soldiers had begun to stream through the gate, in lines of eight abreast. She swore, threw her arms up in despair, turned one hundred and eighty degrees and stomped back towards the cluster of roundhouses.

Tuathal said, "That's her way of welcoming you."

CHAPTER THIRTY-SEVEN

THE tents of the Romans filled the west end of the inner area of the great fortress, set out in neat rows and patterns. Visually it contrasted immediately with the haphazard sprawl of native homes at the other end of the field. Eight men shared each ordinary tent, the centurions and optiones occupying a separate one at the head of each row. As they had marched here along a road, with carts pulled in the rear, each company had the luxury of an extra tent for storing food and spare weapons.

The commanders, Rufus and Tadius had placed their shared tent in the middle of the camp with a decorous extra space around it on each side. Even so, they habitually whispered when they spoke after the evening meal, because they were discussing options for assailing the town, and some options would necessarily place extra risks and even sacrifice on some of the platoons. It was best that the men did not listen in.

Lui Bassus came to the tent and interrupted them. They invited him in and offered him a chair and a tumbler of wine. He took it gratefully and sat down. He was still dressed in his uniform and wore some of his armour, his chainmail jerkin, leather strips over the lower part of his tunic and the senior officer's shin greaves. He had only shed his helmet, cloak and groin protection. The other two noticed that he smelt strongly of horses and lanolin.

"What is it, decurion," asked Tadius.

The small chair creaked as he moved to make himself more comfortable. "Cressido Saenus informed me that the Eighth cohort had suffered a mutiny and desertion of one whole company of Belgic recruits. This happened the day after the Ides of October, which would fit in with my observations. Cressido Saenus appears very embarrassed that he let it happen on his watch. As you know, the Tenth cohort never had a single desertion in the last year. The fact that it happened when he was acting as commander of the Eighth bothers him tremendously. I think he is an ambitious man. He won't be happy until he achieves the position of Primus Pilus, I sometimes think!"

Luti took a sip of wine, and there was a hint of self-satisfied malice in his expression. He went on.

"I think we have found the eighty deserters. The Belgae. They are here, dressed as men of the Durotriges tribe but quite plainly they are not what they seem."

"Something certainly does not seem right," agreed Tadius.

"Have you noticed that all their hair and beards appear, more or less, to be the same length, as if the men of Mai Din all decided to start growing them from scratch on the same day? In my reckoning, their beards are two weeks old, which would just be right if they stopped shaving and cutting their hair around the time of the last Ides."

"One thing is for sure," interrupted Tadius. "The men here are far less uncouth and scruffy looking than we would expect of the *Durotriges*. The men of that tribe are particularly brutish in appearance, and always smell of goats and pig shit. Well, they seemed to be when we were last in these parts, didn't they Rufus, I mean…commander?"

Rufus nodded.

"Precisely, commander," said Luti. "And they do not speak like the *Durotriges*. They make a stab at putting on the accent but forget to do so half the time, and they use dialectic words belonging to the *Belgae* tribe and subgroups which includes the *Atrebates* and *Regnensis*. And, whereas the people of the *Dumnonii* and *Durotriges* have adopted many words from the *Veneti* – the sea traders of Amorica who until recently commanded the Ocean and owned all the ports along the coast – these men here use none of the common words you might expect to hear when they talk of trade or commerce or the price of goods. I tested them by asking some of them who they traded with and what goods they bought and sold, and the price of things, and they all used Belgic words in their answers, not Venetic words. In short, not only are they not of the *Durotriges*, but they have not even been here long enough to know how to *pretend* to speak their dialect. I could do a much better job."

"The deserters stole a ship at the Isca port and set off out to the Ocean," interjected Rufus. "Why would they end up here at Mai Din?"

"Some mishap with the ship? Blown off course? There were storms raging in the Ocean around that time. That was why the merchants' ships were moored up in the port at Isca."

"There is one way to confirm if they are the deserters," said Rufus. "We get their centurion to identify them. They might be bearded and deliberately ungroomed, but he will know if it is them for sure. Embarrassed centurions have long memories!"

"Who is the centurion, commander?" asked Tadius.

Rufus did not know. "You had better ask Cressido Saenus. He disciplined the officer in question."

Tadius looked uncomfortable. "And what then? We will have to waste time convening a court martial and executing them all! There is no room for leniency in the case of mutiny and desertion. Once we start it, we must finish it. They must be publicly condemned and put to the sword. Such a harsh trial and punishment will unsettle the other men, make them disheartened and distracted. Is it really something we want to carry out *now*, when we are just about to storm the town, and we need all the men focussed and with us, and on their finest mettle?"

Rufus agreed with Tadius. Luti did not, and spoke up.

"The *Belgae* are not loved by the other tribes. They are still seen as foreigners, and, ironically, they are blamed for offering too warm a reception to Rome and its culture, not to mention the twenty-four thousand soldiers who landed here one particular year. They are blamed for letting the forces of Rome pass through their lands unhindered, even helped along! No one will shed a tear to watch these lot being put to the sword!"

"And who will carry this out?" asked Rufus. "Are you offering the services of the horse squadron of the Tenth?"

"If necessary. Half my squad are *Carvetii* from the other end of the province. They'll do it without hesitation, if we order them to do so."

"Well, it's not going to happen. Not now. After we have succeeded in ridding the town of Ankows and have set up some proper government there again, we will review the matter," concluded Rufus.

Luti went to say something but stopped himself. Eventually he went on: "You suggest we just pretend we don't know, and leave them be, commander?"

"In the circumstances, I do."

Tadius nodded. "They didn't kill anyone, I hear. They roughed up their centurion and a few subalterns, and tied them all up. A case of injured pride, that's all. We can afford to be pragmatic, not vengeful at this point."

"I have made my decision, anyway," muttered Rufus. "And that means not breathing a word of it, decurion, do you hear?"

Luti nodded and gulped down the rest of his wine. "May I go?" he asked.

"No," answered Rufus. "As you are here, I wish to ask you a few questions. More wine?"

He declined.

"We know you spied for the prefect and possibly the broad-stripe tribune, Luti," began Rufus. "You spied on us, on your own senior officers and comrades."

It was difficult to know whether the man was more disconcerted about this revelation or the sudden and unexpected use of his familiar name instead of his rank. Luti was a stickler for propriety. The conversation had suddenly taken a more troublesome direction and tone. He gave no reaction whatsoever, and just stared blank-faced.

"Now that both your spymasters are dead, you can acknowledge it, Luti. We have known for some time. Indeed, I was *informed* that it was exactly the case. I am not without my connections, myself."

Luti gulped and glanced instinctively at the two thin stripes on the cuff of Rufus's tunic. He seemed to swallow the bait. A film of sweat broke out on his upper lip. Finally, he nodded.

"You have always been intelligent. And no doubt a tremendous help at times with your knowledge and insight," continued Rufus. "But you need to know that the spy was being spied upon, and we let it go because of your special talents which we needed at the time."

Tadius looked at Rufus as if not sure, himself, to what extent Rufus was bluffing now. The air was thick with tension.

"Ulpius Senicianus always spoke about you with great warmth," muttered Luti. "He disagreed with most people about you. He felt that you had been ostracised and overlooked because you upset the senior tribune, and the legate too at times, with your maverick ways."

"My maverick ways," retorted Rufus. "What? Refusing to carry my centurial staff? Refusing to honour every trifling feast day and convention in the calendar? Refusing to bow to the insincere shrines of the Flavians? What exactly was I doing to irritate them?"

"All those things," replied Luti. "And a general feeling about you, that you would cut your own direction if you felt it more convenient at the time, disregarding standing orders and military conventions as it suited you. Your messing about with the soldiers' manual, for instance. Closing up gates in forts, refusing to have archers, keeping the standards locked up and hardly ever parading them, that sort of thing. It bothered people in high places."

"And what about the important things, Luti?" stepped in Tadius. "Plancius Vallaunius's bravery and his cleverness in battles, the fact that the men love him and think him the finest soldier in the land, the fact that, while commanding the outpost at Nemetostatio, he never lost a single man to desertion or sickness? Is that all cancelled out because he closed two portals in the outpost fort and didn't carry a stick?"

"The commander's reputation as a soldier is not doubted," responded Luti. "We are talking here of respect and manners; his reputation for cocking a snoop at his seniors and their sensibilities. It looks like contempt for them simmering under the surface!"

"Thank you for being so honest, at last," said Rufus. "And what do you know about the project to send me to Gaul?"

Luti looked puzzled. "Not just Gaul, Commander. The plan is to send you to *Rome* – with the new lance."

"Why?"

"To present a report about the Ankows, and to present the new lance to the emperor Domitian of course."

Rufus poured himself another beaker of wine and stared at Tadius as if to steady himself. A minute passed in silence. Finally, Rufus said: "It makes sense, I suppose."

"Does it?" asked Tadius.

"Yes, when you think it through. Who else should go? We would be complaining, would we not, Tadius, if some other person got the credit for the victories so far, and for the invention of the new lance? It is our project, more than anyone else's."

"Rufus, they would be sending you to Rome because they are too scared to go themselves! It is not *safe!*" Tadius stopped himself from uttering the fact that the emperor was paranoid and mad.

Rufus turned to Luti, as if conspiratorially, "There is talk that Domitian fears – no, he *predicts* – a coup against him, led by senators. They say the emperor had a dream in which a large army of senators came to kill him, assisted by a legion of monsters! So, the concern is that Domitian will misinterpret the talk about the Ankows and see it only as confirming this prediction and his paranoid expectations. He will believe that the governor and procurator and the three legates in Britannia are raising an army together with the forces of evil in order to march against him. The report about the Ankows will then be seen as nothing less than a subtle, ill-disguised threat! An ultimatum to him to abdicate or fall on his sword, to pass the crown to the consul, Nerva, or else face annihilation."

Luti did not look surprised. He appeared to have knowledge of this already. But now he wondered how Rufus could possibly know as well.

"You are asking yourself, how I should know all this."

"I am."

As I said, I too have my connections."

The decurion looked impressed. "Any more questions?" he asked after a few seconds.

"No, you can go. And, well done about the Belgae. But let's keep it under wraps for now."

The chair creaked again as he stood up.

"Oh, one more thing, decurion," added Rufus as Luti was about to exit the tent. "Now that the camp prefect and broad-stripe tribune are dead, who do you spy for now?"

"Nobody. I answer to the commander, Tadius Naratius, and to you, sir, and of course, *Nerthus*. Things are different now, very different with me. The goddess has other plans for me."

He went to unbuckle the flaps of the tent but stopped. "Commander, I meant to ask your permission for something. As you know, I have a special interest in languages. I have never had the opportunity to study a Druid's speech. I suspect that they speak a more archaic, some might say, *purer* version of the Brythonic tongue. Would you permit me to have an audience with the Druid for that purpose?"

Rufus answered, "If you can find the time for such leisure in the circumstances, which would surprise me, decurion, then I have no objection. We are marching on Duronovaria tomorrow, remember?"

"I will make the time," he muttered, almost to himself. He bowed, said something like, "Be well, commanders," under his breath and left the tent.

CHAPTER THIRTY-EIGHT

AFTER Luti posted a detachment of riders on each of the four roads to the town of Duronovaria to intercept any unsuspecting travellers heading into it, and incidentally to their doom, he returned to the makeshift military camp astride the Mai Din hill. The base was busy with preparations for the big assault. The Belgae were keeping well out of the way and did not appear to have emerged out of their wattle and daub houses at the eastern end of the hill. Luti had noticed something else amiss about the aboriginal community: the absence of any horses. It confirmed his suspicion, if any further proof was needed.

He went to the tent occupied by the two women, Raselg and the Druid. It was situated near to the commanders' tent. Both Rufus and Tadius were away, supervising the preparations and had been gone since dawn. Luti coughed loudly when he was outside the tent, and then said, "Raselg, are you in there? It's me, Luti Bassus. I have come to speak to the Druid."

The flap of the tent opened after a few seconds. Cybele's green eyes were looking out at him, startlingly arresting in the morning light. Luti was momentarily flummoxed.

"What is it, horseman?" she asked.

"A moment of your time, if you don't mind," he stammered.

She thought about it and then stepped out of the tent.

Luti looked around. There was nobody about to listen to them, apart from perhaps Raselg. The Druid seemed to guess his thoughts and said, "The slave woman is not here. She has gone to take food to her master, as he had forgotten to eat this morning. Whatever would you need to speak to me about?"

It should have been difficult to explain but he had rehearsed it in his mind. "I am going into battle today, Druid, but I will survive it. I know I will survive it because She protects me. She has made me the agent for her providence. She preserved me on the Ides of Julius because She wishes me, no commands me, to carry out a great service for Her, and for humanity as a whole. And She wants *you* to help me in this endeavour."

"Me?"

"Yes, it is obvious. There is a design to all this. You were meant to meet us that night on the moor, meant to meet *me* in particular. Look, when this fighting here is over, and I get the chance, I must depart from here to carry out my mission on Her behalf. Will you please help me? You don't need to say, yes, to that right away. All you need do is think about it, convene with Her, and then She will open your eyes and fill you with the same sense."

"What do you intend to do – for Her?"

"I know where She reposes. I am sure of it. I must go there and summons her – allow Her to walk amongst us. Then, She will help us vanquish these devils for once! Rid our lands of them!"

"The Ankows?"

"Yes."

"You speak of *Nerthus*?"

"Yes. I know where Her sacred cart lies! She is waiting for me to awaken Her!"

Cybele did not know what to say to this. Eventually, she said, "I must admit, I have wondered myself where this is all leading. But Nerthus is but a legend amongst some people. We, Druids, do not hold to it with any seriousness. We don't consider God to be earthbound, resting in a so-called sacred cart somewhere."

Luti appeared disappointed. "Nerthus is but one manifestation of the God. The point is that this manifestation of God is for a purpose, and we have been looking at it for years without realising! She always comes amongst us in order to help us in times of great peril! And what better time than now? We need Her, and we need Her as soon as possible! Will you help me?"

"I will think about it and open my heart to Her, as you suggest. I am indeed being led somewhere but I don't know where at present. And I too am being preserved, it seems. Go fight your battle, horseman, and I will be here afterwards. I intend to stay with the commander until I understand things better. Let us hope God preserves him too."

"Thank you, Druid," replied Luti with his particular version of a smile, and then in a hushed whisper: "We are one step nearer now. Ask yourself this: why is Her sacred cart here, on this island, if not for this?"

Cybele nodded and then turned and went back into the tent in order to end the meeting.

Luti felt tears well up in his eyes. He stared at the tent flap for a few seconds until the shouts and blasphemies of officers nearby brought him out of his reverie.

He went back to helping the cavalry prepare for the day's ordeals. The horses were to be kept out of the worst of the affray, and used for scouting and carrying communications mostly, but they still must be draped in leather armour around the shoulders and chest, and shielding the eyes and nose. An Ankow could throw a javelin or spear as far as a slingstone, one hundred yards or more, and even horses on the periphery of a skirmish might fall prey to such a missile.

The horsemen would carry their usual oval shield and plain horse squadron helmets but their legs, normally clad in thin leather trousers only, would be their weakness. Luti had experimented with various solutions, some adopted from German practices, and settled for tin greaves to cover the horseman's thighs down to the knees and a shorter greave over the lower leg. The men looked faintly ridiculous clad this way, and the great Gaius Marius would have turned in his grave to see it, but most of the men concurred with the invention. Only the Carvetii, including Mus, made loud protestations against it, and secretly they promised themselves the option of shedding the extra armour in the heat of battle if it affected their horsemanship.

The foot soldiers were being briefed and steadied mostly by Tullius and Parius. Already they were lined up in their platoons, the air above them bristling with the javelin points as they listened. Nearly eight hundred men, missing only the two platoons of sagittarians, were standing behind their large rectangular curved shields and it looked impressive at first sight. The shields, which were uniformly coloured red, at least gave an appearance of concerted perfection at first glance. The auxiliaries behind them, however, were less consistent in appearance if one looked closely. As they had each been mandated to buy, borrow or steal their own uniforms and armour, they presented a pot puri of variable styles and shades of colour and vintage. There were pieces of armour that may have arrived on these shores with the invasion force back in the days of Emperor Claudius, and perhaps harked back even further to the days of the Republic, such was their antiquity. The men's tunics, visible on the upper arms and upper legs aimed to be red but were just as likely to be unbleached material, or every hue of brown and pink imaginable. The blackberry juice with which some of the men had recently dyed their tunics had produced a purple colour by accident that the governor or broad stripe tribune would have sanctioned had they seen it; for daring to wear the colours of patricians. But the chances were that no one above the rank of centurion would see it before the same men lay dead on the battlefield or rain or laundering had washed it out. The foot soldiers' swords and daggers deserved even less scrutiny. There were auxiliaries who had managed to buy a newly forged weapon up in Isca Augusta or won one on the Gassello course or in other training competitions, but most had had to buy second, third or fourth-hand items. Some swords had been sharpened and polished so often that they were almost as thin as pokers. Many men carried daggers in their sheaths on the left side of their thick leather belts which were actually kitchen knives. The process of *heritable improvement* had not yet begun, this being such a new set of recruits who still possessed their very first accessories. Better weapons and armour would be inherited in course from dead comrades on the field as the cohorts matured. Eventually the more experienced soldiers would be able to satisfactorily pass the most discerning muster.

In every platoon, two men carried a large axe rather than a brace of javelins; this being a feature peculiar to the Eighth and Tenth cohorts, the Ankow-Killers but these were tools that again ranged in size and provenance. Only the two short *Lucullan* lances hanging from the foot soldiers' belts, again on the left side, were all new and consistent in style and pedigree; forged and finished by Dacian smiths in Isca Dumnoniorum very recently.

The centurions and their subalterns walked backwards and forwards, inspecting the men and trying to look satisfied and confident. Their horsehair and feathered helmet crests fluttered in the south-westerly breeze. They tapped the odd offender with their long sticks. The standard bearers stood in the first rows for form's sake, the senior ones wearing moth-eaten cowls made from the pelts and heads of dead wolves or bears. None of them held the staff of a tall standard. Risking the disapproval of his seniors, Rufus had ordered the standards to be left behind today. This was highly unorthodox, but they would not be fighting a conventional battle on the field, and they would not in any sense be fighting anything *orthodox*. Instead of the staffs and standards, they carried something else: firebombs confiscated from the Belgae deserters, made from brittle ceramic amphorae filled with lamp oil, with a rope wick sealed at the top with candle wax.

There was one more faction to add to the assembled troops: the archers. These were still practising over at a makeshift range and would fall into line in a few minutes.

The men dared to turn their eyes from the centurions and optiones when a lithe figure suddenly appeared from the area of tents and began walking towards them. Her long tunic of unbleached linen danced in the rhythm and breeze as she moved, the shapes promising slim, energetic legs underneath. Her arms were folded over a fawn-coloured stole, her dark hair tied strictly into a bun. She stopped around twenty paces from her master, who sensed the rapt attention and almost perceptible sigh emerging from the columns of men spread out on the field. He turned and saw that Raselg was waiting behind him. When he looked at her, she held out a little muslin bag and a flask of liquid. He nodded to acknowledge her and resumed his supervision of the morning's muster for the time being.

Tadius Naratius kept his eyes on her as long as anyone. She deliberately averted hers.

Now the men of the *Coritani* tribe finally ran up from the archery range and formed a line in front of the ranks, shouldering their bows. Everyone was here.

Tadius glanced at Rufus to see if he was in the mood to make a rallying speech. Rufus on cue, removed his helmet.

"We are not at the world's end or even the edge of the glorious empire!" he shouted to the assembled crowd, and he felt every pair of eyes turn to him. "But this *is* a frontier! The front line! We stand on the very border between the forces of Good and the forces of Evil!"

It helped not to look too closely at the expressions of the men at this juncture. From experience, he knew he would see a range of countenances, mostly showing anxiety, concern, fixed concentration, occasionally gratifying expressions of determination and arrogance. Always there would be one or two faces oddly set in scorn, even anger, as if he or somebody else in authority was being blamed for something already. Perhaps these were the men who would die today, and a part of them knew it and hated him for it. Rufus had found letters on the bodies of dead soldiers, addressed to their families, forlornly wishing them a final goodbye. Some even started with the chilling words: "*Today I died.*" It was these faces that Rufus did not want to see so he left his eyes unfocussed.

"Goodness always prevails!" he continued. "The gods ensure that is the case! And, so, we will prevail today! We are the agents of all that is Holy, we are the soldiers at the frontline of Humanity! So, think on this…"

He paused for dramatic effect. A horse whinnied in the distance where the cavalry where assembled. Some crows and jackdaws were whirling in circles in the sky above. In the distance, clothes were flapping on the washing lines over at the roundhouses. Several goats appeared to have stopped chewing to look over towards him. A moment of matchless serenity before the chaos and bloodletting started.

Then a shock went through his body when he turned and saw that Raselg had not returned to the tents but was standing there still, the little muslin bag in her hands. And she was staring at him as if he were a ghost or Ankow already, as if she knew something and was drinking in the last glimpses of him before he departed for ever.

He struggled to return to his train of thought and bring it to the oratorial conclusion. His tongue felt leaden in his mouth and the words would not come. Everyone was waiting but, even so, it felt like his body was being dragged down into Hades already, right limbs first. A dead man was giving a speech and was not able to end it.

CHAPTER THIRTY-NINE

THE collapse of the most senior commander, just at the point he was about to deliver the climactic flourish to his stirring address, created the quantum of prevailing dismay that they might have expected and feared in the circumstances, and despite all efforts by Tadius to step in and end it himself. It was seen as highly ominous. The mood of the soldiers dropped to their sandals. Tadius could not actually see any mouths utter the murmurs and groans, but he could clearly hear it, rising amorphously into the air, the counterpoint to the morale going in the other direction.

Nearby, two centurions organised the heavy heap that had once been the erstwhile commander of men to be scooped up from the ground and carried back towards the tents. Raselg accompanied them in noticeable distress.

Tadius had made a guess at how the speech was to finish and was ready to pick up from the breakpoint immediately. Before he did so, he wondered whether to try to put a positive spin on events first, say something like: "*As with the greatest of generals before him, Gaius Julius Caesar, so it is with our senior commander - afflicted with the same genius and the same weakness*". However, it occurred to him that most of the men listening had probably never even heard of Gaius Julius Caesar, or else they knew him by an entirely different, and less complimentary name. He decided to push on: "As the commander was about to say, so think on this, men: We can count on the greatest gods supporting us today, the gods that love *men* and men's transactions. Jupiter, Mars, Minerva, Mithras, all the gods that love you and love humanity and love soldiering. They march with us, these gods! We will rain down thunder upon our enemy, and turn them into shrivelling lumps of festering, er, festering - er, *shit*!"

He turned and stomped back towards the tents, hearing the attempts of the junior centurions behind him to extract cheers and applause from the foot soldiers, but with dubious success. Such momentum that might have existed when Rufus was in full flow had dissipated from the field.

"Round up the decurions and centurions!" snapped Tadius to Asempero as he passed him.

By the time the officers had arrived at the commanders' tent, Tadius had erected a table in the space outside the front of it. On this, he had placed a neat stack of small wax tablets and one much larger one: the one that Rufus and he had been using to plan the tactics for the assault on the town the previous evening. Tadius gestured the men to scrutinise the large tablet.

"How is he?" asked one of the centurions, whispering.

"I will check on him in a few minutes. First, I need your attention to this. This is the town and layout."

They craned forward and studied the configuration scratched on the wax tablet. Duronovaria was peculiar in that the four roads leading to the gates of the town where not at the usual cardinal points of the compass. This was because of the proximity of the river on the north side of the town, forcing the road from Lindinis to converge with the road from Isca Dumnoniorum just in front of the west gate. On the other side of the town, the road to Vindocladia and the citadel of Sorviodunum connected to the east gate as you might expect. The road to and from the port of Clavinium passed close to Mai Din, and it joined the town at the south gate. The northern ramparts of the great fortress in which they were presently gathered appeared on the map as two curved lines at the bottom lefthand corner of the oblong wax tablet.

"All the buildings in the town are made from timber," continued Tadius. "Hence the firebombs carried by the standard bearers. We will split the infantry into three groups, one group of two hundred and forty men to attack here along the west wall, another group of two hundred and forty men to attack here along the eastern wall, at the same time. All the walls of the town are low, no higher than a man's height and constructed from chalk and turf. The outline ditch outside the walls is shallow and no problem. With the south end of the town on fire by then, the Ankows will have nowhere to go when we push them, except to flee to the north end of the town and over the wall there. They can then be corralled easily. The river will be blocking them on the north side, and the remaining infantry will press in from both sides up here at the north-west and north-east corners."

He looked up to see that he had all the officers' attention still. "The groups along the west and east walls will stand to until they are given the order to move. The firing of the buildings at the south end must be well under way by that point. The wind, as you know, is coming from the south-west today and it will fan the fires and smoke further into the town, pushing the devils where we want them.

"Now, unfortunately, that deals only with the *civilians* in there," he went on. "The soldiers amongst them, if we can still call them that – the vexillation of the Fifth cohort led by Robigalius – can be expected to stay in good order in a close column, perhaps a wedge, and make a push outwards from one of these two sides. My guess is the west side, away from the direction of the river. They will suspect that we have blocked the bridge on the east road, so it is more likely they will force their way out towards the west into open country. The horse squadrons will stand back at the four corners, behind the infantry, ready to pick off stragglers, escapees and any Ankows who attempt to wade across the river to the north.

Wrapping up, Tadius added, "No skirmishers today. Javelins will serve only to furnish them with weapons to throw back at us.

We go in with the lances and axes. Should there be crossbows, we will employ our archers to deal with them. Any questions?"

The ten junior centurions and two decurions made no response at first, except to shake their heads to denote they had nothing to ask for the moment.

"Good," said Tadius. "Here are your orders then."

He handed out the smaller wax tablets. They were each marked with the abbreviated title of the company or squadron that they captained.

"I have a question," said Saenus. "If Robigalius and the Fifth cohort's foot soldiers make a break for it on the west side, or indeed the east side, as the case may be, will the two hundred and forty men on the side that confronts them be sufficient to deal with them? The Fifth will be more experienced than our recruits. Also stronger and faster."

"Possibly not," replied Tadius. "But that is why we have trumpeters and your horsemen. We can adapt as we need to. No set of tactics fully survive the first contact with the enemy, as you know."

"Yes, I know that," said Saenus, testily. "This is Rufus's plan, I take it?"

"Mine and Rufus's."

Saenus leant forward and poked his index finger into the wax tablet. "The ground between the east wall of the town and the river, is probably softer, even marshy in places. It is much more likely that Robigalius and his soldiers will try to thrust out from the *west* side to where the ground is firmer. We should place more men and more horses on the west side."

Tadius was staring at the wax tablet. Saenus's fingernail had gouged a crescent shaped hole in the grey-brown surface on the right side. It seemed to represent a defect in both the map and the plan. He realised with a surprise that he, too, had been harbouring this same doubt in the back of his mind but he had not expressed it to Rufus last night. He had been so willing to defer to his fellow-commander's experience that he had pushed the query to one side. Now Saenus had hit it squarely on its head.

Nevertheless, he decided to defend the plan. "You are only assuming the ground is softer on the east side because it's nearer to the river there. You can't be sure."

"It's a reasonable assumption to make."

Tadius turned to the other decurion. "What do you think, Luti Bassus?"

"I think Cressido Saenus is possibly right, and the vegetation I've observed, albeit from a distance, might suggest the ground is a little boggy in places near to the river."

Tadius sighed. In his mind he was wrestling with a dilemma: the thought that the man he regarded as the best strategist in the army might have missed an obvious factor. "We are all overlooking something, here: the fact that Plancius Vallaunius Rufus knows this part of the world better than any of us. He travelled these parts only four months ago. I reiterate that we cannot be sure where and how Robigalius and the Fifth cohort vexillation will break out of the town. It is quite possible they will do so towards the *east*. We are going to be stuffed if he does so on the east side and we have put most of our soldiers on the other! The whole lot of them will have broken through us and be up the road and hidden in the deep woods before we can do anything about it! We will therefore put an equal force of men on both sides."

"Why don't we ask the locals," suggested Saenus.

Luti and Tadius exchanged urgent glances. The junior centurion of the third company, who had been knocked down and tied up next to the Gassello course when the Belgic recruits mutinied, was standing amidst them, and nobody had troubled to tell him yet that the very same culprits were freely lording it in the roundhouses on the other side of the plateau, no more than three hundred yards away.

"Yes, Queen Belena and her entourage have only our interests and welfare at heart, that's for sure!" retorted Tadius after a few seconds.

The officers laughed.

"There are your orders, let's get moving," concluded Tadius now that he had wrested the momentum back.

They saluted him and dispersed, and Tadius went into the commanders' tent.

Rufus was lying in his bed, seemingly unconscious. Both Raselg and Cybele were sitting next to the bed, on hand to nurse him. "How is he?" he asked.

Both turned an anxious face to him. Raselg pointed to the side of Rufus's face which had drooped. A string of drool was creeping out of the twisted mouth, no matter how many times she wiped it away.

"Apoplexy," Tadius muttered. "Can you do anything?" he asked the Druid.

"He must rest first, before he does anything. It may pass in time."

The tent flap behind him opened partly, and a voice said urgently, "Commander, trouble." It was the voice of Parius, his optio.

Tadius followed the officer out of the tent.

"Some of the men have stolen a goat from the Durotriges and are in the process of slaughtering it to read its liver! They refuse to go into battle until they've divined the will of the gods! The locals are not happy about it."

Tadius swore. "Pay the natives for the goat if it's been killed already."

He followed the optio to where the act of haruspicy was taking place. The animal had indeed been killed, and a soldier with blood up to his elbows was busy cutting out its liver, lungs and heart. A crowd of inquisitive soldiers, at least twenty, were standing around the spectacle, waiting upon the outcome. The liver was smooth and glistening. The man was finding it difficult to hold the slithery object in his two hands as he checked very side of it.

Tadius decided to wait and see the outcome of the divination. Stopping it part way through might do more harm than good in the circumstances. While he watched, he wondered why this soldier, in particular, had put himself forward as a sufficiently qualified augur.

"It's healthy, no disease but, look, the head is missing!" the soldier announced.

Someone answered, "That makes sense!"

Another man commented, "The head is missing but the liver is healthy and full. That is a good omen, surely! What do the other entrails say?"

The man with the liver in his hands placed the large organ down on the ground and then rifled with his fingers amidst the gore and mess he had created. Moments later, he found what he was looking for. The heart was still partly attached to the other evisceration. He struggled to free it from the slime to be able to inspect it. Eventually, he picked his knife up again and began cutting it free.

"Are you actually a haruspex?" asked Tadius suddenly from the crowd when he noticed that the man seemed more hesitant and less sure of himself. The man turned and saw that he had been addressed by the highest-ranking officer still on his feet and he appeared dismayed. Literally caught, red-handed. "No, I'm a butcher."

"Ha! You certainly are!" replied Tadius.

"Fetch the Druid!" a couple of men shouted in turn. The suggestion was taken up by others, and Tadius finally nodded to indicate he approved.

A couple of minutes passed before Cybele appeared, led by the soldier who had fetched her. Her face was ashen with concern. Rather than add an air of confidence to the procedure, she seemed at first to be just as unsure as anybody.

"Can you read this?" asked Tadius, a little impatiently.

Cybele decided to read the faces of all the men around her for half a minute, rather than the animal's entrails. Eventually, keeping the folds of her green robes away from the gore as much as possible, she stooped and stared at the spectacular display spread out beneath her. Another minute passed in silence.

Anyone who knew her father would have recognised her next gesture. She stood up straight again, clapped her hands together in front of her and declared: "The signs are auspicious! Victory is ours!"

Quitting while she was ahead, she then turned and walked quickly back to the tents. The soldiers were muttering contentedly in her wake.

CHAPTER FORTY

QUINTUS Robigalius had been proud to share his origins with the founders of Rome: suckled by a prostitute, otherwise known as a *she-wolf* in slang. Unlike the founders, however, he had been born a slave. His mother told him that he was the child of her master, her pimp. The man was a veteran of the Ninth Hispanic Legion who had taken part as a youngster in the invasion of Britannia. After his leg was crushed by a chariot wheel, Robigalius's father had been discharged from the army and returned to Rome. There he became a prosperous wine merchant who also ran a team of slave-prostitutes as a side-line. At the age of sixteen, Robigalius had been freed out of bondage at his father's deathbed, but on condition that he joined the imperial army immediately. He did so and was sent to Britannia as planned, to serve with the army of Agricola in Caledonia and Brigantia. Rising to a standard bearer in the Fifth cohort of the Second Augustan Legion, he had eventually earned a posting as commander of a vexillation in Duronovaria and was made up to the rank of centurion. This was not an enviable posting but the double-pay was welcome in the remaining years of his service.

The civil town was forlorn and edgy, and its dimensions hardly big enough to house a military unit. The barracks were rickety, cramped and draughty. The stables for the ten horsemen were hardly any better than a pigpen. The town council and other civilians went out of their way to be unwelcoming. The current and previous Roman governors had tried their best to make sure that the resentful and indignant folk of the Durotriges tribe did not take it out on the two-hundred foot soldiers and ten horsemen stationed there. Harsh reprisals, involving multiple beheadings of women, the enslavement of their children and many crucifixions of men ensured that the townsfolk were cowered into submission. It was touch-and go but suited to Robigalius as he was known for having nerves of steel.

He was also very shrewd, a characteristic he liked to think that he had inherited from his hard-nosed businessman father.

His abrupt introduction to the magenta-tinted world of the Ankows was when he woke to the sound of his own cry – the breathless eruption of bad air from his lungs, accompanied by the *vagitus vulgaris* first feral scream of a new-born.

There was no real hierarchy in the world of Ankows, but old habits died hard. Livius Colusanas still thought he was superior because he was of the senatorial class. Ulpius Senicianus and Exuperatus Helius both purported to lord it over him because they were equestrians, and he was just an unpropertied plebeian in his former life. He went along with the pretence of a pecking-order based on previous social standing, partly out of habit, and partly because he knew he could put a stop to it at any time he chose. His two hundred and ten men would answer to him, not some jumped up adjutant who wore purple stripes. Even the five-hundred and seventy civilians would jump at his command he fancied, because they were scared of his soldiers. When it came to fighting, he knew what he was doing, they did not. Old Senicianus, though significantly sprightlier these days, and though he knew a thing or two about real soldiering, was no match for Robigalius and his boys.

Yes, it had been lonely, manning the awful town of Duronovaria over the years, where the inhabitants permanently hated them, but things were looking up now. It was handy having the likes of Senicianus, Colusanas and Helius to confer with. They had intimate knowledge of the enemy that he did not possess.

This was what they knew. The Eighth and Tenth cohorts, under Plancius Vallaunius Rufus and Tadius Naratius respectively, called themselves the *Ankow-Killers*. They carried new lances, tipped with silver and Wolf's-bane, copied from the ancient weapon of the Druids. They fought with axes and fire too. The two commanders were very experienced. They would be no pushover. Rufus and Tadius would be aware by now that the town of Duronovaria was full of Ankows. Helius's slave, Raselg, had disappeared during the take-over; her body never found amongst the victims. It was assumed that she had managed to escape and get word to the Roman authorities about what had happened. Inevitably the so-called *Ankow-killers* would be mobilised and sent here to deal with it. And now they had turned up: around eight-hundred foot soldiers, fifty-two horsemen and nine other centurions amongst the troops commanded by Rufus and Tadius. The Ankows had observed them and counted them as the cohorts made their way up the hill to the citadel of Mai Din to set up their camp there. That was yesterday. Today, the Eighth and Tenth cohorts would be preparing to assail and besiege the town. Robigalius was surprised that they had not started the contest already, as it was now mid-morning. So, he would make use of the time.

As commanders always did before a battle, Robigalius tried to put himself in the boots of his counterpart. What would Rufus do? In this respect, the insight of Senicianus was very helpful. Rufus was a wily fox who would not overlook the special factors. The town was made of wood for instance. The breeze was blowing from the direction of Mai Din in the south-west. Inevitably, the southern end of the town would be targeted with fire.

But first, Rufus would stop his troops in the open land between the old fortress and the town and invite Robigalius to come out to fight in the Roman way, as this is what Roman generals traditionally did. Rufus would also expect Robigalius to ignore the invitation. Two hundred and ten soldiers do not willingly go out to fight eight-hundred and sixty-three soldiers in open land if they can help it. What Rufus was more likely to overlook hopefully was that Robigalius could count on over two hundred civilians fighting with him, as this was the proportion of town folk who were male and between the age of sixteen and fifty. Fighting age. Unless the slave girl was a particularly natural spy, Rufus could not be sure of how many civilians were actually in the town, and therefore how many might join the fight. In any event, Rufus's tactics would be to assume that the Ankows refused to leave the town and that he would therefore have to come in to get them. Robigalius predicted that the enemy would aim to surround most of the town and to wait while the fire at the southern end spread inward to cause panic. Some attempt at herding and corralling the civilian Ankows would be made. Because the defensive walls were ineffective to stop anyone getting in or out, a cordon of soldiers would have to do the walling and corralling. The net would tighten, the civilian Ankows would be pushed into a corner, and then the slaughtering of them would happen.

Finally, Rufus would expect Robigalius, the tribunes and the camp prefect to lead a co-ordinated break-out of the Fifth cohort soldiers, probably on the western side. The woods were closer on that side, the river was further away. Most of Rufus's troops would therefore be on the western side.

Now that Robigalius had estimated what Rufus would do, he could lay out his own plan. And he would be ready.

CHAPTER FORTY-ONE

MUS and his half-squadron of fourteen riders were assigned the station to the northwest of the town. For the next half an hour, however, they held back behind the light infantrymen as they descended the slope towards the southern perimeter of the town.

Quietness was a common feature of Roman soldiers at the beginning of a battle. It was expected to cause dismay in an enemy, especially those who were used to their opponents screaming and issuing blood-curdling curses as they rushed towards them. The silence in contrast was meant to convey purpose, discipline, efficiency and cohesion. Mus had never witnessed it before, not in real battle conditions. The surreal nature of it sent a shiver down his spine.

The first that he was aware that things were going wrong was later, when he and his men had put themselves in their allocated primary position, the river to their left and the north-west corner of the town slightly to their right about a hundred and fifty yards away. They were sitting on their relatively relaxed horses, watching the foot soldiers catch up with them and start to form a line along the western edge of the town. A thicker wedge of soldiers was forming up near the north-west corner. These were the ones who would swing round and block the patch of ground between the river and the wall when the Ankows poured out, thus forming the west fence of the corralling pen. The first smoke had appeared over the roofs of the buildings at the south end of the town, where the incendiary bombs had made their mark. The smoke was growing thicker as more and more of the timber structures burst into flame. But rather than the shouts of consternation he expected to hear from within the town, there was just silence. It was just as surreal in the circumstances as the effect created by the quiet, purposeful Roman soldiers marching into war. So far, Mus was very surprised by the tranquillity of the first stages of battle.

He was not the only one. He could hear foot soldiers question the matter. Most of them were craning their necks to listen out for sounds. Wood could be heard crackling and splintering, and there was an ambient low roar of energetic flames, but that was all. No panic.

All the soldiers and horsemen on the west side of the fort were of the Tenth Cohort. Tadius was in the middle of them, his tall red horsehair arch, very evident. Mus heard a trumpeter blow the signal for the light infantry to scale the wall and enter the town, the blast came from somewhere just the other side of the clouds of smoke, midway along the south wall.

All the foot soldiers, except those assigned to block off the north corners, scrambled to get over the wall quickly. Tadius's helmet was seen, first on the top of the wall and then disappearing over it.

What Tadius found on the other side, explained the lack of panic amongst the Ankows. The ramshackle barracks had all been pulled down and cleared away to create a firebreak, so the fire could not spread beyond the buildings on the extreme periphery of the town. He could see, through the gap caused by the missing barracks, the soldiers of the Eighth cohort similarly pondering the situation on the east side like a mirror image of themselves.

To add to the puzzle, the Ankows, whether soldier or civilian, were yet to make an appearance. For the moment it looked very much like the town was deserted.

Tadius walked cautiously towards the forum in the centre, unsure whether he should spread his men out and start searching the town. He decided to keep them together in one grouping as this had all the hallmarks of an ambush. He spotted the white transverse crest of a junior centurion, and the black and white one of Tullius, Rufus's optio, coming towards him from the opposite side, leading the men of the Eighth cohort.

When they met in the middle, the centurion who was called Maius, said "They are gone."

"I don't think so," replied Tadius. "They are here somewhere. Why else would they bother with a firebreak?"

Tadius contemplated the risky policy of dispersing the men to start the unenviable task of searching buildings one by one, never a safe option in the circumstances. His instincts told him that this was what the Ankows wanted them to do. He was pretty sure that the soldiers amongst the enemy would be together still in one group, as this would increase their strength and effectiveness considerably, but where could such a large body of men hide in one place?

As if reading his thoughts, Maius asked, "Where are the soldiers of the Fifth cohort?"

"Together, and waiting to either break out or to ambush us. My guess is that they're in the forum here. It's the only place big enough to hide two hundred men."

They were of course, standing next to this large enclosed space as they spoke. The buildings forming it were one storey high, forming a square open courtyard: the place for civic gatherings, speeches and ceremonial festivals and markets. Soldiers could parade there, and they could certainly wait there in conventional lines, ready to move out. It was uncanny to contemplate that two hundred foot soldiers might be in there, remaining so hushed, but Tadius could not think of any other solution to the mystery. But, on reflection, would Senicianus and Robigalius be so unwise as to place themselves and their men in a place from which there were only two narrow ways out: through the basilica building or out of the gate at the other side of the square? That would be suicidal, as they would be cut down as they filed out. Unless…

"Ladders," he whispered. They would come over the roof!

Several eyes turned upwards to peer at the roof line. A sickening sense of vulnerability infused the officers. They could imagine a rain of javelins any second. If this happened, they would have to hug the walls of the forum and raise their reinforced shields to avoid being hit.

"Shields up! And spread out and surround the forum!" whispered Tadius.

Signals were given by hand gesture, and the men of both cohorts began to move quickly, their hobnailed sandals unfortunately betraying their intention as they scuffled away. They seemed in irritating disarray as they did so, their shields above their heads and clashing as they found their way up the streets. This was not the neat tortoise manoeuvre they practised so much in open ground, it was more of a free-for-all.

By now, Tadius was beginning to sense that they had lost the momentum of the attack. It felt very much as though they had, instead, fallen into the hands of a carefully laid trap, one that was yet to be sprung. Not only were there two hundred trained soldiers somewhere to contend with and probably about to pounce, but there were several hundred individual civilians of malign disposition and with superior strength lurking somewhere.

When his men and those of the eighth cohort finally stopped shuffling along the streets and around the building, quietness descended again for the time being. The hairs on the back of his neck were prickling with the tension. But still nothing happened.

Tadius needed to use the delay to his advantage, and there was only one thing to do. "Set it on fire!" he shouted, loud enough to be heard by anyone inside the forum. This he expected would surely bring on the ambush. The Ankow-soldiers inside did not know that all the firebombs had been used to start the conflagration at the south end of the town, they would anticipate instead that the forum would be set on fire immediately. Now, surely, was the time to spring the trap.

All eyes continued to scan the eaves of the roof, peering out from the edges of their shields, except those of Tullius and several men who ran off to fetch burning pieces of wood from the fire raging nearby.

Nearly a minute passed before these men returned with the incendiaries. They handed some out and began to use them to ignite the old, rotten timbers of the forum walls. It was soon on fire.

From the distance, a trumpet sounded. It came from outside the town on the east side. It was the signal for *Enemy sighted* but why outside?

The trumpet had been blown by a *cornicene* in Saenus's horse squadron, positioned at the north-east corner of the town. They had spotted the Ankows on mass, coming from the direction of the bridge half a mile to the east of the town. There were hundreds of them, and they were running from the river towards the road that went southward to the harbour of Clavinium, thereby bypassing all the foot soldiers of the Eighth and Tenth cohorts. The light infantry of the Fifth cohort were leading them, and out at the front and just discernible, Saenus could see the helmet crests of a couple of centurions and their subalterns, one transverse crest the red colour of a commander. Robigalius. "Damn it!" he shouted to the riders around him. "They weren't in the town at all! We gave them too much time to prepare!"

The Ankows were well ahead already, and only the horsemen of the Eighth and Tenth cohort could feasibly catch up with them by now. Saenus signalled to give chase, his trumpeter blowing his instrument at the same time to confirm their intentions. The three other groups of cavalrymen would hopefully hear this and join in. Those riders positioned near the two southern corners of the town were now turning to race the few hundred yards to intercept and engage the opponents, but there were only twenty-four of them, including Luti Bassus.

Predictably, the Ankows changed formation when they saw that they were being pursued by the horse squadrons. While the civilians kept on running, the soldiers of Robigalius, stepped out neatly, and turned to face the disparate charge, for the horsemen were coming at them from four different places and over four different distances.

The first flurry of javelins was hurled at the nearest horses when they had closed to around eighty yards. It could only be assumed that the skills of the Ankow skirmishers were much improved by their pitiful metamorphosis because the javelins found their marks with frightening effect. There was hardly a horse that was not struck by this first flurry of projectiles. The horsemen all went down in a heap. The noise of anguished horses could be heard. Somewhere in that heap, and amidst the cloud of dust and clods of turf, was presumably the decurion himself.

Saenus shouted to his men to slow down at once. He was not going to allow them to suffer the same fate. He looked over to see the other group of horsemen who had come from around the town from the north-east corner of it. They were still some way away but quickly catching up, remarkably quickly in fact; a show of horsemanship he had not witnessed in a long time.

Where Saenus and his men had stopped was still three hundred or so yards short of the waiting Ankows with their next waiting javelins, safe enough for the time being.

The other squadron arrived. Their leader, Luti's own optio, Mus, called out to Saenus to give him his view on things.

"We will be mown down if we approach any nearer!" shouted Saenus to him.

Mus nodded. He knew his own men could not throw their own lances as far as the Ankows could throw their deadly javelins back at them. It would be madness to close in any further. There were only twenty-eight of them against two hundred javelins.

"Look!" shouted Mus.

The horsemen whose horses had been felled in the first onslaught and who were unhurt themselves, had mostly scrambled to their feet, and those who had managed to keep hold of their shields and lances were now assailed by Ankows in hand-to-hand combat. The remainder of Robigalius's troops still stood in an impressive line some way back, their next javelins poised in the air ready. Some of the fallen horsemen, those that knew hopelessly that they did not stand a chance without their shields were running towards Saenus and Mus. Thankfully, the Ankows refrained from picking them off with javelins, which surely they could have done easily.

Saenus swallowed hard. He knew they were up against a set of better disciplined soldiers than his own, than any in their own cohorts of auxiliaries. The battle had been snatched from them by shrewder and better-trained opponents. They had started with the superiority of numbers and it had gone spectacularly wrong. It was just like the Ides of Julius battle all over again.

Mus was waiting for Saenus to come up with a plan. The decurion of the Eighth cohort was clearly in charge here until Tadius and Maius eventually showed up. Saenus had spotted the infantrymen finally emerging from the town in the distance, pouring out of the east gate but still most of a mile away. His thoughts were whirling. He wanted to go and help the men engaged with the Ankows two hundred yards away but knew that if they tried to approach any closer, they would be mown down themselves before they even got near. The bilious feeling when he realised that he should stand back and leave his comrades to their own fate was unbearable. Saenus could see it in the anxious expression on Mus's face too. It was illogical and suicidal to order twenty-eight men to charge into a hail of a hundred or so javelins in an attempt to rescue comrades. But at the same time it seemed cowardly not to.

Seconds seemed to pass but it was in reality just a moment, as Saenus wrestled with the predicament. In the maelstrom of this thoughts, the irony represented by Mus's own position suddenly occurred to him. Here was a man of the Carvetii tribe actually contemplating risking his life to rescue men of other Brittonic tribes, men he would not have cared to even look at, let alone greet six months ago. Such were the strange and wonderful systems of the Roman world, a cultural creed that created a blanket of glistening cohesion, like snow could cover and unify a complex and ugly landscape of bracken, stone and mud.

In that instant, the thought of dying for such a wonderful, all-engulfing Roman *adventure* did not seem unattractive. On the contrary, it seemed glorious.

"Come on!" he shouted to everyone around them. "Shields up and at them!"

CHAPTER FORTY-TWO

RASELG had left the Druid to sit by Rufus's bed while she went to the edge of the earthwork to stand on the highest rampart overlooking the town some three miles away. She hoped to see something of the battle, to know the fate of men she cared for in this world: her father, Saenus and Tadius.

She was not alone. Some distance away, standing upon the same high rampart but another part of it, stood Belena and her consort. They too were peering at the distant town and the land between it and the outer edges of the Durotrigan fortress. They glanced at her, somewhat irritably and disdainfully when she came to stand on the earth bank twenty yards away.

Smoke was already lifting up in clouds above the town. Tiny figures on horses could be seen on this side of the town walls, two groups of cavalrymen, waiting no doubt to be called into action. Meanwhile, not a sound could be heard. The breeze was blowing at her back as she stared with her hand covering her eyes against the sunlight. Considering what was probably unfolding in the distant town - the terror, the hacking, stabbing and killing chaos -

the lack of noise seemed disingenuous; a mocking falsity deriding all senses.

The fortune-teller's words had often come back to her during these last few days. It was in today's battle that she feared and even expected that Rufus would die. Yet, today, he was sleeping in his bed in a tent behind her, his twisted, paralyzed body ironically safer than she could ever have anticipated. Is this what the fortune-teller had really seen: the great man struck down by apoplexy and turned into a helpless wretch, forced to retire from the army; a wreck in a permanent vegetative state? Was Fate going to have the last laugh on her and the old fortune-teller? Was the real meaning of the prediction, that Rufus would cease to be the man he was? *That* man would be dead for all intents and purposes. Was this why he would never retire in the normal sense, never marry and have children? Was his predicted perishing, the demise only of the vigorous commander that *was*; to be substituted by a crippled changeling?

Raselg was being called suddenly, snapping her out of her revery. The man and woman on the rampart were calling her by the name *slave* and beckoning her to come to them. She hesitated at first, wondering whether they meant to harm her while they had the chance. She cursed herself for not bringing along one of the spare lances she knew were hidden in the depot tent.

The queen's male companion addressed her in an unfriendly way when she approached them. "How is your master?" he asked, oddly in a Belgic accent. She recognised the accent from the men who used to come to the vicus to trade with her father.

"He is struck down like stone, and sleeps deeply," she answered.

Belena said, "You are of the Dumnonii?"

"I am."

"How did you become a slave? The Dumnonii have never been at war with the Romans. Were you *born* a slave?"

"I was not. My father insulted and caused loss to the very man who sleeps in that tent like a stone. My master now. He punished my father by placing me in bondage. He bought me."

"I don't understand," said the man who Raselg knew as Manann. "If your father insulted and upset your master so much, why did he *buy* you rather than just take you as recompense? You are talking nonsense, slave!"

"My name is *Raselg*. And I am not talking nonsense! Plancius Vallaunius thought the insult and damage worse than it was. It is complicated. I don't really want to talk about it right now. Suffice to say, when it turned out the insult and loss were not as great as he first thought, my master relented and paid my father handsomely for my bondage."

"Will the Romans go?" interrupted Belena, impatiently. "When they have killed all the Ankows, will they leave this place?"

"I don't know. I am not party to such information."

"Yes, you are," retorted Belena. "You are a domestic slave. You stand in the background and listen to all the discussions of the men, although you pretend not to, so you can pour wine in their fancy glasses when they snap their fingers at you."

"Glasses? They only time I saw men drink wine from *glass* was when I went to the governor's place at Noviomagus! My master only has tin and ceramic beakers."

Belena looked Raselg up and down and said slyly. "I reckon your master shares quite a lot with you."

"He does not."

But the two women exchanged knowing glances. "Not information, anyway," added Raselg.

"You must have heard something. Come on, from one Briton to another: how long are the Romans staying in my fortress?"

Raselg had grown bored with the conversation and nothing appeared to be happening in the town in the distance, except a great deal of white billowing smoke. She shrugged and walked quickly back to the tents without saying another word.

Cybele was still sitting by Rufus's bed. He was still, like wood; his face pale and not looking like the man she knew, more like an uglier brother of him perhaps. Cybele turned a sleepy face to the slave. "No change," she mumbled. "What is happening with the battle?"

"Just fire and smoke, that's all I can see."

"I will go and have a look," said the Druid. She stood up, stretched and went out of the tent.

Cybele saw Belena and Tuathal standing on the highest earthen rampart. The remainder of the Britons were milling about the village roundhouses and gave every appearance of waiting for information or orders before they knew what to do, before they could set themselves to some useful purpose. Every time she looked at the Durotrigan men, she was puzzled. There was something not quite right about them. She had never been this far east before now, so knew nothing about how they should look, but their quiet and almost sheepish behaviour bothered her; it was as if they were trying not to be noticed. Only the man who called himself Manann acted confidently, as perhaps he should, being the queen's special companion. Both the queen and her man were now looking at Cybele, watching her approach the ring of ditches and ramparts. Then they turned quickly and peered north-eastward towards the town. Something had attracted their attention.

Cybele rushed to the rampart and looked too. She spotted the dark shape of hundreds of people appearing from the direction of the river to the east of the town. This mass appeared to be heading in their direction but were approximately still two miles away. A Roman road led from the south gate of the town and passed within a quarter of a mile of the outer edges of Mai Din. This was the road she assumed led to the busy port to the south. She had forgotten the name of it. It seemed that the hundreds of people were making their way to this long straight road.

The man with Belena grew excited. He started shouting to the other men to come and have a look themselves. The men obeyed his command surprisingly quickly and assembled themselves in a line, two or three people thick, along the top of the rampart, forcing Cybele to move along so that she was not standing amongst them.

Someone shouted, "There! The Roman *turmae* are coming!"

At first she did not understand what this meant, but then she saw two groups of horses galloping rapidly from the south corners of the town, racing to catch up with the mass of people heading for the road. Twenty or so riders.

The mass of pedestrians now split into two, a larger group continuing to run towards the road, the smaller portion of them stopping to engage the approaching cavalry. The way this smaller group arranged themselves neatly informed her immediately that they were soldiers. Now she understood what was happening with dismay. The Ankows had escaped the town and circumvented all the foot soldiers. Perhaps they had never been in the town at all. They had been expecting this day and prepared for it, had managed to effectively outmanoeuvre the Roman forces and leave them all behind.

The Durotrigan men were jumping up and down and shouting. It was difficult to tell whether they were joyous or anxious, it sounded like a strange mixture of both to her.

Suddenly there was a change to the movements down there in the plain. The first groups of riders had converged together and approached the Ankow-soldiers but, just as they did so, they stopped and seemed to fall in a huddle together. Cybele's hand went to her mouth with shock when it dawned on her she had just witnessed the twenty-odd horsemen being wiped out in one sweep.

Her eye caught more movement further away. Two further sets of horses were now racing towards the conflict. They seemed to have come from either side of the town. The set on the east side were well ahead of the others by several hundred yards.

Now these new groups of riders slowed and converged too, but appeared at least to be in good order, not hurt. They had evidently pulled up to avoid getting too close to the enemy.

Tuathal was shouting at the men next to her. He sounded angry and resentful. The exchange between him and the others became very heated. This lasted all of twenty or so seconds but then appeared to come to some resolution. The men suddenly scrambled off the bank of the rampart and headed back towards their village.

Tuathal was the only one who did not follow them. He headed towards Cybele instead. "Druid, do you have lances?" he asked. "Do you know where they keep the spare *Lucullans*?"

"I know where the munitions tent is," she answered, puzzled. "Whether there are lances there, I don't know!"

"Show me. Quick! We are going to save the soldiers! See, down there, the Ankows are trying to kill the fallen riders! There is a decurion amongst them. They don't have a chance!"

"A decurion?" replied Cybele, alarmed. She thought instantly of Luti Bassus. And he had been so sure he would survive this day. "Follow me!" she shouted.

There were around fifty spare lances in the munition tent. Cybele watched the Britons share them out quickly. When they were finished, there was not a man who did not carry either a *Lucullan* lance or a large axe in his hands.

"Quickly!" she rallied. "May God be with you!"

Her blessing appeared to reassure some of the men. They looked at her gratefully. A second later, they were racing away from her; eighty of them heading to the east gate of the citadel. And then they were all gone within a few more moments.

Cybele picked up the hems of her long robe and tucked them quickly into her belt, freeing her legs of the folds, just as her father had shown her how to do. Sometimes the Druids, including the women, fought naked but she was not going to go that extreme today. She ran to the tent she shared with Raselg and fetched out from it her own poison lance.

Her quick, heavy footsteps brought Raselg out the door of the nearby commanders' tent. "What is happening?" asked the slave.

"Luti Bassus and the riders are being attacked, and I must help save them!"

Raselg was astounded. "No, don't! You will be killed!"

The Druid laughed at this. "So be it, then!"

And with that haughty retort, the Druid was off, running athletically towards the roundhouses and, beyond, to the east gate of the citadel. Raselg watched her until she had disappeared into the convoluted twists of the ditches.

CHAPTER FORTY-THREE

LUTI Bassus had sensed his horse was going to be hit. It stood to reason for he was hidden behind his oval shield, as were his comrades, so any sensible opponent would not waste a javelin aiming for men. On the other hand, the horses' broad chests, ineffectually protected from the javelin points, were an obvious target. And he knew that whichever Ankow was aiming at his mount, it would probably not miss. In fact, there were possibly more than just one Ankow aiming for the obvious man in charge right now. He would be a more valuable target because of the decurion insignia and helmet he wore, and they would have been spotted his rank for sure before he lifted his shield to obscure himself.

So when it came, he was ready. Not the most agile of men, but one who spent his life riding horses, he despatched himself from the saddle as soon as he felt under him the shudder and wave of pain and shock run through his horse. He jumped and landed on his feet like a circus athlete. All around him he heard the terror of beasts, the grunts of men, the thump of those less adept as he was in leaping off the saddle, as they hit the ground topsy turvy.

Twenty-four men jettisoned or urged to dismount violently within two seconds. His senses filled with the awful noise and ground-quakes of heavy, muscular bodies crashing down. A scream went out from a man whose horse had fallen on him, trapping his leg and shattering it. Clumps of dirt and grass were swirling in the air. There was the distinct smell of damp earth and horses emptying their bowels and bladders.

And then, more loud shouts and screams, this time from some of the Ankow-soldiers as they leapt towards them to engage in combat and finish them off. Luti guessed around thirty of the monsters were coming.

His ears, tuned as they always were to the sound of horses, heard more of them approaching behind him, some way off still but the ground was already resonating as if a stampede was heading his way. Surely no more than one hundred to two hundred yards to go for these rescuers.

The first Ankow was upon him already. A sharp point of a sword came through his shield but not enough of it to reach him. "Not today!" he shouted at it, and he thrust his lance at his attacker; wildly and blindly because his shield was largely blocking his view. He felt contact with the end of the lance, and heard his opponent laugh at the ineffectual strike. It must have thought itself immune from the pricking of the lance. The sword withdrew from the shield and, in that instant, Luti had to make a decision: lift the shield to parry a downward blow from the enemy's sword, or lower the shield it so that he could see his foe's face and judge where it's heart was pumping in its chest. The *Lucullan* could only work properly if he could pierce its soul.

He chose right. His enemy must have thought it could cleave Luti's helmet in two. The downward blow struck the edge of the heavy rising shield, sending a shudder through Luti's arm. The impact seemed to dislodge the sword from the Ankow's hand. The blade had become wedged tight in the slit it had scythed down from the outer rim, and the sword now felt free and un-held. Luti dared to drop the shield lower, and face the Ankow that was trying to destroy him – a foot soldier of the Fifth cohort – its face wincing in agony. Luti saw that he had managed to stab it in the neck with the lancehead. The devil was momentarily stunned and sickened by the poison.

With more guesswork than precision behind it, Luti swung up the lance again with all his strength. It had to be an upward strike to find a gap in the iron strips of the chest armour, to find a spot somewhere behind this outer protection, then through the edge of the breastbone a little towards the righthand side, hopefully not hitting a curved rib in the process. One strike, one chance only. Life or death. Much harder than you imagined it would be, so many obstacles in the way. Hardly fair when you thought about it, and you considered what was at stake.

This time lucky though. God be praised! Luti could almost feel the vibration and hiss of a direct hit into the heart. A moment passed while the fiend contemplated what had happened but not yet feeling its true implications. Then the pitiful wail as it dropped to its knees, screaming its last utterance before oblivion and dissolution.

The noises of his surroundings reasserted themselves suddenly. Men and Ankows were fighting all around him in the spaces between dead and wounded horses. Hades had ascended from the underworld and filled the upper plane with chaos and hatred and violence. Ear-shattering noises of men's and horses' shrieks of fear and desperation.

But this time, Luti felt invincible. Every second that went by confirmed his triumph over death. Nerthus held his shield and guided his arm.

His nose was assailed by a horrible stench of decomposition that cast his mind back to that terrifying night at the wharfs at Isca. He tried to keep calm and gather the chaos into some order. How many of his squadron were left fighting? He glimpsed only eight still on their feet. The number of Ankows assailing them had thinned to perhaps the same number. Could that be possible for he was sure he had seen four or five times that number running towards them? About eighty yards further away, a line of skirmishers in Roman uniform stood in good order with javelins poised to throw, and then he noticed that between him and this line of enemy soldiers, there were Ankows crawling on the ground or else staggering back to their diabolical comrades. They were retreating back to safety, and some were evidently struggling with the effects of the poisonous lances. Luti assumed the opponents had been ill prepared for what they encountered, had laughed off initially the threat of being pricked by such little lances, until that is, the pain and nausea had struck them, and their brethren fell and corrupted into slime next to them. And then they realised that the little lances meant either sickness or annihilation. Most had gone back in consternation to lick their wounds.

"Javelins!" he shouted, as he expected these to fly at them any moment. He raised his shield again in readiness and swore loudly. Where were the other horsemen who should have arrived by now to reinforce them? Why were they still fighting alone? He shouted, "Mus!" at the top of his voice, bewildered why his own optio was not fighting alongside him. Then he felt the wondrous rhythm of horses' legs from the ground again, thundering nearer, and he sensed that his plea had been answered.

A whistling, whooshing noise above him at that instant made him look up but flinch. The sky was suddenly full of thin lines, as if God was ploughing the air. Hundreds of javelins were racing across well above their heads. He knew at once what it meant. So many javelins, so many more new deaths.

CYBELE had time to take in the scene as she ran down the slope to join the fray; a solitary figure in emerald-green robes tucked up around her waist, her pale legs running. Pumped with adrenaline, she was not conscious of the ache in the back of her head, the pinch from the wound in her side, nor the bite of the occasional sharp stone on her bare feet.

The young men of Mai Din were well ahead of her, waggling their small round shields as they sprinted and closed in on the four rows of Ankow-soldiers in the flatter land beyond. The men were making a lot of noise and had spread out enough so that axes could be swung threateningly in circles above their heads. Between these men and the enemy soldiers, was the paved Roman road, and further up this road to her right, a group made up of hundreds of former town dwellers had stopped to watch the spectacle. The danger was that these would decide to return to help their fiendish compatriots.

Now two heaps of fallen horses were squirming in the field beyond the road, the first heap she had seen from the top of the fortress ramp, and a second one made up of twenty-odd animals, freshly mown down by the narrow shafts of javelins. Horses' legs and heads were jerking and writhing, and soldiers were rising from the new maelstrom, helping each other extricate themselves from the panicking animals and to pick up their shields and lances. As she got closer, she heard the pitiful whinnying of indignant, terrified beasts.

The Ankow-soldiers were altering shape and even colour as the rear two lines of them turned to face in the opposite direction in response to the approaching, hollering curses and threats of Tuathal and the men of Mai Din. Their lower halves from midriff down became a neat wall of dull red shields.

At the same time, she was reassured to see that the foot soldiers of the Eighth and Tenth cohorts had made half the distance between the town and the distressed horse squadrons. They were jogging but surprisingly disordered for Roman soldiers who were heading to engage the enemy. The white crests of several centurions could be picked out easily at the front, leading the running charge. The Ankows must have seen this too, and noted how the dynamic of the battle was quickly changing against them.

The second band of horsemen, unmolested by further projectiles and any opponents, had collected their weapons and gone to help their cavalry comrades. But a soldier, with a white crest running from front to back on his helmet was being dragged away by two fiends, and was being brought quickly towards the lines of Ankow-soldiers. Cybele knew at once, from the thick waist and the decurion helmet, that this unfortunate man was no other than Luti Bassus.

The Mai Din men had almost reached the spot. Seconds later, they were clashing with the shields of the Fifth cohort. No one was yet paying attention to the mad woman running behind them in the tucked-up green robe.

She headed towards where Luti was being manhandled and dragged along the ground. Now was the time finally to let out the shrieking, warbling Druid's *keen* that was meant to freeze the hearts of Ankows, and had been the conventional challenge to the devils since ancient times. Druid children were taught the special, yodelling note by their parents, but only in the remotest landscapes away from mundane ears; a dreadful scream that was only to be uttered in one deadly situation; a noise meant only for the ears of their darkest foe.

The effect was instantaneous. The Ankows with Luti dropped him and turned to face her. They were clearly disconcerted, baffled and awed by the noise. The front two rows of Ankow-soldiers likewise turned their heads to see where it emanated. Without time to think of how she must have looked at that moment, a lone woman challenging a hundred of the fiends, she closed the gap between her and the decurion's body. The monsters who had tried to drag him into the fold went to draw their swords but spotted the lance in the Druid's hands and decided that discretion was preferable. They ran to join their comrades instead.

Cybele grabbed Luti by the arm and started to pull him away, damning him to get on his feet and run. A lucid expression formed in his dazed eyes finally, and he scrambled on to his legs and let the Druid half-drag him away towards the remainder of the cavalry soldiers.

He fell again, this time at the feet of Mus, who stared down with a wry smile. "Lie there, decurion," said Mus. "As it seems you have a broken leg."

"Do I, Mus?" said Luti, and, looking down, saw that the greave on his right leg was rent in two, and the ankle and foot below it were poised at an unnatural angle. He could not believe that he had just run several yards upon this mangled limb.

"I'll stay with him!" said Cybele.

The foot soldiers, led by Tadius and Maius were now no more than two hundred yards away. They could not throw their javelins ahead of them because of the risk of skewering the horsemen and whoever was fighting the back rows of the Fifth cohort. Neither could the Coritanian archers let loose their arrows. Tadius demanded the men drop their javelins and bows and take up their lances instead.

CHAPTER FORTY-FOUR

THE front row of soldiers had parted, and out from behind stepped the senior officers, Robigalius in the centre, flanked by the camp prefect on one side and the two tribunes on the other. When these undid the straps on their helmets and took off the headgear, Tadius knew what was intended.

He ordered his trumpeter to sound the signal to cease fighting. It was possible that this would have no effect amongst the men fighting at the rear of the Fifth cohort lines; ironically it would only do so if their suspicions were correct, and the men of Mai Din were indeed the former Belgic recruits, into whom every major audible signal of order had been drummed, from the first training days at Isca Augusta down to the finishing of training recently at Isca Dumnoniorum. The sinister soldiers of the Fifth cohort should also recognise the signal immediately. When the tussling petered out at the rear of the lines, Tadius knew they were right. The deserters had indeed heeded the call to stop.

He took off his own helmet, bidding Maius to do the same. The two men walked forward for the parley.

The senior tribune, Livius Colusanas, spoke first. Now that the fighting had ceased temporarily, he was determined to re-establish his superior position. The camp prefect, Senicianus, was busy scouring the faces of the Eighth and Tenth cohorts in the meantime. He appeared so familiar to Tadius that it was difficult to imagine he was anything else but his former, kindly mentor; the arthritic man who had declined the benefits of retirement in order to look after his beloved regiment for a few more years.

Colusanas had noticed the singular absence as well. "Where is Plancius Vallaunius?" he demanded.

Tadius waited a few moments to answer. He was not going to respond like an obedient dog, doing its master's bidding. "He is ill."

"Ha, I knew it," exhorted Senicianus. "Rufus would never have fallen for it, like you did!"

"Before you begin congratulating yourselves, reflect on this," said Tadius. "You have failed to escape. So here you are, herded like the cloven swine you are! What do you bid us do? You have no bargaining power. We outnumber you two-fold, and we have the obliterating lance! You are finished. I have only agreed to this parley out of a semblance of respect for what you once were, Ulpius Senicianus. For we had all loved you in truth."

"I tried to tell them about the lance, Tadius Naratius, but they would not quite believe me," replied the camp prefect, equably.

"Shut up!" shouted Colusanas, harshly. "You have spoken too much, already."

Robigalius came to his prefect's support, bizarrely. "Ulpius Senicianus is a better soldier than you will ever be, tribune," he averred. "You are nothing but a politician, remember?" The centurion and the senior tribune glared at each other with ill-disguised loathing.

It was gratifying to witness the seniors of the Ankow companies, bickering amongst themselves like this but it was not getting them anywhere. Tadius said, "Well if that is it, and the talking is over, shall we begin the process of despatching you finally, so that your shackled souls might find the repose they deserve? Some of you deserve, that is. Robigalius, I never knew you, but I commend you for your command shown today. A fine show, I have to say; worthy of the uniform you wear. I would go so far as say that I hope that my auxiliaries might have learnt something today!"

"Think nothing of it," answered the centurion. "Yes, the plan was mine too. You gave us far too much time to hatch it, commander! What were you thinking of? You left us the liberty to slink out of the fort to the river, and wade along it, crouched and hidden out of view as far as the bridge this morning. And why the Hades did you not secure the bridge?"

"Why take the road to Clavinium?" asked Tadius in return. "You were on the road to Vindocladia surely, if you were already at the bridge."

"A ship, commander. We have booked our passage to Gaul. Our vessel waits for us, even now." It was Colusanas who had spoken.

"You negotiated with sea-traders?" asked Tadius, surprised.

"They are expecting two companies of soldiers to make the journey to Gaul," confirmed the senior tribune. "We paid them handsomely to wait for us."

"I cannot let you go, you must know that."

"Why not? You will be rid of us. You can think of it as banishing us from the realm." Colusanas's voice had taken on an oily, diplomatic texture.

Robigalius spoke up. "Commander, more men will die unnecessarily if you fight us. You know that as well."

"It hinges on your definition of *necessary*, in that case. I happen to think that it is necessary and my paramount duty to wipe you off the face of this good earth."

"In that case…," answered Robigalius, placing his centurial helmet back on his head with grim finality.

Tadius stepped back and did the same. Maius followed suit. The last to put back their helmets were the camp prefect and tribunes.

"One last thing, Tadius Naratius," said the junior tribune next to Colusanas. "The slave known as Raselg, was it she who reported it to you?"

"You know her?" asked Tadius.

"I am Exuperatus Helius. I had the honour of being Rufus's friend."

"Of course, you are," said Tadius. "I should have guessed it. Yes, Exuperatus Helius, you are correct, it was the slave who reported to us about what had happened."

Helius shook his head in seeming admiration. He had not yet tied the fastenings, and the straps swung around loosely. The junior tribune then laughed. "A slave girl. Ridiculous, when you think of it! Ridiculous!"

These were the last words spoken before the slaughtering began.

EPILOGUE

RUFUS lay in a coma for a week beyond the battle. The camp remained in situ for the time being. Their prayers to the god Aesculapius were answered ironically on the day of the next full moon, the fourth day before the Ides of November. On that day Rufus finally opened his eyes. He was paralyzed down his right side, his face slack on that side. When he talked, he slurred his words as if he had overdone it on cheap Cappadocian wine.

Raselg nursed him with extraordinary devotion, and Tadius moved out the tent to make room for her once Rufus revived. She coaxed Rufus out of the bed each day and made him walk backwards and forwards, a little longer each day though he hated it and swore and blasphemed shamefully.

Another regular visitor was Cybele. She sat with Raselg at the bedside, every evening when Rufus was exhausted, and she recounted old Druidic myths in a musical voice. She had been telling these stories even when he was comatose, in the belief that her voice would hold him to this world and lead him home like a beacon. Perhaps it did.

Luti Bassus's leg mended, and within three weeks he was back riding horses, even though he was not yet walking. He put on too much weight again. He stopped wearing his uniform and opted for what could only be described as dour priestly robes. Every day, he went for a ride on his favourite horse, usually along the road towards Clavinium where the air became fresh with the tang of the sea. Sometimes he took the Druid with him. They had struck up an unlikely friendship. Unkind people wondered whether Luti had ever had a real friend before. His leg being so badly mauled, it was reckoned that it would take three months before he was fit for active duties again. He was already in his final year of obligatory service to the army, his twenty-fifth, so, upon his request, he was permitted early discharge and his full pension. A base commander could grant a legionary this in their final year if injuries inflicted in battle meant a long recuperation, and Tadius was prepared to grant it. Luti was not about to depart for his homeland of Germania, however. He wanted to stay in Britannia and travel north to Carvetia on some personal pilgrimage. And he wanted Cybele and Mus to go with him.

Tadius and Maius each earned a shiny torc for bravery which they would pin on their chest harnesses when the awards finally came through from headquarters. The original versions of their written reports went no further than the headquarters at Isca Augusta, as had happened with all previous reports that mentioned the Ankows - or the lance. The reports were *modified* to make them anodyne and less concerning for the Senate and misleading enough just in case they should ever fall into the hands of the emperor himself.

Mus for his own bravery, would have earned promotion on Tadius's and Luti's unhesitating recommendation, but it was his misfortune to lose his left hand in the conflict; swiped off by the sharp edge of an Ankow's sword. Most bitterly, this had occurred in the closing minutes of the battle, when only a few Ankows were left standing. Mus's army career was over before it had really begun. He was distraught and depressed at the thought of being discharged as an invalid and no longer so adept upon a horse. He moped about the camp, bemoaning his plight until one day, Luti took him aside and asked, "Mus, for the God's sake, then what is it you want to do? As you cannot undo what is done! What is your greatest dream if you are not to be a soldier and to earn Roman citizenship eventually? What would be your biggest ambition, say, had you never gone near an auxiliary recruitment office?" Mus replied after a few sullen moments that he would like to start a large horse-breeding depot in Carvetia. He would sell the finest horses to the armies during the looming war in Brigantia, and he would not care which side he sold them to so long as they would pay a good price. "That sounds very, very expensive to set up," mused Luti out loud. "You will need lots of money for land, and for buildings and for good breeding stock. *My* money, perhaps. It sounds like a very good dream, I must say.

And if we become business partners, Mus, you will be able to show me all of Carvetia as well. We will become very rich men there, what do you say?" It was too good a deal for Mus to turn down.

The position regarding Tuathal and the other deserters was tricky. Martial law did not allow for flexibility or amnesty in the case of mutiny and desertion, the penalty must always be death. Yet, it could be said that Tuathal's intervention had turned the tide of the battle, and that he and his men had joined the affray with astounding bravery and put their lives at risk to help their former comrades when they could so easily have taken the opportunity to escape. It was an illustration of the change that had come upon Luti Bassus, the cohort's strictest lawyer, that he was willing to help Tadius find a creative solution to the dilemma. They would say that the Belgic recruits had been on a secret mission to reconnoitre the situation at Mai Din and its nearby town, and that the mutiny and desertion were staged because of the fear of Ankows or spies in their midst. Tuathal and company had then been able to ingratiate themselves into the community living at Mai Din by claiming that they were deserters fleeing the Roman Army. Anyone who doubted this story only had to ask themselves why else the so-called deserters would have put themselves at great personal risk to help their old comrades. When this solution was put to Tuathal it was on the strict condition that he and his surviving company immediately returned to the cohort as if their mission was completed. Tuathal agreed without hesitation, even relief for, Belena aside, life as a fugitive was not that great.

The town residents of Duronovaria disappeared down the Roman road but did not turn up at the port of Clavinium, where scouts had sneaked ahead to warn the port officials. It was assumed that the residents had dispersed into the countryside, Raselg's father amongst them. Cybele was confident that they would never have managed to board a ship, anyway. Her own father and others of her people were keen to ensure that no Ankows ever left these shores and spread their spore abroad. The Druids were carefully watching every port.

Cressido Saenus died of the wounds inflicted during the battle but lingered on for days. At the end, he called for Raselg and she was sent for. He died with her beside him, holding his hand.

AUTHOR'S NOTE

This is a sequel to *Lucullan*, and the events follow closely on from that story. I envisage the opening occurring at the beginning of August in the year 90 *CE*. Raselg's visit to the fortune-teller and the funeral eulogies for Natalinus occur on what we would now call 13th August. Full moons in the seasons in which this story unfolds occur on 14th August, 12th September, 12th October and 10th November. The big showdown occurs just before the last of these full moons.

Historical context for this story includes the newly designed lance made by soldiers serving in Britannia. The governor, Lucullus, would later be summoned to Rome and executed by the emperor for daring to name the lance after himself and not the emperor. The legend of the sacred cart bearing the sleeping deity, Nerthus, somewhere on an island is vague enough to mean Britannia. The Brittonic tribes are real, as are all the places. Britannia at that time can be likened to the American Wild West, full of proud and divisive native tribes and tracts of undiscovered or uncolonized land, admittedly on a much smaller scale.

Roman horses did not have stirrups so fighting from horseback was rather unstable and limited largely to poking with long lances and swords.

The children's game, Hopscotch, was invented or adopted in Roman Britannia by the Second Augustan Legion in the mid-first century, possibly by the legate, Vespasian (Domitian's father), as a tough training course to be attempted in full armour with weapons and full backpacks. No one knows what the soldiers actually called the assault course, so I made up the word *Gassello* to suggest that the aim was to skip over it gracefully like an energetic antelope.

Printed in Great Britain
by Amazon